# Broken Wings

My hand slides over the gun as I place it on top of everything in the box. Yes, I silently tell it, I will be back for you soon.

I put the box back into the long drawer, call the woman in and we both lock it up and take our respective keys with us. I thank her and walk out of the bank, wondering how I can possibly drive home.

I can't. Not yet. I'm not even sure I'd be able to find my way home, as shaken up as I am. I look at the coffee shop across the street and head over. I spend the next two hours nursing a black coffee, turning a muffin into a pile of crumbs and plotting how to kill Uncle Chazz.

My hands stop shaking at some point and I know it's okay to drive. I clean up my mess, half expecting to see napkins littered with murder plots, but no, I'd done all the planning in my head.

On the drive home I turn over all the different ways to exact revenge.

No, not revenge. Vengeance.

Plots and schemes skim through my head, one idea more delicious than the next. I turn down my street and head toward my driveway. The entrance to my safe haven. My nest. A place I hadn't ventured far from for four years.

A soft sound, almost a wail, escapes from me as I realize none of these plans for Uncle Chazz will happen. None *can* happen.

I have finally found my father's killer.

And there's not a damn thing I can do about it.

## Other Titles by Mara Jacobs

***The Worth Series***
***(Contemporary Romance)***
Worth The Weight
Worth The Drive
Worth The Fall
Worth The Effort
Totally Worth Christmas
Worth The Price
Worth The Lies

***Freshman Roommates Trilogy***
***(New Adult Romance)***
In Too Deep
In Too Fast
In Too Hard

***Anna Dawson's Vegas Series***
***(Mystery/Thriller)***
Against The Odds
Against The Spread

***Blackbird & Confessor Series***
***(Romantic Mystery)***
Broken Wings

Countdown To A Kiss
(A New Year's Eve Anthology)

# Broken Wings

Mara Jacobs

Published by Mara Jacobs


ISBN: 978-1-940993-98-0



For more information on the author and her works, please see www.marajacobs.com

*To my mother, Helen.*
You're *just what* I *always wanted.*

# *One*

**I** stare into the eyes of the man who killed my father.

Maybe.

I mean, maybe he's the man who killed my father, not the staring part. Although, to be honest, I'm not really staring *into* his eyes, because I'm looking at a photo of him on a computer screen.

Okay. Let me start over.

I stare *at* the eyes of a man who *maybe* killed my father.

I only knew him for a few weeks before witnessing him murder my father, twenty-two years ago. And, I was only a five-year-old girl, not the most reliable witness.

But yeah, it's him.

I try to calm down. This isn't the first time I thought I saw someone from my past. I've quickly left grocery stores, abandoning my cart mid-aisle, when seeing the flash of a handsome man with dark hair. Only to be embarrassed as I hid in the parking lot and saw a complete stranger walk out later.

But I never thought I'd seen Uncle Chazz before. Until now.

The picture is the desktop picture of my newest acquisition, a used iMac. The man—I knew him as Uncle Chazz though, even at five, I knew he wasn't really an uncle—stands behind the bar in a bar/restaurant. To the right of him, in front of the bar is a young couple standing with their arms around each other. They're more dressed up than the people in the background of the bar, like maybe they've come from somewhere else. They look to be about my age.

The woman is blonde and pretty. The man is handsome with black hair and blue eyes—a combination I used to love on a man. I quickly dismiss them.

I do a couple of quick clicks and realize that the previous owner didn't wipe the hard drive clean. That's not as unusual as you might think. In fact, it's somewhat common. Even after doing this for four years, I'm still amazed at how people can sell their computers without totally obliterating every bit of personal data.

Some don't know how, I suppose. Some don't care. And of course, some computers are stolen, but those are mostly laptops.

The shock value of seeing people's personal things wore off long ago. And there were some shocking things. On one of the first machines I dismantled, I found a folder of the most disgusting pornographic photos I'd ever seen.

I've been around the internet a while, and I've …stumbled upon...a lot of porn. Some made me laugh, some aroused me, some got no reaction, some made me sick. So when I say this was DISGUSTING…well, you know it was bad. A couple of folders down from the porn folder on this machine were all the letters the owner had sent out…to his parishioners.

Yeah, that's right, the guy with all the hard core porn was also a minister.

After awhile I became immune to all the personal docs on the computers I refurbished. Now, I simply don't care enough to look.

I pick up the ebay receipt that was in the box. The seller is an N. Carpenter. There's a hand-written note that I'd tossed aside when I unpacked the computer.

*I hope you like it. It served us well, but time to move on—Nick*

Nick Carpenter from Tennessee sold his Mac on ebay and I bought it. He probably joined the PC nation. Or maybe got a laptop with a new job. Or upgraded to a new Mac. I get a lot of Mac sales that way. Mac users love to have the newest version of everything.

I wonder if the bartender—Uncle Chazz, now, to me—is a part of this Nick's everyday life, or is he just a bartender that happened to be in one of his pictures? The likelihood of him being *my* Uncle Chazz slims in my mind. The bartender has the same basic features that Uncle Chazz had, but that was twenty-two years ago. He would have been in his early thirties then. The bartender looks to be younger than mid-fifties. And hopefully, Uncle Chazz is rotting in prison somewhere. And if he isn't, then he got away with killing my father, is running free, and I really can't imagine him—or any of his ilk—in Tennessee.

Those guys don't leave their home turf unless they have to.

Like I did.

But the more I stare, the more my hand doesn't move on the mouse. I can only see the desktop picture.

And Uncle Chazz.

My mind races as to how I can confirm this. Or, better yet, to eliminate the possibility that it's him. My fingers itch to start Googling, but I know better. No search like that can be traced to this IP address. Or anywhere in the vicinity.

I know there are ways around that, proxies and other stuff, but I don't trust them. I've learned not to.

A thought hits me. The bank. My safe deposit box. I look at the clock, I still have a few hours before my branch closes. Thank goodness they have Saturday hours.

How to do this? I think it through. I don't want the contents of that box in this house. I know it's overkill, but it's how I feel. That life, even the remnants of that life, have no place in this house.

I've been through too much to make sure I had this one, small, safe haven.

I take a screen shot of the desktop and then open it up. I enlarge the pic as much as I can without totally blowing out the pixels. I crop out the blonde and her good-looking boyfriend—presumably Nick Carpenter. I hook up a printer to the IMac and print out a copy.

As if someone is watching me, I quickly fold the picture several times, image inward, and place it on my work table. I run upstairs and change out of my sweats, baggy turtleneck, Hello Kitty slippers—my basic work uniform—and into slacks, a lightweight sweater set and loafers. I have about three such outfits for the rare times I go to the bank or to some other professional establishment.

At home I just wear sweats or yoga pants. To run out for take out or to the store, I usually wear jeans. Or sometimes I just stay in the yoga pants.

Pretty inexpensive wardrobe needs. It makes for an uncluttered closet. And not a lot to have to pack on a moment's notice.

I make the thirty-minute drive to the bank in silence, the print out of the picture sitting on the passenger seat, as if Uncle Chazz is coming for a little ride with me.

I feel a moment of panic at the bank when I pull out my two forms of ID. No reason I should, this is my safe identity. No one outside of this town knows me by this name.

At least no one who wants me dead.

The woman looks at both forms of ID for a while. I don't blame her; they've never seen me in the four years since I got the box. I do my financial stuff at a different bank and most of all my transactions are done online anyway.

The woman finally takes me in the little room and we put our keys into the drawer together and then she leaves to give me privacy. I take the box out and bring it over to the high table in the center of the room. There are four tall stools around the table. I scooch onto one, wishing I was bellying up to the bar to order a brew, not opening the lid on my deadly past.

I turn the key and lift the heavy lid. I open it slowly, as if something inside could strike out at me.

There are only seven items in the box. My birth certificate. My California driver's license. My Social Security card. A stack of hundred dollar bills totaling four thousand dollars. A picture of my father. A gun. And a sealed envelope.

The identification things I quickly move to the bottom of the box. They are no good to me now, and could get me killed. The cash is my safety net, it goes back into the box. The gun…the gun may be needed, but not today.

I finally come to the sealed envelope, not able to put it off any longer. I don't know why the procrastination now, after I'd hurried like hell to get here before the bank closed.

Yeah, on some level I do know why. Because what I find it this envelope may blow my safe world apart.

I take a deep breath and place my finger under the flap of the envelope and quickly slash it across, causing a momentary flash of pain from a tiny paper cut. The envelope flap turns a diluted pink where I bleed, ever so slightly, onto it.

Holding the offending fingertip out of the way, I pull out the contents of the envelope, careful not to let them touch the bloodstain. Two photos. Both single shots of a man alone. Different men. The first is a face I know well.

*Knew* well.

Or maybe, never really knew at all.

I see now that the resemblance to the handsome man in the desktop picture is surface, at best. Black hair, blue eyes, extremely good-looking, yes. But this man…my man…has a gleam in his eye, a charming predator look that draws one in.

Drew me in.

But I flew away.

I swallow down emotion, careful not to examine closely what the exact emotion is, and place that photo back into the envelope. Left remaining is a photo of Uncle Chazz. I take the folded printout of the desktop picture out of my pants pocket. I slowly unfold it, pressing out the creases with my now shaking hands.

I lay the picture from the envelope, a smaller snapshot, onto the table next to the unfolded printout.

He has aged, but it's Uncle Chazz. There are differences, yes.

But even if I hadn't been sure, and I now was, the man in both these photos has a small scar running through his right eyebrow. Very tiny, not very noticeable, unless you were looking for it.

Or looking *at* it. As I had, at five years old, when I saw him standing over my father's body, gun in hand. He'd lifted his index finger to his lips as he watched me watch him, in a "shhhh" motion. It wasn't necessary. I didn't scream. I didn't speak. I only stared at the man who had just killed my father.

My little eyes had followed the line of his index finger as if it were pointing straight up, and saw the scar that bisected his eyebrow. I suppose I was already going into shock because all I could think at the time—and I still remember this, twenty-two years later—was " I wonder how Uncle Chazz got that owie?"

My finger glides over the scar in the printout of the desktop photo, as if it might be embossed, and I could feel the nail in Uncle Chazz's coffin.

I'm not sure how long I sit and stare, but I finally put the snapshot back in the envelope, careful not to look at the other picture in there. I fold up the printout and add it to the envelope. I don't want it in my home. In fact, Nick Carpenter's iMac is going to be nothing but nuts, bolts and motherboard by the end of the day.

My hand slides over the gun as I place it on top of everything in the box. Yes, I silently tell it, I will be back for you soon.

I put the box back into the long drawer, call the woman in and we both lock it up and take our respective keys with us. I thank her and walk out of the bank, wondering how I can possibly drive home.

I can't. Not yet. I'm not even sure I'd be able to find my way home, as shaken up as I am. I look at the coffee shop across the street and head over. I spend the next two hours nursing a black coffee, turning a muffin into a pile of crumbs and plotting how to kill Uncle Chazz.

My hands stop shaking at some point and I know it's okay to drive. I clean up my mess, half expecting to see napkins littered with murder plots, but no, I'd done all the planning in my head.

On the drive home I turn over all the different ways to exact revenge.

No, not revenge. Vengeance.

Plots and schemes skim through my head, one idea more delicious than the next. I turn down my street and head toward my driveway. The entrance to my safe haven. My nest. A place I hadn't ventured far from for four years.

A soft sound, almost a wail, escapes from me as I realize none of these plans for Uncle Chazz will happen. None *can* happen.

I have finally found my father's killer.

And there's not a damn thing I can do about it.

# *Two*

**I** avoid my workroom for the rest of the afternoon and evening, as though if I wait long enough, the iMac will be gone when I go in and I can just pretend that the last few hours never happened.

If only I could pretend the last four years had never happened and I was free to leave my home, my town.

For about an hour I toy with the idea of packing up, getting the cash and gun from my safe deposit box and making a run for it. Getting as far away from Michigan - and not in the direction of Tennessee—that I can. But I don't. Rational thought (ha!) wins out.

You see, I have no fear of Uncle Chazz showing up on my doorstep. I know from experience that he'd send someone else after me it he knew where I was. And that someone else doesn't know where I am, or I wouldn't still be alive.

No, this a safe house, safe identity. And if I don't have the balls to leave it for justice for my father, than I might as well stay put.

Finally, the next morning, it gets the best of me and I settle myself in front of Nick's machine with my coffee and toast. As soon as it boots up I change the desktop picture to a standard Mac background. I only wish I could as easily change out my self-loathing from not being brave enough to hunt down Uncle Chazz.

I wipe my hands on my sweats and reach for the mouse.

Besides the regular folders—applications, system, etc.—are two folders; My Stuff and Carrie's Stuff. I circle the cursor around the Carrie's Stuff folder. Is Carrie is a sister who shared his computer? A roommate? Girlfriend? The woman he has his arm around in the desktop picture? Wife? The note had said served *us* well, so maybe they shared a machine. Which meant they lived together? I double click on the My Stuff folder—there'd be time to get to Carrie's later, if I was still interested.

There are several folders, but the one that jumps out is Pics. I double click on it.

There's something about the folder hierarchy of computers that appeals to me. I loved those Russian nesting dolls as a kid, too. Opening each one, finding another treasure inside.

There are four folders within the Pics folder: Me and Carrie, Family, The Band, Miami. I move the pointer to the Me and Carrie folder, circle it with the mouse. I look at the portable disk drive on the worktable next to the Mac. It has the CD I created to wipe Macs clean. All I'd have to do is plug in the USB cable to the Mac and double click and I'd wipe this machine clean, ready to build up from scratch. I could reconfigure it, get it boxed up, and get on with the other machines sitting on the worktables.

Put Uncle Chazz out of my mind, like I'd tried to for the past twenty-two years.

Put beautiful men with mischievous smiles out of my mind, like I'd tried to for the past four years.

But let's face it, I want to see if Uncle Chazz is in any other photos. Even though I can't do anything about it, I want to know. Even though it'll kill me to live with this knowledge. I almost welcome this pain after so many years of living with a different kind of pain.

It's a kind of digital cutting.

I double click on the picture folder instead of reaching for my wipe out CD. There's a bunch of pics of Carrie and Nick together—all decent, thank God. Carrie is indeed the woman in the desktop picture with Nick. In most of the pictures Nick's black hair is short, trimmed in a fashionable cut. His smile is blinding, his blue eyes penetrating in every photo.

I don't see any with Uncle Chazz in them, but there's a bunch of Carrie alone, most times looking at the camera with a smile. Except, it wasn't really a smile. You know how people say "she smiled with her eyes"? They usually mean the smile was so wide, or infectious, it reached her eyes. That wasn't the case with Carrie. She kind of crinkled her eyes up, even the nose a little bit. If anything, her smiles never reached her mouth.

I'm not sure if the fakish smile masks sadness or some other emotion. She and Nick are both around my age, but that doesn't mean much.

I'm living proof that you can still be young and have a lifetime of sadness behind you.

Carrie's very pretty, but in a high-maintenance kind of way. Lots of hair product, lots of makeup. Her clothes are trendy, and look like a lot of thought had gone into them. Nothing thrown together. Very accessorized.

A couple of photos are obviously taken in the early morning, and she's totally done up. Call me crazy, but I find that suspect.

Or course, I don't even know where my makeup is anymore. Did I even buy any…after?

There's one photo of Carrie without makeup, her hair mussed-up, like maybe she'd just gotten out of bed. She doesn't look happy to have been captured in such a state. Her mouth is forming an N, her tongue on the roof of her mouth, like she's about to say, "Nick!" or "Knock it off!" or perhaps "No!"

Funny, but that's the picture of her I like the best.

I get up and go grab my baby name book from across the room, then return to my seat, already turning through the dog-earred pages.

I look up names in baby name books.

Everybody's done it once or twice. Seen a book in a bookstore and looked up their name, maybe the name of their significant other. Certainly expectant parents use these books. Trying out names, finding the meanings, wondering about the child they'd soon have. The book I held was bought for that reason.

Now, I just use it to look up the names of people I meet online.

*Carrie. From Carol. Carol (French) song of joy, (English) strong, womanly.*

*Nick. From Nicholas (Greek) victorious people. Religion: the patron saint of children.*

They'd probably have lots of strong, womanly, victorious children together.

Other than the photo where she was mad that someone was snapping her makeup-less, there is one photo that stands out.

She is with Nick, their arms around each other. Nick is looking at her, a smile on his face. She is looking at the camera, her smile—for once—reaching her mouth. Her eyebrow is raised slightly in a challenging sort of way. Her lips are higher on one side—not a smirk, more like her smile is soon to become a full-fledged laugh. Perhaps Nick is saying something to make her laugh?

She is wearing a blue gingham dress. It had to be some kind of costume or something. Please, God, let it be some kind of costume.

She doesn't have ruby slippers or a straw basket, but she could be Dorothy in that dress.

A blonde Dorothy with an attitude.

**"Y**ou out there?"

I look down at my laptop screen and see the blinking message. I'm not sure how long it's been there, but it must have been too long because just as I'm about to type my response, a new message appears.

"HELLO?"

"I'm here," I type. "Sorry," I add as an olive branch. I click on the dice icon and roll a three and a two. I move one of my backgammon pieces the five spots and click "done".

Gammon_89 clicks on the dice right away, as if chastising me for losing interest in the game.

"Where R U tonite?" she asks.

"Where I always am—at home," I reply.

"That's not what I mean—UR not paying attention."

I know what she means, and of course my mind is on something else. It's back in my workroom, on Nick's machine, on Uncle Chazz and on the vengeance that I won't find. It was a chore to tear myself away to play backgammon.

I feel bad. Gammon_89 and I have been playing backgammon together every Sunday night for a couple of years. I'm usually right on top of the moves. We also chat as we play. Nothing too heavy. Movies, books, television. Sometimes we talk about guys, but I don't have much to say on that subject.

Not anything I can talk about, anyway.

But tonight we don't chat, or at least I don't. She tries a couple of times, but I don't follow through. Just not in the mood.

"I have to go," she types.

"What? We barely got started," I respond, disappointed.

There is a long pause. I wait. I wonder if Gammon_89 has left, but her icon is still lit up. I almost type again but wait. It is her turn after all.

"Listen…" she finally types. Which is curious, because we are on computers…there really is nothing to listen to. She should have started off with, "Look", but I let that go, thinking I'm already on thin ice with my wandering mind.

"I sense you're in a weird place right now," she writes.

I look around my aunt's house. My house now. Same white walls, same beige carpeting, same cozy stone fireplace. The only difference from when I grew up here is the wall of computers and electronic equipment, overflow from my workroom, that now crowds the cabbage rose-patterned couch and love seat my aunt had adored.

"Nope. Not in a weird place…in the living room," I type back. Normally I watch my tone online, as sarcasm does not always translate through wifi. But Gammon_89 has known me for a couple of years now and she gets it.

At least, I think she gets it. I start to wonder because there is another long pause. Finally I see the "Gammon_89 is writing a message" script run at the bottom of the IM window and I'm surprised at how relieved I am.

"I've sensed a change in U lately," she writes.

"And my backgammon has suffered so terribly that you don't want to be bothered?"

Another pause.

"I don't think your mood is conducive to me being able to concentrate on the game."

It's just a game of backgammon, I think to myself, but the panic I feel at the thought of not having Gammon_89 to play and chat with on Sunday nights surprises me. I backpedal. "I'll be good. I'll stay totally on top of it."

"I'm actually pretty busy," she replies. "I've got a lot of things happening in my life right now."

I get a tickling at the back of my neck. The kind you get when you know you're about to get dumped.

"Are you blowing me off?" I type.

Another pause. A pause that screams YES in my ears.

"I think we need a break," she writes.

A break? We spend two hours together once a week. We're not Ross and Rachel.

But the tickling at my neck has broken into a full-fledged tingling and my fingers fly furiously across the keyboard.

"Look," I start—not pointing out how much more appropriate that is than "Listen". "I know I've been pretty snarky lately, but you've always been okay with that. In fact, you said that was the best thing about playing with me. Are you now going to punish me because of it?"

"It's not a punishment," she writes. I can't help feeling that it is. The worst kind of punishment. To take away something I look forward to, something that gets me through a long Sunday night. The night most people dread because they have to go back out into the world the next day.

The night I dread because I don't.

I don't know a lot about Gammon_89—just small talk while we play—but I do know that she's single, about my age, and has a dachshund named RedHawk that she adores. So, when she shuts down her computer in a few minutes—after she's finished dumping me—she can go walk RedHawk, attend to all the stuff she's got going on in her busy life right now, or maybe call some guy she's interested in.

When I turn off the computer…well…that's just it…I don't ever turn off my computer.

# Three

**"I** think I got dumped last night."

"By who this time?"

I should be insulted by this, but I'm not. I don't even need to respond. As soon as Confessor thinks for a moment, he'll piece it together.

"Oh, right, Sunday night—your backgammon friend," he writes. I smile, though no one can see it. "That one was a long one."

He doesn't add "for you" but I know he is thinking it. So am I.

"Two years," I respond.

"What happened?"

"She said I've changed."

He doesn't respond to that…I don't either.

"What was your screen name with her again?" Confessor asks me.

"AceyDuecey."

"Is that some weird sexual thing?"

I chuckle. "No. It's a backgammon term."

"I suppose you didn't even get to finish your game."

"No, I didn't." I'd gone online and looked for a new backgammon lovers' chat room. I obviously couldn't return to the room I'd met Gammon_89 in. And I didn't want to get sucked back into Nick's machine. I still hadn't made up my mind what to do—wipe it clean or keep poking around and drive myself crazy with Uncle Chazz when I knew it could lead nowhere.

I have a few chat buddies that I watch television with or play backgammon with. But not Confessor. We don't watch TV together. We don't listen to music together. We don't play online chess together.

We talk.

Not chat. Not IM. No cute abbreviations like 4U or R U OK? No emoticons depicting our moods. In fact, after four years, our moods are as transparent to each other as if we were in the same room. Or city. Or state. We may very well be. I don't know.

That's the way Confessor and I want it. Confessor knows all my secrets. I know none of his. Again, that's the way we want it.

"Did you find someone to take her place?" he asks.

I tried, but my heart wasn't in it, still stinging from Gammon_89's words. "No," I type.

"Tell me," he prods, "Confess."

And I start to, my fingers poised at the keyboard, ready to unload the frustration of being cut off from a small pleasure. To try and put into words how hard it is to find someone I can connect with—even if it is only to play backgammon and chat—and then to have it taken away.

But Confessor knows this about me. That I know the pain of having things taken away.

As I start to type all this, the doorbell rings. "Gotta go," I write instead, "doorbell."

"Tom or Bob?" he asks.

I lift the lace curtains and see the big, brown, UPS truck. "Tom," I respond.

"Tell him I said hi."

I smile. "I don't think so."

"I know about him, but he doesn't know about me?"

"Exactly."

"But we're the two most important men in your life."

"All the more reason to keep you apart. Besides, don't forget about Bob," I remind him. Fed-Ex was making nearly as many deliveries as UPS.

"Later?" he asks.

"Depends on how long it takes me to configure whatever comes in this delivery."

"Well, you know where to find me," he writes. "And don't worry about your backgammon chat buddy. It's her loss."

"Thanks. Bye."

"Bye, bye, Blackbird."

Blackbird is my screen name with Confessor. My true screen name. The only one I've ever used with him. And he's the only one I've ever used it with. It's like letting him see me naked, only more intimate.

I walk away from the computer. I know Confessor will be there when I return, whenever that is. I'm not sure what he does for a living. He might work at home, like me. He might have a job that allows him to be online all day. He might not work at all.

I've thought about it, but in the end, I only need to know that Confessor will always be there when I need him. Even if it's only to say "her loss".

*Especially* if it's to say "her loss".

I let Tom in. He's carrying a huge box and I try to help him, but as usual, he rebuffs my offers and makes his way across my living room and into the spare bedroom that I've turned into my workroom. His thinning gray hair slaps across his forehead from the effort.

In my workroom, the four walls are lined with one, long, computer workstation. Table lamps are placed on the workstation every six feet. Computers, printers, scanners, various external drives, modems and wires—lots and lots of wires and cords—cover nearly every inch. The machines are in various stages of dress. Some are complete, some have their cases open, motherboards taken out. Others are only empty shells, the best of their innards taken to make another machine stronger.

Kind of like an organ donor.

I'd moved Nick's machine over to the place next to my own newest Mac. I always leave the first three or four feet of workspace to the left of the door empty for new deliveries. Tom puts the box down there, as he does at least three times a week. He exhales and grunts at the same time—no easy feat—and I once again wish that he'd let me carry the boxes. But, even though he's on the high side of fifty, Tom's a professional, as he likes to tell me often enough, and so I wait patiently for him to catch his breath before I speak. Professional or not, those computer boxes are heavy and the workroom is at the end of the house. And no other delivery person would insist on carrying a box inside for me. At least it's on the first floor. Good thing, or I'd have had to call 911 for Tom by now.

"Morning," Tom finally says.

"Hey, Tom. Thanks for carrying it in here. You should have let me," I say. I *always* say.

"Hmmph," he says. He *always* says. "Anything going out?"

"Not today," I say, mentally reminding myself to finish up my latest ebay sale and get it boxed up for tomorrow.

He pulls his clipboard off the top of the box and we walk back through the hallway and to the living room.

"Coffee's fresh. Wanna cup?"

He shakes his head. "Can't today, thanks. I'm behind."

I nod. About half the time Tom stays for a cup of coffee and a cookie or something. About the other half, he says he's behind. I often wonder about some other stops on his route. If he's having coffee with them on my "behind" days? If that's the reason he's behind, because he's having coffee with them? Does he get behind on the days he has coffee with me and turn them down? These are the things I spend my time thinking about. Pathetic, I know.

"Let me fill your thermos up, then," I say.

He hands me the clipboard and heads out to his truck to get his thermos. I know he doesn't want to seem presumptuous and bring his thermos in with him right away, but he might as well, he always ends up going out to the truck to get it.

I sign the electronic clipboard. I don't even have to look to see where or who the package came from. With online tracking, I know exactly what package is going to show up on my doorstep between eleven-thirty and eleven-forty most mornings.

I hand the clipboard back to Tom and take his thermos, I can feel his eyes sweeping the room and then staying on my back as I walk toward the kitchen. I know what he's about to say before he even says it.

"Such a shame," he says. I'm not exactly right. I thought today it'd be "It's just not right". The wording changes from day to day, but the sentiment is the same.

"What's that?" I ask though I don't need to.

He thinks I don't hear and so raises his voice. "I said, such a shame that a girl like you is all alone."

I fill his thermos in the kitchen. I can see him through the arched doorway to the living room, but I don't meet his eye. "Hardly a girl, Tom."

"You're under forty, aren't you?"

Hell yes I'm under forty! Thirteen years under. "Yes," I answer.

"Then you're still a girl to me."

I chuckle, hoping that the lame joke will keep him from his true mission. No such luck. "A beautiful girl like you should be out every night, searching for Mr. Right."

"What if I find Mr. Goodbar instead?" I ask, but this seems to confuse Tom, even though that reference is more from his generation than mine. His brows furrow, creating even more wrinkles on his already lined face. I see him visibly decide to let it go. I hand him the thermos. He turns. He's nearly to the door and I think I'm about to get a reprieve from his—albeit well-meaning—meddling, when he makes an about face. "You know, my nephew would be perfect for you. Why don't I set something up?"

"Okay," I say, shocking him.

He stares at me, and then as if to pin me down before I can change my mind, he nearly shouts, "When?"

"As soon as my ball gown comes back from the dry cleaners," I say.

He looks at my black, baggy turtleneck, my grey, faded sweatpants, and my Hello Kitty fuzzy slippers and grunts just as I shut the door. I can hear him chuckle on the porch.

As the truck drives away, I have the moment of panic that I do every day when either Tom or Bob drive away. It passes, and I walk toward my workroom, aware that I will probably not speak aloud again until the same time tomorrow.

After four years, I'm used to it. Although, I have to admit, the thought bothers me more lately than in the past. And this was before the heartbreaking knowledge that Uncle Chazz is free, alive and apparently living in Tennessee.

Maybe Gammon_89 is on to something.

I unpack my new delivery—a Viao—and get to work, trying to ignore Nick's machine sitting further down the work surface.

PCs aren't as much fun to me as Macs. I fully admit I'm a Mac snob. But I'm not stupid, and I do realize that we live in a PC world. So, I diversify.

You've probably figured this out by now, but I buy, gut, refurbish, put together, take apart, and tinker with computers. I buy them cheap from internet sites like ebay or at estate sales, or storage places that are seizing property, then I strip them, put new system software on them, sometimes some other, more specialized, software, upgrade the memory, and resell them.

I do it for a living. You'd be surprised how much you can make doing it. Probably not enough to live on, but I don't have a lot of expenses. My aunt left me her house, her car and some money when she died. Not to mention the huge insurance policy payout.

If I live cheaply—and I do—I'd probably never have to work again. Right now I can make ends meet from the computer business.

I haven't touched the insurance money. I don't know if I ever will, but I save it—just in case.

The Viao is a pretty straight-forward job and doesn't take me very long. Like most of the machines I buy, there are still some personal documents on the hard drive. I don't even open them up, but plug my external drive into the machine and run the CD I made that cleans PCs off. I've got the whole thing down to a science by now.

You have to wipe everything clean. As if you're giving it shock therapy. Then you can rebuild it. Kind of like the six million dollar man, but more like a six hundred dollar Mac.

I made a rookie mistake years ago when selling my first IMac. It was a tangerine, clamshell laptop and just the cutest thing, but I'd outgrown it, needed more power. Instead of wiping it clean, I just deleted—or so I thought—all of my personal documents.

A year or so later, as I started getting into the whole buy, refurbish, resell thing, I realized all the hidey holes on the hard drive that probably still held some of my stuff. I didn't have much; some pictures—this was before digital cameras were so commonplace—that a friend had scanned in and emailed me. There were a few email documents that had probably gotten through. Several unfinished drafts of term papers.

I wonder what the person sifting through my tangerine IMac thought. Would they know the dark-haired woman in the pictures was me? What type of person had they come to the conclusion I was by the clues I'd left behind?

Who *was* I then? Someone with friends. Someone taking college classes.

Someone happily married.

# *Four*

The Viao is done, photographed and listed on ebay by the time Tom shows up the next day. I've also got the earlier ebay sale boxed up and ready to go. I stayed up late getting it all done. Confessor wasn't online (odd, but not totally unprecedented—apparently I was the only one with no life whatsoever), and I don't have anybody that I chat with on Monday nights.

Tom stays for coffee today and I tiptoe through his questions about my lack of love life like I'm dodging landmines. Finally he takes the hint and we talk about his favorite subject—besides how my life should be run—NASCAR. I can really only listen and nod, as I know nothing about racing.

I blow off the afternoon by baking cookies—Tom nearly turned his nose up at my store-bought Chips Ahoys earlier—and reading the latest Lawrence Sanders. Yes, I know it's not really Lawrence Sanders anymore, but it doesn't make much difference—I don't know what that says about Mr. Sanders' writing, but there you go.

Later on I look at Nick's machine. I know that with some extra memory that I have on hand and throwing in a printer that I got with a different machine, I can probably get $200 more than I paid for it. Not bad for a couple hours actually spent working on the whole thing.

If I could just wipe it clean. Particularly the desktop photo that included Uncle Chazz. If I won't even Google anything that would connect me to my past from my home machines, it's probably not too smart to keep a photo with his picture on it, even if I did take it off as the default desktop pic.

Even if I don't wipe it clean, I really should be working on other machines and putting up new listings seeing as I piddled the afternoon away (but if you're going to piddle, what better way than with gooey chocolate chip cookies and reading a new mystery). But Tuesday nights I play online backgammon in a league. There are eight of us that met in a Yahoo! backgammon room and we formed our own league about a year ago. Our leader set up our own site that we now use.

Gammon_89 was a member, but dropped out because she was intimidated by one of the other players. That's when she and I started playing on Sunday nights.

I tell myself I have a responsibility to the other seven to show up, and that I can work on the other machines tomorrow.

You may have realized by now that I'm not exactly a go-getter when it comes to work.

When the group convenes there are only six of us. All eight don't show up each week, but I'm pretty much a mainstay as are two other players. We only hope that an even number show up, otherwise we have to do a first-round bye thing and it all gets more complicated than anybody wants to deal with on a Tuesday evening.

I usually play in the living room on my laptop, some music playing, or maybe the TV on. But tonight I play in my workroom on my IMac with the idea that between moves I could at least start writing up listings.

I groan as I see I'm paired with eatmeee!. He's the best player in the group and also the most obnoxious. I don't know for sure, but I think he's the reason Gammon_89 dropped out of the league.

Knowing I won't be able to put up with only his conversation for the next few hours, I pull my laptop over beside me on the workstation.

My laptop is on wifi, and I have three cable internet connections installed in the workroom, all connected to different IMacs. I hold my breath as I tap once on the space bar and up comes my ichat. I release a sigh of relief as I see Confessor's icon bolded.

"You out there?" I ask.

It takes a few seconds, but then I see Confessor typing.

I love the different IM software and how they depict the other person is typing. Smiley faces, thinking bubbles, yield signs, the light bulb slowly going from dark to burning bright. The thinking bubbles are my favorite. It assumes that there is indeed thinking going on.

"Ready to eat meeee, DblSix? LMAO" eatmeee! says.

*Sometimes* there is indeed thinking going on.

"Sorry, I'm going to have to play without IMing. I'm not alone," I blatantly lie to eatmeee! But come on, I'm here to play backgammon, not listen to his trash talk and come-ons. It would only be a matter of time before he mistypes my screen name into DblSex and then asks if I'm interested. He's done it before. A good backgammon player, eatmeee!, but not terribly original.

I look back to the laptop. "I'm here," Confessor has typed. Thank God.

"Time to talk?" I ask as I make my opening move with eatmeee!.

"For awhile."

I came to terms a long time ago with not knowing about Confessor's life. When we first started chatting, I'd ask him the same things he'd ask me, but he was cautious. So was I. I'm a single woman living alone, I'm not stupid enough to give out any kind of info that would allow anyone to be able to find me.

I've hidden from people more intent on finding me than some horny guy on the internet.

But Confessor isn't just a horny guy on the internet. That was obvious early on when he said, "I can tell you all about me if that's what you want. Then I'd be another chat buddy who's info you need to remember. You can ask me how the job's going and I can say good.

"Or… I can be whatever you need. Tell me your thoughts. I'll tell you mine. Tell me your feelings. I'll tell you mine. Tell me things you wouldn't even tell your best friend. I'll keep your secrets. I'll keep you safe."

It was what I needed to hear at the time. What I still need to hear.

So, I did tell him my thoughts—on everything. I did tell him my feelings—whatever they happened to be at the time. I didn't have a best friend anymore, so he was the winner there.

I even told him my secrets. All but one.

Uncle Chazz murdering my father. And so, I obviously can't tell him about the photo with Chazz in it, my trip to the bank, the realization that I cannot leave my safe identity to seek justice for my father.

Instead I ask him, " Big plans?" as I watch eatmeee! roll a five-three combination.

"Not really. Paperwork I need to clean up. What are you up to?"

I don't ask what kind of paperwork—I don't care tonight. Some nights the questions are itching to be typed, other nights, I'm content just to have a friendly voice on the other end. Someone to keep me company while I roll a six and a one.

He wanted to do voice chat when we first met, but I'm glad now that I'd said no. I didn't have the software at the time. I had it soon afterward, but by then it would have seemed weird to put a real voice with Confessor's voice in my head. I really didn't think about him as a sexual being—or even a man for that matter—and to put a voice to him…it just didn't seem right. What if it'd been deep and sexy ? Or worse, high and nasally? What if he had one of those nervous laughs at the end of everything he said? No, for me he is to be drifting, weightless, intangible.

Since then, cameras on computers are much more prevalent, and built-in on laptops, and there's video chatting, Skype, the whole gamut. He's never brought any of those options up, for which I'm grateful.

I double up with the six-one, one of my favorite moves. Liking how safe the neat pile feels to me. I'm a cautious player, and sometimes it costs me, especially with a player as aggressive as eatmeee!.

"Playing backgammon," I answer Confessor.

"Right. Tuesday. So why are you chatting with me? Get an easy draw? Don't need to concentrate?"

"Worse."

"You got eatme? Again?"

"He spells it with three e's."

"My apologies. You do seem to get paired with him a lot, though."

"I know, and our moderator swears he randomly draws the games."

"The moderator isn't eatmeee is it?"

I look at my screen, at the layout of our site with all the different games being visible. "I guess it could be if he was playing under two different screen names, on two different machines. But who would go to that trouble?"

A pause from Confessor as I take my turn at backgammon. Double fours. I smile, I love doubles…security.

Confessor's thinking bubbles are rising higher and higher and finally his message appears. "Right. Because who in their right mind would be so devious as to have various screen names and use more than one machine simultaneously."

"I'm not devious…I'm multi-tasking."

"I hate to break this to you, but neither playing backgammon nor idle chatting are considered tasks."

My eyes glance to the listings sitting on the worktable. That would actually be multi-tasking.

"Okay. Okay. You've hit my guilt nerve."

"Sorry, didn't mean to."

Eatmeee! has just challenged me with the double die. The

cocky bastard. We're only about five moves in—and I've had great rolls—and he wants to double up? My stomach clenches in a mini fight or flight moment. I make my decision.

"Go ahead and do your paperwork, I should really concentrate on the game, it's not fair to my partner."

"Don't EVER call eatmeee your partner—he is your opponent. Big difference."

"Got ya. And by the way, he has an exclamation point at the end…it's eatmeee!."

"Of course he does—how stupid of me not to have guessed that." I can almost hear Confessor laughing.

"Good luck," he says, wrapping it up.

"Thanks. Get to that paperwork."

"Bye, bye, Blackbird." He is gone before I can respond.

I push the laptop away and proceed to get my ass kicked by eatmeee!. As he wins the round, he IM's me. "RU alone now?"

"Why?" I ask cautiously.

"I want to ask U something. Can U talk for a sec?"

Here we go. He's tried to get me to IM separately before, to give him my first name, to phone him…you name it. I'd declined every overture. But the guy could play.

"What is it?"

"Would U be available to play some other time?"

"Backgammon?" I qualify.

"Yes, BG." He quickly adds, "Unless U want to play something else, LMAO!"

"No," I say.

"No 2 what?"

"No to any other games."

"But you'd be willing to play BG more often?"

"Why do you need me to? You can play online with anybody anytime. Go back to the Yahoo! room where we all met."

"I'm in there all the time…it's U I want to play."

"Why?"

"I'm trying to practice against good players, and U R one of the best I've ever played," he says.

I certainly wasn't tonight.

"Except for tonight," he adds.

"Why do you need to practice?" He routinely wins during league. Except for when he plays me—then it's a toss up.

"The National Backgammon Championship is coming up," he says.

"Are you serious?"

"Yes. U didn't know?"

"I didn't even know they had such a thing."

"Oh yeah. They get a huge turn out. It's a two-day event. It's in TN this year. U should totally go."

I look at Nick's machine, having just come from Tennessee. Home of Uncle Chazz. Weird. "I don't think so," I say.

"It'd be great. We could be roommates!"

I laugh. He is obnoxious, but every once in a while eatmeee! makes me laugh. At least, I think he meant it as a joke.

"Count me out," I type, wishing like hell it was safe to travel to Tennessee. Although I wouldn't be playing in a backgammon tournament.

"That's OK—less competition. But can we play more often?"

I guess I could leave one of the IMacs chatting software up on DblSix's username. It would also take the sting out of losing Gammon_89 as a playing partner. And maybe take my mind off of Uncle Chazz's picture. "I guess. Look for me at Yahoo! IM."

"Great. Thx."

"Don't thank me yet, we haven't played."

"I'll find you…and hey…"

"Yes?"

"Bring your A game, will ya? Not the crap you played tonight, LMAO."

I quit out of the software and shut down that machine.

The thrashing I took in backgammon—to eatmeee! of all people—puts me in a sour mood and so I go to bed right afterward. I'm not in the frame of mind to make a decision about wiping Nick's machine clean. I decide to wait until morning to deal with it.

I let the physical reminder that Uncle Chazz is alive—and free - taunt me for one more night of restless sleep. I dream I'm in California, running—always running. I have this dream a lot. But this time I make it to the door of our apartment—which I never have before. But when I open the door, there is Uncle Chazz, looking just as he did twenty-two years ago. He brings his hand up to his mouth, the shhhh motion, but I have no voice.

I need for Uncle Chazz to move, so I can get through the door, but he doesn't. His face morphs into the older version, the one from the picture. His finger comes down from his mouth and I feel like I can finally move when hands slam down on my shoulders from behind.

I wake up in the middle of the night. Very calm, very still, afraid to move.

You know how in the movies when people are having nightmares and they wake up with a start, sitting straight up, flailing about? That's bullshit. How it really happens, when you dream you're being caught, or chased or about to be killed, and you suddenly wake up...you don't move a muscle, you don't make a peep, you prepare yourself to slowly look around the room and make sure the threat is no longer there.

Trust me, I know about nightmares. Ones had while asleep and awake.

I force myself up, out of bed, check all the doors and windows. I even go into the garage and check in the car and trunk. It's the only thing that allows me to get back to sleep when this happens. Of course I find nothing. I never do. But it doesn't make the nightmares go away.

I crawl back into bed, thinking that I haven't had one this bad in a long time.

And cursing the day I booted up Nick Carpenter's computer.

# *Five*

With a quick glance, it looks as though Nick's machine has some software that I'm not familiar with. I feel justified in my decision to poke around some more before wiping it clean. I get a tingle of anticipation. There's not a whole lot of software out there I haven't at least heard of. This has the potential to be good.

I'm not expecting any deliveries today, so I've got the whole day to play with it. It takes away the small disappointment I have at not being able to banter with Tom or Bob.

I head to the kitchen and get a big glass of milk and microwave a plate full of yesterday's cookies, getting the chips to that just-out-of-the-oven level. I bring it all to the workroom and place it on top of the overturned box that held the IMac.

I open the Applications folder, and scroll down the list. Got it. Got it. Need it. Got it. I take out a CD and copy the applications I want and then burn. I scarf down a couple of cookies while the burning executes.

I open up the folder of the applications I hadn't heard of before. One is called SynthoSync, the other SpeakerRay. I play around with SynthoSync just long enough to realize that it's some kind of software that musicians use and to know that it's not something I would ever want for myself. Still, I burn copies of both softwares. I see Garage Band a lot on machines I buy, but am not familiar with these two. Maybe I can configure a machine for musicians.

That's kind of become my secret, how I'm able to sell so well—I configure for niche markets. I'll load up a computer geared for would-be graphic designers with all kinds of Adobe products and desktop publishing software. Or, for students I do lots of word processing, paper-writing stuff. It varies.

It keeps it interesting.

I know squat about music. Or, about making music, anyway. But maybe I can look up this stuff online and see if it's something worth putting together. Maybe, coupled with some other stuff, I'd have something I could package to musicians. A whole other market to go after.

I'm not really ambitious, but I'm not about to let a good opportunity go by without at least checking it out. And yes, I suppose the software police can crash down my door, but those are the people I worry about least being at my door.

I patently ignore the Pics folder, not willing to deal with the conflicting emotions that overtake me when I think about ignoring Uncle Chazz's existence for the sake of my own safety.

Taking a different route, I open the My Stuff folder, curious to see just how far Nick's resemblance to the man in my past carried. Inside are two more folders; Music and Work. I click open the Music folder and see a dozen or so folders.

Each folder is named with what can only be called titles. "Any Other Day" is the first, and I double click on it. There are five files inside, four bearing the SynthoSync icon and one the SpeakerRay. The files are all titled "Any Other Day" and then an underscore and then what instrument or, I suppose, section it is. Like I said, I don't know squat about music. But there was Any OtherDay_lead, "Any Other Day"_bass, "Any Other Day"_drums, "Any Other Day"_keyboard. The SpeakerRay file was entitled "Any Other Day"_track1.

I put the volume of the IMac on—I usually work with computers on mute, who knows what annoying alert sounds people have installed—and double click on track1.

I reach for another cookie as SpeakerRay boots up, liberally dunking it in my glass of milk. A slow, solo acoustic guitar fades in. The rhythm is soft, almost haunting, and catches me right away. A steel guitar joins in, signaling a Country twang, and it loses me just as quickly.

I know squat about music—but I know I don't like Country.

Maybe there is some small justice that Uncle Chazz ended up bartending in Tennessee. No self-respecting goomba from New Jersey would surround himself with Country music.

Bored with the Music folder, I quit out of the software and open the Work folder. Inside is a folder entitled Resumes and Letters. There are eighty-seven Word documents inside. I change my view to date modified. The docs go back four years with the most recent one having been saved six months ago.

I open the doc dated four years ago and take another bite of cookies as the familiar Microsoft icon appears on the screen.

Nick Carpenter
900 Birch Street
Miami, OH 45056
513-477-3323

Mr. James D. Sutton
President, Zephron Records
3020 Park Plaza, Suite 350
Nashville, TN 37219

Dear Mr. Sutton:

I just put down the most recent *Country Times* and the interview featuring you and all you've accomplished at Zephron records. I am soon to graduate from the University of Ohio at Miami with a degree in Music Management, ready to learn from the best. Mr. Sutton, my name is Nick Carpenter and I want to work for you.

The letter then went on to explain Nick's musical accomplishments, instruments played, bands organized and future plans. It was brash without being cocky, saturated with the assuredness of youth.

Nick and I are about the same age, apparently, give or take a year. Was I ever that sure of myself? Could I have ever written a letter like that?

Maybe once. Yes, definitely once. No longer.

Nick's résumé is attached. I skim through it. It reads like most college senior's résumés. Lots of emphasis put on line of study. Not as much on work experience. How could there be, really? But Nick had been working in music in some form or another for eight years already. Clerk at a music store in high school.

Are there even music stores out there anymore? Are there even stores besides bookstores or like Walmarts, that also sell music?

Nick was a busboy in a roadhouse that featured amateur night which he participated in weekly (bet the owners loved that—"Nick, hurry the hell up and finish your song, we're waiting for clean tables").

His various bands are listed. Nobody I'd ever heard of, but I don't expect Nick Carpenter had been in a headliner. He wouldn't be looking for a job otherwise.

I remember the weeks I spent putting together résumés. The book I bought on how to do one correctly. The different drafts. The expectations I had when I sent them out. Knowing the hope Nick must have felt when he wrote these.

I click through the letters, all with attached résumés. It is a chronology of Nick's aspirations.

The first ten letters are all to various music executives in Nashville, all personalized like the Sutton letter with Nick having done his homework on each recipient. All written as Nick neared graduation.

The next group of ten or so are dated six to eight months later. Nick had moved to Mount Juliet, Tennessee. I snatch up my atlas from the shelf—I keep one in my workroom to estimate shipping times and costs. Not to plan trips like most people use them for.

There'll be no more trips for me.

As I suspect, Mount Juliet is just outside Nashville. Following the dream. I tried that once, but had a rude awakening.

The letters are similar to the first batch, but have a follow-up tone to them. Some are to the same executives, some to new people. All to people in the music industry. Country music, I assume.

Some of the companies are the biggies, that even I've heard of; RCA, Epic. Then there are some that I assume are lesser known, maybe specifically country; Planet, Down Home.

A new job has been added to the work experience section. It seems Nick is working at an investment firm, Bertram, Gleason and Young. His title is Account Executive—code for sales.

Somehow, I just don't see young, beautiful, Nick being happy in sales.

Each letter invites the exec to come and see Nick perform on any Wednesday at the Hopeless Heart in Mount Juliet, just outside Nashville.

I sit back in my chair and allow myself to envision the Hopeless Heart. Is it a skuzzy honky-tonk with chicken wire around the stage like in that movie about Jerry Lee Lewis? Or that movie where Patrick Swayze's a bouncer?

I realize all my visions of a Country music place are exactly the same. Lots of rotted wood, people in plaid shirts dancing everywhere, the occasional beer bottle flying across the room (thus, the chicken wire to protect the band), a fight breaking out at any moment.

I'm sure it isn't that clichéd…or is it?

And did Nick have a regular gig, or was it an open mic situation? Or, knowing the turf, did he moon-light from the investment firm as a busboy at the Hopeless Heart? ("Nick, hurry the hell up and finish your song, we're waiting for clean chicken wire.")

And most importantly, is it where Uncle Chazz works?

I don't want to do it, but I call up the desktop picture with Uncle Chazz in it. I try to avoid his eyes, as if they are laughing at me. Instead I take a critical look at all things surrounding the three of them in the picture. There. Just over his shoulder is a rough, wooden sign hanging down from the overhang of the bar. I can only see the right half of it, but what I do see says "ess Heart".

So, mystery solved. Not only is Uncle Chazz alive, free, and a bartender, but it is at the Hopeless Heart in Mount Juliet, Tennessee. Or at least was when this photo was taken. Not that the information does me any good. It feels like salt poured into my wound.

I shut the picture file and return to Nick's life, preferring to immerse myself in his journey rather than lament the lack of my own.

The next batch of letters and résumés are dated about a year later. They contain not only résumés (Nick has been promoted to Senior Account Executive), but apparently a demo CD was enclosed as well. The letter said the CD contained six songs, naming them all.

I go back to the Music folder, and sure enough, there's a folder for each of the songs listed. "Any Other Day" is one of them.

It's a wonder he still keeps trying. He has to be making okay money at the investment firm. Not ever having stuck to anything important myself, my admiration for him grows.

The remaining letters are sporadic. Nothing has changed for Nick. Some of the letters say demo attached, some of them inquire about an executive-type job at the company. Some beg to work in the mailroom, anything, just to get his foot in the door.

The letters are no longer brash, the self-assurance seems to have turned to self-doubt. I can almost smell the desperation in his last letter.

This is a man whose dream is dying.

And where does Carrie fit in? They hadn't been wearing

wedding rings in any of the pictures I looked at the other day. I checked. Is she cheering him on? Or is she one of the reasons his letters seem to take on a tone of desperation?

The last address is still in Mount Juliet, but a different street. Did he need more space? Did he turn one of the bedrooms into a studio? Are the kitchen counters littered with sheet music, Nick's scribbling all over them? Did he and Carrie move in together? Or break up and he moved out? Is that why he no longer needed a computer that they shared?

I force myself away from the computer. It's clear that I'm going to spend some time with this machine—open all the nesting dolls that are Nick and Carrie's lives. Double checking for any photos that may contain Uncle Chazz. But I've poked around enough for one day. I feel too raw after looking at the photo with Uncle Chazz in it.

Besides, it's kind of a delayed gratification thing—something to look forward to tomorrow. And, now that I know I'm not going to wipe it clean and put it up for auction right away, I need to get some other machines up and listed. I try to have at least one or two machines listed on auction sites at any given time.

Later in the afternoon I play two games of backgammon with eatmeee!, winning both. He once again mentions the Nationals (as he calls them). Beating him twice makes my day.

That evening, I tell Confessor about my adventures with Nick's machine and his career woes. I don't mention Uncle Chazz. To even type the name in an IM window feels dangerous to me.

Plus, this is one thing I cannot confess…that I have found the man who killed my father but I'm too concerned about being found that I won't do anything about it. Not a blackbird, more like a chickenshit.

"Those first few years out of college can be rough," he types and I'm brought back to our conversation about Nick.

"Did you always know what you wanted to do?" I ask.

"Hell, I'm still trying to figure it out," he replies. "You?"

I think back. Back to when I had dreams. Back to when I

allowed myself to dream. "I thought for awhile that I wanted to be an engineer."

"Let me guess—you sucked in math and science?"

"No. I was fine there."

"How far did you go before you knew it wasn't for you?"

I never got that far—I always knew it was for me. I still do.

It's as if Confessor is thinking over my life as I've told it to him, because he comes back with "Wait. That's during the time with your ex, right?"

"Yep."

"Were you on track to becoming an engineer then?"

"One semester shy. I was already working on résumés"

"It's never too late, you know. If it's something you really want to do."

I'd given myself the same pep talk many times. But it always came back to the same thing. "Transcripts," I type.

"Oh. Right."

He says nothing more. What can he say? He knows the situation. Most of it.

He changes the subject, returning to Nick's machine. "So, what was the music like? Any good?"

"Country. I didn't listen for very long, but it sounded good."

"For Country."

"Exactly."

"What was the name of the bar he performs at?"

"The Hopeless Heart."

There is a long pause. "Where did you say this machine came from?"

"Tennessee."

"Nashville?"

"Yes. Well, actually Mount Juliet, it's just outside Nashville."

A longer pause. "Do you get a lot of machines from that area?"

I think for a moment. "Not a ton. I seem to get most of my stuff from the Midwest and the West. Why?"

"No reason. Just thought you might have a whole new market with the Hapless Heart."

"Hopeless Heart," I correct him.

"Hmmm. I'm thinking that might be poor Nick's title as well."

"We don't know anything about his heart," I write, getting a little defensive, my fingers clacking just a tad too forcefully. I could care less about Nick Carpenter, but I do applaud his tenacity.

"It sounds like his heart is music and he's sold out for corporate life. Hopeless."

"Everybody makes concessions. Didn't you?"

There is a long pause. "Yes," is all he says.

Now I pause. I'm itching to type "what", but instead I ask, "And are you hopeless? Or just human?"

"Point taken," he writes. "When you think about your concessions, do you think of them as heart-breaking, or just part of growing up?"

I take a sip of pop, my throat suddenly dry. "That's different," I type.

"How?"

"The concessions I made saved my life."

# Six

**I** don't remember my father's face. I know what he looks like because I have pictures. Not many, but some. But I don't *remember* his face.

I do remember his arms. The bristly, dark hair that went past his wrists that sprouted from his knuckles. I would smooth the hair down, sometimes brush it against its grain so it would stand on end. My father's arms as they held me, his voice as he sang to me, are as fresh in my mind as if I'd seen him last night.

Not twenty-two years ago.

I'd sit on his lap, his arms around me, his fingers tapping time against my knee as he'd sing to me before lifting me up and putting me to bed. It was always the Beatles' "Blackbird". He'd sing about broken wings and the dead of night.

When he'd sing the line about learning to fly, he'd lift his arms. Mine would rest on his, so together, we would soar. Together, we would glide to new heights.

And there was more, about waiting for life to begin. When he got to " moment to arise", he'd wrap his strong arms around me, pulling me close against his chest. Shortly after that, he'd turn me in his arms, pick me up and carry me to my bedroom, ignoring my pleading for him to sing again, to hug me again.

For more time.

As he'd tuck me in, I'd breathe in the scent of him. So fresh and clean. And memorable.

For years, I would stand in the soap aisle in grocery stores, lifting each bar of soap, breathing deep, trying to find my father.

I never did.

The next day I drive to northern Ohio for an estate sale. An auction house sends me an email when a particular auction was going to have some electronic equipment. They have auctions a couple of times a week, but it was only monthly, sometimes longer than that, where they'd have much that I'd be interested in.

Sometimes I went even if it was only one computer, more to get out of my town, than for the sale itself.

It is a three-hour drive, a few hours at the auction, then three hours home. A nice little day trip for me. Something I always look forward to.

At the auction, I quickly see that there's really nothing I want. The one computer in the whole lot is an antiquated IBM, the kind that takes up the whole desk. I could jazz it up a little, but nobody would ever buy it. Plus, I wasn't sure I could even carry the huge thing into my house from my car.

I talk with Grace from the auction firm, thank her for emailing me.

"I didn't really think it'd be anything you'd be interested in, but you never know."

"No, you never know."

"Besides, there's some really great stuff at this one, you should take a look around."

I do. Grace is right, it's a treasure trove for collectors, but I'd never been much of one. I think somewhere in the back of my mind I always figured it wasn't wise to become too attached to things. I know from experience that they can be taken from you all too quickly.

That, or I'd have to leave them all behind at a moment's notice. I knew that from experience, too.

I do buy a cute wooden stool. Small, like for a child, with a bear carved into it. I could put it in my workroom. Instead of a child plunking its diapered behind down on it, it will end up holding cables and wires.

On the drive home, I do the same thing I do every time I come to Ohio. I get off the freeway in a mid-size town—I try to mix that up, picking a different town each time. I gas up, paying cash, asking the person behind the counter where I can find the town's library.

Sometimes, I don't even have to do that. I've had times when a coffee shop advertising internet usage will be right on the main drag. That's been happening a lot more frequently lately.

I like when that happens, it fills two of my vices simultaneously, coffee and the internet.

Now, I'm not talking about coffee houses that have wifi where you bring in your own laptop. I don't want that. I want some anonymous machine, in some anonymous town. Those are getting harder to find at anywhere but a library.

I find the library easily enough and wait my turn to use their computers. Finally, an older woman leaves and I sit down. I look around, as I had the entire time I'd been waiting patiently with a magazine at one of the tables. It is late in the afternoon and there aren't too many people. All at work, I suppose.

I can hear a group of children in the far corner of the small building, enjoying story time. Whoever is reading to them is doing a great job, her voice, pure, clear and yet lulling. She's reading a story I'm not familiar with, but then, I didn't have the normal, story time sort of childhood.

I rub my hands on my thighs, leaving nervous sweat marks on my jeans. I caress the mouse, point the pointer to the web address slot and click. My fingers poise over the keyboard. I type in the site for Google. When their home page comes up, I immediately start to type in the search window.

The reader for story-time finishes and the children all applaud. I jump at the sudden commotion. My eyes dart around the small alcove where the computer station resides. Nobody. I continue to type.

My name.

I've lived under two names in my life. No, not my maiden name and my married name. I didn't change my name when I married. I'd been a college student and both my husband and I agreed that it would be easier to keep my maiden name while I was a student. At least, that's why I thought he'd agreed.

I think of the two names as my Michigan name and my California name.

Or, my safe name, my livable name. And the name I was now covertly looking up in an obscure library a hundred miles from my home.

Not so safe.

I click on search and hold my breath. Praying for something to come up.

Dreading for something to come up.

The search only takes a few seconds, as it does every month. And just like every month, when the hits come up, there is nothing. Sure there are hits. For lists that have someone with my first name and someone else with my last name. I'm used to seeing those by now. I can even recite them from memory.

But no hit for me. The real me.

I type in "Uncle Chazz, hitman, murder, mafia, New Jersey", my father's name and any other thing that remotely relates and click on search, just like I do every time I get to one of these places. I never knew Chazz's last name, or don't remember it. Lots of hits, mostly containing the actor Chazz Palminteri, who apparently has played his share of mafia in various movies, but nothing for *my* Uncle Chazz.

I sit back in the chair, I don't really need to Google him anymore, I know where Uncle Chazz is, where he works, or at least worked. I'm just too much of a chicken shit to do anything about it.

I type in one more name, my ex's, going through the same paralyzing waiting process as the machine searches.

Nothing for him either.

I do a search I've never done before on these little trips… I Google the Hopeless Heart. They have a website, but it's pretty bare bones. A picture of the front of the building, its hours, phone and a list of upcoming bands and when they play. I wonder if Nick's band is one of the ones listed.

No mention of any employee names, and no pictures of the staff.

I leave the library, my heart rate finally slowing down to normal. I get in my car and head back to Michigan. Knowing that I'm still confined to my cage. And that Uncle Chazz remains free.

**I** go back to Nick's My stuff folder the next day. I'd only opened one of the Pics folders, and there were three left to investigate. Now caught up in Nick and Carrie's life, I'm so anxious to get to them that I shoo a stunned Tom out the door after he drops off my newest acquisition. I make myself a tuna sandwich and settle in for a little slide show.

My finger—and so the pointer arrow—circles the folders. I decide to open the Miami folder first. The date modifieds on the documents coincide with Nick's years at Miami of Ohio from his résumé.

Guys and girls at football games. Guys playing quarter bounce, eyes bloodshot, smiles crooked. Guys and girls at parties, flashing peace signs and flipping the bird. Girls getting ready for dates. It seems Carrie was in a sorority.

In a bunch of photos, Nick and sometimes Carrie, are with three other men—boys really—who show up repeatedly in the photos. I go back to those photos and look more closely, not sure what I'm expecting to see. The four guys are strikingly different in appearance. One has sandy blonde hair, wavy and shoulder–length. Too long and of no discernible style. He's lanky, self-contained. In every picture he's wearing a t-shirt with different beer manufacturer's logos. He instantly becomes Shaggy in my mind.

The second has white blonde hair, spiky-short. About twenty

years too late to be Billy Idol, but he was trying. In one picture he was even doing a dead-on sneer and the crazy fist-hand pose.

The last man has dark brown hair—chestnut I guess you'd call it—with a tiny bit of natural curl. It settles at his collar. An easy, warm smile, he is looking at the other people in the photos more than he looks at the camera. Taller than the others.

The quintessential boy next door. It is him I like best.

I know most people would go for the drop-dead gorgeous guy—Nick, but not me. Ever since my ex, extremely handsome men make me nervous. Things come too easy to them, they haven't had to build any character. Although, after reading Nick's cover letters, it seems that his one dream—a career in music—is not coming so easily to him.

On a hunch, I open the Band folder next, and, as I expect, it's the same four guys. Some of the photos are staged, maybe to be used for posters? Some are candids taken while they are onstage.

Shaggy is the drummer. Figures.

Billy is the bass player. The boy next door is on guitar. And Nick is everywhere. Playing keyboards in one picture. Front and center with a guitar in another. Demonstrating a bass technique to a watchful Billy. At a recording studio mixing board in yet another.

It solidifies my conviction that Nick is the leader of the band—its heartbeat.

My tuna sandwich sits ignored on my desk as I stay glued to the computer.

I keep coming back to one picture. It was taken at a gig (do they call engagements gigs, or am I hopelessly unhip?) at some smoky bar. Shaggy's face is concealed behind Nick, but you can see his arms flailing mid-beat. Billy is holding the bass in that crazy way that bass players do, with his elbow high, his fingers poised over the strings. He stands to the left of Nick, looking into the audience.

The boy next door—I still don't have a nickname for him yet, I don't want to underestimate him—is to the right of Nick, watching him, a look of envy mixed with admiration on his face.

And then there is Nick.

His eyes are nearly closed, but they still hold a haunting melancholy. His mouth open, mid-note, his cheeks flush, either from singing or the heat of the bar. He seems both in pain and near orgasm.

I minimize the picture and quickly open the folders I'd found the other day. I go to the "Any Other Day" track and play it. As the software boots up, I maximize the photo.

I grew up with MTV—I'm from the video generation—but there's something so stark about hearing a man sing while seeing only a still photo of him. It seems so pure.

Of course, there's no telling what song Nick is singing in the picture. It could be anything from their repertoire, but I imagine it's "Any Other Day".

Nick's voice is deep and resonant. It goes with his face. I know that sounds crazy, but you know how you sometimes see people and then when they speak—or even worse, sing—they don't sound a thing like you thought they would? It wasn't like that with Nick, his voice and face match. Dark, intense.

Something in his voice reminds me of my father singing to me. Something familiar, but I can't place it. My heart pangs as I think of my father singing to me each night. My father would have been about Nick's age then. Had his face held the same raw emotion as Nick's does?

I eat my sandwich as the song plays. Maybe Country isn't so bad. It isn't the Beatles, but hey, what is?

**T**he family folder is the only picture folder remaining that I hadn't gone through. I'd planned it that way. The best or the worst, I wasn't sure.

The thing is, you can leave a band, you graduate from college (or, in my case, you don't) you and your girlfriend can break up. But family is forever.

At least it's supposed to be.

I know seeing family photos will be tough—even if I don't know Nick's family. I polish off my sandwich, wash it down with the last of my milk, and forge on.

It's worse than I thought. It's a complete nuclear family and they seem…happy. The dad is an older version of Nick—which bodes well for Nick—as he's very handsome in a distinguished, graying-at-the-temples kind of way.

The mom has Nick's crystal blue eyes. *Her* smile lights up her whole face. No crinkly eyes masquerading as a smile for mom. She was slightly plump, round…motherly.

There's a younger sister who ages from about fifteen to nineteen in the photos. She'll be a beauty, with her father's—and Nick's—jet-black hair and her mother's stunning smile.

I wonder what it would be like to be Nick's sister. To be a part of this family. Does he tease her mercilessly? Does he grill her prospective boyfriends? Does he protect her?

When they were kids, did the mother have cookies waiting everyday when the kids got home from school? Did she drive them to soccer? Guilt them into eating their vegetables?

Did the father with the graying temples sing lullabies to his daughter when the daughter was young? Does he still? Does she know how lucky she is?

Probably not, no one ever does.

The pictures are all from the last few years—I suppose since Nick got a digital camera. Christmas dinners with Carrie joining the Carpenter family. Some kind of summer home with a huge lawn and a lake in the background, Carrie and Nick surrounded by his family. Birthday cakes. Normal, everyday family life.

My stomach hurts, my heart aches.

I yearn to be a part of those pictures.

Now, normally I'm not a yearner. I know the things that I've missed in life—some were torn from me, and some I ran from—and I've come to terms with it.

Most of the time.

But this is different. These family photos. They're so obviously…normal. It screams at me how far removed I am from that life. How far removed I've always been, even when raised by a loving aunt.

Even when I was married.

Because even then I was keeping secrets.

# *Seven*

"So where does all this take you?" Confessor asks.

"Nowhere I guess. I just thought it was interesting, that's all."

"But you do this for a living, surely you must have come across people's personal stuff before."

"Sure, all the time. I just usually don't take the time to go through it."

"And you've certainly never mentioned it to me. And for three days straight."

It was true. I'd told Confessor all about Nick's machine. Nick's band. Nick's family. He had to be sick of it by now. The question was, why wasn't I?

The one thing I hadn't mentioned to Confessor is Uncle Chazz being in that one photo.

I guess that in itself is the answer to the question.

"Sorry. Too much information?" It isn't a question I ask Confessor often. It seems he couldn't get enough information—about me, anyway. He just seems to have had his fill of Nick and Carrie and the gang.

I have not.

"No. It's just…I don't know whether to be happy you're showing such a strong interest in something, or concerned because it's an interest in…"

He doesn't finish. I'm not sure I can finish that thought either.

Just what is Nick's machine to me? A curiosity? An electronic project? An obsession? A small link to my past? A reminder of how weak I am to stay here safe and sound while my father's killer serves up Rolling Rocks?

I take another route to Confessor's statement. "I have interests in lots of things," I defend myself.

"Name three."

I think. Then quickly type so he won't realize I had to think. "Backgammon. Old movies. Music." I'd just added music. So I only had two…so what.

"You had to think."

It sucks to be so transparent.

"And music was just an add-on. That's not really an interest of yours."

I laugh. Sometimes it's great to have someone who knows you so well.

I think of all the time I've spent listening to Nick's group's music in the last three days. "It's becoming an interest of mine."

"Oh, please."

I know I shouldn't, but I can't help myself. "Oh yeah? What are YOUR interests?" I type.

"That's easy. You."

Is he kidding? Does he mean that in more than the "you're the person I talk to most" way? I take a deep breath, let it out slowly. I poise my fingers over the keyboard, willing them to type something brilliant.

I don't get the chance.

"Bye, bye, Blackbird." He is gone before I can respond.

The next three days are spent on Nick's machine. I don't get anything else done. Machines I'd bought off ebay pile up in my workroom. I blow off my Backgammon league to flip through Nick's family photos again. Eatmeee! sends me an inquiring IM which I ignore.

I spend the most time in the family photos folder. Drawn

back, my mind filled with thoughts of family and what could have been.

Of course I don't ignore Confessor, but that's about the only constant in my life that doesn't collapse from the weight of Nick's Mac.

I even find myself flipping to the Country Music Channel.

That's when I know I need help.

Maybe this is all a sign that I'm ready to start over. To move on. Within the safety of my town.

But where to start? *How* to start?

When Tom delivers my packages the next day, he's surprised when I ask him to stay for coffee. Poor Tom, even he's been a victim to my time spent with Nick's machine.

"So Tom," I begin as I hand him the cookie jar full of Lorna Doones. "About this nephew of yours…"

I don't need to say another word. Within minutes, Tom's made a call on his cell and I've got a date for Friday night.

*Tom. Thomas (Greek, Aramziac) Twin.* Or maybe not a twin, just a double life as my matchmaker?

What can I say about my date with…Steve. God, I forgot his name for a second. Steve.

*Steve. From Steven. Steven (Greek): Crowned.*

You're probably expecting a horror story. A blind-date fiasco.

In fact, it was perfectly fine.

We had dinner. There were a couple of awkward pauses, but not enough to be, you know, awkward.

We went to a movie. Our shoulders brushed in the dark. We shared popcorn, our fingers tangling.

He walked me to my car. We had a quick, but sweet, good night kiss, our noses gently bumping.

He promised to call me. I believed him. I went home.

And felt absolutely nothing the entire time.

As soon as I get home I rush to my workroom. I see my laptop—where Confessor resides—and Nick's Mac next to it.

I'm not sure which one to boot up first.

Having two hands, I don't have to decide.

My laptop—a more powerful machine—comes up first.

"You around?" I type to Confessor.

No answer.

Nick's machine is now up. I've made aliases on the desktop to the four picture folders. I spin the mouse and cursor around and around the folders. Eenie. Meenie.

"Yep, I'm here," Confessor answers.

My hand reluctantly leaves Nick's machine and I give the laptop my entire attention.

"What's up?" I ask.

"Not much. You're home from the big date a little early, aren't you?"

I'd thought about not telling Confessor about my date, but then it would seem like a thing. Like there was some reason that he shouldn't know I was dating. So, I'd told him.

"Not that early."

"What'd you do?"

"Dinner and a movie?"

"And?"

"And, what?" I don't think Confessor wants lurid details, that isn't his style. Besides, there aren't any to give him.

"And…what do you think? Confess."

What *did* I think? I take a deep breath and type really, really fast, the words spilling out of me. "I think that he's a perfectly nice man that I have no spark with whatsoever. And before you say sparks can grow, I know that. And I'll probably see him again if he asks just to make sure that I don't give up too soon. But, ultimately, I KNOW that this is not the guy for me. So, the question becomes, do I waste the time hoping something will grow when I know it won't or do I…" I fist my hands, flex my fingers, but it gives Confessor enough time.

"Do you what?" he asks.

"Do I pursue something…someone…that I feel a connection with?"

'Like you' screams in my head, but I don't type it.

"You mean like Nick?"

I roll my neck, loosening the tense muscles.

No, not Nick, I think to myself. Definitely not Nick. Confessor wouldn't even have suggested that if I'd told him about Nick being a dead ringer for my ex. But I stay silent, waiting to see what Confessor has to say.

"He's not the one for you."

"Why do you think that?"

"Other than the fact that you don't know him. That he has a girlfriend. He lives hundreds of miles away. And, oh yeah…YOU DON"T KNOW HIM!"

"Yeah, other than that."

I can feel his sigh through the computer.

"Besides, how do you know he lives hundreds of miles away? He could be in my backyard."

"I thought you said he lived near Nashville."

"I did. He does." What is left unsaid is how does Confessor know that Nashville is hundreds of miles from me? I wait. So does he. I think back over the conversations I've had with Confessor. There's no way I would have slipped and told him I lived in Michigan. I might have complained about the snow or cold once or twice, but that was all. I guess that's enough to know I'm miles from Tennessee.

I decide to go with that, not allowing myself to think about it too closely.

"If not Steve, and not Nick, then who?" I type. Please say me. Please say me. It is a thought that whistles through my mind so quickly it startles me.

"Anybody." My shoulders sag. "What this is all saying is that you're ready to get out, to live your life again."

I'd thought of that, of course. Thought of nothing but that

since Gammon_89 pointed out the changes she'd sensed in me. Had sensed a change in me even before I saw Uncle Chazz smiling out at me from that picture.

It is a powerful—and scary—feeling. "I think so too," I type.

"Scary?"

"Very."

"It's okay. You're stronger than you think. You'll be fine."

"I know, but still…"

"Yeah, I know…it's the 'but still' that always gets ya."

I smile.

"So, we've established you're ready to start living again. And that this Steve is probably not going anywhere. That's okay. There's lots of ways to ease yourself into this. A job. Friends. Just make sure it's somebody real," he says.

"Nick is real. And the people I meet online are real."

"Okay, he's real. *They're* real. But somebody…"

What? What could he say? Someone I know in person? I don't know anyone.

Partially by design. Mostly by self-preservation.

I've mentioned my aunt. The one who raised me. The one who left me the house I now live in.

At least, they told me she was my aunt. And a five year old who'd just seen her father's murder tends to grasp at whatever straw is thrown her way.

I've come to believe that she wasn't my aunt. Not blood related, anyway. My guess is she was an aging federal agent of some kind, near retirement. That I was put into her custody for the first few years into a sort-of safe house. This house. And it stuck.

Either I was never needed again, or she fought for me, or legally adopted me, or something altogether different—those people have a way of making their own rules.

But, she raised me as her niece, and I believe, loved me. I

know I loved her.

That still didn't stop me from leaving at eighteen.

I thought I could heal my broken wings. That I could fly, soar. But my wings were clipped and I came crawling back home.

My aunt didn't turn me away. I don't know if she ever got in trouble with anybody for my disappearance, or if anyone even cared by that point.

She'd hugged me and tended to my wounds—the physical ones. The others, not all the bandages in the world could cover up.

She died a year later. Car accident, they'd told me. And maybe it was, but I don't believe in accidents too much anymore.

**I** look for Confessor later, but he's not online. He probably doesn't want to keep hearing about Nick's machine.

I eye the IMac, but don't turn it on, trying to see how long I can go without my fix. Feeling restless, needing something to occupy my mind, I boot up the machine that I left my backgammon chatware up on.

Eatmeee! is there, trolling. "Got time to play?" he asks.

I look to Nick's machine and back to my laptop, both dark. "Sure," I say, turning my back on them, facing the machine and the backgammon board.

Three hours later, eatmeee! concedes and I've won the day, 5 games to 3.

"I know I can be an ass some of the time," he says.

"Some of the time?" I tease.

"Whatever. But I do want to thank U for playing with me so much. It's been very helpful."

"You're going to be tough to beat at the Nationals," I type.

"I hope so. U know…"

"Yes?"

"U really should come. It's still a couple of weeks away. Time enough to make plans, get the days off of work, whatever."

I look around my workroom. Yeah, the boss would probably

let me have a couple of days off.

"It's not too late to register. They're still taking people up until the Wednesday before the tournament."

"When does it start?"

He gives me the date. "It's a Thursday afternoon. The finals are scheduled for Friday afternoon-evening."

"And it's just random draws?" I don't know why I'm asking, it's not like I'm really considering going…traveling.

"Random draws for the first round, then it's done in brackets, just like the Final Four."

Could I make it to the Sweet Sixteen? The Elite Eight? I chuckle at myself.

"You said it's in Tennessee?"

"Yep. Nashville. The newspaper there is one of the sponsors, they have all the information on their website," eatmeee! says and sends me the website link.

"I'll think about it, thanks for the info."

"Hope to see you there," he says and logs off. I don't have time to mention that unless he's wearing a nametag that says eatmeee! there's very little chance of us meeting.

I barely glance at Nick's machine as I log into the Nashville paper's website. I have a moment of hesitation about logging into a Nashville site with Uncle Chazz living in Nashville, but my paranoia apparently does have boundaries and I do it, just to satisfy my curiosity about this tournament thing.

There's a sidebar for the tournament and I click on it. Is this just curiosity or am I taunting myself? There's no way I can go. But oh, if only I could. Blow into town, win the National Championship, swing by the Hopeless Heart and take out Uncle Chazz, put my nightmares to rest.

And be on the run for the rest of my life. Would it be worth it? Is my life, as it is now, so great? So worth protecting?

The tournament page comes up, but as I move my cursor to the registration button, something else catches my eye. It's in a right-hand sidebar, along with all the other breaking news stories, and I click on it instead.

A large picture fills my screen. Above it are the words "BREAKING NEWS".

Below it are the words "HAVE YOU SEEN THIS WOMAN?".

I barely register the text; my eyes are so transfixed by the image. Looking back at me, smiling for the camera was a woman wearing a blue gingham dress.

A blonde Dorothy with an attitude.

"So, you don't know that she's missing for sure—didn't you say it was a 'possible missing person' on the website?"

"That's what it said. I've spent the last couple of hours," besides waiting for Confessor to get online, "trying to find something—anything—online. There's nothing else. It only had her name with the photo—her last name is Essex—and just a number to call if you had any information. Not how long she'd been missing. Or even that she was missing. Maybe she's on the run? Maybe she robbed a bank or something." Okay, I was grasping at straws, but that was better than thinking that something really bad had happened to this woman in which whose life I'd become so immersed.

"Maybe you saw something different? That it wasn't really Carrie? You've probably been staring at all those pictures non-stop." True. "You might have just seen a pic that was similar and mentally superimposed Carrie's image onto it." False.

"This is a very particular photo—there's no mistaking it."

"What's so particular about it?"

"She's dressed very distinctly. I've called her Dorothy in my head when I look at it because she's wearing a blue gingham dress."

"Huh?"

"You know, like Dorothy in *The Wizard of Oz*."

"That blue check thing."

"Yep."

"That has a name?"

"Yes…gingham."

"Huh."

Men.

"Wait a minute," he writes. "What do you mean you always thought of Dorothy? Is she wearing that dress in a picture on Nick's machine?"

"It IS the picture from Nick's machine."

"And yet you have the machine in your possession. Huh. That's weird."

"Hello?!! That's what I've been telling you!!"

"Don't use exclamations with me, I'm just trying to sort this all out."

"You and me both."

I start to freak out a little.

"Don't freak out or anything. It's just a weird coincidence," Confessor writes.

I hadn't thought it was anything *but* a weird coincidence. Until now.

"You don't think this has anything to do with me, do you?" He doesn't know about Uncle Chazz, and I can't for the life of me make any connection between Uncle Chazz knowing Carrie, her going missing, and my father's murder. But you never know.

There's a pause. He could be taking a sip of pop, or readjusting his chair, even talking to someone else, but the silence is damning to me. My stomach tenses. I mentally run through what all I'd have to do to be in a car and driving far away from Michigan, never to return. I know I've let my defenses slide, living in safety for the past four years.

"No."

My shoulders sag in relief. Still, I know I have to be more diligent. My life could depend on it.

But Confessor doesn't know about Uncle Chazz. He's thinking about my ex when he says no.

"You got this machine from ebay, right?"

"Yes."

"And you've had no contact with these people before, right?"

"No."

"Then there's no connection."

Logically, I know that. Knew it all along. But I needed Confessor to confirm it.

I grab my business folder, look through until I find the print outs from Nick's machine purchase. Hmmm. "But," I type.

"But what."

"He contacted me. About the machine. I didn't get it in an auction"

"What do you mean, he contacted you?"

"Through ebay. I get that sometimes, people contact me through my ebay account if they want to sell a computer but not go through the hassle of an auction. They see that I buy and sell computers."

"Why wouldn't those people just list it on Craig's list or something?"

"I don't know. Maybe they don't want their info 'out there' so they just contact one person to see if they want to buy. If they have a buyer, it goes much quicker than an auction, and if it's a known buyer, they're more likely to get paid."

"Does that happen a lot?"

"No. Maybe five or six times total."

There is a pause while we both try to think if it means anything that Nick came to me for the sale instead of putting the machine up for auction. Neither of us come up with anything.

"So?" I ask.

"So what?"

"So, what should I do?"

"What do you mean?"

"What should I do about Carrie missing?"

"Why should YOU do anything?"

I think on that. I can't tell him that I know for a fact that Carrie knows—or at least was served at a bar by—a known killer.

"Because." I lamely type.

"Lame."

"It just feels like I should be doing something."

"Relax, Nancy Drew, there's nothing you can do from there, anyway."

It almost sounds like he knows where I am, but that's not possible.

"I know you're right, but…"

"Yeah?"

"I feel…connected…I guess."

"Even more proof that you're ready to get back out in the real world. You want to be connected to something…anything… so you've chosen this."

"Hmmm, maybe." But if feels more like Uncle Chazz chose me.

"What the hell do I know? I could be totally full of shit."

"No. You're probably right."

"So, monitor the Carrie situation, but start concentrating on yourself."

I lean back in my chair. Take a deep breath.

"Besides," he adds, "Are you in a position to come forward to anyone about this? Make yourself known?"

Starting to live again, in my safe little town, under my safe name, is one thing. Speaking out to a newspaper or the authorities of some kind is another thing altogether.

"No," I reply.

There is a long wait for Confessor's answer.

"Small flights, first, Blackbird, small flights first."

The next morning I check the paper's website before I even have my coffee—which is saying a lot. Nothing has changed. The picture and caption are still there, but no new information.

I go to the kitchen, stare at the percolator as my coffee brews, Confessor's words still resonating.

Okay. This is it. I'm going to wipe Nick's machine clean,

load it up with other software and get it posted on ebay. I can monitor Carrie's missing/non-missing status on one of my other machines. I am going to come to terms with the fact that Uncle Chazz is alive and well in Tennessee and there's absolutely nothing I can do about it.

Then I'm going to figure out how to start the rest of my life.

Get a job? Do they do extensive background checks?

Become a volunteer? But what was I good enough at to volunteer to help others?

Thinking about jobs makes me realize I don't know what Carrie does for a living.

Thoughts of wiping the machine clean leave my head as I take my coffee and a plate of cookies into the workroom. I pick through Nick's hard drive, seeing if there's any documents that I missed. I have a Duh! moment. If Nick didn't bother to clear off his documents and pics, could he possibly have left his email untouched as well?

I boot MacMail up. Yep. Completely as Nick left it. All his previous emails are there, but no new ones come flooding in. He must have changed his internet provider, maybe even his email address when he moved but didn't bother to change the settings on this machine seeing as he would put it up for sale.

But what kind of person sells and ships to a stranger a completely loaded machine with all their personal stuff still on it? There's probably a good explanation, but none comes to me.

It makes me wonder if Nick is in a "just don't give a shit" phase of his life.

I know what that was like.

Had it led him to…what? I can't even begin to guess.

**I** spend the entire day reading Nick's emails. He'd saved them all, even from when he'd just gotten the machine (I know this because it says "hey…just wanted you to be my first…email that is. LOL"). The majority of them were to and from Carrie.

There were quick "looking forward to tonight" missives,

to long, rambling "I don't know what I'd ever do without you" letters. From both of them.

But…there was something about their correspondence. Sometimes she'd just drop the smallest…dissatisfaction…with his music. It was subtle at first. In the emails sent during their senior year of college there would be an occasional "when we're out of school, have real jobs and you leave the band" lines dropped by Carrie. I never found anywhere that Nick addressed those snippets.

And she made the plans for them both, that was plain, but I guess not all that uncommon.

She'd emailed him a list of investment firms that he should send résumés to. It was dated about nine months after they'd graduated. All the message said was "Here's that list" then the names. No "Love, C" as she signed most of her emails. I notice that one of the names is the firm that Nick did indeed end up with.

There's an email about two months later. "Congrats, hon. Knew you could do it. You'll look so hot in pinstripes! Love, C".

The love had come back with his gainful employment.

Off on a tangent, I scan through the remaining emails. When she was hinting at something she knew Nick might not like, she signed "C" or sometimes no signature at all. When she was praising him for doing what she'd suggested, it was "Love, C". Subtle. Or passive-aggressive.

Isn't that how you train dogs? Only with kibble?

I try to imagine doing that with my ex. No way.

Finally, I find what I searched for in the first place. Carrie is in sales. No big surprise. She's with a marketing firm in Nashville (her emails to Nick from work have her company's name and address as part of her signature line). Lots of emails reminding Nick he can't play with the band on certain nights because she needs him to go to certain functions with her. "It's good for you too, hon, to make these connections," she writes.

A lot.

I now know what she does for a living. But I know a lot more about her than that.

**"I** think she definitely wears the pants in the relationship. She's obviously pressuring him to give up music." I've told Confessor all about the emails.

"And yet he hasn't. Maybe she doesn't wear the pants all the time."

Carrie's endless legs, tan and pant-less, and now missing, was not a vision I wanted to think about. "I don't like that analogy—wears the pants."

"You brought it up."

"I know. But I still don't like it."

"Okay, let's just say she's the proactive one and he's the reactive one."

Being reactive for most of my life, I was okay with that label.

"It just feels so…"

"Yes?" Confessor prods.

"Familiar," I write, the breath whooshing from my body as I remember.

"Explain," he says gently. Okay, I don't really know if it was said/typed gently, but I imagine it is. How could it not be?

"My ex used the same technique on me. Passive aggressive. Subtly withholding affection when I did something he didn't want me to."

"How did you handle that?"

"I did what he told me to do. For awhile."

"And then?"

I think about what I did and wonder if that's how Nick finally reacted. "And then I snapped."

"My poor Blackbird."

But I didn't want his pity. He knew that.

As if to prove it to me, he quickly comes back with, "Back to Nick and Carrie. People are in the relationships they want to be in," he writes.

I relax, the subject now off of me. "Did you just make that up? That's profound. Total crap, but profound."

"Nah, it was in the movie I watched last night. Some chick flick with the girl from Will and Grace."

Sitting down with a bowl of popcorn for a romantic comedy was so not the picture I had of Confessor. "You watched a chick flick that spouted lines like 'people are in the relationship they want to be in'?"

There is a pause. "It wasn't my night to pick the video."

That stops me cold. Someone else is picking Confessor's videos. I'm silent, my fingers still. I know, of course, that he has a life, that he is not some entity that surfaces when I need him. Even as badly as I want him to be.

I feel like a door I'd only hoped was open is beginning to slowly close.

Confessor skips over his…confession. "And besides, it's not total crap. It's true, in a way. People are in the relationship they want to be in."

I think about that. "But I'm not in any relationship."

"Exactly. And isn't that the way you want it?"

Is it? "Is it?"

"Probably. Or at least it was. Only you can know for sure."

I'm just about to step out on a ledge and type "are you?", but of course, he knows I'm becoming braver, testing my wings. Ready to soar?

"Bye, bye, Blackbird." He is gone before I can respond.

And the door creaks with movement as it inches toward closure.

**I** go back to Nick's machine, opening up Firefox which is the first icon on his dock. I look through his bookmarks, go to a couple of the sites. Mostly music related stuff. Well, on closer look, *all* music-related stuff. I call up his FaceBook page, but he logged out and I'd need his user name and password to get into his account. Same with his MySpace account. He logs out of those but leaves his email untouched? I mentally shrug at that.

The next icon on the dock is for Ichat, the MAC Instant Messaging software. If he logged out of FB, there's probably no reason to…but I open Ichat anyway.

When it opens, nearly fifteen buddies pop up. Nick is logged in as invisible, so I can see if his contacts are online, but they can't see me…well, Nick.

The different buddies icons rearrange, with the ones being online going to the top. Only one is active. Someone with the screen name Bocephus. I take a quick screen shot of the buddies list and then quit out of Ichat.

That name sounds familiar, but I can't quite place it. Greek Mythology? Biblical? I check my name book, nothing. The closest thing is Bo, short for Beauregard. *Beauregard (French) beautiful, handsome, well-regarded.*

But there's no need to guess whom this is. Nick used real pics as icons to his buddies. Bocephus is the nice looking guitar player from Nick's band. The boy next door.

What did Bocephus do that he could be on Ichat in the middle of the day?

I imagine Nick working hard all day, taking crap from clients, writing new tunes in his head in the car on his way from work to the Hopeless Heart or maybe somebody's garage for practice (does every band practice in a garage, or am I again solely drawing from my movie knowledge of bands?)

At practice, he'd take shit from Shaggy who'd forgotten where he comes in with the backbeat (because Shaggy would forget his head if it wasn't attached—or at least, the Shaggy I imagine would).

Billy would once again ask for a bass solo in a totally inappropriate spot in a lovely new ballad Nick had written. When refused, he'd sneer and pout.

And Bocephus?

I don't know. I still don't have a bead on him.

But I know how I could.

All thoughts of starting my life over today are gone. A job? It could wait. It had for four years.

I pull over a laptop I don't use much and open up the Ichat software on it. I want to be able to monitor Nick's buddies on his Ichat. And of course, I'm not willing to log out as Blackbird on my own chat software that I always keep open on my main laptop. I pull a list out of a drawer of all the screen names I've signed up with on Yahoo! or like places, and their corresponding passwords.

I don't worry about having a document like that lying around. For one, nobody comes into my workroom but myself and the delivery guys—when I'm with them. And second, none of these screen names mean anything to me. If anyone found them, they'd never have…a piece of me…the real me.

The only one I've never written down is Blackbird.

Hmmm…what to use for this group? Or should I create something new? Something music oriented would be good, but it should be country and I don't know any female country singers other than the big names.

And something tells me I should be subtler with Bocephus. So, no Shania or Faith or variations thereof.

I end up going with PatsyKlein—a touch of old country with a twinge of humor. I set up a new Yahoo account with that username. I go to Google and find a couple of Patsy Cline websites, looking for a pic I can download and assign to this screen name. Great voice, Patsy, but not much of a looker. I find a pic of Jessica Lange playing Patsy in *Sweet Dreams* and download that instead. What can I say? I am a woman, and if I have to choose between looking like the real Patsy Cline and Jessica Lange…well…I'm not stupid.

I know I'm going to some trouble for something that may not even get used with this group, depending on what restrictions they've put on themselves. If they'll let me—as PatsyKlein—add them to my buddy list or not. Some people click on the "allow any user" permission to add you, some do the "needs permission first".

I log in as PatsyKlein. I print out the screen shot I made of Nick's buddy list. The pics for icons are small at this size, but I'm still able to make out Bocephus, Carrie (who's screen name is CarrieE—some imagination on that one!), Billy (can you believe it…BillyIdolMan) and Shaggy (Russell_2005—Russell? I wouldn't have seen that one coming).

Also, there's Nick's mom and dad (bobcarpenter) and the younger sister (trishthedish—either she had a good sense of humor or an awfully inflated view of herself).

The others are faces that may have shown up in Nick's picture folders, but not frequently enough that I recognize them. I decide to skip all of those.

No picture of Uncle Chazz, but who knows if they have that type of relationship that they'd be IMing. Plus, I can't see Uncle Chazz as the IMing type. But what do I really know about this man and his life now?

Could he have been in prison, all this time? Paid his debt to society for killing my father and is now out? He could have served twenty years and be out.

Would that matter to me? Make a difference?

I honestly don't know.

One by one, I try to add Nick's contacts to PatsyKlein's buddy list. A couple of them allow me to add them without permission. You're probably thinking, what? Are theses people crazy? But you've got to remember they're all using anonymous—mostly - screen names, they don't know that anyone can put them together with who they really are. It's not like FaceBook where you're actively looking for people you know.

You'd be surprised how many people out there don't put the "permission only" preference on for their chatting software. A lot of people don't even know it's an option. I didn't at first, years ago.

Just because they're added to my list doesn't mean I'm automatically added to theirs. They'd have to add me themselves. I have to give them a reason to add me.

I'm not at that point yet. I'm not even sure I'll contact any of them as PatsyKlein, but I want to be ready if I do.

A knocking sound comes from my laptop. Confessor has come online.

"You out there?" he asks.

"Yep."

"Can you tear yourself away from Nick's machine long enough to talk?"

"Ha ha, very funny," I say as I tear myself away from Nick's machine.

"Seriously. Have you gotten anything done in the last few days? Other than monitoring Carrie's…situation?"

I look around my workroom. No other box has been opened, no other machine has been boxed up. Everything is pretty much where it was yesterday. And the day before. And… you get the picture.

"Sure, just sent out a machine yesterday," I type. I believe it is the only time I've ever lied to Confessor.

"Did you just lie to me?"

"I've told you the most intimate details of my screwed-up life, why would I lie about something like that?"

"Exactly."

I feel badly that I lied about something so inane, but he lets me off the hook. "And don't say your life is screwed-up. It's no more screwed-up than anyone else's."

I snort at that, glad he can't hear me. "Besides," he continues, "If you truly think your life is screwed-up, why don't you unscrew it?"

Oh God, he wasn't going to give me pep talk was he?

"Sorry," he says, "I must have been channeling Oprah there for a second."

I smile…there he is…my Confessor.

"Can't stay long," he says.

"That's okay. You go do what you have to do." And I mean it. I don't feel that pang that I normally do when Confessor has to return to his life. Because with Nick's machine by my side, for the first time, I know what I'll do when he leaves.

"Bye, bye, Blackbird." He is gone before I can respond.

# Nine

"**H**ey, does the name Bocephus mean anything to you?" I ask Confessor later that afternoon. I'd meant to Google it, but I'd actually gotten a few things done around the house, and played three games with eatmeee!. He forgave me for blowing off league and took 2 out of 3 (he's going to be a force in Tennessee). But, eventually I'd wandered back into my workroom.

"You mean other than Hank Williams, Jr?"

"Hank Williams, Jr.?"

"You HAVE heard of Hank Williams, Jr., haven't you? I mean, I know he's Country, but he did the—"

"Oh right…are you ready for some football."

"Yeah, that's him."

"And what about him?"

"I don't know, you asked me."

"I did?"

"Bocephus."

"Yeah?"

"Bocephus IS Hank Williams, Jr."

Oh. "Oh."

"But Hank Williams, Jr. has a beard and is kind of scraggly looking, isn't he?" I ask. I'm not a huge sports person, but I have caught the old opening to Monday Night Football a few times.

"Let's just say he's got a face for radio. Incredible guitar player, though."

Huh. So the boy-next-door guitar guy picks the screen name of a not-so-attractive guitar player. Could mean absolutely nothing. Or it could mean that Bocephus—mine, not the recording world's—has some hidden depths.

"Gotta go," Confessor says, drawing my attention back to my laptop. "Bye, bye, Blackbird." He is gone before I can respond.

**S**teve did call, as he said he would. We talked for an hour. Nice, companionable. I didn't think his jokes were funny. He didn't get mine. When he asked me out again, I politely declined. He didn't seem that surprised, or that disappointed.

Maybe I should have said yes. Maybe I need to give it more time, a chance to grow. But I couldn't help feeling that Steve was not someone who would ever get my jokes.

And at this point, I wasn't sure I could change. Nor did I want to, really. Even if he can never be more than my online salvation, Confessor gets my jokes…that's enough. At least for now.

**N**ick wasn't online very often. I'd log in as PatsyKlein, but invisible, in the evenings, just to see when he'd come on, but he seldom did. Probably at band practice or hanging out at the Hopeless Heart hoping to be discovered. Or working late. Or at gigs.

Or out searching for Carrie?

Maybe he doesn't even use chatting software anymore.

Being at home during the days, you'd think I'd be into daytime television. Talk shows or soap operas, but I'm not. Hearing about other people's problems had never been a draw for me. The whole reality show craze has totally passed me by. But now I could see how people could get hooked on it. I had in a way.

Real World—Mount Juliet.

Bocephus is on a lot. Even when no other icons on Nick's Ichat are lit up, Bocehpus' is. The man was online a lot. Or maybe he just never logged off?

Which gives me an idea. Bocephus is a Yahoo! screen name. On a lark, or maybe a hunch, I go to the Yahoo! chat rooms. I click on the "find a friend" button and type in Bocephus. If he's in the chat rooms, I'll be taken there.

I hold my breath. The screen starts to change. He's there, in the chat rooms, and I would soon be there too. But what room? Would I be thrust into a room that PatsyKlein wouldn't be caught dead in?

In my early chat days, I'd checked out the whole scene. Shocked at some rooms, curious at others, bored with some, irritated in others.

It'd been awhile since I'd gone blind to a chat room. What happens is you usually meet someone in a chat room, become friendly, then begin IMing, not needing to go back to the chat room. Kind of like meeting in a seedy singles bar, but then going out to dinner at a nice restaurant the next time.

That's how I'd gotten in the backgammon league—in a backgammon lover's room.

And of course, that's how I met Confessor.

We don't talk about the room we met in. It's embarrassing now that we know each other. We both swore it was the one and only time we'd been to that room. Like I said…he gets my jokes.

Pleasantly surprised, I land in a Country Music chat room. I see my PatsyKlein icon appear in the bottom third of the list, just below MusicMaker88. There's about ten people chatting and they all have names with some sort of country or music flavor. At least, I think they do, I'm still pretty new to the whole genre, even though my clicker does seem to land on Country Music Television more and more frequently.

I just watch the chat for awhile, not introducing myself to the room. I've debated this with eatmeee!—whether or not one should introduce oneself when entering a room. Some people do, some don't.

The decision is made for me. "Hello Patsy, welcome," MusicMaker88 writes.

"Hi all! Just listening, interesting stuff." They are debating somebody's newest album. A group I've never heard of. I write the band's name on a piece of paper, making a mental note to Google them later.

There's a bunch of "welcomes" from chatters, but not from Bocephus.

The conversation continues for a while about the band. Bocephus adds his take and a couple of people agree with him. I'm just about to sign out when Bocephus IM's me privately. "Hey there. First time here?"

"Yep."

"Thought so," he says.

"You must be on here a lot."

"I am."

"Is it always the same group? Am I intruding?"

"Yes, it's usually the same group. We're all in bands. We talk about the music industry mostly. Who's looking for talent, stuff like that. No, you're not intruding."

"k"

"Love your pic." He of course, has seen the pic of Jessica Lange. I congratulate myself on my choice of names and pics… apparently it got his attention.

I look at his avatar, he's chosen a pic of Hank Williams, Jr. No big surprise, but the man in the pictures on Nick's machine is much cuter. Must not have a ton of vanity.

"Thx. U 2." I use the computer slang that I never use with Confessor, somehow thinking it will appeal to Bocephus.

"Thx. I loved that movie. Jessica Lange was so hot."

I've never seen *Sweet Dreams*, but I don't think it's much of a stretch to agree with that. In what movie isn't Jessica Lange hot? Well, maybe that one where she went crazy and had the lobotomy. And the one with Drew Barrymore where they grow old and crazy together.

"So, do you look like your pic?" he asks.

And that's how it starts. I've done the chatting thing long

enough to know. With guys, as soon as they ask for a visual, you know where it's going. To different degrees, of course, but to some extent the conversation is going to veer from our mutual (ha!) love of country music to something more personal.

I feel like I'm doing reconnaissance for some mission that is yet unknown to me. I only know the more information I have, the better prepared I'll be. Prepared for what? I couldn't tell you.

And was this about Carrie's disappearance or Uncle Chazz? I don't know anymore. Knowing I won't—can't - do anything about Uncle Chazz is so painful, that I allow myself to think it's about Carrie this time. I don't really fool myself.

"Not really," I say. I don't look a thing like Jessica Lange. At least not in her blonde, fair, natural state. I'm dark, Italian looking. "U?" I ask.

"LOL," he writes. I guess he would think that's funny. Hank Williams, Jr. probably wouldn't. "You got a pic?" he asks.

"Yep. Hang on a sec."

I scramble to my laptop. I have a bunch of pics from people I've met online. I surf through, looking for a good-looking blonde. Aha. Got one. I pull out a flash drive to transfer it to Nick's machine, but I stop.

Instead, I find a picture of Sophia Loren when she was in her mid-twenties. I quickly load it onto the drive and transfer it onto Nick's machine.

"Sophia, nice to meet ya," he writes after he receives the picture.

I'm a bit startled. Not too many people my age know who a young Sophia Loren is. "It's the closest thing I've got," I type. "I don't have any pics of myself on this computer." Which is true. He doesn't have to know I don't have any pictures of myself on any machine. Or anywhere else for that matter.

Way too dangerous to have something like that potentially floating around cyberspace.

"You look like Sophia Loren?"

"Pretty close," I respond.

"Wait. Grumpy Old Men Sophia or Houseboat Sophia."

"LOL. Houseboat."

"Wow! Bellisima."

"Grazie."

"How about you?" I ask.

I wait. After a minute he sends me a pic of Cary Grant. I think it's from the *Houseboat* poster from some movie site.

The pictures I've seen of Bocephus on Nick's machine do not remind me of Cary Grant. Where Cary was suave, sophisticated, there is something sweet, unaffected about Bocephus.

"Kewl," I type, thinking how much crap Confessor would give me if I ever typed kewl to him.

"A/S/L?" he asks.

Now, for those of you who don't do much online, he's not asking me if I know American Sign Language (which I found out rather embarrassingly the first time I chatted). He's asking for my age, sex and location.

On the list of screen names I use, I write this fictitious information beside each name so I can keep my identities straight. I pull out my list, write PatsyKlein and pick some imaginary info.

"24/f/Vermont," I write, both on the paper and into the chat software. At least I got the right gender. "U?"

"26/m/Tennessee."

"You're only 26 and you've seen Houseboat?"

"Yeah. My grandma loved movies. Fox Movie Channel. Turner Classic. Stuff like that was playing all the time on the TV."

"Lucky you."

"I can't tell if you're being sarcastic or not."

I think of a young Bocephus, his warm eyes, that broad smile, visiting his grandmother, curling up with her to watch a Cary Grant movie, a plate of Oreos on his lap. "I'm not being sarcastic."

"Oh."

I know I should keep him on track, keep him interested so that he'd chat longer and maybe I could lead him to the Hopeless

Heart and Uncle Chazz, or to Nick and Carrie, but instead I ask, "Do you visit your grandmother often?" I feel a small pang of jealousy as I wait for his answer.

"She's dead."

"Oh. Sorry."

"It's okay. And no, didn't visit her often - lived with her after I was five."

"Really? Why?" I ask, curiosity replacing jealousy. I'm probably getting more personal than he wants, but that's the thing about chat rooms. Sometimes people are on to get information about the music industry. Sports, or some other interest. Like backgammon. But sometimes, they're on to find someone to connect with.

Mostly they don't even know the difference.

I'm hoping Bocephus doesn't.

"My parents were killed when I was five."

I stare at the sentence. I look at the author's name. Yep, Bocephus wrote it, but it could just as easily have come from my keyboard.

I start to type and stop. What can I say? I know his pain better than anyone. I know how he felt growing up; the feeling that something was missing, that nothing could ever be completely right. Feeling like an outsider, and guilt for feeling that way because you loved the woman who was raising you.

I take too long with my musings, and Bocephus writes, "U still there?"

I start to write something small, like an "oh, sorry, what a bummer", but my fingers move and the words, "me too" come out.

"U 2 what?"

"My parents were killed when I was five." I don't get into the semantics of never having had a mother, the result is the same; at five, we were both orphans.

Now he is silent for a moment. Probably wondering if I'm pulling his leg. But why would I? He must come to the same conclusion, because the next line to show up on my screen is, "And did YOUR grandmother raise U?"

I think about what I'm about to say, if it's revealing too much? But my ex never knew about my aunt, or that I'd been orphaned at five. He only knew that at eighteen, I had no family of any kind. That's what I'd told him, trying to protect my aunt.

As it turns out, I'd protected myself.

"I was raised by an aunt. One I'd never met before."

"Wow. That's tough, at least I loved my grandmother, had been to visit her."

I look around, trying to remember the first time I walked into this house. Memories and feelings rush to the forefront. Men in blue suits, a woman taking me by the hand, leading me to a bedroom. It was beautiful, with a frilly canopy over the princess bed, a room any five-year-old girl would dream of.

But not the one my father carried me to every night.

I've moved to the master bedroom since my aunt died.

"We did all right She did the best she could."

"Yeah, so did my grandma…but…"

I wait for him to type more. When he doesn't, I prod, "But?"

"But it's not the same, is it?'

"No," I type. I start to make light of it, say something funny, feeling we're both on shaky ground. But I can't. "It's not the same at all. It never has been."

"You always feel like you're on the outside, staring through the window."

"And it's always a family you're looking in at."

"Exactly."

We're both quiet for while. Then he types, "Sorry to be such a downer."

"No, it's okay. It's nice to know I wasn't alone—wasn't the only one that felt like…"

"An alien?"

"Yeah, that's as good a word as any."

"Anyway," he writes, "I was raised by my movie-loving

grandmother, that's how I know Sophia Loren and Cary Grant."

"Now I know," I type.

"And knowing is half the battle," he answers.

A childhood memory flickers and before I can stop myself—surely he won't get the obscure reference?—I type, "Yo, Joe!"

And am shocked to see Bocephus has simultaneously typed the exact same thing, only with two exclamation points (must be a guy thing, lots of exclamations).

"You know GI Joe?" he asks.

"Yep—loved it," I answer.

"Really, a girl? That's so cool!"

"Watched it every day after school. Even when I outgrew it and watched MTV, I'd turn back to USA at the top of the hour to watch the PSAs at the end."

"You know they've got a bunch of those on YouTube."

I do, I've seen them. There're some pretty creative voice-overs done to the GI Joe team. "I've seen 'em—too funny."

"Favorite character?" he writes.

"Lady Jaye," I quickly type, a smile on my face as fond memories rush over me. "You?"

"Duke."

"Did they ever defeat COBRA?"

"I think they're still fighting the good fight."

"Freeing up the world for truth, democracy…"

"And the American Way!"

It's nice to talk to someone my age, someone who watched the same after school program I did. I've never talked with Confessor about that kind of stuff. Who knows if he'd even get the reference?

I can almost feel Bocephus reminiscing along with me, and I know that if we're anything alike, the memories will inevitably lead to pain. I want to spare him that. Even if I can't spare myself.

I change the subject. "So, you said that most people in this room are in a band. RU a musician?" The chat in the room has continued while I IM privately with Bocephus, but I haven't kept up with it, too engrossed in our shared memories.

"Yep."

"RU famous?"

"Not yet."

"Soon? Will I be able to say I knew you when?"

"Any day now. But you'll have to tell me your name to be able to say you knew me when."

"LOL," I write, even though I'm not close to laughing, out loud or otherwise. "You can just call me Sophia," I type.

"Shy?" he asks.

"No. Cautious."

"I can respect that. A lot of crazies out there."

I can vouch for that, I was married to one.

"Are you married?" Bocephus asks.

"No."

"Boyfriend?"

"No."

"And you look like Sophia Loren? How can that be possible?"

Through hard work and diligence. "Haven't met the right guy," I write.

"Are you looking for him?"

No. Because even if I found him, how could I ever be honest with him? How could I put someone else in danger?

Thoughts of my past put me on edge. "I've got to go," I type. I need to think about this. Do I really want to delve so deeply into Carrie's disappearance that I'm chatting with her boyfriend's band mate? A man who shares the pain that I've deeply buried?

I need to talk to Confessor.

"Did I scare you off?"

Yes, but not in the way he means. "No, not at all, I really have to go. Some other time?"

"Sure. U online a lot?"

"Not in chat rooms much, but online a lot. IM?"

"Great, I'll add you to my buddy list—make sure you ok me, lol!"

"I will. Bye." I don't tell him that he's already on PatsyKlein's buddy list.

**I** spend the next hour trying to find something new on Carrie.

There's something on the newspaper's website. It was a bigger item, but with the same pic of Carrie in the Dorothy dress, Nick cropped out, but his arm around her. As if he'd been amputated, with only his hand dangling from her shoulder.

Carrie's full name—Carolyn Essex—was listed now. And a plea for anybody with any information on her whereabouts.

It says the paper had received the item anonymously, the photo emailed into the paper from an untraceable email account. The same email was sent to a smaller paper in Mount Juliet, and the police.

When Nick was questioned, he'd denied that Carrie was missing, saying she'd left him a voicemail that she'd needed to get away for a few days and that she'd call him when she got back. (Even I think that sounds fishy and I don't even know these people). But, there was a lot to back up Nick's story.

Her work place confirmed that she didn't show up for work on Monday, but she had scheduled time away from the office a while ago. She had several weeks of paid time coming and had left her plans open-ended.

Her parents hadn't come forward at all. And apparently hadn't been contacted. Or at least they hadn't been mentioned.

And no mention of a bartender being questioned, not that I thought there would be.

There really is no reason to assume she was missing other than the anonymous tip. And the fact that no one knows where she is or had heard from her.

So, to me, it seems that the mystery isn't so much where Carrie is, but who sent the anonymous email? And why?

The item in the paper called the "case" baffling.

Uh, yeah, I wouldn't be sitting in my workroom chatting with unknowns, work piling up around me, for less than baffling.

# Ten

**"S**o, I told you that I'm single. Are you?" I ask Bocephus the next time we chat. We've already compared notes on our favorite GI Joe episodes and realized we both owned second-hand Commodore 64s when we were in middle school. I'll admit it; I'm intrigued with this guy.

I think back to the pictures of Bocephus on Nick's machine. In most, he's with Nick or the other members of the band. There aren't any of him with the same girl twice. A heartbreaker? A player? Gay?

"Yeah, I'm single."

"How is a guy who looks like you single?" As soon as I hit the return key I realize my mistake.

"How do U know what I look like?"

I think fast. "You mean you DON'T look like Cary Grant? I'm shocked!"

"LOL," he responds. Whew, dodged a bullet.

"Besides, you could be a total troll, but if you're in a hot band, girls are going to flock."

"I'm not really interested in the type of girls that flock."

"Isn't that why guys join bands, to get chicks?"

"Maybe some guys."

"But not you?"

There is a long pause. "No. Not me. I'm in it for more than that."

"You mean there IS more to it than getting chicks?"

"LOL. Yeah. I don't expect you to understand."

"Because I'm not a musician, or because I'm a girl?"

"Both."

"Make me understand." I almost say, "Confess," but I can't. It would feel like a betrayal.

"I want music to be my ticket to fame, but I also believe in the music, in the songwriting."

"Why do U want to be famous?" I ask. The notion is so far from my sphere…I crave—need—total anonymity.

"It's going to sound stupid," he says.

"Try me."

"When I'm up on stage, and people in the crowd are singing along, I feel like I finally belong, like I'm part of something."

A little breath of air escapes through my lungs and my fingers fly across the keyboard. "Like being part of a family."

"Yeah," he admits. "And I guess I feel like as the stage, and the crowds get bigger, so will the feeling of…"

"Belonging," I finish his thoughts, his feelings.

My feelings.

"Yeah. Like I said, stupid."

"No. Not stupid. Just human."

"Anyway, that feeling is so rare for me, so precious, that I can't share it with just anyone. Certainly not a woman who's into me just 'cuz I play in a band. Or one who wanted the lead singer but settles for me 'cuz he's taken."

"That makes sense, I guess." And it does make sense to me. I know those feelings, they're not ones you can share with just anybody. I feel honored Bocephus shares them with me.

"Besides the groupies—which I'm not interested in, and it's not like there's tons of them, anyway—girls don't think of me like that."

"Like a man?"

"Right."

"They think of you as a woman?"

"Ha. Ha. Very freakin' funny."

I smile to myself. I find myself doing that a lot lately. When I'm online with Bocephus.

"So, how do girls think of you?"

"Like a pal. A buddy."

"Oh, you're that guy."

"What guy?"

"The nice guy."

A long pause. "Yeah. I'm that guy." I can almost hear the resignation in his voice. "I'm not dangerous or brooding. I'm 'sweet', or so all the girls I've ever been interested in say."

I'd had enough of dangerous and brooding. Sweet sounds pretty good to me.

"Don't worry, most girls realize that the bad boys make fun boyfriends but the nice guys make good husbands."

"When?"

"LOL. They start figuring it out in their late twenties."

"You're in your early twenties and it sounds like you figured it out."

That's right, I'd skimmed a few years off my age. It doesn't matter. At twenty-four I knew the score. "I did. The hard way."

"Ahhhh.... So that's why you're single."

"Yes. And why I know the value of a nice guy."

"Just how is it that you're online so much?" I ask him the next day.

"I could ask you the same thing."

"I work at home."

"What do you do?"

A lie easily comes to me. "I'm an accountant. I do the books for some of the local businesses out of my home office."

"So, shouldn't you be balancing columns instead of chatting with me?"

"I keep kind of irregular hours. I'm here, and can answer their questions during the day, but I do most of the actual work at night." I put my hand to my nose. I can almost feel it growing.

"I understand that. I keep crazy hours myself."

"So, there's still a need for a day job? Music isn't supporting you yet?"

"In a way it is. I do a lot of studio jobs."

"What's that?"

"There's lots of recording studios around here. If someone needs a musician, I'm on a list. You show up when they call and do a good job, your name moves up the list."

"How high are you?"

"I'm probably the third or fourth guy they call when they need a guitar player. A little lower down for other instruments."

"You make sure you show up."

"Absolutely."

"And these calls are enough to get by?" I think of Nick, slaving away at the investment firm. Does he bear the brunt of the band's expenses? Is Bocephus a mooch? That doesn't fit with the man I'm coming to know.

"Close. A few more months and they probably will be. I live pretty cheaply. The only things I spend money on are instruments. And I pick up stuff during the day. Some construction, I help out around the bar where we play, hell, I've even walked dogs."

Aha. The bar where they play. How to latch onto that one? "Where you play? What type of stuff do you do there?"

"I build stuff for Johnny sometimes during the day when they're closed. I built the stage we play on."

My heart rates skips up a notch. I take my fingers from the keyboard, think, but nor for too long, then answer, "Johnny?"

"The manager of the bar we play at…Hopeless Heart. Johnny Campos. He's been really good to us."

"That's nice. Has he been there a long time?"

"Yeah. Since it opened. Like twenty years or so, I think."

So, not in prison for the last twenty. If Johnny Campos is even Uncle Chazz.

How to type, "does he have a scar through his eyebrow and

look like a hitman for the mob"? No way that I can see, but I grab a pen and one of the scratch pads I leave lying around the office and write "Johnny Campos" down. Like I'd ever forget it.

**M**y mind races, wishing I could Google Johnny Campos right now. But no, I can't, not from here. Never from my home machines, this IP address. Like I said, I know there's ways around it, changing proxies, clearing your cache, all that stuff. But, have you ever done a search for, say, a motel in Arkansas, and then the next few times your on Facebook or wherever there are advertisements, ads for Arkansas hotels come up? And you start remembering all those Orwellian, Big Brother type things?

Yeah. No, not taking the chance.

I look back to the screen, even scroll up a little as I forgot what we were talking about. Oh yeah, part-time stuff he does at the Hopeless Heart. "A waiter? Aren't all starving artists waiters? Or is that just actors?"

"LOL. Nope, never been a waiter. I couldn't commit to a regular schedule in case a recording session came up. I don't want to do that to anyone."

I bungled that, but there's no way to gracefully bring it up again. "Very responsible for the slacker generation."

"U R not a slacker."

I look around my workroom. Three machines lay bare, their cases off, keyboards askew, motherboards partially out. Yeah, I kind of am a slacker, but I don't care about that—all I can see is the name Johnny Campos laughing at me where I wrote it down.

"I better get going," I say.

"LMAO. Did I hit a nerve?" He did, but not the one he means. The nerve he hit is much larger than he thinks, much closer to the surface, and throbs so badly at times I want to puke just to ease the pain, as if it was a migraine.

"Yeah."

"Now I know."

"And knowing is half the battle," I answer.

"Tomorrow?" he asks.

"Definitely," I type without even thinking about it.

"Tell me about your band." Nick's band. The one that plays at the Hopeless Heart. While Uncle Chazz tends bar. Or while Johnny Campos manages.

"It's me and three other guys," Bocephus types.

We'd been chatting every day since we met. Sometimes for a few minutes, sometimes for hours. We chat about music (mostly me listening there), food, television, shared memories. And always old movies.

Sometimes we flirted, sometimes not. It wasn't as meaningful as my relationship with Confessor, but it was coming to mean a great deal to me.

I had to discipline myself. There's an element of discipline for anyone who works at home, but now I really had to step it up. Bocephus was online a lot during the days because of the odd jobs and recording studio schedules. If I wanted to, I could be chatting with him all day long.

I didn't allow that, though I would have enjoyed it. I limit my time on Nick's machine to a couple of hours a day. I still kept his Ichat up all the time, but just, you know, to see what was going on.

I caught up with my machines. Poor Tom had to carry three out on one day. I thought the guy would have a heart attack. When I offered coffee, he'd looked at me with pity in his eyes and shook his head. I guess Steve had told him we were a no-go. He'd started to bring it up, but I cut him off. He let it drop, and in a couple of days, we were back to coffee and cookies.

I kicked butt in backgammon league (it helped that eatmeee! wasn't on that night). I caught a matinee of a thriller I'd wanted to see.

And yet…And yet, I was always drawn back.

"What's your band's name?"

"We've had a bunch over the years."

"How long have you been together?"

"I met Nick when his family moved in next to me and my grandma. We were both eight. His family was kind of like my second family. His dad would always include me when he played ball with Nick, his mom had me over for dinner a lot. Stuff like that."

"That's so nice," I say, meaning it. Wishing I'd had neighbors like that. But my aunt and I didn't live close to anyone, and she didn't socialize much. Of course, later I figured out that was all part of the plan.

"Nick got a guitar for Christmas when he was twelve. God, we'd play that thing for hours, taking turns. Finally his parents took pity on me and bought me one of my own. It was the nicest thing anyone's ever done for me."

I take a drink of pop, urging the lump in my throat to go down.

"We started a band in high school. The other guys were goof offs, but we took it seriously. We hooked up with Russ and Billy in college."

High school. He'd been Nick's band mate for nearly ten years. How long had they known Carrie?

"So, what's the name now?" I, of course, had named Nick's band The Carpenters. Confessor had gotten a chuckle out of that one.

"The River Rats," he writes.

Hmm, it didn't set off any bells, but I don't know a lot about band names. I guess it'd look okay on a marquee. Or a CD case.

"Great!"

"It was my idea." It sounded like maybe the others weren't.

"Catchy."

"Thanks."

There is a pause.

This is the point in our conversation where he'd turn it personal. He'd been doing it for the last few days. We'd talk about music, or work (what would those businesses do without me to balance their books!) and then it would turn personal. And I don't mean the personal stuff we'd already discussed. I mean personal as in romantic.

I'd been ducking him so far, avoiding questions, steering him back to safer topics. I don't know how long he'll stay with me if I don't cough up something soon.

And he was my connection to Carrie and Nick. And possibly Uncle Chazz.

Plus, I was drawn to Bocephus. Drawn in a way that was becoming more important each day.

"You told me you're not seeing anyone. It sounds like you've been burned before, but you're awfully young to not be out there looking. Why is that?" he writes.

Images of the small number of men in my life rush through my head. My ex. A high school boyfriend. Steve. My father's dead body. Uncle Chazz putting his finger to his pursed lips, forcing my silence.

No image of Confessor, but he is there. He's always there.

I wait, willing an answer to come. I've been chatting for a long time, though it's been awhile since I've chatted with anyone this often but Confessor. I can spontaneously come up with a totally different personality and life history in a matter of seconds.

My favorite thing to do, back in those days, was pick an old movie character, and make that my life story. The Bette Davis movies were great for that. Lots of melodrama that played pretty well in today's world. I even managed to pull off the one where her twin marries the man she loves then dies and she secretly assumes the twin's identity so she could be with Glen Ford.

I think by the end of that chat I'd been busted, but the guy was hoping I'd let him talk dirty to me, so he'd played along. Guys will do anything if they think you'll let them talk dirty to you. Even more if you'll talk dirty back.

But nothing pops into my head to tell Bocephus. I certainly can't call on an old movie plot—he's seen them all. I'm tempted to stick as close to the truth as possible, but that doesn't seem like a safe thing to do.

And it seems like a betrayal of Confessor.

I split the difference.

"You're right, I was burned before—very badly. So now, I'm taking my time, being cautious."

"Caution is good. Caution is wise. But…"

"But what."

"But sooner or later, if the right guy comes along, you might just want to consider throwing caution to the wind. And…"

"And?"

"And I might just feel a breeze coming on."

**"I'm** asking again—where is all this going?" Confessor asks me after I bring him up to speed on Bocephus' and my most recent conversation. "Are you expecting him to lead you to Carrie? Keep you updated on a situation you're not supposed to know anything about? Is that why you're chatting with him so often?"

At first that's what I'd hoped. That's why I originally contacted Bocephus—to learn more about Carrie and Uncle Chazz. But now…now I very seldom think about Carrie when we're chatting. And I don't allow myself to dwell on Uncle Chazz never having paid for killing my father or I'll go completely insane. I keep all that to myself. "Does it have to go anywhere?"

"If it's not going anywhere, why are you investing so much time in it?"

Hah! Does he see the irony of *him* asking me that?

He must, because he quickly comes back with, "Scratch that." Yeah, I guess so.

"But here's the thing," he types.

Oh no, does there have to be a thing?

"I've sensed the change in you lately."

Since Nick's machine. And seeing Uncle Chazz.

"Even before you got that stupid machine."

Huh. Really? Then I remember Gammon_89's comments about my attitude. And even eatmeee! had asked if something had happened recently. I'd assumed knowing Uncle Chazz is alive was the catalyst, but maybe it is just the final straw.

But of what?

I look to Confessor for answers. As always, I'm not disappointed.

"I think you're ready."

He's right, I feel it too. But ready for what? His words sound ominously like a therapist trying to break it to their patient that they won't be treating them any longer.

"You're not…you're not…" I can't finish the thought.

There's no need, he knows where my mind goes. "No. No. Not that."

I want him to type "Never that", but he doesn't.

"So, I'm ready for what?"

"Only you can answer that for sure…but I think…"

"Yes?"

"You're ready to take your broken wings and learn to fly."

I'd never told him about my father singing Blackbird to me every night.

**T**he thing I've found with Beatles fans—and I mean real fans, have every CD, read all the books—is that they tend to gravitate into two classifications; Pauls or Johns. I've been to a lot of different Beatles chat rooms over the years and if you talk to someone, it becomes clear very quickly which they are. Even without them mentioning either one. It seems that the more hard-core fans are Johns. The Pauls are a little more laid back about it all, the Johns can get almost defensive. It is a true character distinguisher. It's quite interesting, really.

Confessor is one of those rare mixes. He has a John's intensity, but a Paul's sense of humor.

I never knew which my father was.

**"W**anna hear something spooky?"

"What?"

"Houseboat was on Turner Classic Movies last night."

"I know, I watched it."

"Me too. I thought about you."

"Same here."

**"U** there?"

"Yes."

"Quick—turn on Turner Classics."

"Why?"

"Just do it."

"Ooooh…Desk Set! I love that movie."

"You got time to watch it together."

Of course I do. "Let me get a couple of things done. BRB."

I have nothing I have to do, but hey, a girl's gotta keep some sense of mystery…only if it's five minutes worth.

# *Eleven*

**"Y**ou know, you never told me your name," I say to Bocephus the next time we chat.

"I didn't? I thought I told you that first day we met."

"Nope. We started to and then we got off on a tangent."

"That's all we've gotten off on…tangents."

He is getting impatient. Frankly, if he wanted a cybersex buddy, I don't know what he was still doing with me. You could find those easily enough all over the internet. If you knew where and how to look. And as much as Bocephus was online, he'd have to know where to look.

Yeah, yeah, I'm online a lot, too. Just never you mind.

Maybe he wants more than that. The question is do I? *Can* I?

His thinking bubbles come on, and I reach for my baby name book.

"My name is Colin."

*Colin (Greek) A short form of Nicholas (Irish) Young cub.*

Too weird—a short form of Nicholas. Or was he more the Irish than the Greek translation? A young cub?

"Colin… I like it," I type.

"Thx."

"How'd your band practice go last night?"

"It wasn't practice with the whole band, just me and Nick trying to write some songs."

Huh. For some reason I'd assumed Nick wrote all the band's original stuff solo. I think back. I guess there was nothing that pointed to that. "You and Nick write your songs together?"

"Yeah. Well, we're listed as co-writers on everything, but mostly he writes alone and I write alone."

Just like the Beatles!

"We haven't come up with anything new for awhile, so we thought if we got together maybe we could spark something."

"And did you?"

There's a pause, then Bocephus'—Colin's—bubbles start rising.

"Sparks flew—but we didn't get anything written."

"You guys fought?" Again, just like the Beatles!

"Yeah, we got into it a little bit."

"Over the songs?"

"No, over Nick having his head buried so far up his ass he can't even make a decent chord transition."

I don't know what a chord transition is, but I assume it's something that Nick could handle on any given day.

But maybe not if his girlfriend's missing.

I take a deep breath, willing myself to retain ignorance in my response. "Maybe he was just having an off day? Or has this been going on for awhile?"

There's a pause. He's probably wondering if he wants to go down this road with me. Introduce supporting players into our unfolding relationship. He must decide yes, because he soon types, "No, not long. His girlfriend's doing a number on him."

"Oh. That sucks."

"They lived together for awhile, then she told him he had to quit the band and get married or move out."

"And?"

"He moved out."

That explains the change of address from his résumés to the return label on his computer. Also, probably why he sold the computer. Maybe even why he didn't bother to fully clean it off—

totally wiping Carrie out of his life.

"So, they broke up?"

"Ha."

"That's a no?"

"They stopped living together, but it didn't stop him from sniffing around her all the time."

"But she held firm to her ultimatum?"

"No, she slept with him all the time. Until recently."

"Recently?"

"Yeah. And it's not the first time she's done this, either, but the guy can't see it."

"Done what exactly?"

"Took off on him."

"What do you mean?"

"Told him she needed time alone."

"Oh, that. That's a girl thing."

"But then went totally incommunicado—with everyone."

"Oh. That seems a bit drastic."

"Yeah, Carrie's a drastic kind of chick."

"You sound like you don't like her."

"I don't like what she does to Nick."

"You're a good friend."

"Yeah, maybe. Or maybe I'm just selfish."

"In what way?"

"When she does this to him, he's not worth shit to the band."

That did sound selfish, I guess, but I can see his point.

"What does she tell him when she does this—takes off on him?"

"That she's 're-evaluating'."

What the hell does that mean?

"Whatever the hell that means."

"What do you think it means?"

A long pause, then the thinking bubbles start to rise. "She had a real unstable upbringing and when she and Nick started dating she really latched onto his family. That's the life she wants, solid, nine-to five, hi honey I'm home shit."

"But not Nick?" I ask.

"No. Not yet, not until we exhaust every avenue with the band."

"And that doesn't go over real well with Carrie?"

"Carrie has been yanking Nick's chain for years. I kept hoping he'd get sick of her and cut her loose, but he just keeps hanging on tighter and tighter."

"Bummer," I say.

"Yeah. It pretty much sucks. It's been hell for him, and yet he can't seem to give her up. She's like a drug habit to him."

Just what kind of crazy tricks was Carrie performing in bed?

I so don't want to think about that. I change the subject, even though we'd finally gotten to the subject for which I'd originally sought out Colin. "So…Carrie drives Nick to distraction. What drives you to distraction? What can make you miss a chord transition?"

"Are U applying for the job?"

"Is there an opening?"

"Yep."

"And the job description?"

"It's tough, rigorous work, but there is hazard pay!"

"LOL!"

"What do U say? Should we move this up a notch?"

"How do we do that?" I know what's coming next. It's come with every guy I've ever chatted with no matter in what capacity. Every guy except Confessor. They all wanted to see a pic, and then, when they'd charmed you a little bit, they went in for the kill.

"Let me call you."

There it is. So predictable.

"That's probably not a good idea."

"So, you are seeing someone."

"No, that's not it."

"Then what? You can call me if you're worried about giving

me your number."

Obviously, I'd never give out my number to anyone. I suppose I could give my cell number, at least that couldn't be traced to my address. And I know there's a way to call someone so your number doesn't show up on their caller ID. But even if I took every precaution to be untraceable, I'm hesitant to do it.

But I'd really like to hear his voice. I know he sings back-up on the tracks of The River Rats that I listened to over and over, but I can't really distinguish his voice from the blend.

I read somewhere once that the most arousing thing about a woman to a man is her hair, and the most arousing thing about a man to a woman is his voice. I can believe that. Although, by the number of men I meet online who want to talk on the phone, I'd say voice ranks right up there with them, too.

"It's not that either—although I would call you if we went that route. It's just…do you really want to muddy the waters right now? It sounds like you've got a lot on your plate, with Nick and Carrie and all."

"The water's so damn murky with them anyway it would make the Creature of the Black Lagoon feel right at home."

"Exactly, so why add me to the mix?"

It's quiet for a bit. He's probably thinking "she's right… what am I thinking…I need to stop this nonsense and get back to making music with Nick" and then come back with a goodbye for PatsyKlein. The thought makes me sad. And that makes me realize that maybe it would be a good thing if he ended it here and now, because obviously I won't.

I tell myself that it's keeping a connection to Carrie's disappearance open. A way to find out if Uncle Chazz is Johnny Campos.

But the truth is I'd come to enjoy my little chats with Bocephus. Colin. And I didn't want to give them up.

"Because I really like you. I enjoy chatting with you. I look forward to it. You have an honesty that's so refreshing," he says.

Ha!

"You're different from anyone I've ever met online before. Or in person for that matter."

Yes, I am, but not in the way he thinks.

"And we have so much in common –the whole parents thing for starters."

Yes, we did share the painful orphaned-at-a-young-age bond.

"And, Sophia..."

"Yes?"

"You're not a girl who flocks, are you?"

"No," I say truthfully.

"Now I know," he says.

"And knowing is half the battle," I finish.

"Think about it," he writes. "That's all I'm asking. For now."

I do.

Colin is not online the next morning. Neither is Confessor. Nor eatmeee!. I'm semi-caught up with my work, so I boot up Nick's machine. Just to look around, see if there's anything I missed…in my gazillion times on before.

And I do find something new. Based on Colin's confirmation that Nick and Carrie lived together, and thus probably shared this machine, I move down the dock and open Safari instead of Firefox.

A complete different set of bookmarks. Lots of shopping ones, celebrity gossip, the usual. Carrie used Safari and Nick used Firefox. A good way to share a machine, I suppose.

There's a bookmark for a webmail url and when I open it and find something unnerving. A batch of emails. Conversations between Carrie and someone with the email address barabino@hotmail.com. They're in a folder within a folder within a folder the webmail account, which apparently she didn't log out of before Nick took his machine when he hit the road. Hidden.

My love of nesting dolls pays off.

I hit the date modified menu bar and sort them oldest to most recent. I flip through them, starting with the oldest, completely transfixed.

The band. The band. The band. I'm not sure how much more of this I can take. Any ideas? This from Carrie to barabino.

Surely he'll see he has to make a choice. From barabino back.

Ah. Carrie had an ally in her quest to make Nick choose to leave the band.

I try to think if the name barabino means anything to me, but very few names have actually been unveiled in my travels through this machine. Nick hadn't labeled her pictures.

I open the next two emails. They were sent on the same date.

I'm sorry I was such a total bitch today. I didn't mean to snap at you. Carrie wrote to barabino.

I know you didn't mean it. You're dealing with a lot right now. From barabino back.

So barabino was a woman. No man would let a woman off the hook that easily when she admitted being a bitch.

Or ever utter the words you're dealing with a lot right now.

The next two emails were dated a few weeks later. About a month before Nick sold his machine.

He blew off a dinner I had with clients last night to write with Colin. A dinner he knew would be good connections for him. He just doesn't care about anything but the fucking band. From Carrie.

I know it's hard. But time will help. From barabino.

An unease washes over me. Did Carrie feel time was running out? Was she willing to strike out?

I know about striking out.

And being struck down.

There are only four emails left, dated a week before Nick put his machine on ebay. I don't want to open them. I don't want Nick to be like my ex. I don't want Carrie to be a woman in jeopardy.

I don't want to be reminded of my own past.

But, of course, I open them. I take a long sip of my coffee, carefully return the mug to my desktop, stalling while the documents appear on the screen.

I've had enough of this. He's going to have to make a choice. I'm telling him he has to quit the band or move out.

Barabino responds: Don't put something into action that you're not prepared to follow through on.

Carrie writes back: I have every intention of following through. It will work. It has to.

Barabino responds: What if it doesn't?

From Carrie: It will. But if not, I've got a big presentation at work in a couple of weeks and then I'm going to get away for a while. Think it out. Make him think about it, too. Something's got to change.

Barabino: That could blow up in your face.

Carrie's last email reads: It won't blow up, it never has before.

Barabino's reply is short, succinct, and perfectly sums up how I feel.

Be careful.

So, she gave Nick an ultimatum. And he didn't cave—he moved out. She sounds determined to play it out until the end. But what will the end be?

You never know how people will react when backed into a corner.

I'm living proof of that.

# Twelve

**"S**o, what do you think about the whole thing now?"

"I don't know, I'm so confused," I respond to Confessor.

"Your perception of these people has shifted."

"Yes."

"Do you think Nick had something to do with her disappearance?"

I rub my hands against my pajama bottoms. I was still in bed, my back against the headboard, my laptop stacked on a pillow. I hadn't even taken the time to get up before reaching for my laptop. Reaching for Confessor.

"I think he's the reason she's disappeared," I hedge.

"You're hedging."

"Yes."

"Because you want to believe in Nick."

Not so much believe in Nick, but believe lightning doesn't strike twice. That not all beautiful men with black hair and blue eyes want to hurt the women they profess to love. I could tell him that Carrie knew, on some level, a former mafia hitman, and perhaps he's involved. But I only answer, "Yes."

"But you—of all people—know that people aren't always what they appear to be."

My fingers are heavy on the keyboard. "Yes."

"And the name barabino doesn't ring any bells? It's not anywhere else on Nick's machine?"

"Nope."

"Well, it's an unusual name, it wouldn't be hard to trace. If it's their real name."

"Yeah, she could just be a Welcome Back Kotter fan."

"What?"

"Barabino. John Travolta's character."

"That was Barbarino."

"Oh. It was before my time. I only know about it because of TVLand."

I notice he doesn't add that it was before his time too. Or not. Nothing to tip his hand either way.

"Are you near Nick's machine right now?"

"No. I'm still in bed."

There's a long silence. Is Confessor thinking of me in bed? Or just taking a sip of coffee, spreading his newspaper across his desk?

"When you get to the machine, send me those email documents."

Not thinking of me in bed, thinking of our next move. "Why? I just told you what they said."

"I know, but you gave me your interpretation of them. I want to read them as someone who isn't involved. Maybe I'll get a different take on them."

"I'm not really someone who is involved," I write, though my heart isn't in it.

"I'm not even going to comment on that," he writes. "When you get out of bed, send me those emails."

"All right," I answer. Then I think on it. "Should I send them to someone else, too?"

"Like who?"

"Like the authorities in Mount Juliet?"

"No. Wait on that."

"Why?"

There is a long pause. I reach for a non-existent coffee cup. Brush the hair out of my eyes. Run my tongue across my unbrushed teeth. I really need to get out of bed.

"Are you really in a position to get publicly involved in this? Have your name on a police report somewhere?"

My fingers slide up and down the space bar. "No," I finally type.

"It's Tuesday morning. Give it a couple more days before you make a decision like that."

"I don't know. I feel like I should be doing something. Something to help."

"Just send me those emails, I'll look at them with an objective eye. And then stay the hell away from it for a couple of days."

That's the first time Confessor has told me what to do. Even when I'd asked before, he'd always give me some "what feels right to you" or "do what you think is best" bullshit answer. And now he was giving unsolicited advice.

"That's the first time you've ever told me what to do," I say, still slightly stunned.

"It's the first time I felt your instincts were out of whack."

"My instincts have been out of whack my whole life—that's what's gotten me to this point."

"Your instincts have kept you alive."

True.

**"F**avorite Cary Grant movie?"

"Do I have to say Houseboat?"

"No. Unless that's really your favorite."

"Hmm, no probably not."

"So?"

"Bringing up Baby? Maybe Philadelphia Story. U?"

"Lots too choose from. I'd have to say Arsenic and Old Lace."

"Ahhh, I forgot about that one."

"Can't forget that one."

"What about North by Northwest."

"Doh! Forgot that one too!"

Which leads us into a Hitchcock discussion that lasts all

afternoon.

That night, Grace from the auction company in Ohio emails me and says that they're having an auction the next day. She writes that she would have emailed me earlier but she'd been off for a few days and had just now seen the docket with the merchandise listings. There were some MACs and PCs and she didn't think it'd be very well attended because the girl who took her place while she was off forgot to put the ad in a couple of papers that they usually got a good response from. She says that it could be a good chance to pick up a few machines at low prices.

I decide to take a quick trip to Ohio tomorrow.

"Have we talked about Casablanca yet?"

"I think we've missed that one."

"Missed Casablanca…how could we!"

"Best line? 'Play it again, Sam' or 'Here's looking at you, kid'?"

"Or 'We'll always have Paris'?"

"Forgot that one. Tough call."

"Gotta go. I got a studio call tonight."

"K. Play well."

"Thx. Hey…we forgot one…"

"Forgot one?"

"I think this is the beginning of a beautiful friendship."

I know he is quoting Casablanca, but I type, "I think so too."

He is not gone before I respond…he sees every word.

The auction is a success; I bag two bare bones machines that I can load up with memory and software and sell for a tidy profit. I talk to Grace for a bit then head back home. I almost pass the exit I took last time for the library, but at the last moment I turn off. It hadn't been that long since I'd last checked, but I still drive to the library. Plus, this time, I have another name to Google.

It probably isn't a good idea to go back to the same place two times in a row and normally I don't, but… okay, I know this sounds corny, but I'm kind of hoping that the woman who was reading to the kids will be there again. Something about hearing her soothing voice, and the children's laughter had made the process easier.

Luck is on my side, not only is she there reading, but nobody is on the computer and I'm able to slide right in. I call up Google, rub my hands on my thighs, and then type in Johnny Campos, Hopeless Heart, Mount Juliet, Tennesee. For good measure, I add in New Jersey. I sit back in the chair and listen to the woman (I can't see them once I sit at the computer station) as the search engine chugs. She's reading them Rapunzel, I think. That's the one with the woman in the tower with the long hair, right? My knowledge of children's stories is seriously lacking, my father preferring to sing Beatles' tunes than tell stories.

A few hits come up. I do some digging, some false leads, and finally get an address for a Johnny Campos. I look around for something to write it down, or to send to the printer, but I stop. I don't want that address in my house, taunting me. Haunting me. What can I do with it, anyway?

My throat constricts, and I fight back tears, knowing I'm playing it safe, staying in my nest in Michigan. Telling myself that's what my father would have wanted—for me to be safe. And yet, I feel like I've let him down, the only person who ever, truly, loved me.

I start to leave, and then realize I didn't search for my name. So engrossed in Uncle Chazz, I forgot the usual reason I came to the library. I scoot my chair back in, bring Google back up again and then type in my name.

The search results come up and my breath catches. A new hit. I notice the url is for a Nevada newspaper and I swallow hard. This is what I've waited four years to see.

I click on the link. An intro page comes up touting the paper's newly archived editions going back for fifty years. No wonder I'd struck out until now.

And there it is, a small article about a one-car accident along the highway. No drugs or alcohol seemed to play a part, but the driver was pronounced DOA at the town's hospital. They mention my name, age, and that I was from California, but had no other details.

My death notice.

The children applaud as the story ends and I jerk out of my trance. I feel like cheering with them, but I keep my cool. I quickly glance around to see if anyone is looking at me, or could see the screen, but there is no one. I can hear the rustle of chairs and general body movement from around the corner and know that children—and presumably their parents—would be coming by soon. I hit print on computer, gather my purse, grab the printout. I erase my history from the machine and head to the door. I pay for my printout and leave.

My hands shake on the steering wheel and I can barely get the key in the ignition. I sit back and just breathe for several minutes until I feel strong enough to drive. Finally, I pull out of the library's parking lot.

For the last time. There is no reason to go back, I found out what I need to know.

Faking my death four years ago worked. The world thinks I'm dead. I can live my life again.

But where to start?

When I get home, my mind is racing. I take the printout and read it again. And again. Then I burn it.

I rush to my workroom, needing to share my news with Confessor, but he's not online. Probably just as well. Now I can think about how much I should tell him. How much is safe to tell him.

"So, have you thought about it? Calling me?" Bocephus asks the next morning.

"I have. I just haven't decided."

"That's okay. And if all you're looking for is a chat buddy, that's cool, I can do that. There's just such a connection between us, it seems like a waste not to follow up. But you need to decide what you want." He almost sounds like Confessor. Almost.

"Is there a time factor involved here?"

"No, I guess not. You just seem to be on the fence. I thought I could give you a nudge."

"In your direction, of course."

"Of course, LOL."

"Let's change the subject."

"Okay. Okay. What do U want to talk about?"

While I try to figure out a way to slide the name barabino into the conversation, his bubbles start to rise.

"OMG I haven't told you yet!"

"What?"

"I was so hoping you'd decided to let me call that I forgot."

"What?" I ask again.

"A scout from Planet Records showed up at the Hopeless Heart last night. To hear us."

"No way!"

"Way!"

"What'd he say?"

"He said he liked what he heard, wanted to keep in touch, gave us his card, and said he'd come back on Saturday to hear us again."

"OMG!!! That's so great!"

"I know. I could hardly believe it."

I see an opening here and I take it. "Are you managed by anyone? Who sets up your gigs, like at the Hopeless Heart? Or do you just have a good relationship with the people there that you can play when you want? Like that Johnny guy you mentioned?"

"No manager for the band. Not yet. So far, Nick and I set all the gigs. And yeah, we've been at HH for a while. We have a standard gig on Wednesdays and Saturdays, but Johnny calls us first if another band flakes."

"That's so great. I'm so happy for you."

"We've been after these guys to come and hear us for years. Of course he'd have to show up now."

"What's wrong with now?"

"Nick is so distracted with this Carrie thing, it really affects his playing."

"Did he mess up last night?'

"No. Thank God. But this thing has got to turn around. She can't just leave him dangling like this. He's going crazy. He knows it, too."

I want to type that maybe she's afraid to come back. That maybe Nick is tied up with guilt over his behavior towards her. That maybe it's better if she just stays away. Safer.

I don't type any of those things. "He'll pull it together for Saturday."

"Yeah, but this goes beyond Saturday. It looks like it could really happen for us this time. Nick has to be prepared for that—long term."

"Maybe they'll work it out when she comes back," I write, wishing for everybody's sakes that it could be true.

"Maybe," he says. Of course, I can't hear his voice, but I know there is doubt, skepticism in it.

"I need to get going," he writes. "I want to burn a CD of our stuff to give to Will on Saturday."

"Will?"

"The guy from Planet Records."

"Oh." I don't mention that I have a CD burned of all The River Rats' songs.

"Hey, think about it. Calling me, I mean."

"I will. I have," I answer truthfully.

"I really think this might be something."

I rub my fingers together, and then place them back on the smooth keys. "So do I," I type.

Nobody is online the rest of Thursday. Late that night, awoken by a nightmare, I make my way down to my workroom. I flip through photos on Nick's machine. I skim over the dock going for the system preferences icon to change the desktop picture to one of the band. My finger releases too quickly and the Yahoo! IM icon next to it opens instead.

That's the one thing I don't like about OSX, the dock has such a soft trigger.

I wait for the software to come up so I can quit out of it.

When it opens, I'm automatically logged in. As Carrie! Oh, so not only did they use different web browsers, but they used different chat software as well.

The different buddies icons rearrange, with the ones being online going to the top. Four are active. I'm just about to quit when the IM window comes up. "Who are you?"

The IM is from Colin…well Bocephus. I quickly quit out. Hopefully, he'd just think it was an ichat blip. Rotten luck that he was online at exactly that second.

But good luck as I now log in as PatsyKlein and prepare for a few hours of good conversation.

Late Friday afternoon I play a few games of backgammon with eatmeee!, my chat software up, idle, waiting. No Confessor or Colin online at all today.

"Hey, I might not play you again before I leave next week," eatmeee! says as he beats me in our fourth game.

"Leaving?"

"To go to Nationals."

"They're next week already?"

"Yep, and thx to U, I feel prepared."

"That's good."

"I'll be taking my laptop, I'll check in with you, let you know how it's going."

Eatmeee! drove me crazy most of the time, but I really did wish him well in this.

"Good luck," I write.

"Why don't you come? I'd love to kick your ass in person."

I smile. I'm about to talk trash back, but my heart isn't in it. "You said they're in Nashville?"

"Yeah. Are you thinking about it?"

I thought about Nashville, and a select few of its citizens, all the time, but I didn't tell eatmeee! that.

"Nah, can't do it," I write, though I wouldn't have an answer if he asked why.

"Too bad. Well, maybe not. Who needs the competition!"

We say our goodbyes. I'm strangely saddened by the thought of not seeing eatmeee! on line for several days.

Neither Colin nor Confessor are online that evening. Thinking of eatmeee!'s unasked question—why couldn't I go to Nashville—I head to the newspaper that is hosting the tournament's website. It's bookmarked, of course, for updates on Carrie, although I hadn't checked it in the past few days. Colin had become my updater on that front.

As the page comes up, my eye automatically goes to the lower right corner, where the sidebar about Carrie has been before.

It's gone, replaced by a blurb about a new arrival to the city's zoo. My hand tightens against the mouse, my eyes dart to the top of the page. To breaking news.

I stare at Carrie's smiling face, her gingham dress crisp and clean, Nick's hand wrapped around her shoulder.

I try to swallow as I read the headline, but my mouth is dry.

"Body of missing woman found."

**"S**o…I'm going to Nashville." I end my story to Confessor Saturday morning.

"Whoa, slow down."

"I really feel it's something I have to do."

"Playing Nancy Drew? Or playing Colin? Or is it the compelling draw of beating eatmeee! to become our National Backgammon Champion?"

"Backgammon," I type a little too quickly. He doesn't need to know that the one reason that beats all of those he mentioned is finding Uncle Chazz. And making him pay.

"This is me you're talking to," he says.

"Okay. All three."

Carrie's body had been found, but she hadn't been dead all the time she'd been missing. It looks like she'd done exactly what she'd told barabino; secluded herself in a small cabin. Part of several rentals called The Range View Cabins, in the foothills of the Smokey Mountains. The rental staff had seen her a few times. The cleaning woman found her body Friday morning. The coroner put her time of death between eight and ten p.m. Thursday night.

She died from a blow to the back of her head. She'd fallen onto the andiron at the fireplace. The police were trying to determine whether she fell or was pushed.

I know it probably wasn't an accident.

Nick had probably, finally, pushed back.

I take it as a sign from the universe. The Perfect Storm of signs, actually, starting with Uncle Chazz's picture on Nick's machine. Then meeting and getting to know Colin. Carrie's emails. But the one thing that shouted it was time to go, time to end this all, was knowing that my faked death four years ago had worked and that to the world I no longer existed.

Freedom to leave my nest. Freedom to start again.

Freedom to kill my father's murderer and get away with it.

"Blackbird…" Confessor starts, but I interrupt.

"I'm going for the tournament, but how can I not at least look into this? I mean…Carrie's dead…Nick did it. And he could get away with it." I kind of don't care anymore if Nick did it or not. He probably did, isn't it always the boyfriend or husband? But I want Confessor to think this is all about Carrie's case for me. No need for him to ever find out about Uncle Chazz.

Especially now that I'm going to...

I trust Confessor, but there's no way I will tell anyone about the real reason I'm going to Nashville.

"And YOU're going to prove it?" he asks and I have to remember my train of thought. Oh yeah, me proving Nick killed Carrie.

"No, I can't prove it absolutely."

"But you think you can?"

"I don't know. All I know is that Carrie was pushing at the end…she was making demands…"

"And?"

"And somebody pushed back."

"Just like you did, that's what you're thinking isn't it? But when you pushed back it was by running away."

"Yes. And that's what Nick could have done. Walked away. Called it quits. But he didn't. And I don't want him to get away with that."

"Like your ex got away with hurting you?"

"Yes."

"And then will the lambs be silent, Clarice?"

"Very funny," I type, but I can't help but wonder if that might be part of it. I may not hear lambs screaming, but my dreams were filled with other scary things. And part of that might go away once Uncle Chazz is gone.

"I'm going," I write.

"Okay. Okay. Let's talk this through."

"Okay, but I'm going."

"Okay. You're going. But give it a few days. Wait till Monday."

"Why?"

"Because anything could happen in that time. It could be determined an accident. Or if not, somebody could be arrested. Or some suspect might be eliminated. You'd have a lot more information to go on."

He was right about that. And Uncle Chazz would still be there then. But two days sounds like an eternity. Weird, because the last four years had passed at a snail's pace.

Then it hits me. Not only do I *want* to go, I'm *excited* to go. Even without the vengeance part. The thought of leaving the safety of my home, my city, is not as terrifying as it should be. I've either made progress, or let down my guard.

One is a breakthrough. The other deadly.

But, I really can't leave until Monday, anyway. I have something I need to get from the bank. Something that can't fit through the ATM. And even though my bank has Saturday hours, I'm expecting a delivery from UPS this afternoon and don't want Tom to wonder about my not being here.

"You're right. I'll wait until Monday." Let him think it was his cool rationale that made me wait.

"You weren't going to go until Monday anyway, were you?"

I smile, my tense mood broken.

"I need to get some things in order here."

"That sounds ominous. You are intending to return, aren't you?"

I hadn't thought of it—not returning. But, I guess I hadn't

thought of much beyond getting to Nashville and…and what? I wasn't sure. But really, what did I have to come back to?

The truth is, I could have relocated at any time in the last four years. What I did I could do from anywhere. I could sell the house. The name I live under now is not in any danger. Or, at least, that is what I have come to believe. The fact that I'm still alive proves it.

I was so happy to find a safe refuge after my ex, that I'd never really thought of leaving.

I look around the living room where I sit with my laptop. "It's not all that great here…I don't know that I'd be giving up anything much."

"Don't play dumb. You know what I mean."

I did. He meant the environment I'd created here. The safety.

"Are you willing to leave your nest, Blackbird?"

"What if I said yes?"

There is a long wait for his answer. I look around the room again, my stomach clenches at the thought of making myself so vulnerable again by leaving Michigan.

"I'd say great. Do it. Get a job outside of your house. Move to Florida for the sun. Anything. But don't leave your nest just to avenge Carrie. To make sure justice comes to a woman you never met. That will either happen or it won't without you."

"What if it's for Colin?"

"Is it really to that point with him?"

Is it? "I don't know," I say. "Lots of happy people meet their mates through internet relationships," I point out.

"True," he says.

"Would you ever meet someone you met through the internet? Not like a dating site or anything where that's the goal, but like through a chat room?"

I've left an opening the size of the Grand Canyon.

"No," he says. "I would never do that. I can't do that."

The door bangs shuts.

It hurts a little—okay, a lot—but I know I'll survive.

Confessor has been my salvation for the last four years.

That doesn't mean he has to be my future.

I don't know that Colin is either. In fact, that seems highly unlikely if I do what I set out to do. If I do, I'll have to get out of Nashville and never return. And my determination to do this... to see Chazz pay for his sins...to make my nightmares go away, becomes stronger.

Resolved, my fingers heavy on the keyboard, I type, "I'm sure I'm coming back. But...would it matter? If I didn't come back?"

"Of course."

"Why? We'd always be just a laptop away."

"Would we?"

Of course we would. I can't imagine Confessor not being a part of my life, even if I was in a relationship. I start to tell him this, but I don't get the chance.

"Bye, bye, Blackbird." He is gone before I can respond.

**W**hen I left my ex—and California—I cut myself off from the world. I'd had to, or he would have found me. I hadn't left many friends behind—he'd been my whole world—so it wasn't too difficult.

How to rattle off the details without going back emotionally to that time? It was something I put behind me. Something that I didn't want to dredge up.

Other women have miscarriages. Other women have their marriages break up.

But how many women find out their husband had been hired to kill them?

**"T**om, can I ask you something?" I say later that afternoon. There must be something different in my voice, because Tom stops his cookie halfway to his mouth, sets it back on his plate and gives me his attention.

"Of course, you know you can ask me anything." Before I can phrase what I want to ask he says, "This isn't about my nephew is it? He didn't do anything he shouldn't have?"

There is such concern in his eyes that a lump rises in my throat. I've felt so alone these last few years, but I know that Tom is a good friend. If only one I see every few days for a few minutes.

I reach across the table and touch his arm, then put my hands around my coffee mug. "No. It's something totally unrelated."

Tom waits. I take a sip of coffee, then a bite of cookie.

"Do you know if you have to have a credit card to rent a car?"

His brows furrow. "That's it?" I shrug. "Well, that's an easy one. Yep, you need to have a credit card and a valid drivers license. And I believe you have to be twenty-one."

My mind starts to race. I can't rent a car to drive to Tennessee. I don't want my Michigan name "out there" in any way. I don't think anyone's looking for me now that I've seen my death notice, but using a credit card in that name would be waving a red flag. Any credit cards I had in my California name have long since expired.

But I don't want anybody to trace my car back to this address either.

"Taking a trip, honey?" Tom asks pulling me out of my logistical quandary.

"Yes, I'm taking a trip. I'm leaving Monday."

"How long you planning on being gone? If you want, I can drive by your place and check on things."

I look around the kitchen. Nothing's happened here in four years, I don't expect anything to happen in the next week. "That's okay, Tom, but thanks. I shouldn't have any deliveries coming in." Because I haven't gotten anything listed, I've been so engrossed with Carrie's disappearance. And then with plotting my vengeance.

"Maybe I'll just swing by once or twice anyway," Tom says.

I know better to argue with him. If the man won't cave

about carrying sixty-pound boxes, he's not going to give on this. "Thanks, that would ease my mind."

He waves away my thanks. "And you were going to rent a car, but you don't have a credit card?" I know where his mind is going. He totes in several boxes a week of things bought online... of course I have a credit card.

"I have one, for my online business. But I try to only use it for that."

He looks at me for a few minutes, scrutinizing. Uncomfortable, I rise and refill his mug and mine. I bring the cookie jar over to the table from the counter. This could take awhile.

"Are you flying in somewhere? Would they maybe have a shuttle service or something?"

"I'm driving," I say.

His brows furrow. "And you don't want to just drive your car?"

"It's not that. It's just I don't..."

He waits for me.

I bite my lip. In for a penny... "I don't want anyone to know it's my car. My license plate number." I take a deep breath, let it out slowly. "Where I'm from."

Tom has been a part of my life for a while. Surely he's wondered at my reclusive existence. But he's never asked. And he doesn't now.

He watches me again. Seems to think for a minute. Drinks some more coffee.

I'm just about to tell him to forget the whole thing, but then he sweeps the paisley curtain back from the window next to the table. He nods to my car. I always drive it around to the back of the house out of habit. "You know, your car looks like a rental car."

I look out at my car. It's only two years old. When my aunt was killed, her car was totaled. The insurance company paid for a new one. I was still so in shock I just bought the same kind of car she'd driven—a white Taurus. There's less than three thousand miles on it. It looks brand new.

"Does it?"

"Yep, sure does. Course, they use all kinds now, but the majority of those rental companies' fleets are still basic sedans by American manufacturers. That Taurus would sure pass for a rental car…if that would help any."

"So, I could just go somewhere and if anyone asks—for whatever reason—I could say it was a rental?" It would probably never come up, but I like the idea of Colin thinking that I was in a rental, especially if I was coming all the way from Vermont.

"Well, yeah, I guess so. Vacuum it out good, take all the personal stuff out."

No problem there. I'd never been one to live out of my car.

"Don't rental cars have stickers on them?" I asked.

"Some do. Some don't. They took them off a few years back when rentals were being targeted in Florida and tourists were being held up. I think now they just have the bar code stickers."

"What's that?"

"On the driver's side and the back passenger side they have stickers on the inside with a bar code and number on it. I think they just scan those when you return the car."

"Oh," I say, defeated.

Tom takes a bite of cookie, chews thoughtfully. "Seems like you could make one easy enough on one of those computers of yours."

"Yeah?" I say, interested.

He nods. "In fact, they're about the size of your mailing label you use on your return address. Just make up some numbers and do a fake bar code. Nobody will know the difference, unless they're looking close, and maybe not even then."

"Nobody will be looking close." I can't imagine in what scenario anybody would. "What about license plates?"

Tom shrugs. "Well, rental cars get returned all over the place, so what state you're in doesn't necessarily have to the be the state on your license."

"But I don't want to have my plate on it."

"Change it once you get to the state you're headed to."

"Change it? Change it with what?"

Tom looks away, thinks. "What about an abandoned car? Or like in a scrap yard? Or maybe a lot where they bring repossessed cars. Nobody's going to miss those plates."

"Do they leave the plates on cars going to the scrap yard?"

"Sometimes. But they'd probably be pretty old and beat up. You'd have to really look to find one that looks like it'd be used on a newer rental."

I don't like the idea of tromping through a junkyard in Tennessee, but I may be running out of options.

He leans forward, places his hand on mine. His look tells me he's guessed some about my past. Maybe he's just been waiting for a time when I'd need help. "Honey, just be on the lookout for a junkyard or abandoned cars once you cross the state line. You'll be shocked how common they are."

I cover his hand on mine with my other and gently squeeze. "Thanks, Tom," is all I say, but he knows I mean more.

He pulls back, embarrassed. "Just have a good trip, honey, you deserve it. All these years…" he lets his thought trail away.

He gets up. I start to rise, but he motions for me to keep sitting, so I do. He comes to my side. He leans down and places the softest kiss on the top of my head. "Be careful," he whispers into my hair.

My throat tightens and all I can do is nod. He moves to the archway and turns back to me. "It's time," he says then turns and leaves. I hear the door front door close softly behind him.

He's right.

The rest of Saturday is torture. I pack. I unpack. I pack again. I get all the information on the Backgammon tournament. I'd have to give a legitimate name; they needed a driver's license at check-in. The good news is I can register online as late as Wednesday morning. I don't know if I'd be in Nashville that long, but I print out all the information.

I keep my laptop at my side every moment. Confessor never shows up. When he finally comes back online he'll be greeted with about twenty "You out there?" messages.

If he comes back online.

But I won't allow myself to imagine that he has left me. That he's seen my desire to meet Colin, to go to Tennessee as a choice made. That it is either him or Colin.

I don't feel that way. Besides, this trip is not about Colin, the tournament, or even Carrie for that matter.

This is about me taking care of business.

My mind whizzes with all kinds of thoughts as I try to sleep, my laptop on my night table, up, ready, waiting.

Sunday is even worse.

I pack my bags again. Keep them packed. I'm going. Even if I find out that the mystery has been solved, the killer arrested in the next twenty-four hours, I'm still going.

For my father. For justice.

I go to Nick's machine, hook it up to a printer. I start to filter through the documents, trying to decide what might be of importance later. Things with addresses on them, phone numbers. Of course the emails between Carrie and barabino. I even print out the logs of the chats between Colin and me.

I end up printing out everything, figuring what the hell—too much information is better than not enough. I find the Hopeless Heart's address online. I now had Carrie's home address as well as Nick's home address, his office address and the Hopeless Heart's. I Mapquest them all, as well as the directions to the place where the backgammon tournament is being held (turns out an auditorium of some sort).

Unwilling to turn Nick's machine off for good, I take a cable and transfer everything from his hard drive to my laptop. I also burn a CD of the contents, put it in my laptop bag. Overkill, probably, but at least I'm now able to bring myself to shut down his machine.

Sunday night I hear the knock from my laptop that someone new has entered my IM software. I nearly trip over myself lunging for it.

"You out there?" Confessor writes.

I let out a breath of relief. "I'm here," I answer.

"Where, exactly are you?"

I pause. He's never asked me something that would let him in any way pinpoint me. He must realize this, because he quickly adds, "You're not in Nashville are you?"

"No. I said I'd wait until Monday."

"And you're still going?"

"Yes," I reply.

There is a pause. I suppose he's putting together his argument against it.

"Okay," he says.

Huh. "Okay?"

"I can't really stop you, can I?"

Well no, of course not, but his opinion carries a great deal of weight with me. For better or worse.

"But, I need to ask you some things, and I need you to be really honest with me."

"Okay—shoot."

"How are you going to go about this?"

"Register for the tournament, go, play, kick some geek's ass."

"Ha ha, very funny. Be serious."

"Oh, you mean the Carrie thing."

He doesn't respond. Okay, not in the mood for that tonight apparently.

"I have an idea on how to get close to Nick. I'm hoping I can wing it from there."

"Colin."

It's not a question. "Yes."

"Are you sure you want to use him that way?"

I'm not sure meeting Colin would only be to get to Nick. In fact, I know it wouldn't be, but I don't say that to Confessor. Besides, I'm planning on using Colin for more than getting me close to Nick. Or for getting me close to someone *besides* Nick.

"And what name are you going to use?" he asks.

My hands are poised over the keyboard. I breathe deeply. I try to type, but I can't. Not even for Confessor.

"I don't mean for you to tell me the actual name. I mean are you going to use the name that you live under there? Do you think that's wise?"

I exhale, relieved.

"No. I have another set of identification. That's what I need to get to the bank for. Why I had to wait until Monday."

"The name you used when you were in California?"

"Yes." That was the only other set of identification I have. I don't have a passport in every European capital like somebody out of a Robert Ludlum novel. Or John LeCarre. I always get those two mixed up.

"Not a good idea," he says.

"I know, but it's the safer of the two to use."

"Do you think so?"

I tell him about finding my death notice, and all that entailed.

"Let me get this straight. You've been Googling yourself monthly for the past four years waiting to see if you were dead or not?"

"That sounds kind of dirty," I say.

"What does?"

"Googling myself."

"Like—stop Googling yourself or you'll go blind," he writes.

"Exactly. Or if you keep Googling yourself you'll grow hair on your palms."

There was a pause as I imagined Confessor smiling as I am.

"And you're sure this name is safe to use?"

"Not long term, no. I would never do that. But for a few

days, it would be better to have a name, that if traced, goes back to a dead woman." It was one of those thoughts that had kept me awake nearly continuously since Friday.

**I** was five years old when I came to live with my aunt. She said we needed to change my name so the man who hurt daddy couldn't find me. I was scared and alone and I clung to whatever my aunt said.

Three months previously my father had been murdered.

And I'd seen the murderer. Uncle Chazz.

When I left my aunt's home at eighteen, I didn't expect to ever return. I was spreading my wings. I sent her notes now and then, calls to let her know I was okay, but never let on to anyone in my new life that I still had an aunt—and a different name—in Michigan.

Shortly before my eighteenth birthday, I'd found a box in the attic that, according to the postmark, had been shipped to us a few years after I'd come to live with my aunt. It didn't contain much, but it was all I had of the life I barely remembered.

It affected me deeply. Confused me, then made me stubborn. Determined to stand on my own.

When I graduated from high school, I took my birth certificate, and my father's picture, and left.

It wasn't out of rebellion, or that I didn't love my aunt. It was out of some other need. The need to find something of my own, I suppose. She'd understood. I suppose she always knew the day would come when I'd leave her.

I don't know if she'd needed to clear it with anybody, or if she took any heat for me leaving—she never let on if she did, and I'm eternally grateful for that. I couldn't have piled guilt on top of all the other emotions that came into play.

Mainly fear.

When I got to California, I got a license and all the other stuff under my real name—the name my father gave me.

The name I Google every month.

The name of a dead woman.

**M**y only alternative to my California name is to use the name I live under now. My Michigan name. And risk giving up my safe haven.

Besides, I figure I'll only be in Nashville a few days, a week at the most. Not enough time for an obsolete name to be found and tracked. If anyone even still wanted to find me. I wouldn't use credit cards, or anything so traceable. I didn't think the backgammon tournament would be putting their registrants online. Into some kind of database, sure, but only for the purposes of the tournament. I'd get enough cash from the bank to pay for everything.

**A**pparently Confessor goes through the same thought process that I do.

"I guess it's better than the name you live with now," he writes.

"That's what I figured."

"Unless…"

"Yes?"

"Unless you really don't plan on coming back."

"Why then?"

"If you're going to start a new life - and I don't mean in Tennessee—but after, you should probably use the name that you know is safe. The one you live under now."

I don't know for certain that any name is safe. But then, I don't know for certain that anybody is looking for me, either. Under any name.

"Think about it," he says. Like I haven't been thinking about this non-stop since Friday night. Not coming back doesn't really feel like an option, but it had opened up thoughts about what I would do after I am set free from my past.

What would be safe for me to do?

"We probably won't talk again for awhile," he says.

The thought unnerves me. "I'll be taking my laptop."

"But you'll be traveling during the day. Then trying to make contact with Colin."

"But…" I don't finish the thought.

"I'll be around," he says. "But it might be harder for us to talk."

I'm relieved. I'd always find a way to talk to him. As long as his connection was open.

"Promise me one thing, Blackbird."

Anything. "Yes?"

"Don't let anybody clip those wings of yours."

"I won't."

I feel I should say more. That we're at some sort of turning point in our relationship. That things may never be the same, that the dynamic has shifted. I'm not the frightened baby bird with the broken wings any longer.

"Bye, bye, Blackbird." He is gone before I can respond.

# Fourteen

**"I'**ve thought about it," I say to Colin later that night. I'd almost given up on him coming online before I went to bed. Before I'd leave in the morning. But at eleven forty-five I heard the knocking from PatsyKlein's Yahoo! IM and nearly broken my neck diving for the keyboard.

"About us?" he asks.

"Yes."

"And?"

"I think you're right, we should move it up a notch," I say.

"You want to call me?"

"I could do that…or…"

"Or?"

"I know you're in Tennessee, are you anywhere near Nashville?"

"Yeah. Just outside of it. Why?"

"I have to be in Nashville this week, for a conference on accounting for small businesses. I thought maybe we could meet."

"RU kidding me?"

"Nope, I'm flying in tomorrow."

"How long R U staying?"

I wasn't sure if he was getting that anxiousness men get when they feel they might be cornered, or if he was asking because I couldn't stay long enough to suit him. Probably neither, just curiosity. "I'm not sure. The conference is only a couple of days, but…"

"But if I'm a troll you'll be leaving right after that?"

"LOL! No. BUT…I gave myself a couple of days for sight seeing and anything else I might want to do. I'm leaving it open."

"Open for sightseeing or open for me?"

"I was thinking for sightseeing, but I suppose for both."

There's a pause. He's probably thinking of some excuse why we can't meet. This has just gotten bigger than just a few phone calls. Of course he does have a good excuse—his best friend's girlfriend is dead and his best friend is probably guilty—but I don't think he'd tell me that one.

"Shit," he types, "The timing of this stinks."

"It's okay," I respond, hiding my disappointment behind the toneless keyboard. "We can just stay as is—online only. I'll IM you when I get back."

Thoughts of how I was now going to get close enough to the Hopeless Heart and Uncle Chazz without Colin travel through my head as his bubbles rise. "Wait," he says.

"Yes?"

"I just meant that I had a lot going on right now—but I still want to meet."

The pleasure that courses through me has nothing to do with getting close to Uncle Chazz or looking into Carrie's death. "Great," I type, meaning it.

"How do you want to do this?"

"I'm traveling tomorrow, and will probably just want to crash tomorrow night," I write. I don't like the idea of wasting any time sitting in my room, road-tired or not, but I think it's better to give Colin some time to digest this all. Plus, anything could happen to Carrie's case in twenty-four hours. I'd want Monday night to get up to speed.

"So, Tuesday then?" he asks.

"Is that alright?"

"At this point I'm not sure what my schedule is for Tuesday."

Of course not. He'd want to be up to speed as much as I did.

Probably figured he'd have to bail out his best friend that day. "I'm taking my laptop, I'll IM you tomorrow night from the motel. That sound okay?"

"Yeah. I might not be on until late, though, but I'll be there."

"OK. And if you're not…"

"Yeah?"

"Then I'll know that the timing was wrong—or that you changed your mind—no harm, no foul."

"I'll be there—wait for me."

"Okay," I type, and sign off.

I hook up my laptop, the one I'll take with me, to a printer and get online. I take the sheet of paper where I wrote Johnny Campos when Colin and I had chatted. In the last few days, I have doodled dark blue scrolls around his name as I thought about what I was going to do. Came to terms with what I'm going to do.

I rip off the top sheet. Then, because I've seen too many copy shows, I tear off the next few sheets also, so nobody can do the pencil etching thing to find out what was written on the top sheet of a pad. I put the sheets of paper in my laptop case. I'll tear them up and throw them in the garbage at some stop along the way to Tennessee.

If something goes wrong in Tennessee, and people—I'm not sure who, good guys or bad guys—come to my house, I don't want them connecting me with Johnny Campos' name.

I break my cardinal rule and Google Johnny Campos, Hopeless Heart, Mount Juliet, Tennessee. I do the same links I did at the library and get the address that I wouldn't write down at the time. I'm not sure it's current, or for the right Johnny Campos. Hell, I'm not even completely sure Johnny Campos *is* Uncle Chazz. But I MapQuest the home address from the Hopeless Heart, print it out and put it in my laptop case.

I get rid of the history and clear the cache and all those things from my laptop, but I know the laptop will be with me, so I figure if the machine is looked at by somebody it shouldn't be, the shit has already hit the fan.

Monday morning I leave my home. I put a thing in my mailbox holding my mail for a week. I don't get a paper, so they won't stack up. I don't have anything coming in as far as computers go (I'd been so busy obsessing about Uncle Chazz and chatting with Colin that I hadn't purchased anything).

I go to the bank and get my safety deposit box. It's a different person than the one that was there only a few weeks ago. My God, was that only a few weeks ago that I'd booted up Nick's machine and changed my life? Yes, the change had started that day, but what really gave me the freedom to do this was the trip to Ohio library and my Google results.

I have to remember to send Grace from the auctions a thank you note when I get back.

If I make it back.

Finally, I'm in the little room alone with my safety deposit box. I turn the key and lift the heavy lid. I take all my identification that is in my real name, the stacks of money and the gun and put them in my tote bag. I lock the box, leaving my father's photo and the envelope with my ex and Uncle Chazz's photo, and walk out of the little room. I don't want to have his photo on me if for some reason things turn sour. I mean Uncle Chazz's photo, but that could just as easily apply to my ex and my father's photos as well.

I go a few blocks away, to a different bank. I take about half of the cash and buy traveler's checks. I figure if I pay cash at hotels it might raise some eyebrows, but traveler's checks are still somewhat commonplace. And not as traceable as credit cards.

I go back home and load up the car. I'd packed for more than a few days. I'd told myself it was because I wasn't sure of the Tennessee weather—that at this time of year the evening probably became quite cool—but the truth is I'm keeping my options open. If I do play in the tournament, and do well, I'll be there until the end of the week, anyway.

And if things went horribly wrong, I might be away for a while. Or forever.

The last thing to pack was my laptop. I'd left it on as long as possible waiting to see if Confessor came on. He hadn't.

He probably figures I'm on the road by now. I hope that's all it is. That his 'Bye, Bye, Blackbird' last night wasn't truly goodbye.

I make good time, stopping only to gas up and use the restroom, eating junk food while I drive. There's nothing like eating crappy gas station food—it feels legal in a car. Where as if you eat the same things at home you feel like a total slob. It's about the only time I ever eat Cheetos.

I do check my rearview mirror an awful lot, but I don't know what I'm looking for. If anyone is following me, then they knew where I was all along. That thought doesn't sit well with me.

Midway through Ohio the enormity of what I plan to do hits me. Well, that's the thing, there really is no plan. Except to find Uncle Chazz, let him know who I am moments before I put a bullet through his head, just like he'd done to my father.

And oh yeah, somehow let the authorities know about Carrie's email where she's fearful of Nick without getting myself involved.

Plus, meet up with Colin, let him lead me to Uncle Chazz, and try not to get too attached to him in the time it takes me to commit a murder and solve another one.

And, how could I forget…win the National Backgammon Championship (or at least beat eatmeee!)

But it all fades away, becomes a very distant second, third and fourth to taking out Uncle Chazz.

I don't ask myself if I'll be able to do it when the time comes. I know I will. And if a moment of hesitation creeps in, I'll just remember my father's lifeless and bloody body. Or the face of my ex the last time I saw him, because that all started years ago with Uncle Chazz.

I cross into Tennessee just as the sky grows dark, which is what I hoped for.

I'd thought long and hard about Tom's idea of getting a license plate from an abandoned car or a junkyard, but I felt that would be leaving too much to chance.

You really don't see abandoned cars or junkyards from the freeway. So, before I left Michigan, I came up with a backup plan.

It's not a plan I'm really comfortable with, but I think it will work. If I can just suck it up and do it.

I pull out the Mapquest pile from my bag. I'd looked up five different small airports between the border and Mount Juliet. I want one small enough not to have great security yet large enough to have a long-term parking lot. Surely one will be what I'm looking for.

The first two have security cameras over the long-term lots. I keep going.

An hour later I get to the third airport. A shiver of dread runs through me as I realize it's exactly what I'm looking for. So, I'm really going to do this.

I enter the lot and park in the last row, out of the line of sight of the person in the toll booth. I pull out the fake bar code stickers I made and tape them inside my windshield in the places Tom told me about.

And then I wait.

I'm no criminal, and what I'm about to do doesn't sit real well with me, but I try to rationalize it. A small inconvenience for one person versus a stronger chance of survival for me. (this from a woman who has no compunction about planning to kill someone—but that's different!)

It's no contest, and yet I can't think of a time that I've ever broken the law. Not even a parking ticket.

Oh, well, wait… I guess faking my own death wasn't exactly legal. And I suppose I'm now in for, at the very least, conspiracy to commit murder.

Funny, but those are easier for me to live with than swiping a license plate.

It's all in how you look at it, I guess.

I watch as several people come, park, unload and head to the terminal. I don't make a move. Too many people around. I need a late arrival.

Which is exactly what I get a half-hour later. A woman arrives in a Lexus. When she gets out I can see she's dressed in a suit and has a laptop case slung over her shoulder. I'm thinking an overnight business trip until I see the amount of luggage she has. That's what I'm aiming for; somebody who's going to be gone longer than a few days. She stacks the bags on top of each other in a manner that speaks to her frequent traveling. She hustles off to the terminal and the lot—or my back section of it, anyway—is empty of people.

My stomach churns as I reach for my screwdriver. It slips from my sweaty hands. I wipe them on my jeans and grab for the screwdriver. I reach for the door handle, my hand trembles.

Oh, get on with it all ready, it's not a capital crime. Kids have been doing crap like this for years.

I leave my Taurus, walk to the Lexus. As I reach the back, I drop a coin and bend down, pretending to retrieve it…just in case anyone I can't see is looking.

The screwdriver slips the first time, gouging my thumb, drawing blood.

Penance.

I make sure there is no blood on the Lexus. I'm careful to only touch the plate, not the car itself. I don't think my DNA or blood type is on file anywhere, but I don't take the chance.

I finally find the thread of the screw and get it off. Then the other. I quickly return to my car and replace my plates with it, all the while watching for new cars entering the lot.

The whole thing takes maybe five minutes but it feels like an eternity.

I get in my car and start to put the key in the ignition but my hand pauses halfway. I look at the Lexus again, guilt bubbling up inside of me. I pull a pair of plastic gloves out of the glove box. The kind that comes in hair coloring kits. My aunt always had a pair in her glove box in case she had to change a tire or she hit a deer or something.

At least that's what she'd said. Looking back, maybe she had other uses for rubber gloves.

After I grapple with the gloves, I reach into my purse, grab my wallet, and take out a hundred dollar bill from the middle of my stack. One that only the bank teller would have touched.

Last time I bought plates in Michigan they were around sixty dollars. I don't have any idea what they are in Tennessee, but it can't be more than one hundred. The rest can go for the woman's inconvenience.

And to ease my conscience.

I make my way back to the Lexus and wedge the bill into the plate area through the screw opening. It wouldn't show to just anyone passing by, but when the woman went to replace her plate she'd find it.

I give it another tug, making sure it won't fly away when the car leaves the airport. Who knows how long it will take before the woman even realizes the plate is gone.

How often do you look at your license plate?

The woman at the toll booth takes my ticket and punches it in. "You should have been in the short term lot," she says through her gum chomping.

"Yeah, I just realized that," I say. "Charge me for that rate if there's a difference."

She cracks a bubble, her tongue swooping out to wipe the excess gum from her lips. "Nah, it don't matter none." She collects my money and I leave the airport, quickly getting back onto the expressway.

I whisper "I'm sorry" to the woman in the Lexus who will never know me.

And drive toward my future.

**I** reach Nashville by eight p.m. I bypass the city and drive to Mount Juliet where Uncle Chazz works. Where Carrie lived. I'd gotten three motel addresses from Mapquest that were all close to the Hopeless Heart. In the center of things.

They are clustered together, all three with vacancy lit up. Fast food joints and a couple of strip malls surrounding them. Two have signs that tout high-speed internet access. That's convenient, but not what I base my decision on.

I choose the one that has outside entrances to every room. It's just one story, about forty units. I drive around back. Near the far end, a light bulb is burned out. That's good and bad. It would be hard for me to make out somebody outside. But it would also be hard for someone to see me clearly as I made my way to my room. The scale tips in favor of the latter.

The clerk is an older woman, the owner, she tells me as I check in.

"I'm here to get some work done and I was hoping to have a quiet room. Would it be possible to get something in the back, away from the street? Maybe in the far corner?"

She looks at her registry. "You're in luck, the end unit is open."

From the looks of the fairly deserted parking lot, I don't think it's luck so much as law of averages. As I leave the office I ask the woman if there's a car wash nearby.

"About two block down. Right next to the Chick-Fil-A."

Two birds. One stone. And we don't have those in Michigan.

I drive around to my room and unload my car. Then I head to the car wash. I get rid of my food wrappers from the day's drive and anything that is remotely personal. I take my registration and insurance information from the glove box and tuck them in my tote bag. I take my Michigan plate and put it in the trunk, underneath the carpeting, with the spare tire.

I vacuum out the car and then run it through the wash. I go to a drugstore and buy a pre-paid cell phone, having left mine—purposely—back in Michigan. Then I hit the Chick-Fil-A drive-thru.

When I get back to the motels, I drive past mine and park in the lot of the one farthest away of the three. I then take my bag of food and walk to my room.

I take a look around as I put the key card into the slot. Nobody.

I enter my home for the next few days. My first overnight foray outside my nest in four years.

**I** unpack my laptop and set-up the cell phone as I scarf down dinner. Great shakes, by the way. Why don't we have these in Michigan?

"You out there?" I type to Confessor. Nothing.

I spend the next hour trying to find something on Carrie. There is some more news on the investigation. Police now feel that the force of trauma (their phrase—force of trauma—sounds so clinical, which it is I suppose) is severe enough that it must have been caused by Carrie being pushed, that her body weight and gravity alone would not have caused such a deadly injury.

Police had interviewed her boyfriend (though Nick is not mentioned by name), whose whereabouts at the approximate time of death are accounted for. Nobody at the cabin rental place had seen anyone else visit Carrie on that day.

On that day. Does that mean they'd seen visitors previously? And who would that be? Had Nick known where she was all along? Did barabino? And I musn't forget about the Uncle Chazz connection to these people. Maybe he's involved somehow. I can't make up my mind if that would be better for me, or not.

So, Nick has an alibi. Or claims to have one.

Yeah, right. And I died four years ago in a fiery car crash in the middle of the desert.

I close out my web software, keeping only my chat software up, waiting for Colin. I flip through the television channels, nothing catching my eye. I glance at the book I'd brought along to read, but can't focus on the words.

I return to my laptop, open my Nick folder where all of his machine's contents reside. I go to the pictures folder. Instead of pictures of Colin or Nick and Carrie or even Nick's family, I keep open only the photos where Carrie is featured. I finally come to the one where she's wearing the blue gingham dress. I close the others and enlarge that one.

I think about Carrie, so pretty, so young. Just wanting a secure future with the man she loved. Trying to take control of her life, trying to get Nick to take control of his. Pushing too far.

And now she lies somewhere in some morgue on a cold slab, plastic over her fine features. A wound on the back of her head.

I slide the laptop off my lap and rush to the bathroom, vomit up all the greasy food I'd eaten all day. I lay my forehead on the cool tile of the vanity for a full five minutes. I brush my teeth—twice—and wash my face.

I stare at myself in the mirror. In this strange motel room, in this strange city, expecting a stranger to stare back. But no, it's just me. Unchanged, yet changed.

I head back to my bed, check the laptop.

"U there?" Colin asks.

I sit down, slide the computer to my lap, close the picture of Carrie, watching as her face disappears so quickly. I try not to think of the symbolism of that. I position my fingers on the keyboard, the familiar dents on the F and J a sweet reminder on my index fingers.

"I'm here," I respond to Colin, knowing the words were true on so many levels. "Yes, I'm here," I repeat.

"Great," he writes, "I was worried you might change your mind."

"Nope. I haven't. Have U?"

"No way."

My stomach, in turmoil from its recent purge, calms. "So?" I write.

"Will you have your business wrapped up by 3 tomorrow?"

Ah yes, the conference that I'm attending. "Yes, I'll be done by then."

"I have to be somewhere until then. And at three I have to pick up some work at my buddy's office to bring to him later, but that won't take long."

"You want to meet somewhere after you go to his office?"

"There's a place nearby that would be good. I thought you'd might feel better meeting somewhere in public."

"Yes," I say, wondering if he means the Hopeless Heart. Will I be able to scope out the place so soon? Find out if Johnny Campos is Uncle Chazz?

"It's just I'm not sure how long it will all take. I could be just picking stuff up or I could be there a while."

"We could meet at your friend's office," I offer.

"If you don't mind doing that, it would probably work best. I could pick up the stuff and then we could go get some coffee or something before I head over to Nick's"

"Oh, your partner in the band? That Nick?"

"Yeah."

"It's his office we'd meet at?"

"Yes."

"He out sick?"

I wait, seeing just how much Colin is willing to tell me. If he's thinking it's just going to be a quick cup of coffee between us, he'll say yes and leave it at that. If he's thinking we could be something more, something longer, he'll tell me at least some of the truth figuring I'll learn about it anyway if I'm going to be in town for any length of time. Carrie's picture is bound to be all over every paper if it isn't already.

They'd use the picture of her smiling, of course, the one where she looks the prettiest. Carrie's image is the stuff the media go wild for. If her case isn't wrapped up in a couple of day, this is going to be big national news. For now, it's big Nashville news.

"I want to be honest with you," Colin writes and I'm curious to see his idea of honesty in a completely anonymous (he assumes) situation. "Remember I said Nick's girlfriend took off?"

"Yes."

"Well, she's been found. Dead."

"OMG"

"Yeah, it's been really hard for Nick."

"Did she have some kind of accident?'

"Sort of. She fell and hit her head."

Ah, so he wasn't going to let on it was more than an accident.

"Or so we thought. The police told us today that she'd been pushed."

"Somebody murdered her?"

"Somebody pushed her and she fell on a heavy object. I don't know if it was murder or an accident. Nobody knows."

"Who did it?"

"They don't know."

"This is so sad, I'm so sorry."

"Thanks, but it's Nick that's really going through hell. He feels pretty helpless."

"Of course he does. Now I know what you meant about it being a bad time to meet."

"Yeah—it had nothing to do with not wanting to meet you, believe me."

"We don't have to do this now," I type, but I'm hoping he doesn't agree with me.

"Do you get this way for business often?" he asks.

"This is my first time," I answer truthfully.

"No telling when will be the next time?"

"I actually don't travel all that often." That's also true.

"Then let's meet, see if there's anything here that we want to pursue. Who knows, you might get one look at me and run screaming back to Vermont."

"I doubt that," I type.

"How will I know you?" he asks.

"I really do look like Sophia Loren," I say. "How will I know you? Should I be looking for Cary Grant?"

"Let me send you a pic," he says. I minimize his picture in the background of my laptop and wait for the file to arrive.

It's one I've seen before. One of the band. The other three guys are cropped out and it's just Colin.

"You're adorable!" I say, meaning it.

"Oh, Jesus, not adorable."

"Adorable is bad?"

"I was hoping for studly, gorgeous, a hunk of Greek God."

I think of my ex who fits that description. As does Nick. "Believe me, adorable goes a lot further with me."

"Now I know," he says.

"And knowing is half the battle," I finish.

"Let me give you the address to Bertram, Gleason and Young, that's Nick's firm."

I don't tell him I already not only have the address but the directions mapped out. The address he gives me matches what I have, as I knew it would.

"Okay, I'll meet you outside the building at 3 tomorrow," I write.

"Good. If I'm running really late, you could go up to Nick's office and wait. His secretary's name is Jennilee. She's a real ditz in the office, but she'll let you wait for me there."

I grab for my baby name book. Why I'd felt the need to pack it, I don't know. But it felt good to have it nearby.

*Jennilee. (American) A combination of Jennifer + Lee. Jennifer. (Welsh) White wave. White phantom. Lee. (Chinese) plum. (Irish) poetic. (English) meadow.*

A ditz or a phantom? I probably won't get the chance to find out.

"I'll be fine outside," I say. I'd love to go through Nick's things without Colin, but I don't really want to deal with the ditzy phantom on my own.

"Okay. C U then."

"K—bye," I type, my fingers close to the command Q to quit out of chat.

"Hey," he types and my fingers change configuration.

"Yeah?"

"Are you nervous?"

I rub my sweaty palms on the bedspread. "Yes."

"Me too. You know why, don't you?"

"First date?"

"No. I mean, yeah, but it's more than that."

"Because?"

"I've never met somebody that I've felt so connected with. And I want..."

"Yes?"

He doesn't seem to be able to put it into words any better than I can. But I feel what he does. The anticipation, and also the dread. Because it's been so good so far, can it live up to expectations? And I don't mean looks.

Even though I know it can't go beyond this week, beyond when I find—and...confront - Uncle Chazz.

"I'm really looking forward to this," he types.

"Me too," I confess.

# Fifteen

**I'm** up at the crack of dawn on Tuesday morning, which is odd, because I'm more of a night owl. I'd say I'm like a kid on Christmas, but that would imply excitement, and I don't think you could classify what I'm feeling as excitement.

But what is it, if not excitement? Dread, I suppose. And guilt that knowing passing on Carrie's emails might help the police's investigation but not willing to come forward to do it. Rationalization for what I plan to do to Uncle Chazz. But that emotion is ever present.

Terror, that at any second my ex is going to come breaking through the door.

And yeah, I guess excitement. Or at least excitement to finally be meeting Colin.

I walk next door to the McDonald's and get some breakfast which I take back to my room. And three coffees. It was going to be a while before I left the motel.

After throwing up last night, the food doesn't appeal and I push it aside and reach for the coffee.

My laptop is still on the night stand. I move it to the little desk/table thing. Confessor has not responded to any of my IMs.

I refuse to believe he is cutting me off, but I can't remember a time that we'd gone more than twenty-four hours without talking. No wonder he'd become my touchstone.

My fingers slowly trace the space bar.

Enough.

I pull out all my stuff from my tote bag and spread it out on the table. It soon becomes too much for the small table to hold. Wanting to organize it anyway, I push the table to the corner of the room, move the two side chairs out of the way and spread the papers out on the floor.

I organize the piles as I take long, satisfying gulps of coffee. Emails to and from Carrie in one. Résumés and cover letters in another. Band notes in still another. Anything work related in a fourth pile. All the other emails from miscellaneous people I pile altogether.

I start with the Carrie email pile. Skimming each one as I put them in chronological order. I've read them all before, of course. But that seems like ages ago. Before Carrie went missing, ended up dead. Before I knew Colin (I know, I know—I don't *know* him now—but you know what I mean).

My stomach back to normal (besides the butterflies over meeting Colin), I go back to McDonad's and get lunch. I go for a swim in the outdoor pool at the motel, trying to calm my nerves. Even though it's cool out this time of year for Tennessee and I'm the only one in the pool, it feels pretty good compared to Michigan. But neither food nor exercise do the trick.

I hop in the shower, then start to get ready. I take extra time styling my hair, and actually put on makeup (hastily bought at a RiteAid in Michigan after I realized mine had all died of old age and non-use). I dress, fighting with my pantyhose (from the same RiteAid). I put on the skirt and sweater set I'd brought. After all, Colin thought I was coming from a business conference. I slip on my pumps, the height unfamiliar. I look longingly at my Hello Kitty slippers next to the bed.

*All your life you were only waiting for this moment to be free.*

Somehow I never thought my leap from the nest would be in three-inch heels.

I put my notes and a couple of tablets in a leather portfolio I brought from home. They'd be in my car if Colin happened to look in. Or in case he actually got in.

One last look in the mirror. If he looks for a Sophia Loren look-alike, he'll spot me in a crowd.

No problem of me not spotting him - he doesn't know I spent the last three weeks studying him in excruciating detail in hundreds of pictures.

I take the gun out of my tote bag. Weigh the risk of taking it now, and possibly having Colin find it, with the chance that a perfect opportunity will present itself.

I end up finding a hiding spot in the room for it and leaving it behind.

I grab all my Mapquest info and the map I'd bought at a gas station last night and leave. Closing the door of the motel room isn't quite as scary as closing the door to my house in Michigan, but it has the same kind of …closure… to it.

On to something new.

I find the offices of Bertram, Gleason and Young fairly easily. It's a large building, five stories high, lots of flourishes, lots of windows.

Lots of money.

There's a large parking lot across the street. Several empty spots have signs that read "For guests of Bertram, Gleason and Young". Not customers, guests. Classy. I pull into one of the spots, figuring I'm a guest of a guest so I sort of qualify.

I step out of my car, cross the street. I take a deep breath.

Here goes.

**A** van pulls into the lot a moment later. I can't see the driver, but somehow I know it's Colin. The driver gets out, comes around to the front, to the edge of the street.

We are directly across the street from each other. Colin looks away from the passing traffic and sees me. Cars and trucks speed past, breaking up our vision, but I can clearly make out a soft, sweet smile creeping across his face.

I can't hear him over the cars, but his lips, clearly form the syllables, "So-Phee-Ahh". I return his smile and then lower my head, embarrassed by the intiMacy.

My attention is returned by the shrill sound of a car horn and screeching brakes. My head jerks up to see Colin stepping back onto the curb, shrugging at the car's driver who flips Colin the bird and then speeds off. Colin looks both ways—this time—and crosses the street as traffic clears.

He's wearing worn jeans (but not holey—thank goodness—I hate that look) that fit him perfectly, and a white cotton shirt, sleeves rolled up. His chestnut hair is slightly disheveled like maybe he just rolled out of bed. Or was having a bad day and had run his hands through his hair a thousand times.

His tall body ambles toward me. He seems both shy and excited.

"Patsy. Sophia!" he says to me in greeting as he nears.

He stops, close to me, but not too close. "Colin," I say, my voice raw, unused. I clear my throat. "It's great to meet you," I add.

"Great to meet you, too," he says. He looks me over, head to toe, then meets my eyes. "God, you're beautiful."

I smile, "Well, you're certainly no troll." It's true. As sweet and friendly as he looks in pictures, he's that much more genuine in the flesh. And what adorable flesh it is.

There's an awkward moment where I raise my hand to shake and he raises his arms to hug. We both sense it, laugh and drop our arms, still untouched.

"Come on, let's get this over with then we can go somewhere to talk," he says, opening the door to Nick's building for me.

"Hey, Joe," Colin says to the security guard at the front desk in the opulent lobby.

The guard greets Colin warmly, spins a clipboard around for him to sign. The guard vaguely reminds me of Tom, which I take as a good omen—but maybe any man in a uniform with a clipboard to sign has a soft spot in my heart.

Colin signs the sheet, motions to me and says, "She's with me."

Joe nods. "How's Nick doing?" he asks Colin.

Colin shrugs. "Not so good. He's pretty broken up about it."

"Yeah," Joe says, "It's tough. Tell him we're all thinking of him down here."

"I will," Colin replies.

"And tell him we know he didn't do anything wrong."

Colin nods. "I'll tell him that, too. Thanks, Joe."

Joe's head is slowly bobbing, he mumbles something that sounds like "Fine young man," as we walk to the elevator bank. I'm not sure if he's talking about Nick or Colin.

The elevator glass is metallic inside and acts as a mirror. I get in, staring at myself, not recognizing the woman in front of me. She looks like someone who knows what she's doing. Someone who has plans, who just came from a business meeting. Who knows what she's making for dinner. Who knows accounting inside and out.

Colin enters, the doors shut and my focus shifts to his reflection. He hits the button for the fourth floor then leans back against the railing. Our eyes meet in the reflective door. His body turns to mine, I turn to him. We face each other, our sides resting against the back of the elevator.

Now confined, I can make out his scent. It's not too heavy, faint, but definitely male.

He smiles softly. "This is weird, hey?" I nod. "I feel like I know you, we've chatted so often, you look just like I thought you would—which is beautiful, by the way."

"Thank you," I say softly, watching his mouth as he continues on. "It's just weird to be standing with someone you never met physically and yet feel like you have such a connection with. You know?"

I nod again. I know just what he means. Colin doesn't feel like a stranger to me. After all we've shared with each other, he's someone I feel I know well, and yet I'm in an elevator with a body that I've never met before, never touched, never smelled.

Colin reaches out, takes my hand in his, brings his other hand up, taking mine in both of his as if to shake it. But he doesn't, he just holds it.

His hand is warm, tender, but not soft, he holds mine gently, as if he's trying not to scare me.

I look at our hands, they look right together. I look up into Colin's face.

"Let's try this again," he says softly. He begins to move his hand in a hand-shake motion. "Hello, I'm Colin James."

I take a deep breath; terrified to utter words I haven't spoken in four years. I return the pressure of his hands. Not a squeeze, exactly, more like a claiming.

Placing my trust in his hands.

My life in his hands.

"Hello, Colin. I'm Raven Moldano."

*Raven. (English) Blackbird.*

# Sixteen

"Raven." Colin's voice is soft, but firm. He says my name with reverence, awe almost. "Beautiful name. It suits you."

To hear my name—my real name—on a man's lips is both joyful and terrifying.

"Raven, my little Blackbird," my father used to croon to me.

"Raven, you're killing me," my ex used to say to me while we made love.

The spell of Colin's gaze is broken by the soft ding of our arrival on the fourth floor. Colin's hands slide from me, slowly, it seems like reluctantly.

We step off the elevator and to the front desk of Bertram, Gleason and Young. The desk is more of a counter, really, made of expensive looking marble (is there any cheap looking marble?). The woman behind the desk/counter is young and pretty, but dressed very conservatively, her hair pulled back into a bun.

She looks up and sees me, "Welcome to Bertram, Gleason and —" Colin steps from behind me and the receptionist's expression changes, a friendly smile brightens her face, a comfortable drawl replaces her smooth tone, "Hey, Colin, how y'all doing? How's Nick?"

Colin smiles at the woman, but I notice it's not the same

smile he'd given me outside. "He's doing okay, Kelly, thanks. Getting by, I guess."

"It's just awful what happened to Carrie," Kelly says.

Colin sighs. I imagine he's been doing this a lot, being the go-between for Nick. "Yeah, terrible," he says. "This is my friend, Raven." I shake hands with the receptionist and we do our hellos. Colin places his hand at my back and begins to steer me down a hallway. "Jennilee's expecting us," he says to Kelly. I hear her say something back, but we've rounded a corner and I can't make out the words.

We round another corner and step through a door into a smaller receiving area. A woman sits behind the desk and behind her is an open office door. Nick's office.

"Hey, Jennilee," Colin says.

The woman looks up from her computer, startled. "Hello Colin," she says, recovering. Her face doesn't become friendly from his presence, I notice, like the receptionist's and the security guard's. In fact she looks nervous. Her fingers fly from the keyboard, as if she'd been caught doing something.

I don't know what I was expecting from the ditzy phantom, but it sure wasn't this. Mousy is the only way to describe her. She's about my age. Straight, non-descript brown hair hangs to her shoulders. She wears a light blue blouse with one button undone and a tiny gold cross peeking through. She has on navy either pants or skirt (I couldn't tell for sure with her sitting down). Small gold post earrings. A tiny bit of lipstick on an otherwise unmade-up face. She was just so…plain.

And obviously very upset about something. Colin? Me being here with Colin? Thoughts about Nick? That maybe she'd lose her job if Nick was arrested and fired?

She chews on her bottom lip and actually—I kid you not—wrings her hands. "I'm so… Oh, I'm so…"

Colin steps to the desk, places his hand on her shoulder, she seems to recoil, and he takes his hand away. "I know. We're all pretty upset. This is Raven Moldano," he says, turning back to me.

I nod at Jennilee, she nods back. "Nice to meet you," we say at the same time.

Jennilee studies me, trying to figure out where I fit in. I don't help her out. I'm not sure myself. At least she's stopped wringing her hands, though they flutter over things on her desk, straightening already straight items.

"You have the stuff that needs to go to Nick ready?" Colin asks her.

She nods once, gets up (it's a skirt, straight and shapeless) and walks into Nick's office. Colin follows her. I'm about to sit in one of the side chairs when he calls, "Come on in here, Raven. I want you to see something."

I enter the office. Colin and Jennilee are behind Nick's desk. She's pointing out the different piles, mentioning the things that Nick needs to sign, the ones that just need to be looked at. Colin murmurs his understanding.

I look around the office. It's standard office furniture. Nice office furniture, but pretty much what you'd expect.

But, instead of the obligatory paintings of flowers or landscapes on the walls (or worse, those motivational things with pictures of mountains and quotes about perseverance or something as banal), there are photos of old country music stars. They're great shots, all kind of candid, or in concert. No staged headshots. They're all in black and white and framed in black suede frames.

Now that I've done a little research into country music I can recognize some of them. Hank Williams Sr. walking along a dirt road. A very young Johnny Cash singing. A group identified by the sign behind them at a country fair as The Carter Family singers. And even…and I take this as a sign, of course…Patsy Cline, a beer in her hand, a saucy smile on her face.

My kind of woman.

I hear Jennilee say she needs to make a couple more copies

and heads out the door, back to her area.

I feel Colin come up behind me. His body doesn't touch mine, but I still feel him.

"Great photos," I say, motioning to the wall.

"That's what I wanted you to see. Thanks"

"You took them?" Of course not, Raven, you idiot. Some of these people have been dead for thirty or forty years.

He doen't seem to hold my gaffe against me. He only chuckles. Good, maybe he thought it was a joke. "No. Not took them. I found them. Archives. Garage sales. I've been collecting stuff like that for years. The old-timers. I put them together, chose the frames, stuff like that."

His arm reaches past my shoulder, he points to the photo of Patsy Cline, "There's my girl," he says. I laugh. It sounds strange to my ears. Sure, Tom and I have an occasional chuckle over coffee and cookies. And I've laughed out loud at some of Confessor's one-liners. But this is different. This is shared.

"You've got a great eye." I turn to look at him. He's staring at me, not the photos.

"Yes, I do," he says quietly.

Jennilee bustles back into the office. "This is the last of them."

Colin's fingers brush mine, and then he turns and heads back to the desk. He takes the stacks from Jennilee, thanking her.

I take a step forward, look at Nick's desk. It's your regular desk, computer, calendar blotter, paperweights. Nick's watch is lying by his keyboard. He probably didn't expect to be away so long. I'm about to ask Colin whether or not he should take that to Nick as well when I see the photograph sitting on the desk. It's not front and center, but off to the side, positioned behind one of those in and out stacking things.

Its back is to me, I can't see it. I have to see it, I just have to. "Well, the pictures are great. Just great. They really add to the whole office." I swing my arms a little too widely, encompassing the office walls and knocking the photo frame over.

"Oh, I'm so sorry," I say as I start to reach for it.

"That's okay. Just leave it," he says.

No way in hell.

I pick up the frame and flip it over, ostensibly to right it. Before I even look, I know what it will be. It is, of course, the picture of Carrie in the blue gingham dress. Man, the woman genuinely smiles in one photo and it's circulated like the *New York Times*. But this time, unlike the photo on the newspaper's website, Nick is not cropped out.

They stand arm in arm. Together. United.

Ironic.

"She's very pretty. Is this…is it…" I leave the sentence unfinished, my voice rising to a question. Both Colin and Jennilee nod. "That's Carrie," she says.

"I'm so sorry. You must have known her pretty well, working for Nick and all," I almost reach for Jennilee, to touch her arm in understanding, but remembering her flinch from Colin's touch, I don't.

"We...she and I…yes, I knew her well."

I suspect she wants to say more, but her expression closes off. She steps to the door and then to the side as if to usher us out.

I put the photo back on Nick's desk. I accidentally jar the keyboard, which makes Nick's watch fall on its side.

The light is shining right on it and I can make out the engraving on the back.

"It's *our* time now. Love, C"

Probably a graduation gift. Or maybe when Nick got his promotion. Either way, Carrie had played her passive aggressive game. Not the band. Not the boys. It's our time. She'd even had it in italics.

I must have spent too long at the desk because Jennilee says from behind me, "It was nice to meet you, Ms. Moldano," definite dismissal in her voice.

"Raven, please," I say stepping past her as she moves out of Nick's office and back to her desk.

Colin comes out of the office behind me, juggling the papers for Nick.

Jennilee looks to Colin. "Tell him…"

"Yes?"

She shakes her head, dismissing her thought. "Nothing. Just tell him to call me if I can do anything. I'd be happy to go to his apartment and pick these up tomorrow."

"We'll get them back to you," Colin says.

Jennilee looks away, nods slowly. "Yes. Of course. That will be fine."

Colin is silent in the elevator, as we cross the street to the parking lot, he says, "Thanks for going in there with me. I really didn't want to deal with her alone."

I don't see Jennilee as someone that you'd need reinforcements for, but I don't know any of the subtext. Yet.

"No problem," is all I say.

We reach Colin's van, parked next to my car. "Yours?" he points to my car.

"Yes."

"I figured. Rental." All the guilt from stealing the license plate leaves me. Somehow I knew Colin would be the type to notice things like rental stickers and plates.

"Let me throw these in my van. There's a coffee place just around the corner, that sound okay?"

"Coffee always sounds okay." I'm disappointed that it's not the Hopeless Heart that he wants to go to, but I do like the thought of getting to know Colin in the flesh without having my radar up and looking for Uncle Chazz.

"Ah, a slave to the bean?"

"That's me," I admit. He smiles, takes my hand and we head down the block.

Just like normal people on a first date.

**An** hour later, lulled by the coffee, good, easy conversation, and many laughs, I blurt out, "I can't believe I'm really here."

The meaning is much deeper for me than Colin can possibly understand.

"I can't believe you're so gorgeous. I figured for sure you were putting me on. Nobody who looks like you has ever… " He doesn't finish his thought.

I wonder if he's thinking that only Nick gets the good-looking ones?

I duck my head. He probably thinks out of shyness, but it's not. It's out of guilt. He doesn't know that I've been staring at various pictures of him. But the real thing is even better. He places a single finger on my chin, lifting it. I meet his soft, brown eyes.

"It's just icing on the cake," he continues, "Incredible icing. Red velvet, cream-cheese frosting, but I knew this was going to be about more than just looks. I knew it from the first day."

"That seems so long ago," I say.

He nods. "It does, doesn't it?" He looks toward the window, his eyes not really focusing on the outside. "So much has happened in such a short time."

"Listen," I start, but Colin starts to shake his head.

"No, I know what you're going to say. And it's sweet. And yeah, there's a lot of shit going on right now. But, I really want to get to know you, spend some time with you."

I feel my breath slowly leave my body as he adds, "The connection isn't only online. At least not for me."

"Me either," I admit.

He gets off his stool, starts cleaning our mugs up. "Good. I have to bring that stuff to Nick's place. Why don't you go with me?"

"I don't think that's a good idea. I don't want to intrude on him, not with all he's going through." The truth is I don't want to come face to face with Nick. Not yet. It will remind me that I'm here, in Tennessee for reasons beyond meeting a boy I met online. Just a little more time of being normal before I'll have to seriously start planning how to take out Uncle Chazz.

"He's been stuck in that apartment all day. The last couple

of days, really. It'd be good for him to be around somebody else. Somebody not connected to this whole thing. Besides, we'll just drop the stuff off, stay for a few minutes and then go grab dinner or something."

"Okay," I reluctantly agree. I guess I should be happy. This is exactly what I want to happen, to get close to Nick. Get into the inner circle. Find a way to get those emails to the right people. Let them lead me to the Hopeless Heart and Uncle Chazz. But now faced with it, I suddenly want to forget about Nick and Carrie and even Uncle Chazz altogether. Pretend Carrie is safe somewhere and I'm out on a date with Colin.

"Come on," he says. We walk in silence back to the parking lot, our arms touching, his fingers sweeping past mine with each stride.

"Why don't I follow you," I say when we reach our cars. "In case you need to stay or something."

"Still being cautious?" he asks.

I shrug.

"That's okay," he says, "That's really smart, in fact. I wish Carrie had been more cautious."

He opens my car door for me, I slide in. "Follow me," he says, shutting my door, heading toward his van.

"I will," I say to his retreating back.

I lose Colin at a light and panic. I know where Nick lives, have his address memorized and could find it easily with my map, but Colin doesn't know that. I can't just show up there. The light turns to green and I surge forward, not sure what to do. Colin's van is pulled over a half a block away. When he sees me near, he pulls in front of me, gives me a wave and we're off again.

I follow him into Nick's apartment's parking lot. There are two spots empty next to each other. I get out of my car and walk to Colin's door. He is writing something on a scrap of paper and hands it to me as he gets out. "Here. This is my cell number. When I lost you at that light, I thought 'Holy shit, I could totally lose her, she'd have no way of getting a hold of me'."

"There's always online," I tell him.

He's shaking his head. "I don't like the thought of having to wait until you're back at your computer." His lips slowly start to turn up, his straight, white teeth showing through his soft smile. He leads the way into the building.

**A**t Nick's door I get cold feet. I turn to Colin. "Why don't I just wait for you at the cars, or some restaurant nearby."

He's shaking his head. "No, it's okay. I'd really like for you to meet Nick."

"I…but…"

He takes my shoulders, turns me toward him. "Nick didn't do anything wrong. He would never do anything wrong. I know that we just met, but trust me."

It's not Colin that I don't trust, but I just nod and face the door as he knocks.

The door swings open and is filled with Nick.

I know what he looks like, of course, but I'm still startled. He's wearing a plain white dress shirt, unbuttoned at the collar, sleeves rolled up. Grey dress slacks that are terribly wrinkled, hang on his hips. It looks like he got dressed for work, realized he couldn't go and went back to bed in his clothes.

His hair—that jet-black hair—looks rumpled and untamed. He has beard growth of several days. Probably since Friday, I think to myself.

He could be the younger brother of my ex.

I take an involuntary step back, then, not wanting to show my true feelings, step forward again.

He looks from me to Colin and back again, as if one of us has the secret to all of this.

One of us does, but I'm not telling.

Besides, he's probably keeping secrets, too.

# *Seventeen*

"What's going on?" Nick asks Colin.

Colin takes my hand and moves past Nick, taking me with him. Nick has no choice but to move aside. "Nick, this is Raven Moldano. Raven, Nick Carpenter."

I've already been led past Nick, but I stop, take my hand from Colin's and force myself to extend it to Nick. "It's nice to meet you, Nick. I'm really sorry that it couldn't have been under better circumstances."

He shakes my hand automatically, murmuring his thanks for my condolences. He looks at Colin who shrugs and says, "I told her…about Carrie."

We walk into the living room of a typical apartment. Living room, dining room, galley kitchen and a hallway that I assume leads to bathroom and bedroom. Three doors; must be a two-bedroom. The furnishings are the stuff you expect to see in a young, male, professional's place. Lots of expensive stereo equipment. Hundreds of CDs stacked all around it. A large television, a leather recliner, and then, like it's an afterthought, a small couch, a chair and what looks to be a second or third-hand dining room table, with four non-matching chairs. There are still some boxes—presumably unpacked—stacked here and there, from Nick having just moved here not so long ago.

Sitting at the dining room table, a textbook in front of her, is Tricia Carpenter. Her head is out of her book, looking to see who's arrived. She looks exactly like the pictures on Nick's machine. Cute, spunky.

She sees me and smiles hesitantly, not sure if I'm friend or foe. I imagine the last few days has put everyone in Carrie's circle on alert.

Colin steps past me and Tricia's whole body changes. She sits up straighter, shoulders back, her hands fly through her hair, smoothing, poofing.

Oh, so that's how it is. Colin was wrong, not *all* women see him as just a buddy.

Colin heads over to the table. He ruffles Tricia's newly smooth hair. "Hey, Squirt," he says.

Oh, so that's how it is.

"Hey," she says.

Colin introduces us. I step over to the table, say my hellos. I don't say much, but it's enough for her to realize I'm not from around here.

"Where are you from?" she asks.

"Vermont," I answer.

"Brrrr," she says.

"You can say that again."

"Brrrr," she says and flashes me a grin so big and goofy I start to laugh.

She holds her hand out for me to shake. "I'm Tricia."

*Tricia (Latin) An Alternate form of Trisha. Trisha (Latin) Noblewoman.*

It fits her. She does seem noble, strong, a presence. Someone who wants to be noticed and carries herself as such. But not in a bitchy kind of way. Or in a strictly beautiful way. This is someone you want to be friends with, tell your secrets to.

I can't tell my secrets to her, but I'd like to.

"Raven," I say for the second time today. It rolls off my tongue more easily. Sounds almost natural.

"Sit down," she says, gesturing to the chair next to her. "Even talking about Vermont would be better than studying this dry stuff."

"Hey," I say, full of laughing indignation.

"Just teasing," she says. "I've never been, I've heard it's beautiful. All that maple syrup, right?"

I nod, wishing I'd done a bit more research on my *home* state. "Are you a student here?" I ask, pointing to her book.

She shakes her head, her sleek bob swaying against her neck. Nick's hair.

"I'm at University of Georgia."

"A ways from home."

She nods. "Yeah. I came up here to be with Nick, he's going through some heavy shit right now."

"Colin told me. It's all so horrible," I say, meaning it.

She just continues to nod her head.

"So, how do you know Colin if you're from Vermont?"

I look at Colin, he's joined us at the table, Nick is a few feet away, getting two Rolling Rocks out of the fridge, but he looks at me also, waiting for my answer. Colin nods his consent.

"I'm in town for a few days for a conference," I say trying to lend some legitiMacy to my appearance in their lives. Tricia raises her brows, waiting for me to answer her question. "Colin and I met online a while ago, have been chatting ever since, and since I was going to be in town, we decided to meet in person."

Tricia takes a moment to process this, looking from me to Colin and back again. Nick has turned his back to us, opening the beer bottles at the kitchen counter. I can't see his expression.

I know thousands, probably millions of people meet online. There are hundreds of flourishing online businesses for just that purpose. But I still feel a little cheesy telling our story.

"You met online?" she asks, a tone of disbelief—but not distaste—in her voice.

We both nod.

She looks at Colin. "You're using an online dating service?" More disbelief and this time just a touch of hurt in her voice.

He shakes his head. "No, we met in a chat room."

Somehow that sounds worse. "A music chat room," I clarify.

Nick brings Colin and me beers, and takes the seat directly across the table from me. He starts looking through the folder of papers Colin had placed there.

I take a long drag from the beer. It's icy cold and feels good rushing down my throat. "We talked about music a lot at first. Colin's told me all about your band. It's too bad I won't get to hear you all while I'm here." It's the only way I can think to start the conversation in a direction that might ultimately lead to the Hopeless Heart.

Nick nods, but continues going through his papers. Tricia drops all pretenses of studying and shuts her textbook, sliding it into a gigantic book bag near her feet. Colin tilts his head at me, questioningly. "You don't have meetings tomorrow night, do you?"

"No, just in the afternoon," I lie.

"Then you'll hear us. We play on Wednesdays at a bar near here, the Hopeless Heart."

Yes, I know, I think but only nod.

Nick's head jerks up from his work. "You didn't call Johnny and cancel?"

Colin shook his head. "No. We cancelled on Saturday. I didn't want to cancel tomorrow, too. Not with Will interested."

Nick leans back in his chair, brushes his hands through his thick hair, making it even more disheveled. "Colin—" he begins, but Colin has his hand held up.

"I know the timing sucks, but there's a scout that's coming to hear us play and we are going to be there."

"But how will that look?" Nick asks.

Guilty, I think to myself.

"Like a man who is mourning the death of his girlfriend is keeping a long-standing commitment to the bar."

Nick waves that away, "There are thirty bands that would step into that spot with ten minutes notice."

"And to his band," Colin adds.

They look at each other, no words pass, but the connection is so strong none need to. Finally Nick bows his head in defeat. "Fine. But you know I'm going to sound like shit."

"No you're not, 'cuz if you do, I'm going to kick your ass."

They both chuckle softly; a shared joke cultivated over years of friendship and fights.

"What do you think?" he asks Tricia.

She shrugs. "On the one hand, it's a good idea to play. To get on with your life, let the cops see you have nothing to hide, that you're not sitting in your apartment feeling guilty."

I look at Nick's appearance. That's exactly what it looks like he's been doing.

"On the other, it could look like you don't feel bad enough," Tricia says softly.

"Christ," Nick says, burying his hands in his handsome face.

I want to leap across the table and shake him. Scream at him. Tell him I know that Carrie was pushing him. Ask him if he pushed back. Instead, I take a long swallow of beer and ask, "So what are you going to do?" I mean about the band, although I guess that had already been decided.

Nick looks at me, mistaking my question for the larger picture. "Nothing. I mean, I don't know what to do. My dad was totally pissed that I even talked to the police without a lawyer. But, I didn't have anything to hide, you know?"

I keep silent.

"They're coming up tomorrow—my folks," he continued.

"Oh shit," Tricia says.

He eyes her beer bottle. "Yeah, you're going to have to straighten up."

She scowls at him. "It's not that. They don't even know I'm here."

Nick sighs. A big brother exasperated sigh, I suppose. Never having had a brother—big or otherwise—I wouldn't know for sure. "Maybe you should just head back tomorrow, then."

"No way," Tricia says, reaching out, placing her hand on

Nick's arm. "I'm not going anywhere till they find out who did this to Carrie."

I like Tricia, I really do. She's going to be devastated when… I don't finish my thought, not sure how any of this will play out. Maybe Nick will get away with it.

Others have.

On some level, I'm hoping to myself…get away with killing someone.

"Your dad's right, you can't talk to them again without a lawyer," Colin says.

Nick nods. "I know. He's lining up some guy from Nashville for me…in case…"

Colin shakes his head, his brown eyes intense. "There's no 'in case', you didn't do this, there is no way you could have done this."

Colin's defense of his friend is touching, but I wonder if it isn't misguided.

"Besides," he adds, "You have an airtight alibi. You couldn't have done it."

I look at Nick. I know this isn't the right time, that I'm an intruder here. But when will I ever get the chance to question the suspect (ha! Nancy Drew, eat your heart out) again?

"What exactly is your alibi?" I ask, trying to sound nonchalant, like I ask about people's alibis everyday.

Nick opens his mouth, but Colin beats him to it. "He was with me, at my apartment. We were practicing."

"Oh, well if there's three other guys that can corroborate your whereabouts" (I just couldn't stop with the detective speak!), "then you're in the clear."

And I won't have to somehow get those emails to the authorities. Which will leave me to the real reason for my trip to Nashville.

"No, not the whole band, just me and Nick. We write songs together, and we write a lot without Billy and Russ there—we get too distracted otherwise."

That made sense, that they'd do that, write without the other two guys present.

So, there *is* an alibi. I am just about to question my belief that Nick pushed Carrie when Nick looks over at Colin and I see Colin give the tiniest nod to Nick, his brown eyes staring into Nick's blue ones.

They're lying. Colin is lying for Nick, giving his friend an alibi.

My admiration at Colin's loyalty is matched by my fury at Nick for putting Colin at risk. And now I'm back to square one; how to make the stuff on Nick's machine known without making myself known?

Yes, I could send copies of her emails from a public email account. But sooner or later someone would put it together that those email came form Nick's old machine, and then they'd start looking for shipping records and other things that would lead them to my safe house in Michigan.

"What..uh…arrangements have been made for Carrie?" I ask.

"Arrangements?" Colin asks.

"She means a funeral," Nick clarifies and I look at him, nodding.

"Her mom's on a trip to India. She's at some ashram or some kind of new-agey thing. They can't get a hold of her. She doesn't even know yet. That's why they're holding off on any kind of…" Nick's voice cracks a little. "Funeral plans. They're not letting me be involved in any of it. I'm totally cut off, the person who knew her best."

"Her father?" I ask.

Nick shakes his head. "He's never been in the picture. It's just been Carrie and her mom."

"And her mom's a class A flake, always has been from what Carrie's said," Colin adds.

No wonder she was so desperate for some stability in her life. She was probably drawn to the normalcy of the Carpenters.

I can understand that. I am too, in a way.

Colin takes a long drink from his beer and changes the subject. "Will call yet?"

Nick shakes his head. "No." He lets out a heavy sigh, "He's probably scared off—who could blame him."

I see Colin's hand tighten around his beer bottle. He looks at his watch—one with a large face and a beat up leather band. "It's still early. He probably had a late meeting."

"Maybe," Nick says. I can hear the doubt in his voice.

"Yeah, that's probably all it is, a late meeting," Colin says. There's no doubt in his voice at all. I'm not sure if that's to convince Nick or himself.

"I need to use the bathroom," Tricia says, getting up from the table.

Colin raises his eyebrow. "Thanks for keeping us in the loop."

I chuckle. I look across the table at Nick studying me. I stop chuckling.

"Has anyone ever told you you look exactly like Sophia Loren?"

Colin and I share a smile and I say to Nick, "Not many people our age know who Sophia Loren is."

"I'm not like most people," he says. It feels like a warning.

"Neither am I," I say, rising to his silent challenge.

He nods, like he'd figured that out already.

"And you just got to Tennessee? Today?"

I nod. "Well, last night, actually."

"And you and Colin have been chatting how long?"

"Almost a month," I say, looking at Colin for corroboration, feeling like the tables have turned and now I'm the one being questioned.

Nick gives his head a little shake. "Why? What?" I ask.

He shrugs. "Nothing…I just…it seems like weird timing is all."

I'm relieved when Tricia comes back from the bathroom. "What'd I miss?" she asks.

Nick looks at me, says nothing. "Nothing," I say to Tricia, but my eyes stay on Nick.

Colin gets up from the table, holds out his hand to me. "Raven, I want to show you something." Grateful to leave Nick's stare, I take Colin's hand, leave the table and follow him down the hallway. He opens the first door down the hall, steps into the room and switches on the light. The room is a bit cooler than the rest of the apartment, and I fight the urge to shiver. Colin notices, runs his hand across my back. "Yeah, we keep it a little cooler in here for the instruments."

The room is full of musical equipment. Several guitars, sheet music everywhere. A brand new G5 MAC sits on a small table, hooked up to a large electronic piano keyboard.

"Wow," I say, looking around.

"Yeah, this is where we start the process," he says, looking around with pride.

"Nick's neighbors must love him."

"That's why he got this place, it's on the ground floor, and the lady above him is nearly deaf. We don't play too loudly here—we have a space for our rehearsals. This room is mostly for writing." He points to the computer. "We just got that a few months ago, state of the art synthesizing software."

"But this is what I really wanted you to see," he says, pointing to the walls. "Since you seemed to like the ones in Nick's office so much."

It's another set of vintage photographs, these matted in beige with gold frames. "Very nice," I say, meaning it. After studying the photographs for a few minutes, I turn to Colin. "So, you guys write here," I point to the computer, "record what you're working on?"

He seems pleased that I've taken such an interest. "Yep. We lay down a keyboard track and a guitar track and process it in the computer." He starts to go on with explaining the electronic process but I cut him off.

"But the night Carrie died you were writing at *your*

apartment?"

His eyes narrow at me "Yes," he says, but there's a question behind it.

"Is that unusual?"

"No."

"You have all this great equipment here, the computer, but you write at your place?"

"We write here, we write at my place, we write at the IHOP over pancakes if we're just doing lyrics. We have pretty busy lives with our day jobs, we write whenever and wherever we get the chance." His voice turns defensive at the end and I'm almost sorry I questioned him. Almost. He looks at me like Nick did at the table.

"I'm sorry. I'm just trying to think like the police will," I say.

"Why?"

Because a woman is dead, and whether it was an accident or not, the man who probably did it is having a beer in the next room, planning his musical career. "Because, even though we just met, I feel like we know each other," I say.

"We do," Colin says, moving toward me.

I nod, I feel the same way. "And I just don't like the idea of you becoming involved in something…something…that maybe you shouldn't."

He smiles, his face transforming from suspicion to affection. "That's sweet, really. But don't worry, Nick didn't do anything wrong."

I notice he doesn't say that he's just telling the truth, or that Nick *couldn't* have done anything wrong, but I let it go. If Colin is lying for Nick it will come out sooner or later.

"Raven," he whispers as he steps to me. His eyes sweep down my body. His hand touches mine. He leans forward and I realize he's going to kiss me—and that I want him to.

The doorbell rings and his head lifts from mine, his brows furrowed. "I wonder who that is?"

I shrug. "You should probably go see," I say.

He chuckles, low and throaty. "Saved by the bell," he says as he turns and leads me out of the music room.

I'm not so sure I want to be saved.

Colin looks over his shoulder at me. "For now," he adds, his voice full of promise.

**W**e walk out of the music room. I turn the other way. "Let me make a pit stop. I'll be right out."

Colin nods, drops my hand and heads to the living room. I turn the other way. I'd love to go into Nick's bedroom, but that seems like too much of a risk. I go into the bathroom, shut the door and turn on the water full blast to create as much noise as possible.

I look around the small room. Typical male bathroom, though I don't have much experience with them. The towels match and are large and fluffy, new. Lots of toiletries scattered about. I take a peek in the medicine cabinet. Just your usual stuff; aspirin, antacids (guilty stomach?), deodorant.

I don't know what I expect to find, but there is nothing out of the ordinary here. I flush the toilet and let the water run a few more seconds. When I turn it off, I can barely hear the tail end of Colin and Nick talking.

"It's just the timing is all," Nick says.

"And I'm telling you, we've been chatting for a long time, well before any of this started," Colin answers. Actually, I looked Bocephus up online the day after the first anonymous tip about Carrie surfaced. I'm hoping Colin doesn't remember the timing.

"Okay, fine. But do you have to bring her around now, while all this shit is happening?" He has a point there. If I were Nick, I'd want as few people around as possible.

Less people for whom to keep my story straight?

"She's only in town this week. I've wanted to meet this girl since the day we met. And she finally feels comfortable enough to get together. There's no way in hell I'm going to give that up. I know the timing sucks, man, but you didn't do anything wrong.

This is all gonna get cleared up soon. I'm not gonna blow it with this girl."

Nick says nothing to that, or at least nothing I can hear.

I make a lot of noise with the bathroom door and coming down the hallway. The voices stop.

As I enter the living area I take a quick look at everyone. Tricia is chagrinned (she probably knows I was listening in), Nick ignores me completely, Colin flashes me his bright smile.

And a man who hadn't been there before rises from his seat, looks me dead in the eyes and says, "And this must be Raven."

# Eighteen

"**R**aven, this is Will Fredrickson, he's with Planet Records."

I shake the new addition's hand. It's large and rough. In fact, that's how you could describe Will Fredrickson as a whole—large and rough. Oh, he had on a nice shirt and slacks, a leather jacket that looked worn from use, not from the manufacturer, but Will has a physicality about him that neither Nick nor Colin possess.

He tops Colin by an inch or two, Nick by at least three. He is older than all of us too, maybe in his late-thirties, early-forties. His hair is sandy-blonde and just a tad too long—but it looks good on him. His face doesn't hold the earnestness that Colin's does, nor the beauty of Nick. But it has strength—a sense of character that I suppose comes with living a few more years than we have.

There is a small scar creasing his top lip. The scar reminds me of Uncle Chazz, and the real reason I'm here.

Will's presence seems to fill up the room, and he's in a room with two men that have been perfecting their presence on stage for years.

He doesn't look like a record executive, but how do I know what one should look like? I guess I thought they'd all wear shiny suits and slick hair like that one Mariah Carey married. And divorced.

"I was just telling Nick that I stopped by his office earlier, but his assistant said he hadn't been in. I'm not surprised, with what you've been through. And I know it's probably not a good time, but I thought I'd stop by and pick up that CD, and see how things were progressing as far as…" He doesn't finish his sentence, but then he doesn't have to.

"I'll go get the CD," Colin says. "Can you stay and listen to some of it?"

Will looks at his watch. "Yeah, I can stay for a little while."

Colin heads back into the music room and reappears with a CD in hand, which he takes to the stereo. Nick grabs a beer for Will and pulls another chair to the table.

"Why don't I order some pizzas?" Tricia asks Nick. He nods and she heads to the phone.

We all settle in at the table, sipping our beers as Colin brings the stereo remote to the table with him.

"What we've done on the CD are all original songs that are different from the ones you heard last Wednesday at the Heart."

Will takes the CD case from Colin, looking at the song sheet. "There's seventeen songs on here." Colin and Nick nod. "You guys played two hours of original stuff besides the hour of covers at the bar the other night." Colin and Nick both nod again. "You have that much original material?"

They both grin, looking at each other. They look twelve-years-old, the age when they got their first guitars, first hatched this plan to be music stars. The look is so sweet, so endearing, that for just a moment I forget that there's a woman lying in a morgue somewhere in this city waiting to be buried.

"And all the stuff we'll play tomorrow—besides the hour of covers—will be different from all of these."

Will's brows raise. "You guys are going to play at the Hopeless Heart tomorrow?" He looks at me as if I might have some comment on that decision. I keep quiet. "With all that's going on?" he asks Colin.

Colin shrugs, like a murder suspect in the band is no big deal. Nick leans forward, a worried look in his eyes. "Do you think that's a bad idea? That it'll look bad, like I don't care?"

"I can't answer that for you," Will says.

"Screw how it looks," Colin says. "Those people don't need to see your pain, they don't get to know that you're wracked with grief about her. How you deal with it isn't anybody else's business."

"That's true…" Will says, drawing it out

"But?"

"What have the police said lately?"

Nick leans back, runs his hands over his gorgeous face. "They won't tell me squat about the case. As soon as they found out I was with Colin at the time of death they shut me out."

"Probably checking out the alibi," Will says.

"What do you mean? They asked me if Nick was with me, I said yes," Colin says.

Even I'm not that naïve. "There's more to it than that," Will explains. "They'll be checking with your neighbors, to see if any of them saw Nick coming or going, or heard the two of you in your apartment. They'll be driving from your apartment to the cabin where Carrie was killed to see if Nick could have made it there and back in the time frame that they've got. They'll be checking every angle. The fact that they haven't come back since that first questioning probably means they haven't finished with all of that yet."

I take another look at Will, study him. He seems like he knows what he's talking about. But I suppose anybody who watches a lot of crime shows knows this stuff.

"Jesus," Nick murmurs.

"Nick, a girl is dead, they have to check out everything. You want them to find out who did this to Carrie, don't you?"

"Do I?" Nick asks.

Everybody looks around the table at each other at this, and then all eyes gravitate back to Nick, needing an explanation.

He sighs, looking more tired than he had just an hour ago. "Of course I want whoever did this to Carrie to pay. But look, they found no signs of forced entry, whoever did it had likely been invited in. So, she tells me she needs time away, she goes to this cabin for a while, and someone that comes there—with her or to see her, but either way it's not me, the man she supposedly loves—gets into a fight with her and pushes her."

We know all of this, of course. I just always pictured Nick in the starring role. It's fascinating to hear him tell the tale as he wants people to see it.

It's almost believable.

Nick's voice pitches low, we all lean forward to hear him.

"I'm so pissed at her for taking off, maybe being with someone else. I'm sick inside that I've lost her, that she's gone, that I'll never see her again." He looks at us all, his crystal blue eyes glistening with unshed tears. "And I'm scared to death that this is somehow going to get pinned on me."

I almost buy it, and then I remember the look that passed between Nick and Colin about the alibi. The fake alibi.

Tricia lays her hand on his arm, soothing, comforting. Nick pulls away, brushes at his eyes. "This is so fucked up, I can't even mourn my girlfriend, 'cuz I'm waiting for the police to knock on that door any minute."

There is nothing but silence for a minute, and then I say softly, "It's probably good for you guys to play tomorrow. Try to put some normalcy back in your life. Sitting around here with all that conflicting stuff going on inside of you will drive you crazy."

Colin nods his agreement. Tricia gives me a small smile. Nick's face is buried in his hands. I look at Will who is studying me closely. He's probably wondering about the timing of me showing up right now, too, just as Nick had.

"You have a lawyer ready?" Will asks, turning his attention from me back to Nick.

Nick pulls his face from his hands and nods. "My dad knows somebody up here, supposedly pretty good, he's talked to him, filled him in. He says he's ready to go if I need him."

"That's good."

"My parents are coming up tomorrow."

"That's good. Family. A show of support," Will says.

An awkward silence crosses the table. Will takes off his jacket, slings it across the back of his chair, takes a drag from his beer and says, "Well, let's take a listen."

**A**n hour and a half, three pizzas, and several beers later, Will looks at his watch and declares it time to leave. "I still need to check out a band before closing time."

Both Colin and Nick look dismayed at the news of competition.

Will smiles, his green eyes crinkling up at the sides, his brow raised. "I wouldn't really be doing my job if I only listened to one band, would I?"

Coliln looks chagrined. Nick looks pissed off. "I suppose not," Nick grudgingly admits.

"Besides, I plan on going to the Heart tomorrow night to hear you guys," Will adds, stepping behind me.

He's close enough for me to smell him. His scent is different from either Colin or Nick. A hint of musk, but not overpowering.

The contrast of these three men staggers me.

Colin; solid, the boy next door. Someone you'd curl up on a couch with and while away a Sunday afternoon watching old movies.

Nick; beautiful, a little bit dangerous, who sees everything. Someone you'd ride off on the back of a motorcycle with while Bob Seger blared.

Will; strong, with a quiet intensity. Someone you'd...well...I don't know what you'd do with Will. But Will is not a man to underestimate; that much is clear.

"You're not from around here?" I ask him. He didn't have a distinct accent, but he definitely wasn't from Tennessee. If I had to guess, I'd say East coast, but not in a New Yaawk-y kind of way.

"No," Will says.

"What brought you to Nashville?"

"Probably the same thing that brought you," he replies.

I highly doubt that.

"The job," he says.

"Oh. Right. Yeah, me too."

He nods, waiting. I'm not sure what else I'm supposed to say. My small talk skills are basically nil and I've used all of them up with Nick, Colin and Tricia.

In fact, all this banter, especially with Colin at the coffee shop, would have been so much easier for me on a computer. At home. Alone.

Once or twice I even caught my fingers poised over a non-existent keyboard.

But I'm proud that I've done it. That I'm making conversation with people in the flesh, not with those using passwords and user names.

I realize how much I've missed it. Not that I was ever a social butterfly.

My ex saw to that.

**He** called me Snow White. I thought it was because of my black hair, though my skin wasn't fair like the cartoon.

"Mirror, mirror, on the wall," he'd say when I was putting on my makeup or doing my hair. "My Snow White's the fairest of them all."

I'd smile at him, but he wouldn't smile back. "You're prettier without any makeup," he'd say. I'd wipe it off.

We'd go out, but never stay out late. He said he was jealous, that he couldn't stand to see other men look at me. I didn't believe him—he wasn't the jealous type. He knew I'd never stray, he was the only man I ever wanted. But I didn't push it.

We stayed in a lot, which was fine with me. I only wanted to be with him.

He told me later why I was Snow White to him. It really had nothing to do with me, so much as him. He was the huntsman. The one that was sent into the woods to kill Snow White but couldn't go through with it, so he brings a deer heart back to the wicked queen.

Though at the end, he'd have gone through with it—if he'd found me.

Colin collects the CD from the stereo, puts it in the case and gives it to Will. Nick rises to see Will out. They all shake hands.

He waves across the table to Tricia. I am still sitting and he places his hand on my shoulder. His hand is heavy and warm. "Raven, it was nice to meet you. I'll see you tomorrow?"

"I…I…yes, okay," I say, like I was thinking it over. Of course I'd be there.

He moves his hand away, and it takes a couple of strands of my hair with it. I watch as his hand moves back to his side and my dark hair continues, then slips off and falls back into place. But not quite. Those few strands crackle with electricity and hover above the rest, as if reaching for Will. I put my hand out to smooth them just as Will starts to do the same and our fingers tangle. He puts his hand up, out of my way. I put the hair back in place and look up at him. His eyes are still on my hair, then follow my hand as I lower it back to my lap. Then he looks into my eyes. He opens his mouth as if to say something, then shuts it. He waves to us all and leaves the apartment.

I follow him out with my eyes, still trying to get a good reading on him. When I turn back to the table, Nick and Colin are discussing their play list for the next night.

Tricia grabs for her book bag. "I guess I'd better hit it. I still have another chapter to get through."

"We'll try to be quiet out here," Nick says.

Tricia shrugs. "Whatever." She heads to the bedroom, comes back out with a pile of bedding that she places on the couch for Nick.

"See you in the morning," she says to him. He nods. She looks at me. "I'll see you tomorrow night?"

I look at Colin. His soft eyes are questioning, inviting. "Yes," I say. Tricia nods and heads to the bedroom, Colin smiles at me.

"I should get going too," I say. Colin looks up at me,

disappointment in his eyes. I motion to the tablet of song titles he and Nick are looking at. "You guys have a lot of stuff to do." I point to the folder of work we brought over for Nick that had been relegated to the kitchen counter. "Don't forget about those," I add.

Colin gets up, defeated. "Okay, let me walk you to your car."

I tell him it's not necessary, but he insists. Nick and I say our goodbyes. It's awkward. He's shown so much emotion tonight, the total gamut, and I'm just a stranger to him.

But he's not to me.

I lead the way to my car. The parking lot is dark and I'm glad Colin's with me. "Thanks," I say as we reach my car. "It wasn't really necessary, but I appreciate it."

"Us Southern boys are raised right," he says, faking a drawl.

"I'm glad I got to meet Nick and Tricia," I say. True, but not for the reason Colin probably thinks.

"He's a great guy, my best friend. It's a shame he has to be going through this."

I don't answer that. I lean against my car door. "Tricia's got it bad for you, you know," I say before I can stop myself.

I don't know what I expect. Denial? Smugness? But Colin sighs heavily. "I know," he says with defeat.

"For how long?" I ask.

"Forever," he replies. Then he looks at me, puzzled. "You don't think I'd ever…with Tricia?"

"She's a very beautiful girl."

"She's a kid."

"She's only a few years younger than me," I say. Or the age I'd told Colin I am.

"Yeah, I guess that's true. But you seem a lot more worldly to me."

Before I can ask what, exactly, he means, he adds, "Besides, Tricia will always be my best friend's baby sister to me…that's all she'll ever be."

"That's not how she feels," I say. There is concern for Tricia in my voice, not jealously, although I have to admit it is there, just a tiny bit, lurking.

He nods his head. "I know. I love her like a sister, but that's all it will ever be. I thought by just ignoring it maybe she'd grow out of it. What do you think? Do you think I should talk to her about it? God, I wouldn't hurt her for the world." His concern for Tricia is endearing, heartbreaking.

"I…I don't know. I have no idea how you should handle it. It's really not my place to say," I add.

He looks at me with puppy-dog eyes. "It can be. It can be your place to have a say in my life."

I smile. He shakes his head. "You're okay with that? With Tricia?"

I shrug. "It's not your fault she has a crush on you. You don't seem to be leading her on. You're aware of the situation…what else can you do?"

He looks at me, his brows furrowed. "Wow. Beauty. Brains. And common sense. What have I done to deserve you?"

I smile. "Maybe nice guys don't always finish last, Colin."

He leans toward me. It would feel good to be kissed by Colin, safe, I know that instinctively. But I put my hand on his chest to stop him.

"Too soon?"

I swallow. "Too soon," I say on a whisper.

"Fair enough," he says, taking a step back.

I unlock the car door and open it.

"How about I show you around tomorrow," he says.

"Really? That'd be great. I don't have meetings until the afternoon. But don't you have to work?"

He shakes his head. "I've got nothing in the morning. Where are you staying? I'll pick you up."

"Here, in Mount Juliet." I'm just about to give him the name of the motel but I stop. I'd been careful too long for something like that to just roll off my tongue. "Why don't I meet you at the IHOP. I'll buy you breakfast."

"You don't need to buy me breakfast."

"It'll be your tour-guide payment."

He smiles. His grin is soft and lopsided. "Remember this offer when I shovel down twenty pancakes."

I laugh. "A small price to pay."

I get in the car. "Eight?"

He shuts the door for me. Holds up five fingers on one hand, four on the other and mouths, "Nine."

I nod and start the car. I back out and watch as he walks back into Nick's apartment building.

**B**ack in my room, I hop in the shower and try to digest all that's happened in my one day in Tennessee.

How meeting Nick was not what I'd expected. He seems like a guy who has just lost his girlfriend and is truly torn up about it. Of course, if it had been an accident—pushing Carrie in the heat of an argument—he'd be justifiably torn up. But if it had been an accident, why not just come forward?

Because nobody would believe him, I admit to myself.

Mostly I think about Colin. Going out on a limb to give his best friend an alibi. I'm both proud of him and scared for him.

I put on the boxers and tee-shirt that I sleep in, slip my feet into my slippers. I boot up my laptop and get online.

Nothing has changed on the newspaper's website, but I hadn't expected it to. I'm now on the inside, I'd know before the papers would.

I make a final decision and register for the backgammon tournament. I'd have to be there by noon on Thursday to register in person. The first matches begin at one.

If I'm able to get close enough to Uncle Chazz tomorrow night, I might be gone by Thursday afternoon, but if not, I might need the distraction.

I pick the room up a little bit. I'd only been here a day, but all of Nick's computer print outs are lying around. So are the remains of my breakfast and lunch.

As I'm clearing away the numerous empty coffee cups, I hear the knock-knock of someone entering ichat from my laptop.

I scrape my shin on the dresser as I leap for the laptop.

Confessor.

I know it'd been kind of an emotional couple of days for me—leaving Michigan, having people calling me by my real name, meeting Colin and Nick. Dealing with the reality of what I plan to do. But all that pales in comparison with the sheer… relief…that rushes through me when I see Confessor's thinking bubbles rising. I hate to admit it, but I can feel my eyes tearing up.

I knew he wouldn't leave me.

"You out there?" he asks.

"Yep." The messy room forgotten, I climb onto the bed, put one pillow in my lap and another behind my back. I carefully place the laptop on the pillow—like any jarring or sudden movements might cause Confessor to go away.

"Are you in Tennessee?"

"Yes," I answer.

"Tell me," he says. "Confess."

So I do… confess everything…as is always the way with Confessor.

"So, it's Colin for you and Nick for the slammer?"

My fingers slide across the keyboard, the magical, safe, feeling of the keys under my fingers.

"Yes. No. I don't know. Maybe."

"Glad to see you're so on top of it."

"I never claimed to have a handle on any of it—sheesh—even I know I'm just one step away from being a full-fledged stalker with these people."

"You actually think you're a step away?"

"Haha."

"I'm serious."

Oh. Was I a stalker? And if so, of who—Nick or Colin?

"I'm not going to hurt anybody, I just want to make sure that whoever hurt Carrie pays for it." That wasn't all I wanted.

Not even what I wanted most, but I'm sticking with the decision not to tell Confessor about Uncle Chazz. As much for Confessor's protection as mine.

"And you're still sure Nick's involved?"

"I'm sure," I say, not quite as sure as I was a day ago. Then I see the print outs I'd just picked up lying on the table. Carrie's emails to barabino. The emails of a woman playing games. Deadly games.

"Yes," I add. "But maybe it was an accident."

"And Colin?"

"What about Colin?"

"Do you get the sense that he thinks Nick's involved?"

I think of Colin and Nick's covert glance as the explained Nick's alibi. "I'm not sure," I say. I should feel disloyal to Colin, doubting him after the day we'd spent together, having made plans to spend tomorrow morning with him. Feeling the way I do about him. Beginning to feel more.

But, this is Confessor, it isn't just that I *want* to be honest with him—I *have* to be. I wait and watch Confessor's icon. No bubbles. No bubbles. Finally he types.

"I think your new wings have carried you far, Blackbird."

The stress of the last few days hits me and I feel the tears streaming down my cheeks.

"I think so, too," I answer.

"Promise me you'll be careful. These guys may seem like some good ol' boys, but something strange is going on. You don't want to poke your nose into something that could bite it off."

He didn't know that any threat is much more likely to come from an old goomba than a good ol' boy. "I'll be careful," I type.

"Good. I—" the bubble stop, his thought unfinished.

"Yes?" I prod.

"I can't lose you, Blackbird," he types.

My fingers are poised, but how to answer? Tell him how distraught I'd been over the fact that he might cut off communication? Why not? He had to suspect how much he meant to me.

But, of course, I don't get the chance to tell him anything more.

"Bye, bye, Blackbird." He is gone before I can respond.

# *Nineteen*

When I enter the IHOP at nine, Colin is waiting for me in a back booth.

Before I even set my purse down, the waitress is there with her coffee pot. Bless her.

Colin starts to speak, but I hold up my finger "one minute" style. I take a deep sip of the scalding, black concoction. Strong, fresh, I would dive in and swim in it if I could.

"Not much of a morning person?" he asks.

I shake my head and take another gulp.

"Me neither." I notice the stubble, the tired eyes, the baseball cap hiding what was probably a bad case of bed head. I know because I wear a Tennessee Volunteer's cap I'd bought at the gas station Monday night. My hair in a ponytail laced through the back opening. Somehow, on him, it makes him look sexy.

"You look beautiful," he says. I nearly choke on my coffee. I raise a brow. "Well, maybe not beautiful." I raise my other brow. "But very sexy. Very 'I just rolled out of bed'."

"I did just roll out of bed."

"And you wanted to meet at eight."

"What was I thinking?" Oh yeah, I'd been thinking that I was here on business and would want to get cracking before my afternoon seminar.

"I'm trying to figure that out myself," he said, taking a sip from his cup and watching me with those all-seeing eyes.

"Huh?"

"What you were thinking. What *are* you thinking. What's going on up there, Raven?"

Oh God, where to start? I'm thinking you may be the sweetest man I've ever known. I'm thinking that I'm in over my head—that I haven't swum in these deep of waters in a long time. I'm thinking that I wish you could be a part of my life. That Nick would be found out. That Carrie would have justice.

That you didn't live in a town where I'd have to flee, never to return to, in a few days.

"I'm thinking we should have met for lunch instead of breakfast," I say.

He smiles, but he continues to study me. After a second or two, he shrugs and opens his menu.

"Do you have any thing in particular you want to do or see, or are we winging it?" He asks as we get into his car after breakfast.

"We're winging it," I say. Oh, were we ever.

"Great, then we'll start with my dream house," he says, a lopsided smile spreading wide on his face.

"The utilities on this place must be a bitch," I say. I twirl around, taking in the vast cavern. We're standing on the stage at the Grand Ole Opry. The stage is dark, but the set is still in place. A huge barn frame that matches the sign outside the building.

Colin chuckles. "Yeah, the heating bill alone would probably do you in."

He knew the elderly woman who gives tours, and although it wasn't anywhere near the time for a tour, she'd just opened the door and waved Colin in when we'd entered. I got the idea it wasn't the first time he'd done this.

She'd called him honey and looked like she'd wanted to pinch his cheeks.

He steps to the center of the stage. Looks out onto the empty seats in the audience. He closes his eyes and I know he's seeing the place packed, the River Rats front and center. His hands twitch, as though to go to his non-existent guitar. He seems to be breathing the image in, storing it.

He is mesmerizing. His good-naturedness overtaken by an intensity I hadn't seen in him before.

He opens his eyes, turns to me. "It's close, Raven. It's so close this time, I can feel it." His voice is filled with passion, determination. I think about how hard it must be to be a struggling artist, praying with each demo you send out that this one with be *the* one. Each time a stranger comes to hear you play wondering if he could be a scout.

With Colin, so much more is at stake.

"Because of Will?" I ask.

He nods, walks towards me, takes my hand loosely, plays with my fingers. "He's the real deal. He knows his shit. We could go all the way to the top with him."

I squeeze his hand. "And then you'll belong," I say.

He pulls me into his arms, holds me tightly. "I feel like I belong now. With you."

I am caught up in his excitement, but I've been disappointed too many times in my life to not go into anything—everything—with some trepidation.

A feeling that it's all going to be pulled out from under you.

I push that feeling aside and hug him back. "Me too," I whisper.

He lets me go, steps back. "Okay, we've seen my dream house, now let's show you Nashville."

Three hours later we're back at the IHOP. We'd seen most of the sights, but my eyes had rested mostly on Colin at the wheel.

"Thanks so much," I say, turning to look at Colin. He puts the car in park, keeps the engine running. "It was really nice to see your town."

"So what are you going to do now?" he asks.

I shrug. "Go back to my motel. Get ready for a seminar I

want to attend this afternoon. Check in on some things."

"Things back in Vermont?"

"Uh-huh," I say and look away. His eyes are just normal eyes, I tell myself, but I can't help but feel that they see right through me. Right through the lies I tell.

He reaches over and touches my chin, tilts my head to look at him. "Are any of those arrangements back in Vermont a guy?"

I shake my head.

"You didn't leave anyone behind to come down and check me out?"

Only if you count my UPS man. "No," I say. I wasn't leaving Confessor behind, he came with me. And anyway, he's different.

"How is that possible?" he asks.

I shrug again. "I told you, I was burned a while back. I'm being cautious."

"Gun shy, hey?"

Literally. "I guess a little." I take a deep breath, sit up straight. "But not anymore."

His lips crack at one side. I already know the start of his smile. Yep, here it comes…the other side tugs up, then the lower lip opens ever so slightly. Soon, a small dimple forms in his right cheek, just under his cheekbone. And then the lips ease back and there come those pearly whites.

Adorable.

I can't help but smile back at him, he's so infectious.

"Good to know," he says as he leans over. Kisses me. His kiss is perfect. Sweet. Tentative. As if it's his first kiss.

His hand comes up and lodges under my hair, around my nape.

"Raven," he murmurs as we break apart. "Ah, Raven." Oh God. To hear my name used so sweetly after all these years. It almost—almost—makes me forget the harshness with which it was last used.

He kisses me again and I twine my arms around his neck, playing with his hair, knocking his baseball cap off. Really sinking my hands in.

He's pulling me toward him and only the console jabbing my hip keeps me from doing something totally stupid. Like sleeping with a guy I'd just met. In broad daylight. In a car.

In an IHOP parking lot.

"Wait, we have to stop," I say, pulling back, trying to catch my breath, to slow my rapid heartbeat.

"Why?"

"Why? Why? We're in an IHOP parking lot!"

He puts his hand on the gear shift. "That can be easily changed. Let's go to my place."

I shake my head.

"Your hotel?"

I shake my head.

He drops his head on the steering wheel, causing a soft thunk. I laugh. "Thanks again for the guided tour," I say, reaching for the door handle.

His hand flashes out, stopping me. "Wait," he barks.

I flinch. I can't help it.

He sees my reaction, his brow furrows, and then he gets a look like he's figured something out. Figured me out. And maybe he has. Or part of me, anyway.

His voice softens. "I just want to make sure you're coming to the bar tonight."

I nod. "I'm coming."

He smiles slyly. "Good, because if you count last night, it will be our third date."

I quirk a brow. "You're counting pancakes at the IHOP as a date?"

He chuckles. "Hell, yes, if it'll mean tonight is our third date."

"What if I'm a fifth date kind of girl? Or sixth? Or seventh?" I don't really know what I am, it's been so long since I've been in this position. But if it means kissing Colin again, I'm certainly willing to fudge our timetable a little bit.

He touches my hand, his skin rough over mine. "We can take this slow, Raven. There's no rush. We've got all the time in the world."

I get out of the car and head to my own. His taste on my lips. His last words ringing in my ears. Wishing they were true.

I take a long shower, and a short nap. When I wake up I reach for my laptop. "You out there?" I ask Confessor. Nothing

A vision of Colin on the stage at the Opry drifts through my mind and I reach for my laptop. I Google Planet Records and find their website. I'd never heard of them, but then, I don't know any record companies outside of the really big ones like Sony and... okay, I guess I only know Sony.

They've got an impressive client list with artists I have heard of, most of them in Country. I do a little digging and find Will Fredrickson and his bio. In the picture, Will is wearing a suit and although it's a good picture of him, it seems off, not natural. He's much more in his element in the bars, in casual clothes. In a suit he looks like someone's banker father. Or older brother.

I read through the list of bands that he's developed over the years and agree with Colin; the River Rats have a very good chance of going all the way with Will.

**I** park my car at the back of the lot at the Hopeless Heart even though it's early and there are lots of empty spaces closer to the building. My gun is back at the motel. This is just re-con.

My eyes sweep the outside of the building, taking in the security cameras attached to the two furthest corner eaves and pointed toward the parking lot. On my way here, I swung around the back of the building. There were no cameras there. Just one, steel door, with no outdoor handle. The kind that you see on mall stores, that have to be opened from the inside.

So, if I do this....*when* I do this...if it's at an off time, I'll need to approach and leave the building from the back. Which might be hard to accomplish with that one-way door.

Or, I could park in the back of the building, and enter through the front at just a regular time, maybe with a hat or something to distort my appearance for the cameras, then wait until the place was deserted, and once I was finished go out through the back.

Different thoughts and scenarios rush through me as I walk across the parking lot, keeping my head down, pretending I'm playing with my hair, but positioning it in front of my face for the cameras. I take a deep breath outside the doors. This is it. What the last twenty-two years have led me to.

How to describe the Hopeless Heart? It's your basic large, somewhat of a dive, bar. The décor's country, of course. The waitstaff are dressed casually in jeans and western shirts. There is a large, circular bar in the middle, back part of the bar, a stage and dance floor in front of the bar.

I'm disappointed to see absolutely no chicken wire anywhere near the stage.

I sweep the bar first, looking for Uncle Chazz, but there is only a young, female bartender and a few waitresses. I then scan the rest of the room, but see no one who remotely resembles the man from Nick's desktop picture.

But I do see someone I recognize from Nick's machine. I'd know Mr. Carpenter anywhere. Not just because I'd seen his pictures all over Nick's machine, but because his son is the spitting image of him. He's probably in his mid-fifties, very distinguished but still has that devastating beauty that oozes from Nick. He's wearing a sports coat, dress shirt and Dockers-style slacks and looks way over dressed for the Hopeless Heart.

Mrs. Carpenter is wearing a khaki skirt—the long kind that has buttons down the entire front—and a baby-blue sweater set. And pearls. Honestly. Mrs. Cleaver pearls.

Tricia is with them and when she sees me, she waves me over.

She introduces me to her parents as their new friend. I'm somehow touched that she sees me as a new friend and not just a friend of Colin's.

As my name rolls off her tongue I mentally tally the number

of people who know me by my real name. I take a deep breath, trying to calm the urge to walk out the door, get in my car and not look back.

But there's no turning back now. Besides, Colin has probably already Googled me now that he knows my name. Maybe he's been too busy to. Even if he had, he'd only find the obituary of a woman with the same name. The ages wouldn't match, because I lied about mine. And that Raven died in Nevada, nowhere near the Northeast I'd said I lived all my life.

Tricia pulls out a chair next to her own. "Here you go," she says.

"Oh, no. I don't want to intrude," I say. And it's true. Nick's parents have made a long drive to be here for their son. I don't want to get in the way of some family strategy meeting. I start to walk away—Mr. & Mrs. Carpenter seem quite alright with that—but Tricia balks.

"You're not intruding. Come on." She motions to the empty chair and sits back down in her own.

I smile apologetically at Mrs. Carpenter and sit down. Now that it's a done deal, Mrs. Carpenter's good southern manners come out and she asks me all about myself.

I give her the same story as I have to everyone else. It now rolls off my tongue.

"Colin's backstage," Tricia says as she catches me scanning the room. I'm not looking for Colin.

"And Nick?" I say, trying to throw off the scent.

"Nick too," Tricia says, but her smile says she's not buying it. "Colin's hot for Raven," she says to her parents.

"Oh, Tricia, really," her mother says.

She laughs. "Sorry. Colin is quite taken with Raven."

I wave her off, like she doesn't know what she was talking about.

"Is that so?" Mrs. Carpenter asks.

Something about her eyes—Nick's and Tricia's eyes—pins me. "I…I…I don't know. We've been communicating for a while, but we just met yesterday."

"I know. He's hot for her," Tricia says, teasingly.

"Nick and Colin have been friends a long time. We just think the world of him. We practically raised Colin, too. Sometimes I think those two are joined at the hip."

I know that of course, from Nick's machine and chatting with Colin. But I pretend I don't. "Really? They've been friends that long? That's really nice."

A smile that speaks of fond memories comes over Mrs. Carpenter's face then she seems to remember the mess her son is in and turns to look over her menu.

"Have you eaten yet?" Tricia asks.

I shake my head. "I've had my mind on a burger all day," I say. And it was kind of true, when my mind wasn't on the real reason I am here.

"That's good," Tricia says. "They don't have much on the menu here, but they do a great burger."

It *is* a great burger, juicy, sloppy. Just as we finish dinner and our waitress clears the table, Colin and Nick appear from a door that leads backstage. I crane my neck to see anybody else behind them. There is a shadow of somebody, but the door swings shut before I can make anything out.

"Hi, Raven. I see you've met my parents," Nick says. He's wearing a pure white tee-shirt, faded Levi's that fit him like he was born in them, and biker boots. Very James Dean. Very dangerous. I nod in his direction.

Colin steps around Nick and heads for me. "Hey there, beautiful," he says. He's wearing jeans, worn cowboy boots and a western shirt. Very country. He leans over and kisses my cheek. He rests his hands on my shoulders, standing behind me.

Nick's parents and Tricia look at each other with a "I guess that settles that" look. Tricia's look to her parents is gloating, "I told you so". I look at her closely, trying to see if this was too much for her, if it broke her heart. She's been very nice to me.

But there is nothing. I suppose she could have had a crush

on Colin for so long that it was second nature for her to be around him and his…careful now, I'd be including myself in whatever word I used next…female interests. I didn't like the label, but wasn't dumb enough for the word girlfriend to be popping into my head. Well, not popping, anyway, more like lurking.

I reach up and touch Colin's hand on my shoulder. I can't help it. I know it looks like a caress, but it's really just reassurance that this all is happening.

Michigan seems very far away right now. Maybe that's good.

Maybe it's deadly.

Colin entwines his fingers with mine. "We're on in ten. Any sign of Will?"

Both Tricia and I shake our heads. "When he comes, see if you can get him to sit with you guys," he says.

"Why?" Nick, Tricia and I ask in unison.

Colin shrugs—I can see because I've tilted my head back, causing it to push into his hard belly (do men have bellies if they're hard—or is it just beer bellies or abs?) "It'd be harder for him to leave if he's with people." That makes sense. "Besides, you guys can talk us up to him." Tricia's eyes light up—she'd be good at that, and she knows it—a born PR specialist.

"Are we going to have to, or will your music be able to talk you up?" I tease.

"That's right, you've never heard us play. Other than the CD last night. But not see us in person. You weren't even here last week."

No, not last week, but I've been listening to your music constantly. I could probably get up on that stage and play it myself.

He bends down so his cheek is next to mine. He has some stubble, the sexy kind—not the I'm too lazy to shave kind—and it grazes my cheek. "I'll see you after the show—to finish our third date," he whispers in my ear.

I duck my head, embarrassed. He grins, nuzzles my cheek with his nose, then straightens. "Enjoy the show," he says and walks away.

Nick is still looking at me funnily. He opens his mouth to say something, but shuts it. He turns his wrist, as if to look at the time, but his wrist is bare. He looks puzzled, then shakes it off. I start to tell him that his watch is at his office, that I'd seen it there yesterday when I was with Colin, but he speaks first. "I'll see you all after the show. We can talk more about Carrie then," he says to his parents.

They must have been talking about Carrie before I got here and then he'd had to go backstage. Darn. I should have gotten here earlier. Or spent less time casing the joint for an exit strategy.

No, that is more important. I'd like to be able to help in Carrie's murder, but I won't lose sight of why I'm really here.

And it's not to finish a third date with Colin, although I'd be happy to include that.

His father responds with a stern, "Yes. We will." His mother has a worried look that she tries to wipe off her face with a "Have a good, show, honey." Tricia adds, "It's all going to be okay. Just wipe it out of your mind for a couple of hours."

All I come up with is a lame, "Break a leg."

Nick smiles—a small, not quite real, smile—at us all and walks off. His shoulders a little low, his walk hesitant. He looks over his shoulder at the table once—at his family—and then disappears behind the door.

I look around me and the feelings I had when I first opened the picture folder titled "family" on Nick's machine assail me again.

Yearning. Pure, unadulterated yearning.

Mr. Carpenter reaches out and places his hand on his wife's and gives it a squeeze. Tricia gently rubs her mother's back. "It's going to be fine, Mom," she whispers. "Nick didn't do anything wrong."

Mrs. Carpenter—Rose she'd asked me to call her over our burgers—nods, but I can see the moisture gathering in her eyes.

I feel like an intruder and yet I can't tear my eyes away. The dealings of a family are so new to me, I'm mesmerized.

And furious. I'm furious at Nick for putting his family through this.

Growing up, Colin and I hungered for a family like his. How could Nick not think of them? Even if killing Carrie was an accident, doesn't he know it will kill his mother when he gets caught?

Will steps up to our table. I didn't even notice him come in I'm so entranced by the Carpenters. The family breaks away from each other and puts up a united front. Rallying for Nick. Tricia introduces Will to everyone. Mr. Carpenter—Bob—gets a chair for Will. Rose makes some small talk.

We all scoot our chairs around the table so we can see the stage. I notice a lot of other tables do the same. The River Rats have a good following. I sit on the end, with Will between Tricia and me. Bob and Rose are on the other side of Tricia. From my position I can see not only the stage, but am able to keep an eye on the door leading to the kitchen and the one that leads backstage.

Tricia gives me an encouraging look, and I realize she expects me to help out "talking us up" as Colin had put it.

"Have you seen the band before?" I ask Will, even though I know he was here last week. Colin had been so excited on line the morning after.

Tricia gives me an approving smile—I've gotten the ball rolling.

Will nods. "Yes, I was here last Wednesday, but I've been meaning to for a while now. I've heard good buzz about them. We've been talking about them at the record company for quite some time. But I'm the first one to get out here and listen to them.

"They didn't play on Saturday. Obviously."

Tricia's bobbing her head in a go ahead fashion. But something in what Will says catches my attention.

"Why do they still call them record companies? Nobody makes records anymore."

I catch an exasperated eye roll from Tricia over Will's broad shoulder.

Will gives me a funny look. "I guess I never thought about it."

Of course he didn't. I'm the only geek who thinks about stuff like that. And maybe Confessor.

The band comes onstage to great applause. I notice Nick looks over to the table and nods to his parents, then sees Will and smiles, nods again. Colin looks to our table and his eyes go immediately to Will. He doesn't smile, but his shoulders relax a tiny bit. His gaze turns to me, and his shoulders go back up. He smiles that slow, lopsided grin, and I can't help but smile back.

Billy and Russ amble to their positions, take up their instruments, never looking into the crowd.

Russ clicks his drumsticks together for a count, and the band strikes up. The songs are the same as I've been listening to, but it's so much different to watch them actually playing as opposed to staring at still pictures on Nick's machine.

The two of them—Nick and Colin—are so different onstage, and yet you can see what's kept them together all these years. They are a perfect compliment for each other.

Nick is all passion; you can feel every note he sings. But not in the affected, hands fluttering, strutting way of a rock star. More in an understated, real way. He never steps too far from center stage, letting the lyrics do the work. Half the time he has his eyes closed, letting the music penetrate him.

Colin is precision. His eyes dart constantly, but in an all-seeing way, not furtively. He watches Nick constantly, admiration and something else, playing across his wholesome face. When Nick comes to a particularly poignant part, Colin looks to me and I stare back at him. He breaks contact first, launching into an intensely brooding guitar solo.

Onstage, Nick is fire, Colin ice.

I look around at the Carpenters. Here to support their son, so sure of his innocence. They'll be devastated when the truth comes out.

Realizing this would be a good time to get a better lay of

the land, I rise, ostensibly to go to the bathroom. Will pushes his chair back and rises to let me pass. My purse strap slides down my shoulder, and Will reaches for it, puts it back in place, an electric shock startling us both.

"Sorry," he says.

I wave him off. "Don't worry about it. Sorry I shocked you."

He chuckles, his green eyes crinkling at the corners. "Believe me, in my line of business it takes a lot to shock me."

Visions of rock stars trashing hotel rooms, underage girls and heroin addicts dance in my head. "I can only imagine," I say.

His smile fades away. "No, you can't even imagine."

Something in his voice startles me, and I look closer at him, but his attention has already returned to the band.

I slowly make my way across the large room. I see a security camera above the bar and note that it is pointed downward, to catch the action at and around the bar itself. Probably in case of a hold-up, that's likely where it would take place. Or to make sure the bartender isn't giving away extra cherries?

Regardless, it's the only camera of any kind I see on the floor. Not that there couldn't be hidden ones, but I'd work on the assumption that there isn't.

So, if I came in through the front door, as long as I kept my distance from the bar area, and left through the back, I'd really only have to worry about being caught on camera as I approached the front door. And even then, if I came around the side of the building, and edged my way to the door while staying below the eaves, I might not be detected at all.

There is a short hallway between the door to the kitchen and the door to what looks to be an office that leads to the restrooms. I step into the hallway, turn and check out the line of sight. Two paces in and I can still see, and therefore can *be seen by*, the tables closest to the kitchen area. I take two steps backward. Now the only thing visible is the hallway itself. I look down and mentally take stock of where I become invisible to the rest of the room. I file it away.

The bathroom has three stalls and no windows. I'm assuming the men's room is laid out the same as they would share and outside wall.

When I come out of the bathroom, I edge around the back of the room, intending to come at our table from behind. As I pass the kitchen doors, which do not have windows, I stall, waiting for someone to come out. Finally a waitress does and I sneak a peek inside as the door swings shut.

Typical bar backroom. Some stainless steel, counters, people milling about. I don't see anyone who resembles Uncle Chazz.

Not wanting to be noticed, I keep moving along the periphery of the room until I am at the back, in one corner of the large room. Everyone in the room has their back to me, facing the stage. Even those who hadn't originally moved their chairs when the band took the stage have now moved.

I take in the band. Right then, Colin steps up to his mic and joins Nick in backup. They nail a heartbreaking harmony on the chorus of "Any Other Day".

The song still hits me. I suppose it's from listening to it hundreds of time. But, seeing them sing it in person, makes it all the more…personal…I guess.

I suppose that's why people pay astronomical prices to go to concerts and sit in the nose-bleed section rather than listen to their favorite band's CD and watch their videos. The connection.

Some movement makes me look at the corner directly to my right, the other corner in the back of the room. A figure is in the shadows. I move forward a tiny bit to be able to see better.

It's Jennilee, Nick's assistant. Her hands are in front of her, clasped together, like they'd been frozen mid-clap. She's wearing another prim outfit, this one a dress with a lace collar. Her hair is pulled back in one long braid that falls down her back.

She's watching the band—watching Nick?—with what can only be described as rapture. Her face is so expressive. Her eyes follow Nick's every movement. Her lips sing the words as he does. From this far away I can't tell if she's truly singing along, or simply mouthing the words, as if to help Nick out.

I start to walk toward her, to say hello. The song ends. Before the band can even introduce the next song, Jennilee's head is down and she's heading for the door.

I stay where I am. She obviously doesn't want anyone to see her. The door closes behind her as the band—Nick—says goodnight and thanks the crowd.

I don't even know it was their last song. But Jennilee does.

I turn to make my way to the table and stop dead in my tracks. Ten feet away from me, in the corner of the room I'd just come from stands Uncle Chazz.

Staring right at me.

# *Twenty*

**I** wait to see what he does, braced for anything, but he does nothing, just watches me and then turns and heads toward the office door, which the band is now going through. He pats Nick on the back, but I can't hear what he says to him.

In a daze, I make my way back to our table. Emotions are pouring over me. Relief that he's here, that I haven't ventured out of my safe haven for nothing. Determination.

And fear. There is always fear. From as far back as I can remember there has always been fear.

And it all began with Uncle Chazz standing over my father's body.

But I tell myself there's no way he could know me, recognize me. Unless my ex had…

"You missed the end," Tricia says to me, interrupting my thoughts.

"I was able to hear it," I answer. That mollifies Tricia and she turns to speak with her parents.

Will is watching me—was watching as I approached the table I now realize. "You okay?" he asks.

"Mmm-hmm," I answer and slip my shaking hands under the table. Breathe deep, Raven.

He looks closely at me, then turns his attention to the office door which has just opened.

Nick and Colin are quickly at the table, leaving poor Billy

and Russ to deal with the equipment. The crowd thins out some, last call is announced.

Colin and Nick greet Will who seems very positive, if cautious, in praising the band. "You have a really strong stage presence," he says to them both. "Great for small clubs like this. If it got to the point where you were playing arenas, we'd probably have to look at ratcheting it up a notch or two. Adding a keyboard player, some dancers, stuff like that."

"I play keyboards," Nick says.

Will shakes his head. "We'd never put you behind a keyboard. You need to be front and center. The audience loves you. They can feel every note you sing."

I look at Colin, expecting resentment, but he's nodding his head in agreement. He knows Nick's the lead.

"Bigger venue, bigger show, yeah of course," Colin says as if this makes perfect sense.

Billy yells something from the stage and Nick turns, waves to him. He turns back to us and says to Will, "Can you hang out for awhile to talk? We have to help Billy and Russ. And you'll want to meet them too."

Will looks at his watch and nods. "Sure. I've got time."

Nick says something to his parents that I don't hear, and they nod to him. He comes and stands next to Colin. "Let's go," he says.

For a minute I think Colin is going to stay, but he leans over to me, kisses my cheek and walks back to the stage. Nick follows him.

"So, you and Colin?" Will asks me.

I shrug. I'd been barely listening to them all, my mind on the man backstage. "Sort of. I guess," I say.

He chuckles, a warm, inviting sound. "That sounds like a guy talking. Very noncommittal."

My full attention turns to Will now. I give him a small smile. He's right. "It's all pretty new."

"Have you ever dated anyone in the music industry before?"

Will asks.

I shake my head. "No. Nothing even close," I say, thinking of my ex.

"They're a different breed," he says.

As opposed to hitmen, who are so normal.

"How so?"

"Well, the hours for one thing. The struggling. The egos. The road. The groupies." He stops and looks at my expression. "Should I go on?"

I shake my head. "No. It's okay. It won't get to the point where I need to deal with that anyway."

He looks puzzled. "You mean you and Colin won't get to the point that you'd have to deal with it, or the band won't ever get to that point?"

I mean Colin and me. I like him. A lot. But he's nothing in the grand scheme of things. Avenging my father is—has to be—my only true focus.

Besides, I can't afford to be Raven Moldano for any length of time without my ex finding me. Even if I am thought dead. *Especially* if I'm thought dead.

But I can't say any of that.

I also can't say that I don't think the band would ever get to the fame stage. Not to the man who could get them there.

"I mean…I guess I don't know what I mean. Just that I hadn't given it that much thought." Me, who over thinks everything.

Will narrows his eyes at me. "I find that hard to believe."

"Why?"

He shrugs. "I don't know you very well, but you seem like the type of person who puts some thought into everything."

I narrow my eyes at him. "What makes you think that?"

He puts his hand on my shoulder. It's warm, comforting. "No reason. You just don't seem like you'd jump into the unknown."

If only he knew how right he is.

Colin and Nick come back to the table then, with Billy and Russ in tow. Introductions are made for both Will and me.

My eyes are firmly on the door leading to the backstage area, but Uncle Chazz has not reappeared.

"I'm not prepared to talk specifics tonight," Will says after we were all settled at the table, chairs pulled up, drinks ordered and received. "But I'd like to hear what kind of career path you have in mind for The River Rats."

Nick and Colin do all the talking. It is a thing of beauty, the way they tag-team their vision of the future. Nick starts a sentence, Colin finishes, and then Nick would have an add-on. Billy and Russ nod all the while.

After about twenty minutes, and still no sign of Uncle Chazz, Will holds up a hand. "Okay, I think I have a good bead on where you're headed. I think Planet Records could make that happen." Smiles appear on every face at the table. "Like I said, I'm not prepared to offer anything concrete at this point. But I want to stay in close contact with you all."

Colin leans over and gives me big kiss. "We're on our way," he says. "Hang on for the ride of your life." The words scare me—the only wild ride I want is to finish this whole thing off and get home—but his grin is infectious.

I smile back. "Do I get to say 'I'm with the band'?" I joke.

"Damn straight."

"And get an all access pass?" I laugh.

"Hell yeah," he laughs along.

The mood is catching. Billy and Russ start punching each other on the arm—a guy thing, I guess. The Carpenters all beam at each other. All except Nick who is watching Colin and me.

Colin gives me another quick peck and leaves for the bathroom. Nick quickly slides over to the seat next to me.

"Listen," he says.

I hold up my hand. "I know. I know. This is where you sell me on Colin. He's your best friend. Great guy. Etc., etc. You don't need to, Nick. I know Colin's a great guy."

His brows furrow. "That's not what I was going to say."

"What then?" I ask, aware that Will can overhear us, though

he doesn't appear to be listening.

"You're right about Colin," he says. "He is a great guy. He hardly ever dates. It's all about the music for him. That's his entire focus."

After chatting so much with Colin, and then seeing him on the stage at the Opry, I'm not surprised. "Then what's your concern?"

He sighs. "I'm just letting you know that Colin doesn't bring women around. For you to be here—for him to want you here—that's a big deal. I've never seen him be so demonstrative before. I guess I'm just saying that Colin may seem easy going, but I think he's pretty serious about you. And it's happening really fast."

I look closely at Nick, trying to see any hidden messages in his eyes. Is he thinking that he just got rid of one impediment to the band—Carrie—and another one comes along? I could put his mind at ease, tell him Colin and I have no future, but I don't. "And that would be…good? Bad?" I hedge.

"I guess that would be up to you," he says. His blue eyes go almost gray as they narrow on mine. "I will say this. Colin is my best friend. And if anybody ever hurt him…"

I feel Colin behind us more than hear him. Nick senses him at the same time. He slides back to his own chair, much to my relief. He smiles up at Colin. "Just keeping your date warm, bro."

Colin takes his seat, taking my hand in his, placing them both on his knee, the denim of his jeans scratching my knuckles. "I can keep her warm just fine." There is a smile on his face, but no humor in his voice. "Let's dance," he says, standing again, tugging my hand.

I meet Will's eyes as I get up. I can't read his expression, but it stops me. Colin pulls on my arm. "Come on," he says gently.

The jukebox is playing as the bar winds down. It's a slow song, a cover of some country song I heard on the radio on the way down here. Colin pulls me into his arms, one hand taking mine, the other wrapping around my neck the way I'd seen people dancing on CMT. It's been years since I've danced. Since I've been held by a man.

We start to move lazily around the floor. He smells good. Clean and…safe.

We're only one of four couples on the dance floor. I feel exposed. When we turn so I'm facing our table, both Will and Nick are watching us. As we turn toward the other side of the room, Uncle Chazz steps out of the office door. His eyes go directly to our table, and then scan the room and land on Colin and me. As if he's looking for me.

I tense and Colin must feel it because he pulls back so he can see my face. "You, okay?"

I nod. I motion my head over toward Uncle Chazz. "Is that Johnny?"

"Yeah. You want to meet him? He's probably wondering who you are. I never bring girls to our gigs." He starts to break his hold on me, but I pull him closer. Maybe I am just being paranoid that Johnny seems to be watching me. Maybe he's just curious about Colin dancing so closely with a girl. Either way, being introduced as Raven Moldano is not going to help the situation. "Later, I just want you to hold me for now."

"That I can do," he says, pulls me closer and we dance in silence.

After a moment he asks, "What are you thinking, Raven?"

A plan races through my head. Get Colin out of here, now. Take him back to my room, be quick about it and…afterward… while he's asleep (I know I have some Ambien in my bag, that I use on those nights that I hear the lambs, which I could slip in Colin's drink), come back here and take care of Uncle Chazz. Surely he'll be here for a few more hours doing books, or dishes, or whatever he does here. It's still half an hour until closing time.

Then I'll go back to the motel, crawl into bed with Colin. Stay another day or two, so there's no red flag with my sudden disappearance when I said I'd be here the whole week for my seminar, and then head home.

If anything goes wrong, Colin will be my alibi.

Another alibi he'd be lying about. Only this time he wouldn't know it.

I give Colin my best come-hither smile and answer his question. "I'm thinking that I'm a third-date girl after all."

**He** smiles, takes my hand and walks me off the dance floor, well before the song ends. He's in a hurry too, but for a different reason.

As we approach the table, the doors open and several men enter. Two in uniform, a couple in sports coats and ties. Police. They scan the room. My breath holds as they pass over Colin and me. Their gazes keep going, and I release my breath. In unison they all land on the Carpenters' table. The men start walking to the table.

Shit. This is not going to play into my plan.

"Shit," Colin says as he speeds up.

We reach the table just as the police do. The Carpenter men have risen. As have Will, Billy and Russ. Mrs. Carpenter is still sitting, her husband's hand on her shoulder. Tricia sits next to her mother. I see her reach for her hand and my heart pangs for them both.

"Don't say anything," Mr. Carpenter is telling Nick. He reaches for a cell phone. "I'm going to call Bert." He starts pushing numbers. I don't know who Bert is, but I assume it's the lawyer Nick's dad found for him.

"Dad, I can handle this," Nick says. He turns to one of the policemen in the sports coat. "Hello, Detective Mosley, is there something I can help you with? Has there been a break in the case?"

"You might say that, Nick," Detective Mosley said.

Nick stares at the detective for a moment then shakes his head. "Are you going to tell me what that might be?"

"I see you're not wearing a watch, Nick. Do you normally?"

Everyone at the table—except for Mr. Carpenter who is still on the phone, his back partially turned away from us—turns their heads to Nick's wrist. His naked wrist.

His right hand skims his empty left wrist. He looks at the detective, wondering if this is a trap. *I'm* wondering if this is a trap.

"I…I…lost my watch," he says.

"Lost?" the detective says, doubt in his voice.

"Misplaced," Nick clarifies, though I don't really see the difference between lost and misplaced.

"Misplaced?" the detective mimics.

Nick nods.

"When did you misplace your watch, Nick?"

"I don't know. I'm pretty sure I had it this weekend."

I want to say that it's lying on his desk at the Bertram, Gleason and Young offices, but I don't. I'm not sure where this is going yet, and I don't want to get in the detective's way. And I certainly don't want to draw the detective's attention to myself. I look to my right, at Will. His eyes are glued to Nick, watching him with a close scrutiny. I turn to my left, to Colin. He's watching the detective.

"We'd like you to come back to the station and answer some more questions," the detective says. The other men, who'd said nothing at all, begin to move, to spread out, edge closer to Nick, as if he might make a break for it right here in the Hopeless Heart.

"He's not going anywhere without an attorney," Mr. Carpenter says before Nick can answer.

"His attorney can meet us there," the detective says.

Nick and Mr. Carpenter exchange looks. "It's okay, Dad. I didn't do anything." He makes a move to leave the group. To step outside its protection.

Mr. Carpenter glowers at the police officer. "Of course you didn't do anything wrong. That doesn't stop these people from twisting the truth to make their case."

I look at the police officers. They show no sign of emotion at Mr. Carpenter's words. "Have Bert meet us there, okay?" Nick says to his father. Mr. Carpenter lets out a sigh and drops his son's arm. He turns to the policemen. "What's this all about anyway?

Why are you dragging my son to the station at this time of night? He's told you everything he knows. What can't wait until the morning?"

"We have some new evidence in the case," the detective says. He's trying to hold back a sneer, and doing a poor job of it.

"What kind of evidence?"

"We found a towel that we believe is from The Range View. The words 'The Range' are clearly visible. There's blood on it that we're testing against Miss Essex's."

There is shock and then relief on Nick's face. "That's great. That's a real lead."

The detective nods again. Pauses. Then says, "It was tangled up with a man's watch. The engraving says 'It's our time now –'."

"Love, C," I say to myself as the detective says it out loud.

# *Twenty-One*

Nick and his father leave with the policemen, telling Tricia to follow along with Mrs. Carpenter. The moment the men leave the bar, Mrs. Carpenter bursts into tears and falls into Tricia's arms.

This is what I wanted. To see Nick led away. To see justice for Carrie. All without having to come forward with her emails to barabino. But now, faced with the pain the Carpenter family is feeling, I rethink my motives.

I step to Colin, to tell him about seeing Nick's watch yesterday in Nick's office, but he doesn't see my movement. He moves to Mrs. Carpenter and Tricia, puts his arm around them both, whispering something low into their ears. Mrs. Carpenter clings to his arm, looks at him with pleading eyes.

Like Colin can make it all go away.

Maybe he can if he tells the truth about Nick's alibi.

I feel like an intruder—I *am* an intruder—and I take a step back, away. I bump into Will's chest and he steadies me, his hands strong on my shoulders.

Billy and Russ look at each other, at the Carpenter women, at Will and I, then each other again. Clearly they are used to Nick or Colin calling the shots.

Colin resumes his role. "You guys go home," he says to Billy and Russ. "I'll call you in the morning." They nod and amble off together, their heads down.

Mrs. Carpenter breaks her embrace with Tricia. "Excuse me

for a moment," she says and heads to the bathroom. To pull it together or to totally lose it, I'm not sure.

Colin puts his arm around Tricia; gives it a squeeze. "It's going to be okay, Squirt. We both know Nick would never do anything wrong." He says it to Tricia, but his eyes are on Will, as if it's him he needs to convince.

Will clears his throat behind me, a low, rumbling sound. "Be that as it may, you guys have got to get this worked out. No matter what I say to the company, there's no way in hell they'd touch you with a ten-foot-pole with something like this hanging over your head."

"What about the old saying 'there's no such thing as bad publicity'?" Colin asks hopefully.

"Not when you're starting out. If you're established, maybe. But not even then could you have a dead girlfriend hanging over your head. The public forgives its celebrities for sex scandals and drug habits, not murder."

Tricia gasps. I'm so glad Mrs. Carpenter is only now returning from the bathroom and didn't hear that. "Sorry," Will says to Tricia. She waves away his explanation. Her look is far away, as if this is all just hitting home.

I know how she feels.

I'm convinced Nick killed Carrie, whether on purpose or by accident. But I know I saw his watch—the same watch the detective had just mentioned—on Nick's desk yesterday.

Is someone framing Nick?

"Why don't I drive you both to the station," Colin says to Tricia and Mrs. Carpenter.

Tricia shakes her head. "We should probably take Nick's car. He'll want it when this is all through." She looks at Colin. "He will be able to go home tonight, won't he?"

Colin doesn't say anything, just shrugs his shoulders and looks over to Will and I for help.

"If they had anything substantial, they would have made an arrest already," Will says. "They told him about the evidence like that in front of his friends and family, where he plays music, to try and shake him. Did you see how closely the detective was watching him? Now they want to question him while he's still rattled, see if he trips up," Will says. We all nod, as this seems to make sense to us. "Not really professional, though," he adds.

He sees we're all hanging on his every word, hoping he can make sense of it all. He throws up his hands. "That's all just a guess. He'll probably be able to leave tonight. But they'll make it a long night."

At that, Mrs. Carpenter seems to gather her strength. Her shoulders shoot back, her chin goes up. "Tricia, let's go." She looks at Colin. "You'll meet us there?" Colin nods. She then turns to Will and I. "Raven, it was nice to meet you. I hope to see you again."

"You will," Colin says before I can speak. I smile at Mrs. Carpenter, trying to convey my concern. She nods, then nods to Will, and then she and Tricia head out the door, arm in arm.

I feel a pang of emptiness for the mother I never knew.

**I** know what you're thinking by now…where's her mother in all of this? The truth is I don't know. The scary truth is…I don't want to know.

I said before I don't remember my father's face. But I do remember his voice when I asked him why I didn't have a mommy. "She's with the angels, watching over you." What scares me about knowing the truth about my mother is the tone my father used whenever he said this to me. There was no sadness, no wistfulness, no pain. It was a soft monotone, rehearsed, as if he had practiced different versions to tell his small child and this was the winner.

And maybe he had. I suppose any parent put in that position might practice what they'd say to their child. But there was never any wavering, any change in his inflection the many times I'd ask him this. Finally, I stopped asking, content with my vision of a dark haired angel with my face and beautiful wings, and my father's undying love.

My father was my only link to my mother and that link was broken when I was five years old.

I know that I could find out about my mother now. With the internet it wouldn't be hard. I'm not a hacker or anything, I couldn't do searches of hospital records or government agencies, but I could probably find out something about her.

Her name, for one thing. Whether she and my father were married. If she's still alive.

But it was the other things that I wanted to know. Things you couldn't find out on the internet, no matter how computer savvy you are.

Whether she'd wanted me.

If she knew how much I'd needed her all those years.

In the end, my trust in my father is what kept me - keeps me - from looking for information about my mother. There was a reason my father was attempting to raise me alone. It couldn't have been easy for him, a man alone, raising a small girl. But he did it, or tried to, and he didn't want me to know anything more than my mother was in heaven.

Sure, he didn't know he'd be killed so young. And maybe he had every intention of telling me about my mother when I was older, when I could handle whatever the truth turned out to be.

There were no things of my mother's in the belongings that I'd found when I was eighteen. This fact confirmed my convictions about my father's intentions. For some reason, he didn't want me knowing about my mother.

I tell myself it's the trust I have in my father that keeps me from looking. That's true, but the other part is fear of the unknown.

I have learned that knowledge can be the death of things. The end of good situations.

Who was it that said ignorance is bliss? He had the right idea.

**I** wonder if I would be going to the police station with Colin. If he'd want me to go? If I'd just be in the way?

He turns to me. "I'll walk you to your car on my way out." Guess that decides that. I'm relieved. And disappointed. I don't want to intrude on the Carpenters, but what if it all comes out tonight? What if barabino had come forward, was the one that found the towel and the watch?

Not to mention my own plans for later this evening. Where does that stand now?

We say our goodbyes to Will and head to the parking lot. At my car, Colin pulls me into his arms and hugs me tight. I'm not sure if he's looking for comfort, or to give it. Regardless, I relax into his body. This has just gotten a little scarier and it feels safe in his arms.

"This isn't how I expected this night to end," he whispers in my ear.

I pull back and look at him. His smile is small now, strained. "Me neither," I say.

He leans in to kiss me, but then pulls back. "I'd better not start something I can't finish."

I nod, my head drops to his chest. He takes a step back. "Tomorrow?" he asks.

I nod yes. "Tomorrow," I say.

I get in my car and he walks away. He is gone before I realize that he doesn't have my cell number, or any idea where I'm staying. I hadn't offered it.

I go to my car, wondering if I can still pull off my Uncle Chazz plans tonight without Colin as an alibi? There's still quite a few cars in the lot, so I decide to leave and go back to the motel and think it out. Besides, my gun is back in my room. As I pull out of the lot, Will is walking to his car. I pull along-side and roll down my window a little.

"Goodnight, Will."

He motions for me to stop, which I do. I put the car in park and roll the window the rest of the way down.

"Raven, I know you said this was all new to you, this whole

music scene…"

I nod. "It is."

He puts his hand on the roof of my car, leans over to my level. "This is not a normal part of it. Whatever's going on with Nick's girlfriend. This is some crazy shit."

I sigh. "I know. What do you think will happen?"

He straightens, but leaves his arm on the roof. He glances around the parking lot. Searching for something or just searching for words? He bends over again, his green eyes soft and concerned. "I don't know what to think. I've seen perfectly nice people who did some really nasty things in my life. You can't always know what a person is really like."

I think of my wedding day, when I'd been so certain that I was going to be with this man for the rest of my life. "I know that," I say.

"It might be time to cut and run," he says.

I look at him but don't say anything.

"You're young, not from around here. This might not be the group you want to…" He doesn't finish. What is the appropriate verbiage for what I'm doing with this group of people? I don't know any more than Will does. He drops his hand from the car and steps back. "Just a thought," he says.

"Thanks for the concern," I say.

He nods and turns away. I put the car in drive and head back to the motel.

**W**hen I get back to the motel I take a very long shower. I wash my hair twice, trying to get the smoke from the bar out of it.

I throw on a bra, tee-shirt and panties. I'm not sure I'm definitely in for the evening, but I don't bother putting street clothes back on yet. I pull my gun out of its hiding place. Check that it's loaded. Hold it for a very long time.

Finally, I set it aside and, perched on the edge of the bed, I grab my laptop.

"You out there?" I ask.

His bubbles are immediately rising. "Finally," he types.

"Finally?"

"I've been waiting for hours."

"You have? For what?" It seems so odd that Confessor would actually be waiting for me to come online. What a role reversal.

"For an update. To make sure you're okay. To find out how the saga of Nick and Colin is playing out."

"That would make a good Country song, 'the saga of Nick and Colin'," I type.

"A gay country song."

"Maybe Nic—for Nicole."

"Yeah, the Dixie Dicks could do it."

"I told you—they're the River Rats!" It wasn't the first time he'd called Colin's band the Dixie Dicks. Normally I got a chuckle out of it. Not so much tonight.

I brought him up to speed.

"Blackbird, maybe it's time to fly home."

I'd been thinking the same thought myself. I want out of this Carrie mess. But I can't leave without doing what I came here to do. My fingers caress the keyboard. I'd missed it the last few days, and yet my fingers were touching such new and different textures. Colin's skin. Nick's hand. Tricia's arm. A cold beer bottle. The rough wood of the tables at the Hopeless Heart. Colin's hair. Will's hands on my shoulders.

The trigger on my gun.

"I have to stay. I have to see where it ends," I say, knowing Confessor will think I mean Colin and the crew.

"Where what ends? Nick and Carrie or you and Colin?"

Neither, but I don't answer, and that's answer enough for him.

"Do you really think there's any future with Colin?"

No. There never was.

"I know how Colin and I will play out," I say. And I do. It breaks my heart, but I do.

"How?"

"We'll spend a few more days together and when this whole thing with Nick and Carrie is solved, I'll leave and go back home, resume my old life. I'll tell him I'm heading back to Vermont and that I'll talk to him soon. He'll never hear from me again."

"And you'll be able to leave him?"

"I'll have to, I can't risk staying around. Not only would my safety be in danger, but so would all those around me."

"Ah…my poor Blackbird."

I think about Colin. How much he's come to mean to me in such a short time. I don't feel sorry for myself often, but I do now. I wallow in it, wrap my arms around myself.

And yet, I will gladly give that up—give him up—to complete what I set out to do.

There is nothing for a moment, and then Confessor types, "And Nick and Carrie, how will that play out, any ideas?"

"None," I say, glad he's pulled me out of my Colin-induced pity party. "At first I thought it was done in cold blood. That Carrie'd pushed him too far and he pushed back - literally."

"And now?"

I think about the bloody towel and Nick's watch that the police found. "Now, I don't know."

"These might not be people you want to be around," he says.

"Will said something similar tonight."

"Which one's Will? The drummer?"

"No, that's Russ, Will's the record company guy."

"Right. Sorry, can't tell the players without a program."

Thinking of Will makes me ask Confessor, "Why do they still call it a record company? They don't make records anymore." I didn't really expect more of an answer than I got from Will, but I was trying to get Confessor off the topic of my leaving. Or not leaving.

"Because 'I'm being scouted by a CD company' doesn't sound nearly as cool."

I laugh. I'll have to remember to tell Will that, so he'd have a pat answer if anybody else asks. If I ever see Will again. He may have run as far away from the River Rats as possible.

I'm trying to think of a response when he types, "I have to go. Bye, bye, Blackbird."

Of course, he is gone before I can respond.

**A**t two-thirty I am still awake and restless. Even though I don't like the thought of walking through my motel's parking lot to the one where my car is parked, I do just that. An aimless drive, I think to myself, but already the car is heading toward the Hopeless Heart, and I'm pulling out Uncle Chazz's Mapquest directions.

There are three cars in the front parking lot. I park across the street and wait. In a few moments three waitresses come out, Uncle Chazz holding the door for them, waiting as they walk to their cars. I'm in my car across the street, in an all night drugstore lot, surrounded by other cars, but I still hunch down a little. He waits until all three drive away before he turns and goes through the door, I assume locking it behind him.

Such a model of concern. I mentally snort.

Where was his concern for me when he left me without a father?

A few more minutes later two cars come from around the back of the building to the main road. They stop at the intersection and I can clearly see they are younger kids. The two cars turn in different directions.

Shortly behind them is a large, red, Ford pickup truck. When it stops at the intersection, the light shines down on Uncle Chazz. He turns right. I take a look at the Mapquest directions. Yep, right, then a left in about a half mile.

I follow him, at a discreet distance, until he makes his left hand turn. I turn right and then I take another right at the next cross street and pull into a convenience store's parking lot. I check the clock on the dash and force myself to wait a half hour before I start the car and drive to Chazz's address, using the Mapquest directions.

Ten minutes later I get to a residential area and a thought

hits me. What if when I get to his address it screams family man? A lawn strewn with bikes, bats and balls.

Am I prepared to take a father away from children like he did to me?

I swallow that thought as I come to the end of my directions and turn into an apartment complex parking lot. It's been a half hour since Chazz would have pulled in, so I feel it's safe to drive through the lot. There's only one red Ford pickup. The carport spots are numbered and I write down Uncle Chazz's number and wonder if it corresponds to his apartment number.

Driving through the complex I take note of the fact that there isn't one mini-van in the lot, and no toys on the balconies of the various apartments. The majority of the cars are on the mid to high price range, and somewhat sporty. A complex for single professionals?

As I make a circle around the lot and start to head for the street I notice the security cameras at the door of each building. I look up. Yep, at the top of each building, too. And in the eaves of every other carport cluster.

I pull out onto the street and head back to the motel. Shit, tight security. I'd feel very safe living there. But maybe not the best place to…confront Uncle Chazz.

Finally in my bed, my mind races with what I know of the comings and goings of Uncle Chazz. Trying to piece it all together. If I did it at the Hopeless Heart, police might think it was a break-in gone bad. Where as if it was at his apartment, to go through all that security, and only target one apartment? That would be seen as more personal.

It couldn't be any more personal, but no need to point that out to the police.

# Twenty-Two

**I** wake up starving. I grab my tote bag with most of my information in it and drive to the IHOP.

I take the table at the back—Colin's and mine—and the blessed waitress from yesterday is right there with the coffee pot.

"Nice to see ya, again, honey. That cute boyfriend of yours joining you?"

I open my mouth to correct her, but just shake my head. Maybe he is my boyfriend. As much as I could have one. "He has to work," I say. I don't know that to be true. He could still be at the police station for all I know.

She rubs her back. "Yeah, most of us do. I'll be back in a sec to take your order."

I'd bought a paper on the way in and I scanned it for any news on a possible arrest of Nick. Nothing. But then, the paper would have already gone to press when all hell broke loose last night.

I put down the paper and pick up my menu to figure out my order. As I lift it up, my eyes are drawn to the door where Will is walking in.

He greets the hostess and she leads him to a table. As she's about to sit him at a booth a few down from me, I sit up straighter and wave a little to get his attention. He stops mid-stride, his surprise evident.

"Hi, Raven. What are you doing here?" he asks. I raise my

coffee cup in answer. He smiles. "Of course. I guess you just surprised me that's all."

"Are you meeting clients here?" I ask.

He chuckles. "No, I don't do business over breakfast. I take it too seriously."

I laugh. "Me too, I was just about to order. You want to join me and see if you can outdo me?"

He mock pushes up his sleeves. "Oh, this sounds like a challenge."

I bring my utensils up, poised over a non-existent plate. "Let the best man win."

He thanks the waitress, and slides into the seat across from me, tossing his leather jacket onto the seat beside him.

Don't you just love booths? They're so much better than tables. I know it isn't practical, but I think all restaurants should have nothing but booths. The thick, padded kind like at IHOP. The kind that when they rip they just put a strip of duct tape across it.

The waitress comes to take our order and fill Will's cup. He orders. Then I do. I order a huge breakfast—the recon work effect—and then dessert.

The waitress is nonplused and leaves, but Will's eyes grow huge. "I think I just got conned. What are you, some kind of breakfast ringer? Travel from town to town hustling breakfast pros?"

I almost snort my coffee out my nose. "Thanks. I needed that laugh."

"At your service. Things are pretty weird right now, hey?"

I'm in a town I have no business being in, using a name that could get me killed. In the name of helping, I'd gotten mixed up with people that may have done some very bad things or to whom I could bring a killer down on. And, oh yeah, I was planning on killing someone. "Yeah, pretty weird," I respond.

He leans back and stretches. His black tee-shirt goes taut against his well-formed chest. He sits back and takes a gulp of coffee, watching me. He puts down the cup and leans forward, his arms on the table.

He'd worn long sleeves the two times I'd been with him before, when he'd been on duty, so to speak. This is the first time I've seen his arms. I suppose it's because of my father, but I find myself fascinated by men's forearms. Will's are muscled, the tendons and veins forming a sinewy combination. The skin is tanned and the hair is light, a sandy blonde, lighter than the hair on his head. Lighter than Colin's. Much lighter than Nick's. Maybe he spent a lot of time outdoors but with a hat on.

"Just as long as you know what you're doing, Raven," he says.

I lean forward too, my hands nearly touching his. "Does anybody really know what they're doing in stuff like this?" I ask. And I mean it. I'm not trying to be a smart ass. Does anybody really know?

His hand inches forward, to mine. He opens his mouth to respond, but we're both startled apart by Nick's appearance at the side of the table. "Hey you two. This is weird. I didn't know you guys were…" There is a question in his voice.

"We're not. We met here by accident," Will says. "Both big breakfast people."

Nick looks from Will to me then back again. I guess with all he's going through I wouldn't take any explanation at face value either. I nod my head in agreement. I scoot over on my bench and Nick sits next to me.

The waitress comes with our food and a place setting for Nick. He waves it away and places a large order to go. "I'm headed to my parents' hotel. I thought I'd bring breakfast," he explains.

"So, Nick," Will says. "Are you able to talk about what happened last night? Just how much trouble are you in?"

I see Nick thinking about how much he should tell Will. Will must have seen Nick's apprehension too because he quickly adds, "I'm not asking as your possible rep, just concerned, that's all."

Nick relaxes, his shoulder brushes mine as they sag. "The police found that towel and my watch in a Dumpster a block from Colin's apartment."

"So they are doing a full-scale investigation, canvassing the area around your place, and where you were that night?"

Nick shakes his head. "That's just it. They aren't. Well, they weren't anyway. They are now."

"So somebody found the towel and watch and turned it in?" I ask.

"No. They got a tip. Another god-damn anonymous tip. From another bogus email account. It told them where to find the towel."

"That doesn't make any sense. That looks like a total frame job," I say. I look to Will and he just shrugs.

"The police do think that; that someone is out to get me. The emails and the fact that I have an alibi point to that. Or that I did it, raced back to Colin's place to have an alibi and dumped the stuff near his apartment."

"They'd be testing time frames for that scenario, like I said the other night," Will says. I nod, urging Nick to go on.

"Their latest theory is that I…I…did it, but that I wasn't alone. That I had help."

"And now that help is turning on you," Will finishes. "You need to think about who the hell could get your watch."

"I've been thinking about that nonstop since the police station."

"And?"

"I don't know. I leave it off sometimes; at work, when I'm playing guitar. Lots of people could have had access to it." Nick rubs his hand across his face, and only drops his head, shaking it.

"Have you gone to your office since Colin and I were there Tuesday afternoon?" I ask.

He looks at me, his eyes narrowing. "No, why?"

"Because your watch was on your desk that afternoon. I saw it when I was there with Colin to pick up your papers. I noticed it when I knocked over your picture of Carrie." Nick winces and I feel like I'd physically hurt Carrie. But that's impossible.

"So, who had access to your office since Tuesday?"

Nick shrugs. "Lots of people. People at work. We all share files all the time. Jennilee said some friends stopped by looking for me, seeing if there was anything they could do. Colin. Jennilee." He looks at me. "Raven." He looks back at Will "You said you had stopped by."

"It's great your friends want to support you. But one of those friends could be the person who got you into this mess," Will says.

Nick lets out a sound. Something between a chuckle and a snort. "In that case, you two would be my prime suspects. You've both only been in my life a short time, right when all the trouble started."

I keep my mouth shut.

"Good point," Will says. "But the truth is, you need to look at everyone around you, from work, the band, the bar, everywhere you have connections. Everyone, Nick."

Is he trying to say something?

"Are you trying to say something, Will?"

Will sits back, placing his arms along the back of the booth. "If I knew something, Nick, I'd tell you."

That seems to satisfy Nick. He looks at his wrist. The remembrance of where his watch was puts an agony across his face that is unbearable to watch. But is it a look of guilt or of grief? The waitress brings Nick's food to him bagged and ready.

"I really have to go," he says. He turns to Will and says, "I'll think about what you said."

"That's all I'm asking," Will says. They shake hands.

He starts to leave and then turns back to us. "Believe me, much as I hate the idea of someone close to me doing this to me—framing me—I'm hoping like hell it's true."

I give him a puzzled look.

He sighs. "Because the alternative—that Carrie was with another man… that someone she was cheating on me with did this to her," His voice cracks as he continues. "It's not something I can even think about."

He seems so genuine, his pain so real. He walks out of the restaurant. I watch him.

Will watches me. "Do you believe him?"

I look at Will. I should show my faith in Colin by saying yes. "Colin says Nick was with him the night Carrie was killed," I hedge.

"You're hedging. Do you believe Nick?"

Two days ago I would have said no.

"I'm not sure," I say.

**W**ill finishes his plate and then I finish mine. He tips a non-existent brim of his hat to me, I do the same to him. We have another cup of coffee, and fight over the tab, which Will picks up. Just as we're readying to leave, Will takes a business card from his wallet. He pulls a pen from his back pocket. He writes something down on the back of the card and then hands it to me.

"This is my cell number. I never give it out, but I always have my phone with me."

I nod, not really understanding.

He touches my arm. "Please use this if something—anything—happens." His hand leaves mine and brushes through his wavy hair. "Neither of us knows what's going on here. Both of us would like to help. Nick said it right; we've known him for the shortest amount of time. We might be able to see things that people close to the situation can't. It would make sense if we hooked up."

I raise my eyebrow.

"To team up. To find out what the hell is going on."

It makes a weird kind of sense. I nod. He gets up and stands at the edge of the table.

"One more thing," he says. "Don't tell Colin any of this." He turns and walks away before I can ask why.

# Twenty-Three

It's not an auditorium, or an arena. Turns out the National Backgammon Championships are being held in a Nashville high school gymnasium.

The gym smell assaults me as I walk in. It's a scent they could put under your nose at the age of ninety-four and you'd know in an instant—high school gymnasium.

There are about two hundred contestants. And yes, it's a total geek-fest. Well, I shouldn't say totally. There are some normal looking people. I count myself amongst that group. But for the most part, it's exactly what you would imagine.

I pay my fee, get my pairings sheet and a name tag. I said earlier that the thought of a crowd doesn't bother me—that being alone with one person seems scarier to me than being in a large room with two hundred. Safety in numbers.

But I hadn't counted on the name tag. If you hadn't had to show identification to register I would have just written Jane on it, but they already had one made up for me. Raven, large and bold in a forty-eight point font.

I step up on the bleachers so that I can see the whole floor. I scan the crowd. I don't know what I'm looking for. Or who.

Yes I do. My ex.

I let out my breath, silently chiding myself for being beyond cautious—for entering into paranoia.

Like my ex is going to read about a backgammon event (a

game I tried to teach him several times to no avail) and come from California on the off chance that I might come out of four years of hiding to play a couple of games. Besides, he thought I was dead.

I start to step off the bleachers, then stop myself. I take one more look around.

You never know.

I wonder if I will know eatmeee! if I see him? I look around for someone who stood out. Gold chains? Slicked back hair? What did online obnoxious showboat translate to in real life?

The first match is just one game, to get the number down to a bracket-friendly amount. After that, each match is a best of five games total. So, some matches could take a half hour, others hours. It could be a long afternoon. The first three rounds would be played today. Another three, tomorrow afternoon, and then the championship game, expected around five tomorrow night.

If you win, you move on, if you lose, you go home. It's probably why people aren't swarming here from all over the continent. It's a long way to go to be done in an hour.

I won't bore you with the play-by-play. The first match was an easy win against an eight-year-old whose mother acted like he was a child prodigy. He wasn't anywhere close.

The second match took longer, but I still won in four games.

The third match went all five games, but the first two games were quick ones.

Anyway, a little while later I'm heading out the door, ready to come back tomorrow, relieved that I can put off Uncle Chazz for one more day. As I turn the corner into the hallway, I see a flash of long braid taking the corner ahead of me. "Jennilee," I call out, and run down the hall. I get to the corner, but she's gone. I scan down the pairings sheet in my hand, and sure enough she's on it.

Huh, Jennilee is a backgammon player. I'm not sure if that makes me feel like more of a geek or just not quite so alone. If she was here this long, then she probably won, so chances are I'll see her tomorrow. She's on the other side of the pairings, so I'd only play her if we both make it to the final game. I don't think there's much chance of that, but maybe I can find her before the games start and talk to her. Ask her about Nick's watch.

**O**n the way back to the motel I swing past the Hopeless Heart. There are no cars in the lot. I drive around back and park in the back lot for the party store that is kitty-korner from the Hopeless Heart. It's mid-afternoon, and they don't open until five. Probably not a lot of prep works need to be done for the limited menu that they have.

Still, it seems like somebody…just as that thought starts through my head Uncle Chazz pulls up in his red, Ford pick-up. I check my watch for the exact time. Three o'clock on the dot. He takes his keys and opens the back, metal door. I notice again that the exit door is just that, an exit. No handle, only the deadbolt lock and a small knob to pull the door open with just under the lock hole. You have to either have a key or have somebody let you in to enter from the outside.

So, Johnny opens the place up by himself. Is it at three every day? What time do others come in? I sit in my car, making a mental note of everything. I notice the party store does not have a security camera in the back of the store which points to this lot. I see that there is very little traffic behind the buildings on this access road.

At three fifteen, he comes out of the back with garbage bags in his hand. He props open the metal door with a plastic milk crate that sits next to the building, ostensibly for that reason—to be a door stop. He walks to the Dumpsters that the Hopeless Heart must share with the business next door. It is in the direction away from my car, but I have a clear line of sight the whole time.

It occurs to me that this is how I could do it. Be in my car, wait for him to come out, shoot, and be gone.

But I know I won't. For one thing, I don't trust myself with that kind of shot. I'll need to be closer. But more importantly, I want him to see it coming. To know *why* it's coming.

To say my father's name as I pull the trigger.

After dumping the garbage. Uncle Chazz goes back in and the door slams tight. I sit for another thirty-five minutes. If I had my gun with me, I could go to the door, knock and deal with this right now.

But, I hadn't expected on needing the gun when I set off for the backgammon tournament, and so I sit empty-handed. Stupid. I should be more prepared.

I have a vision of Mandy Patikin in *Princess Bride*, searching for the six-fingered man so he could someday say, "Hello, my name is Inigo Montoya. You are the man who killed my father. Prepare to die."

Inigo, now he was prepared. Me, I'm stuck here watching my prey empty-handed.

The absurdity of how close my life is to a children's movie nearly brings me to tears.

At twenty to four he steps out of the building again, propping the door open with the milk crate. He lights up a cigarette, takes a deep toke and exhales slowly, toward the sky. I watch as he slowly smokes his cigarette, staring up at the sky the entire time.

I wonder what's going through his head. Is it thoughts of tonight's business, of the band that's going to play? Is there enough Pabst Blue Ribbon in the storeroom? Is he thinking mundane thoughts that we all do…like do I have enough clean underwear to put off laundry for a couple more days?

Or is he thinking of his past, of the men he's killed (I assume there was more than just my father, but I could be wrong)? The families he's destroyed?

The children who grew up without their father?

He stubs out his butt, looks at his watch and turns toward the door to go back in. As he does he looks in my direction. The sun is in his eyes, so I know he can't see me, or at least can't make me out, but I sit perfectly still and wait until he goes through the door before I breathe again.

This time, though, he puts the blue milk crate back in place, keeping the door open behind him. I look at my watch…about ten minutes to four. It's another five minutes before the first car pulls into the parking lot. A young kid, maybe still in high school, driving a total beater. He's wearing jeans and a tee-shirt. Kitchen help, probably, or he'd be better dressed. He steps over the milk crate. A couple of minutes later another car pulls in and parks. Two kids, a little older, maybe college age, and car poolers apparently, get out this time and go into the building, again leaving the crate in place.

At ten after a third car pulls into the lot and a girl gets out. She, like the others, is dressed in jeans and tee-shirt, not the western-style shirts the waitresses and bartenders were wearing last night.

So, the kitchen help comes on at four, at least on Thursdays. And Johnny leaves the door open for them. It's about a ten-minute window assuming no one shows up extra early for work. But these are kids with part time jobs, maybe after class or school or something, I can probably count on them showing up right when they have to.

A half hour later the wait staff starts showing up. A couple park in back, but when I start to leave, I see that there's a few cars now in the front lot, toward the back of the lot, parked under the light posts. Probably the people who'll be closing up.

One waitress is hurriedly rushing to the front door and enters, it is unlocked. I check my watch again.

Yeah, there's a ton of variables here. Is this a regular day? Are weekends different? Can I count on workers showing up when they're supposed to and not earlier?

But I feel better as I drive to the motel. More in control than I have during all of this.

Tomorrow, I'll bring the gun with me and leave it in the car during the backgammon tourney. I'll have packed my bags, but not checked out. I've paid through Sunday, and I might want the motel to think I've been there all weekend. Maybe I'll put the Do Not Disturb sign out. And when I get beat out at backgammon,

I'll swing by here and wait for Uncle Chazz.

Then back home to my nest.

**"H**ow was the conf 2day?" Colin asks me when I boot up later that evening and find him online.

"Good. What did U do all day?"

"Had a PT session gig."

"How'd it go?"

"OK…but can't wait till I don't have to do it anymore."

"When?"

"When Will signs us."

Oh, right. "Heard anymore on that?"

"Nope. He said he'd be in touch."

I don't tell him that I had breakfast with Will. Either Nick didn't tell Colin he saw us, or he did but Colin doesn't want to bring it up.

"What are U up 2 tonite?" he asks.

"Nothing, just hanging out. U?"

"I have to meet with Nick, his parents and the lawyer."

"Oh."

"Yeah. I'm sorry, I'd luv to be hanging with U instead."

"Me too."

"Really?"

"Yes," I type and mean it. There was no future here with Colin. I'd be leaving tomorrow evening if all went well. What would one night with a sweet guy who really likes me hurt?

Besides, I'd come to really care about Colin. I know it can't lead anywhere, but it doesn't mean I don't want it to.

"I thought that maybe you'd changed your mind about us. Or were sorry we met."

"No. Y would U think that?"

There is nothing for a moment, and then he types. "On Tuesday, I gave you my cell number so you could reach me, but you didn't give me yours. I don't even know where you're staying. The only way I have to reach you is online."

Which is exactly how I want it. I have nothing to say to his comment, and as I try to come up with something, he writes, "You ARE involved with someone, aren't U? Married?"

"No. I was honest about that," I hit "reply" before I realize how it sounds.

"About THAT?"

"LOL, about everything. Not married. Not involved. Just cautious."

"Yeah. Very cautious."

"Colin…it's all I can give right now."

There is a long pause before I see him start to type. "I know. And I'll take what I can get from you. I think we could build something. I have a flexible schedule, I can do a few days in Vermont here and there. Just tell me you're not throwing in the towel. Or, if you are, tell me for sure right now."

If all goes well, I'll never see Colin again. But if it doesn't, if I need to stay longer… "I'm not throwing in the towel."

"Phew"

"LOL"

"And you'll be here through the weekend? So we'll have lots of time once your conference is over?"

"I have the room through Sunday."

"But you could stay longer, right, you work for yourself."

"I could stay longer…" If it takes that long.

"Gotta go. Nick is texting me. I'm supposed to be over there by now."

"Then you better get going."

"Yeah. I'll look for you online when we're done. Maybe it will still be early."

"Okay. Bye."

"Bye."

I shut down—Confessor still hadn't shown up—and go out for some dinner which I bring back to my room. I think about keeping the computer up in case Colin or Confessor show up, but I lay down on the bed instead and quickly go to sleep.

I dream of large black and white backgammon tiles that are spilled all over the floor so that I can't get any traction as I try to run to Colin. I'm being chased, but I don't know by whom. I have a vague feeling that it's Uncle Chazz, but then I see my ex's beautiful face. I reach out for Colin, finally safe, but grab onto the sleeves of Will's leather jacket.

That's all I remember when I wake up, covered in sweat.

This is it. This is the day. It will all be over. I will avenge my father.

I can't get back to sleep after my dream, so I lay in bed, playing over what I saw at the Hopeless Heart, putting me and five minutes alone with Uncle Chazz into the scene. Finally, having visualized it several times, I fling the covers off and start the day.

I run over to the McDonald's for my coffees and breakfast. I take them back to the room and boot up my laptop. The first thing I do is call up my ichat and log-in as Blackbird. Confessor's icon is unlit. I need some distraction to get me through the morning.

It seems so odd to be doing regular things like McDonad's breakfast on this day, when all I can think of is what I'll be doing later, but I think the normalcy is good for me.

I check my various email accounts. There's an email from eatmeee! addressed to my dblsix account letting me know that he'd made it through the first day of the tournament and was still in it. He said that no opponent he'd faced so far was as much a challenge as I was. That makes me feel good.

So, at least I know he wasn't one of the people I played yesterday. Somehow I know he wasn't the eight year old non-prodigy. That's about all I can be sure of.

Well, maybe not even that.

"You out there?"

I quickly minimize all the other windows and answer Confessor. "I'm here."

"Didn't know if you'd be up this early," he says.

"I'm up."

A pause, then he asks, "Are you alone?" Did he think I was sleeping with Colin? And would that be so bad for him to think that?

"Yes, I'm alone"

"And you're still up this early?"

"I'm almost becoming a morning person." I take a gulp from the third coffee. Almost.

"Really?"

"No, not really, this eight a.m. crap sucks."

"That kind of attitude's not going to move you up in the accounting world."

"Very funny,"

"Take another gulp of coffee."

I take another gulp of coffee.

"Now, Confess."

I tell him about meeting Nick and Will for breakfast. Will's offer of help. The backgammon tournament. Chatting with Colin last night. That's all. I obviously don't tell him about my stake out at the Hopeless Heart.

"So, think you have a chance to win today?"

There will be a victory of sorts, but not the kind he means. "I guess I never really thought about it. I honestly thought I'd chicken out and end up not going."

"Wrong species."

"Huh?"

"You're a Blackbird, not a chicken."

Corny, sure, but it makes me smile.

We talk about Nick's predicament a while longer, neither of us having any ideas about how I could move the case along without turning over all I had from his machine.

"I think this Will guy had the right idea, though," he says.

"What do you mean?"

"He said that you shouldn't try to do anything on your own, right?"

"I guess. He gave me his card, said he thought we should

work together if we came up with anything."

"Can you trust him?"

"I think so. As much as anyone else in this whole mess."

"Then take him up on his offer. Or somebody else. Just don't do anything alone."

"Okay."

He pauses. "Promise me," he finally says.

"I promise."

"Bye, bye, Blackbird." He is gone before I can respond.

**Y**ou would think that the crowd in the gymnasium would be a quarter of the size it was yesterday, that's how many contestants had been eliminated. But no, people came back to watch. To watch!

I don't see Jennilee until we're all seated and the first game begins. She looks nervous, her hands twist within each other in between moves. I try to catch her eye, but she's pretty far across the room and doesn't see me. I'm not even sure she'd remember me if she did.

I try to shake the thought that my car is out in the parking lot, all my stuff in the trunk, and a gun in the glove box. I immerse myself in the game.

My first match takes a while, but I pull it out. The second one is much the same. One more victory and I'm in the championship match.

I try to find Jennilee but can't. I go to the large board that has the entire bracket and see that she lost while I'd played my last match. I hadn't seen her go. A failed opportunity, but I don't know that Jennilee could tell me much anyway. And it won't matter in the long run. If I leave right after I…well, right after, then I won't be any help in Carrie's case after all. Maybe I could stop somewhere on my way back to Michigan, and send an email with all the contents of Nick's machine?

No, because then I'm back to them tracing Nick's sale to me in Michigan.

I've finished sooner than my future opponent, so I sit in the bleachers and wait. Finally, the other game ends and I get up to play my next match. I'm introduced to my next opponent, Kevin.

*Kevin. (Irish) Handsome.* Oh, this poor kid does not live up to his name. He barely looks old enough to have driven himself here. Maybe he didn't. I look around for hovering parents but don't see anyone in Kevin's corner.

All the other players I played had at least one or two people with them, cheering them on. Kevin and I, it appears, are the only ones going it solo. I wonder if Colin would have come and cheered me on if I'd asked him to?

I smile to myself, knowing he would. He'd be cheering me on from the front row.

Kevin is thin and pimply, his fine, blonde hair laying flat against his pale scalp. He's wearing a plaid short-sleeve shirt and chinos that hang off his tiny frame. He's taller than I am, but much thinner.

I'd like to beat him in backgammon and then take him out and feed him.

He can barely meet my eyes when he shakes my hand. His palm is clammy. In a gymnasium full of geeks, this kid takes the crown.

We sit at the table. The other two contestants begin at the table next to us. Some of the contestants have left, the others that have stayed to see the last matches gather round the remaining players. It feels a little weird, all the attention focused on just these two games.

Kevin and I begin our match. We each quickly take a game. He's aggressive, taking chances. I'm my cautious self, playing defensively. One of us will get tripped up in the other's strategy.

I have one checker on the bar when I roll a five and a four. I anchor my checker from the bar on the five-spot with my checker from the one spot.

"Ah, yes, the Barabino," Kevin says and starts to shake his dice cup.

"What did you just say?" I ask.

He looks up at me, squints, "Huh?"

"You called me barabino. Why?"

He looks puzzled. "Not you, your move."

"What are you talking about?" I ask, my voice rising.

Kevin looks around, not sure what to make of me. "The five four combination," he points to my previous move. "That's called a Barabino."

"It is?"

"After Rick Barabino, the famous backgammon player."

I don't even know there was such a thing as a famous backgammon player, let alone one named Barabino. My eyes once more search the crowd for Jennilee but she's long gone.

Is Jennilee the barabino from the emails with Carrie?

Kevin lets out a small sound of delight over his roll and my mind returns to the task at hand. We each take another game, but these take longer. Kevin is a good opponent, the best player I've had here.

I hear a whoop from the crowd and realize that the players next to us have finished already. Whoever wins our match will be playing an elderly man that looks like he just stepped out of a Harvard English Lit classroom where he waxed poetically about Byron. Who knew people still wore handlebar mustaches?

The tournament committee starts moving tables aside, putting one last table on a raised dais. They set up video cameras around the table and a large screen is dropped from somewhere above. They'll be showing the final match on the big screen.

They bring up a little table and put a large trophy on it. A smaller, less impressive trophy is placed along side it. Several photographers seem to appear from thin air, setting themselves up by the championship match table, jockeying for position.

It hits me. I can't be in the finals.

Even if I don't win, there's a chance I'll be in some of the photos. That consolation prize trophy would be presented, and the runner-up would probably have to pose with the winner.

Sure, it's an obscure pastime, but it is a National Championship (I'm pretty sure there are no rings that go with it, though). It will probably hit the papers, certainly here in Tennessee. Maybe picked up by a wire service? On the internet? Who knows where this could end up if it's a slow news week?

I have a flash of my ex picking up his morning paper and the first thing he sees over his corn flakes is my very alive face holding a trophy.

Yeah, sure, I should have thought of this all before, but I hadn't. It didn't occur to me that I'd actually make it this far. I play with the same eight people online. I win most of the time, but not enough to make me think I could waltz in here and take the championship. Who knew those other seven players are so good?

I have to throw the final game.

Throwing a backgammon game should be easy. I suppose it's the same as taking a dive in the fifth for boxers. But, never having done either, I don't know where to start.

Then I see my opening. Feigning aggressiveness, I make a play, and hope like hell Kevin rolls a five or a two.

Kevin picks up the dice. He looks at me with a question in his eyes. He knows it was a bad play. I pretend I don't see his look.

He rolls a five two combination.

The crowd groans (it's kind of nice to know they were on my side—takes the sting out of throwing the match—sort of).

Kevin looks up, stunned, but quickly recovers. He smiles and makes his move. Under his breath he mumbles, "eat me!"

I nearly fall out of my chair.

The rest of the game is just a formality, but I play it like I could come back. Both of us know I can't.

When he wins, he shakes my hand, and this time he meets my eyes.

"Congratulations," I say. "Good luck in the finals."

"Thank you. I think this was probably the hardest match I played."

I accept the compliment with a nod of my head. I turn to go, but can't help myself. "You know, it would have been a different story if I'd just had a double six."

He looks at me, confused. He looks down at the table, mentally replaying the game, trying to see where a double six would have made a difference. It wouldn't have.

"Because, there's nothing like a *double six*," I say, emphasis on the last words. I look at him, wait…wait…here it comes.

His eyes go wide. He looks at me like he hadn't seen me before. His eyes shoot to my nametag, but I've already peeled it off. He'd already seen it, of course. And even if he hadn't, he could get it anywhere, but in about two hours Raven Moldano will cease to exist. Again.

"Hey," he says as I disappear into the crowd.

I can hear him yell for me—for double six—but I'm already to the door. His adoring crowd swallows him up. More polyester in one place you'll never see. Not quite the same as a rock star, but hey.

I get in my car and start to leave the parking lot, to go to the Hopeless Heart. Two girls are leaving the gymnasium and I wait for them to cross the walk. They look to be about Tricia's age—college age.

They're cute, lively, and I silently wonder if something besides the backgammon tournament is being held in the building.

They're both in jeans and tee-shirts. One an Abercrombie-Fitch, the other a red tee-shirt that reads "Redhawk's Chi-O". It has the University of Miami logo on the back. The Chi-O is in the Greek font that sororities use.

I'd seen that shirt somewhere before.

Something clicks and I wish I hadn't packed my stuff in the trunk. I need my laptop.

I look at the clock. The matches went quickly, so I still have an hour before I would need to get to the Hopeless Heart. I could do this in any parking lot, but I don't want anybody to see me.

I still have my room key, hadn't checked out. I have to drive by the motel to get to the Hopeless Heart anyway. The privacy of a room would be better, plus the high speed internet cable if needed. When I reach the motel, I park right in front of my room, not taking the time to do the safety thing.

I grab my tote bag and computer bag from the trunk, leaving my suitcase with my clothes. I rush into my room and boot up my laptop. I grab my tote and pull out the CD I'd burned of all the stuff from Nick's machine.

My hands tremble as I load it into my laptop. I click on the folder entitled Miami. There are so many. I select them all and hit open. I sit back and try to slow my breathing as they all open one on top of each other, accordion style. Checking my watch as I do.

I'm clicking the photos close until I finally come to the photo I want. It's of Nick and Carrie, obviously taken at a party in someone's house. Carrie's wearing her Chi-O tee shirt, but she's not the only one. In the background, in the corner of the kitchen, is a woman looking at the backs of Carrie and Nick. Her lanky brown hair hides her face. Her hands are clasped in front of her. Her body language screams out of place, awkward. She's wearing a Chi-O tee shirt similar to the one the girl in the parking lot had on, and the same as Carrie. But this woman doesn't look like sorority material.

She hasn't changed one bit in the few years since this picture was taken.

Jennilee is Carrie's sorority sister.

Being an only child, and never a member of a sorority, I can only hypothetically ask; what would you do for your sister?

Or better yet, what *wouldn't* you do?

# Twenty-Four

"So what does that mean, other than she went to school with them all?" Will asks me as we sit in his car.

After my discovery, I'd called him and asked if he was up for a Friday afternoon stake-out. He hadn't said a word, just asked me where he should pick me up.

I put off Uncle Chazz for one more day.

I could give you all kinds of rationalizations. This is one way I might be able to help out with Carrie's murder without tipping off my identity. This way I could still see Colin tonight. I could go on and on. But, if you must know, it doesn't really bother me to put off killing a man, even if I was doing it for the right reasons.

Even if I want it done, it doesn't mean I want to do it. You know?

So now, Will and I sit outside Bertram, Gleason and Young's offices hoping Jennilee went back to work after busting out of the backgammon tournament. My bet is that she's just conscientious enough to do it. She was wearing work clothes at the tournament.

I'd had to fudge a little bit on how I'd come across the knowledge that Carrie and Jennilee had been sorority sisters in college. And that she'd been out of the office for a few hours already this afternoon.

He hadn't pushed it. I could tell he wanted to, but he didn't. Maybe he didn't want to know too much. Just enough to get a potential new band out of a fix and into a recording studio.

Not enough to testify at a trial.

I'd had him pick me up. I'd sacrificed caution for speed and told Will at which motel—which room—to pick me up. Somehow, on some level, I knew I could trust Will with my whereabouts.

He drove a black SUV—an Envoy I think, but I didn't really pay attention. I'd just gotten in, and directed him to Nick's office building.

It is now ten after five. People are beginning to stream out, but so far no sign of Jennilee or Nick. I don't even know if Nick is back to work yet.

"Raven?"

"Huh?" I say, startled out of the haze I'd fallen into watching people leave the building.

"I said, what does Jennilee and Carrie being sorority sisters have to do with anything?"

It doesn't seem like such a big deal now. But when I realized that Jennilee could be—probably is—barabino, and then saw those girls in the parking lot at the backgammon tournament, and the memory of the photo clicked, I felt like it untangled a piece of the puzzle.

Now I'm not so sure.

I look across the console at him. "Probably nothing. It's just nobody ever mentions Carrie and Jennilee in any kind of conjunction together. And if they were sorority sisters, and one of them had been killed…" I was losing my thread. Finally I just shrug. "It's nothing. Do you want to scrap this?" I ask, waving my hands in an encompassing way around the parking lot.

He shakes his head. He's wearing a tee-shirt and jeans again. White shirt this time. His leather jacket is strewn across the backseat as is a Baltimore Orioles cap (in case we have to go incognito? Should I have brought my Tennessee cap?). He rubs a finger across the scar on his lip absent-mindedly. His hair is tousled and I wonder what (or who) I'd torn him away from.

I'm struck again by my good fortune on this trip to be

surrounded by so many good-looking, yet vastly different men. Eatmeee! (sorry, Kevin, you'll always be eatmeee! to me) excluded.

If you're only going to immerse yourself within humanity every four years or so, I highly recommend doing it amongst gorgeous guys.

"No," he says. "Let's play out this hunch of yours."

As if on cue, Jennilee exits the building. She heads to her car—a dependable little compact, I'd expect nothing else—and drives away, Will and I hot on her tail.

She lives just outside of Nashville proper, but not quite to Mount Juliet. She pulls into a modest apartment complex. The parking lot is nearly empty. She goes into the building as Will and I pull up to the curb across the street.

We look at each other.

"Now what?" we say simultaneously. My smile is sheepish, his laugh deep and throaty.

"I haven't been on a stake-out since I thought my high school girlfriend was cheating on me," he says.

"Was she?"

He nods.

"Stupid girl," I whisper. He heard, I can tell, because he smiles and looks out his window.

"How about you?" he asks after a moment.

"Which? Stake-outs or cheating?"

"I meant stake-outs, but whatever you want to tell me," he teases.

"Only one. Stake-out, that is." I don't count Uncle Chazz and the Hopeless Heart, I only count the one from years ago, with my ex.

"And were you successful?"

I'm here. Alive. "Yes," I say.

"And the other?"

"Nope. Never cheated."

He nods. "Yeah, I don't really see you as the cheating type." There is almost…regret? …in his voice. Before I can analyze it any further he asks, "So, you and Colin? How's that going?"

I take a deep breath, let it out. "My conference is over. I thought I'd do some sight-seeing over the weekend, then head back to Vermont. I don't think there's any reason to stick around after that." Cryptic as hell, but let him read it any way he wants to.

If he wants to know if Colin and I have a future because he's interested in Colin as a potential client, now he knows it's not going beyond this weekend. If he wants to know for any other reason? Well, there's no future there, either.

And that thought upsets me more than I thought it would.

He looks at me. Hard. His green eyes penetrating mine. Then he just nods and looks away.

"Listen," I say. "Why don't we call it a day? A hunch that was nothing. A—" He cuts me off by pointing. I follow his direction while he starts the car.

Jennilee, dressed more casually—but still a frump—is coming out of the building and heading for her car.

"Maybe not so bad a hunch, after all," Will says, putting the car in drive.

**S**he drives away from Nashville, heads for Mount Juliet. Will seems to know what he's doing following her—close enough to keep her in our sights, yet not too close for her to "make" us. His words, as he explains his technique to me.

She drives, past the Hopeless Heart, past the turn off to Nick's neighborhood, through Mount Juliet completely.

"I hope she's not headed away for the weekend," Will says. "I didn't bring a change of clothes." He smiles at me and I try to smile back.

"Neither did she," I point out. "She came out empty handed, so hopefully this is a short trip."

It turns out that way. In the next town past Mount Juliet, Jennilee pulls over on the main drag and heads into a coffee shop called The Country Grounds. Will drives past, makes a U-turn and parks across the street where we're able to see in.

I look at the sign in the window and feel an eerie tingle.

"Twenty minutes of free internet with each Grande," the sign reads.

We watch Jennilee get a coffee from the counter—looks like a Grande, no surprise—then head to one of the three computers. She is facing us, but her eyes are glued to the computer screen. We can see the movement of her elbows. I know that movement. She's typing. Fast.

"Maybe she doesn't have a computer at home," Will says.

"She has a computer at home," I say.

"How do you know?"

I look at him. "I don't. Not for sure. But she didn't come all the way out here just to use a computer. She came out here to use a computer that no one would ever know she used."

Will looks at me for a second. He looks like he's going to ask me about that—how I'd know that, I suppose—but he doesn't. He looks back at Jennilee.

"I think we know who sent the anonymous emails," I say. I don't tell him my suspicions that Jennilee and Carrie corresponded right up until Nick sold his machine. Probably after, too. I just didn't have access to those emails. I can't explain how I'd come by that information so I leave it unsaid.

But I do tell him about seeing Jennilee at the Hopeless Heart the other night, and the longing looks she gave Nick. How she snuck out as the band ended without anybody seeing her.

I know Jennilee is involved in this all somehow. And my doubt that Nick is involved begins to grow.

After a minute or two, Will reaches across me to the glove box. His arm brushes my knees and I breathe deep, liking how Will smells. He pulls a tablet and a pen out of the compartment, shuts it, moves back to his side of the SUV and flips the tablet open. He looks at the coffee shop, writes something down. He cranes his neck, looking down the street in front of us, and behind and writes again. I peek at the paper. He's written the name of the coffee shop and the address.

Apparently he's come to the same conclusion I have. Somebody needs to know about Jennilee.

I reach into my tote bag, pull out the slip of paper Colin gave me the night we met and my prepaid cell phone. I haven't used it so far, but I'm glad I have it now. I'll chuck it somewhere along the route back to Michigan when I'm done here.

"Who are you calling?" Will asks.

"Colin," I say as if it's obvious.

"Do you think that's a good idea?"

I look at him, stunned. "He'll know how to get a hold of Nick. How could it not be a good idea?"

He shrugs. "I don't know. But let's think about it for a second. We should probably wait and follow Jennilee home, anyway."

"Okay. Talk."

He looks out the window. The sky is getting dark now, but the coffee shop is well lit. We'll be able to see Jennilee leave. Will sighs. "What do we really know now that we didn't before?"

I look at him like he's crazy. "What, are you crazy?"

"No, really."

"We know Jennilee sent those emails," I say.

"Not necessarily. What else?"

"We know that if she wrote the emails she put the towel and Nick's watch in that Dumpster."

"No, not necessarily. Whoever wrote the emails could have seen someone put the towel into the Dumpster. What else?"

"We know she had access to Nick's watch."

"So did a lot of other people, including you and Colin, his co-workers. Even me. Nick said so himself. Lots of people. What else?"

I open my mouth, but he stops me. "That we didn't know before," he cautions.

My mind races. I come up with nothing. I let the phone fall back into my lap.

A few minutes later, Jennilee leaves the coffee shop. We follow her home, and watch her go into her building. Then Will starts to take me to my motel.

He puts a CD into the drive and Billie Holiday's tortured voice comes out.

"Mind if we turn that off," I ask, already reaching for the knob.

"Not a Billie Holiday fan?"

I look out the window. "It reminds me of somebody," is all I say, thinking of my ex.

We ride the rest of the way in silence. We hadn't come to any conclusions by the time he pulls in front of my room, so I wait. My cell phone still sits in my lap. I pick it up.

"Put it in your bag. Go into your room. Get a good night's sleep."

He sounds so calm. I want to do what he says.

"But," I say.

"I know a guy I can call. He can find out what's been sent on that machine back in the coffee shop. But he'll need a few hours to do it."

"You know people that can do stuff like that?" I ask, impressed, and just a little bit suspicious.

"Are you kidding? With all the music pirating going on? We've got the best hackers in the business on our payroll, so does every record company these days."

That makes sense. And makes me feel just a little bit guilty for the few MP3 files I'd illegally downloaded in the past.

" I'll pick you up in the morning, and we'll go poke around Jennilee's place. If we don't figure it out by the afternoon, we'll call the police and tell them everything we know about Jennilee."

"Another anonymous tip," I say, liking the irony.

He smiles. "Exactly. Full circle."

I start to get out of the door, but stop. "This doesn't feel right," I say.

"What?"

"Not calling the police. Or at the very least, Colin."

"I thought we just went through that."

"You know how in every movie, when someone finds a dead body?" Will nods. "And they leave to go find somebody to tell, or to follow the killer?" He starts to smile, he's seen the same movies I have.

"And the body's gone when they get back," he finishes for me.

"Exactly."

"But the body's already been found in this case."

"Even more reason to wrap this up now. So there aren't any other ones."

"Do you want to wrap it up with so many questions left hanging?"

"Waiting 'til we see Jennilee may not answer those questions."

He shrugs. "Maybe not, but I don't think waiting until then is going to make the case against Nick any worse."

"No, I suppose not," I say, "It's not like she saw us, that she's on to us and feels she has to skip town or anything.

"And selfishly," Will says. I look at him, waiting. "I'd like to see if all this could be wrapped up with minimal fuss."

I stare at him, not getting it.

"I'm going to sign these guys. I want them coming to Planet with a clean slate. No arrests even if the charges are never made. I'm just protecting my investment."

Ah. I can't argue with that. I want to protect Colin, also, if I can. Sort of a parting gift. And that means protecting Nick's alibi.

"Eight tomorrow?" I ask.

He nods, relaxes. "Eight. I'll see you then."

I start to get out of the door, then turn back. "Thank you. You didn't have to do any of this. I want you to know how much I appreciate it."

He reaches out to touch my cheek, but lets his hand drop. It falls on my hand instead. He gives me a lopsided smile that makes me want to crawl back into the SUV. But I don't.

"Raven, nobody should be completely alone," he says.

His words hit me with a force that nearly knocks me over.

"Not to figure out something like this. For people she just met," he clarifies.

"Oh. Right."

"Besides, if Planet signs the River Rats…" he lets the sentence finish itself. It's just good business.

I nod. "Right. Well, thanks anyway."

I slide my hand out from under his, wishing…oh, just wishing. I get out of the car, go to the door, enter the room, wave to Will and shut the door behind me. He waits until I have a light turned on, then I hear him drive away.

Once I'm sure he's gone, I go out to my car and grab my suitcase with my clothes, glad I made the decision to not check out.

Unsettled, I check my room thoroughly. I don't know if I am more afraid of the thought of Uncle Chazz or my ex showing up. I peek into the closet and behind the shower curtain. Even under the bed, though only a small child could possibly fit under it. I don't know why I feel so uneasy in the room. Maybe it was having just spied on another person. Or that my car, for once, is parked in front of my door. I make sure the drapes are shut tight, no slivers of light. I lock and chain the door.

I consider changing rooms, even changing hotels, but decide against it. Will is picking me up here in the morning. I'd be safe enough until then. Besides, if Uncle Chazz shows up now, maybe it would just save me some time.

I toss my tote bag on the desk, then take a shower, leaving the bathroom door open and my gun within reach, resting on the tank lid of the toilet.

After I dry-off, do something with my hair and have my tee-shirt and boxers on, I boot up my laptop. "You out there?" I ask. Hope. Wish. Desperately need.

"Yes. Where've you been? I've been dying to hear about the tournament."

The tournament? That seems like a lifetime ago.

"Oh, that. I lost in the quarter-finals."

"Poor Blackbird. Did you ever figure out who eatmeee! is?"

I smile, my mood suddenly lighter. I tell him the Kevin story.

"So, did he win? Is eatmeee! our national champion?"

I chuckle at the thought, picturing Kevin hoisting that big trophy, his scrawny arms quivering with the effort. "I don't know. I left before the final game."

"Really? Couldn't stand to see the winner if it couldn't be you?"

I think he's kidding. I hope he knows me better than that.

"I'm kidding," he types. "I know that's not you."

A wave of desolation washes over me.

It makes no sense. I'm out there. I'm meeting people, becoming involved in other people's lives. Letting them in—as much as it's safe to do. For goodness sakes, a great guy seems to really like me.

And suddenly I feel more alone than I have in the past four years.

Because, still, only Confessor really knows me.

And who knows where he is? Who he is?

"I gotta go," I type.

There's a pause. "Why? What's going on? Is it Colin?"

"No. Nothing. I'm just tired."

"Okay," he says.

"Good night," I say and quit out of ichat.

I cross the room, taking the chair from the table and placing it under the door, even though the dead bolt and chain are on. Then I turn off the laptop and crawl into bed, placing the gun on the table next to me. I remember I was supposed to contact Colin, that we had planned to get together tonight. I look at the laptop on the bedside table. I pull the blanket tight around me, cocooning myself. As I turn off the light I realize it's the first time that I ever left the chat room before Confessor did.

# *Twenty-Five*

Will picks me up at eight. We both sport wet hair, tee-shirts and jeans. His leather jacket in strewn across the back seat and I throw my denim one back there with it. "I don't know about you, but I can't do any sleuthing without coffee," he says as he pulls out of my parking lot.

"Bless you, my son," I say.

He shoots me a look, questioning. I can't figure out why, but after a second he turns his attention back to the road.

"IHOP?" he asks.

"Fine," I say, wondering if they have a frequent eater card of some kind.

In front of the doors to the IHOP are the lines of newspaper machines. I stop in front of the local paper. In one of the sidebars is the teaser for the story about the backgammon tournament. It's just a tiny blurb, directing people to the lifestyle section, but there is a pic.

You guessed it. There he is, holding the trophy. His shiny face boasting a huge smile.

I smile, and buy a paper. I put it in my tote bag. I'll read it later. I hadn't seen any photographers taking pictures while I was there. I'd assumed they wouldn't start shooting until the championship round. Still, I'll look at the pictures to make sure there aren't any crowd shots with me in them. Or that my name is mentioned. Though there isn't much I can do about it now.

I keep moving into the restaurant. I've got other things on my mind.

Once again I'm led to the back booth. Is it now mine and Will's booth? I don't care, I only know my waitress is on duty and she brings over the coffee pot before I'm barely seated.

"Getting to be a regular, hey, hon?" she says. She looks at Will, then back at me, a small smirk on her face. "Good for you," she whispers under her breath to me as she fills my cup.

"I wasn't sure you'd be working on a Saturday," I say, raising the cup, taking a deep draw.

"Yep, I'm off Mondays and Tuesdays," she replies.

I nod, like I'll remember that bit of information. The fact is I won't be here on Monday or Tuesday. I need to do what I can to help out with Nick, Carrie and Colin this morning, but after that, it's time for me to take care of business and get the hell out of here. I don't want to spend another night with a gun on my bedside table.

We order breakfast and try to come up with a game plan.

"My guy says that the first email that went to the newspaper came from that IP address," Will says. "The second email, tipping off the towel and watch only, went to the police, so I don't have access to that IP address, so I don't know for sure. But I suspect it was also from the coffee shop."

"You have access to the IP address from the email that was sent to the newspaper?"

"I called in a favor with the music critic there—he hooked me up with the Metro editor."

I set down my coffee. "So, it *is* Jennilee."

"That machine anyways. We can't prove it was Jennilee that sent the emails."

I shake my head. "Why? Why would she do that? Send those emails, she must have known suspicion would fall on Nick."

Will shrugs. "I can think of only one reason she'd want the suspicion to fall on Nick if she cares for him as much as you think she does."

"Why?"

"So it doesn't fall on her."

"She pushed Carrie," I whisper, my voice not really questioning.

Will leans forward, his arms on the table, his strong hands gently holding his coffee cup. "Hear me out. Carrie goes away to make a point to Nick…"

"Right. To make him quit the band," I finish. That's consistent with Jennilee's—barabino's - emails with Carrie. I don't tell that to Will.

"Nick's quitting the band?"

Oh-oh. I start backtracking. "No. No. He loves the music, the band. It's just that Carrie's been pressuring him about settling down with something more stable. That's what I think this whole 'I need time to think' thing was all about, to make him jump the fence."

He looks closely at me, his green eyes darkening. "Colin told you all this? Or Nick?"

I flutter my hands. "Mostly Colin when we were chatting online, but I've picked up pieces from both of them. And Tricia. It's not hard to put together if you're listening."

He seems to buy it. Our food comes and we both begin eating, but we quickly return to Will's scenario. Between bites, he says, "Okay, so Carrie goes away to make a point to Nick. She checks in with Jennilee, her old sorority sister, to secretly see how Nick's doing."

"Colin and I were chatting by that time. He said Nick was getting sick of Carrie's games."

"So, if Nick's not coming after her, playing to her tune, she ups the stakes."

"The first email," I say.

Will nods, takes a sip of coffee. "Either she went to that coffee shop and sent it, or, more likely, she had Jennilee."

"But why would Jennilee send an email that puts Nick into the spotlight?"

"What happens if Nick gets nervous about the email and goes to find Carrie? He probably knew or had a good idea where she'd gone. If he had to find her, he probably could have. He just didn't before then because he wasn't going to play games anymore. But if he has to…and when he does, either Carrie wins and he leaves the band—"

"Ensuring Jennilee still gets to work for him, see him everyday," I point out.

But Will is already nodding. "Or Nick says enough of this shit and breaks it off for good with Carrie."

"Freeing Nick up. At least in Jennilee's eyes."

"Right. Win-win for Jennilee."

"So she sends the email for Carrie. She's smart enough not to do it from her own house. And the police come sniffing around."

"Which kills Jennilee—she doesn't want to see Nick suffering. But she knows Carrie is safe and sound that nothing really bad is going to happen."

I'm nodding, finishing his thought. "But it goes on too long. Starts to maybe get sticky for Nick. So she goes to confront Carrie."

"They have a fight, struggle, Carrie falls. It's an accident, but Jennilee panics, leaves. Maybe she even tries to clean up with that towel, then takes it with her. Then she starts thinking about how bad it'll look that she left, so now she has to divert the attention away from herself."

"The towel, the watch and the second email."

"We know she had access to Nick's watch."

We don't say anything else, just finish our breakfasts in silence.

I have to admit, I like it better, that Jennilee pushed Carrie. That Nick is truly innocent. I never wanted to believe that Colin could be so close to, would cover for, a man who could have done something like this.

But the one thing that I've learned in my lifetime is that you never really know anyone.

We leave the IHOP and drive to Jennilee's apartment. Her car is parked in the spot she'd left it in last night.

"Are you sure you want to do this? We could always do what you wanted to last night and just call the police?" Will asks.

"We probably should, but I'd like to just talk to Jennilee first. Let her know we know about the computer, that she's involved. See if she slips up somehow. If she does we can let her know that we believe it was an accident. Maybe we can somehow resolve this whole thing without anybody getting in too much trouble." Or me having to speak to the police myself.

"You really think this is going to get wrapped up so neatly? That we'll walk in there with a hunch and walk out with a confession?"

I look at him closely, and then look away. "No. But I can hope."

He looks away, and then back at me. "I've never met her. I didn't see her at the Hopeless Heart. All I have to go on is your gut instinct."

I take a deep breath. "My gut says she wouldn't purposely hurt anybody."

He nods. "Then let's go see if we can't talk to her. Clear this whole thing up."

I don't tell him that my gut had been deadly wrong before.

Will parks in an empty church parking lot across the busy street from Jennilee's apartment building. "Ready, Starsky?" Will asks as he opens his door.

I laugh weakly. "Ready, Hutch."

We take a few steps away from the car and I stop. "Wait, I forgot something."

Will hits unlock on the car and I go to my door. I open it and grab my tote bag on the floor. I pull out the gun I'd put in earlier. I have no idea why. I'm not expecting a shoot out or anything.

That's just it…I have no idea what to expect.

Should I put it back in the tote and just bring the whole bag? Stick it in the waist of my pants? Though it looked cool in movies, the idea of that cold, deadly metal against my skin did not appeal to me at all. As I'm trying to figure out what to do with it, where to put it, Will peeks over my shoulder.

"Have you got a tape recorder? That's probably a good idea—" He doesn't finish as he sees the gun. I hear the breath leave his body.

He snatches the gun out of my hand so quickly it takes me a second to realize it's gone. He spins me around, pushes me against the side of his SUV. "What's going on?"

I shake my head. "Nothing. I don't know."

I can feel his strong body leaning into me, I should be scared, but I'm not.

"What do you think is going to happen in there? Why do you need to bring a gun? Why do you even *have* a gun?"

I look him straight in the eyes. The sun is out in full force now and I can see golden flecks within his green irises. His lips are pressed together with emotion, causing his scar to turn a deathly white. "I brought the gun from home, for protection. It's been in my bag, I hadn't intended to bring it here, but I thought…I don't know what I thought."

He lets me go. Takes a step back, scrubs his hands over his face. "I don't know what to think, either." He sighs, looks around the deserted church parking lot. He looks up to the steeple. Praying he'd never met me? Met any of us?

He doesn't ask how I got a gun on a plane. Maybe he doesn't know that I supposedly flew here from Vermont. Maybe that will come to him later. After I'm on my way back to Michigan.

He looks down at the gun in his hand, his fingers curl around the trigger with a natural ease. I expect him to put it in the car, lock it up, or throw it in the bushes. He sticks the gun in the back of his waistband then grabs his jacket from the back seat, pulls it on covering the gun.

I gotta admit, that move looks pretty damn sexy.

He grabs my hand and turns back to the apartment building. "Let's go." He hangs on to my hand until we cross the highway, then he drops it, like a parent who'd seen their child safely across.

Is that how Will thinks of me? A child he has to keep an eye on, lest she gets hit by oncoming traffic?

I expect to wake Jennilee up, that she'd come to the door in her pajamas, sleep in her eyes. That's surely how you'd find me at nine o'clock on a typical Saturday morning.

But this isn't a typical Saturday morning.

Jennilee answers the door dressed in her usual prim attire. A dachshund prances around her feet (as much as a dachshund can prance). She looks blankly at me for a moment and then it comes to her. "Ms. Moldano?"

"Raven," I say.

"Raven," she repeats.

I point to Will. "This is my friend, Will Fredrickson." They nod at each other.

"Yes, I remember you from when you came to Nick's office," she says. Will just nods again.

She looks back to me. "I'm afraid I don't understand. You were at the office with Colin the other day, right? Does this have to do with the papers for Nick?"

I hold up my hand. "No, this has nothing to do with business."

Her confusion is evident. I guess that's good. It means she doesn't know I've become involved in any of this.

"It's about Carrie," Will says gently. "Can we come in and talk to you for a minute?"

She goes deathly white. Her hands clench together, wringing. Probably not the best poker player, Jennilee. She steps aside, letting us in and shooing her dog away. It waddles down a hallway and out of sight. She leads us to the kitchen, which isn't a long trip in the tiny apartment. "I just made a pot of coffee, would you like some?"

"Yes, please," Will and I say simultaneously.

She gets us coffee and we all sit at the tiny table. "I'm sorry, I don't have anything else to offer you." Her hands are clenching her mug so tight I expect it to break into shards, the coffee erupting like a volcano.

"The coffee's fine, really," I say.

She looks so uncomfortable. I wish I could put her at ease, but I'm not really sure where to start.

Will seems content to watch her squirm.

Finally, she says, "You said this had to do with Carrie?"

"Yes," I say.

"Should we call Nick? Maybe he should be here?"

"We're going to call Nick next. In fact, we're going to call Nick as soon as we leave here, Jennilee," Will says firmly.

We are? Oh. He seems to know what he's doing, so I let him go.

"And we want you to know that," he adds.

I'm not following him.

"I'm not following you," Jennilee says.

"When we leave this building, we are going to call Nick and tell him that the anonymous emails were sent from a coffee shop just the other side of Mount Juliet."

Both Jennilee and I gasp.

"We just thought you'd like to know that. In case there's anything you'd like to get straightened out," Will says.

Ah. He was either giving her an out if it was an accident, or enough rope to hang herself if it wasn't. Or both.

I desperately want to play bad cop, but I'm not sure that Will is good cop. Is he helping her out or setting her up?

After a moment, when Jennilee still hasn't answered him, he gets up and motions for me to join him. We cross the apartment. I turn at the door, to thank her for the coffee, but she is deep in thought, a million miles away. She's tidying up, moving our cups to the sink. She pushes all of our chairs in, the scraping against the floor sending a shiver through me. She stands there, staring into space, her hands working themselves into knots. I leave her alone with her demons.

Across the street, we get in Will's SUV. I reach for my phone.

Will places his hand over mine. "Not yet," he says.

"Why?"

He nods to Jennilee's building. "Let's just wait a few minutes and see if she goes anywhere."

"Like comes out with a suitcase and guns blazing?"

He smiles softly. "Something like that."

Exactly one half hour later Will taps my hand that's still tightly wrapped around my phone. "Okay. Doesn't look like she's going anywhere. Let's call Nick."

I hold up the piece of paper that Colin gave me the day we met. "I only have Colin's number. I was going to call him and see if he's with Nick."

Will digs out his wallet, thumbs through and pulls out a business card. He hands it to me. "Here, Nick gave me his cell and home phone." It's Nick's business card. On the back he'd written "The River Rats" and every possible number imaginable for reaching him.

Will starts to put his wallet back in his pocket, but stops. He pulls out another business card and places it on his thigh, face down. Then he puts the wallet back.

I call Nick on his cell phone. He answers on the third ring. Thank God.

"Nick, it's Raven."

"Raven? What's up?" I can hear the confusion in his voice.

"Where are you?"

"I'm at my apartment. I'm just about to leave to meet my parents at my lawyer's office."

"Tell him we'll be right there," Will says.

"Who's with you?" Nick asks when he hears Will's voice.

"Will," I say.

A pause.

"Where are you?"

I tell him where we are. "Can we come over?"

"What, you mean now? Why are you at Jennilee's?"

"Yes. Now. And we'll tell you when we get there."

"I told you, I'm just about to leave for my lawyer's office."

Will hears that and says to me "Tell him to have his lawyer come to his place. His parents, too. This will be better to do on his home turf."

I repeat Will's instructions to Nick.

"What's going on, Raven?"

I look to Will, who had his ear close to mine. He nods. "We know who killed Carrie."

"Holy shit. Are you sure? Who?"

"I'm sure. Call your lawyer and have him come there, we'll be there as soon as possible. We'll explain it all then."

His voice is stunned. "Just tell me who."

I look at Will, he shrugs. "Jennilee," I say quietly.

There is silence on the phone for a full minute. "I…I don't…I can't…"

"We'll be there in just a few minutes to explain it all," I say. Then I ask, "Is Colin with you?"

"He's out of town at an auction. There's supposed to be a bunch of music equipment for sale. I was supposed to go, but I have to meet with the lawyer." Something warms inside me at the thought of Colin as an auction shopper. Wonder if he likes ebay? "He's probably on his way back already. He may even be home by now. I'll call him. He's not going to believe it was Jennilee any more than I do. This is so unbelievable."

"I know. But it's true. We'll be there as soon as we can."

The phone goes dead. I turn it off and drop it into my lap.

Will starts up the SUV and we drive to Nick's. As we pull into Nick's lot, Will hands me the business card that had rested on his leg. "Call," he says.

The card is for Detective Mosley.

"Are you sure?" I ask. He nods. "What about protecting your investment?"

He sighs, brushes his hand through his hair. It has dried,

now, and the waves fall back in place as his hand drags through. "I am. Hopefully we gave them enough time to get his lawyer here, but…"

I nod, and dial the phone. The detective doesn't even seem that surprised when I tell him that we know who killed Carrie and that we'd meet him at Nick's. He says he'll be there immediately.

"How'd you have his number, anyway?" I ask Will.

"He gave me a card that night he showed up at the Hopeless Heart."

I don't remember that, but I could have missed it. Or, maybe Will had gone to the police station that night. Protecting his investment.

A car pulls into the lot next to us and Mr. and Mrs. Carpenter get out. So does a man I assume is Nick's lawyer. He quickly walks toward Will and I.

"All right. What's all this about young lady?"

I don't get the chance to answer. Two police cars, sirens blaring, one a black-and-white, the other unmarked except for its siren on the dashboard, peel into the parking lot.

# Twenty-Six

We all go up to Nick's apartment. Tricia is sitting at the table, drinking coffee, bleary-eyed and dressed in sweats and a tee-shirt. Looking like she just woke up.

Nick is dressed in work clothes, a crisp white shirt, neatly pressed pants and a tie. He is freshly showered and shaved. Looking like he is on his way to work. Or to see his lawyer.

Tricia gets up from the table, starts taking coffee mugs out of the cupboard, filling them up. Mrs. Carpenter, a bundle of nerves, goes to help, looking over her shoulder at Nick as if he might disappear at any moment.

Just like the other night, Nick gets extra chairs and we gather around the table. Detective Mosley pulls out his tablet, looks at Will and me. "Okay, let's have it," he says.

I'm so glad Will is with me, that I don't have to tell the story alone.

Two hours later everyone's questions are answered. Nick fills in Jennilee's crush on him, which I knew from seeing her at the Hopeless Heart. He calls it a crush. I call it obsession, but who am I to throw stones.

Detective Mosley sighs loudly. "Motive, opportunity, access to the watch. She was seen at the place where the emails were sent from."

Will and I look at each other. So, the second email was sent from the same place, just like we'd figured.

The detective takes another big sigh, this one more satisfactory. "We'll check everything out, of course, the coffee shop, see if we can get any prints off the machine, the watch. Show Ms. Andrews' picture around at the cabin where Miss Essex was staying. That sort of thing."

He looks at Nick. He doesn't come out and say Nick is off the hook, he can't at this point, there's still too much to wrap up, but everyone in the room understands that Nick can breathe a little easier.

Nick runs his hands over his face, through his hair. I thought he'd look jubilant, triumphant, but there is still the haunted look in his eyes. Yes, he is no longer a "person of interest", but the woman he loves is still dead.

His father and the lawyer are speaking with the detective, hashing out details, I suppose.

Mrs. Carpenter gets up from the table, starts to clear away our coffee mugs. She takes the three steps from the table to the kitchen, puts down some mugs and breaks down into tears. Tricia jumps up, wraps her mother in her arms and the two women sway back and forth in the tiny galley kitchen, each one softly patting the other's back.

My heart aches for them.

To be them.

**T**he whole thing feels like a Scooby Doo ending. You know, how at the end of every Scooby Doo episode the gang and the curator of the museum (or whomever) explain how the whole thing happened. Loose ends are all tied up. Motives given. Usually accompanied by a, "And I'd have gotten away with it too, if it weren't for you pesky kids!"

Except nobody is calling Will and me pesky kids.

And the museum curator is back at her apartment. For now.

I watch as Detective Mosley says something to a uniformed

officer and then heads to his car. "Come on," I say to Will, pulling on his sleeve. "Let's go."

Will follows my gaze, realizes what I'm after, and starts to head for the door.

Nick grabs my arm. "What's going on?"

"Detective Mosley is probably going to Jennilee's."

"So?"

"So, I want to be there when he talks to her."

"Why?"

I shake my head. "I'm not sure, it's just something I have to do. I think she's pretty scared right now. I'd like to help if I can."

He lets go of my arm and runs his hands through his hair. "It looks like she's off her rocker. She's already killed once. I really don't think you should be going there."

His concern touches me. This is a man I'd believed a murderer, and now he's looking out for me. "It'll be okay. Will and Detective Mosley will be there. I may not even see her, but I feel I should be there."

He nods and then lets me go. We rush to Will's car.

**W**e're about twenty minutes or so behind Detective Mosley—he does have sirens, after all.

When we get to the building he is walking out of it. I look to see if Jennilee's car is gone, but it's there. Could he have finished questioning her so fast? Wouldn't he have placed her under arrest? Or at the very least, taken her in for questioning?

We walk up to the building. Detective Mosley is on his cell phone. "Better get CSI down here," he says. "And have them send someone from the morgue, too," he says, and then closes his phone, noticing us heading his way.

Oh, God.

I start to run. Detective Mosley lunges for me, but I pull away, dart past him. I take the stairs two at a time. I round the corner and see Jennilee's door open. A man with a large set of keys is leaning against the wall a few doors down…weeping.

Oh, God.

I hear Detective Mosley on the stairs behind me. "Do not go in there!"

I hear Will closer behind me. "Raven, don't."

I turn into Jennilee's apartment, take one step in and then stop.

She sits at the kitchen table, where we'd sat with her this morning. Hours ago. Her coffee cup is smashed and she'd used one of its shards to slash her wrists. Blood covers the table, her lap, the floor. Her hands, for once still, hang by her sides, her head lolls to one side.

She's dead. Very dead.

Will enters behind me. "Christ," he says and pulls me to him. He turns me around, crushes me to his chest so that I can't see her lifeless body.

Too late. In those few seconds, I memorize every detail. Her body on the chair, my and Will's chairs still pulled out, as if ghosts sat at the table with her. Our cups still on the table, blood encircling their bases.

So much blood. I would see it for the rest of my life.

Detective Mosley has reached us, herds us out of the apartment. I move in tandem with Will, unable—unwilling—to let go of him just yet. We move down the hall, away from the man—the super, I suspect—and toward the stairwell.

"This is now a crime scene. You can't be in there."

I feel Will nod. I remember something and stop, Will and Detective Mosley bumping into me. "Wait, she had a dog. There was a dog this morning. Someone needs to make sure the dog is okay."

The super steps forward. "I've taken the dog, miss. I brought Red Hawk to my apartment, my wife has him."

I nod and turn back, take a few more steps and stop again. I turn back to the super. "Did you say Red Hawk? Her dog's name is Red Hawk?"

The super looks at me oddly, nodding. "Uh-huh. We're really

not supposed to have pets in this building. But Red Hawk's just one of them wiener dogs, don't take up much space. And Miss Jennilee loved that dog, she did." His voice starts to crack and he fishes out a soiled handkerchief from his back pocket.

"Is the dog relevant somehow?" Detective Mosley asks me. He and Will are shepherding me outside once more.

"No. It's just…I know…knew… somebody with a dachshund named Red Hawk," I say, thinking of Gammon_89.

"And you think it's the same dog?" Will asks.

I nod slowly. "I think it's the same person," I say and my despair deepens. She had said she had a lot happening in her life right now. I thought it was just an excuse to stop playing backgammon with me.

Maybe if I'd tried a little harder, got her to talk about her problems…would it have stopped any of this? Would she still be alive?

Would Carrie?

"She left a note," Detective Mosley says.

"So, you're sure it was a suicide?" I ask. I don't think it was anything else, I guess I'm just in denial.

"As sure as we can be without an autopsy. There were no marks that she'd been forced, like she was trying to get loose, or had second thoughts, the cuts were true and deep. Nothing under her nails at first glance."

Oh, God, he'd looked at her fingernails.

"What did the note say?" Will asks.

Detective Mosley pulls out his tablet. He must have written it down and kept the note where it was. At the table where we'd sat and shared coffee?

"I'm sorry. It wasn't supposed to happen like this. I loved him."

There are more questions—thankfully outside of the building—but there's not much else Will and I can say—we told the detective everything we knew at Nick's place.

Well, not everything I know, but the things I knew from Nick's machine won't help now anyway. Will gives the detective his name and number as contact information for the both of us. The detective takes him aside for a while.

Had she started to kill herself while we sat across from her building for a half hour after we left? As the detective and Will talk, I try to replay this morning, but without coming here. Would Jennilee still be alive? Would someone else have gotten hurt instead?

Did we save someone, or kill someone? We'll never know.

**W**ill drops me off. Putting the car in park in front of my door.

"My gun," I say, holding out my hand.

He watches me for a moment, then sighs and reaches under his seat. At some point he must have put my gun there. He hands it to me. "Put it away. Far away," he says.

I nod. I look at him, fighting for something to say. He holds my hand, the gun between us. He's right, there are no words left to say.

I stick the gun back in my tote bag, leave his car, and walk away from him. Once inside, I hear Will pull away. Carrie's murder has been solved. And another girl is dead.

And it is only early afternoon.

**I**t is my first impulse to talk not to Colin, nor Nick, nor Will. The person I need the most is Confessor.

He's not online.

I sit, dazed, for a half hour. Feeling awful for poor Jennilee. Happy that it wasn't Colin that had been hurt. If her obsession was turning deadly, I guess it was for the best that she be the one to die.

I wonder if my coming from Michigan made things worse or better for them all. I still have no answers by three o'clock.

I just know that now, finally, it is time for Uncle Chazz.

I load all my stuff in the car again, but still keep my room key with me. I drive to the Hopeless Heart on auto pilot. It is three fifteen when I pull in to the lot behind the party store. Uncle Chazz's truck is the only one in the back lot of the bar. I don't know if a Saturday schedule is the same as Thursday. The kitchen help could come earlier or later than four, and I certainly don't want to time it so close that they arrive while I'm still here. I can't count on Uncle Chazz doing both the trash and taking a smoke break. I have to be ready whenever he makes an appearance.

If he makes an appearance.

I take my gun from my tote bag and leave my car, walking quickly across the access road and to the back corner of the Hopeless Heart, wedging myself between the Dumpster and the back of the building. The reek assails me and I breathe through my mouth, but I stay where I am. Barely seconds after I'm in place I hear the back door open. From the corner of my eye, I see the blue milk crate slide toward the door. Seconds later I see the toes of cowboy boots nearing the edge of the Dumpster. I wait until I hear the drop of the bags into the bin and the boots turn back toward the door. Drawing in a deep breath, I step out of my hiding place, take two quick steps and just as Uncle Chazz is about to turn around and see what he just heard, I jam the point of my gun into his spine and say, "Walk slowly through the door."

My arm is tense, waiting for him to twirl around, pounce, attack. But no, he just does what I say and slowly walks through the door. I use my foot to slide the blue milk crate away and the door slams shut behind us.

We walk about five feet into the building before I say, "Stop. Now, take five steps forward." He does, making him out of reach. "Slowly turn around."

As he turns, I brace myself, but of course I know what he looks like. He's wearing a western shirt, jeans, and boots, just a good ol' boy. He must be in his mid to late fifties but he looks young for his age. And I have to admit, he is a handsome man.

But then, I'd thought so years ago.

I look at his eyebrow, see the scar, confirming to myself I have the right man. But I needn't have bothered, for he confirms it himself.

"I wondered when you'd show up."

# *Twenty-Seven*

"You knew I'd be here," I say, my throat raw, and I clear it with a cough. I aim the gun higher at him and motion for him to raise his arms, hold up style, which he does.

I briefly glance around me to get the lay of the land. It's your basic back room to a bar. A small kitchen area with stainless steel counters. A large grill. Stacks of red, plastic baskets that burgers are served up in. Cases of liquor and beer are stacked along one of the long walls. Two doors. One that leads to the main floor, and the other looks like a large, walk-in refrigerator.

I can see both of those doors clearly. I don't turn around, but I know the heavy door leading outside closed behind me, because the sunlight disappeared. I turn my attention back to the man standing in front of me.

"I didn't know what day, what month, what year. But I knew you'd show up someday."

This confuses me. He knew before the night he saw me here with Colin and the Carpenters? "You didn't think I was dead?"

He snorts. "Nobody thinks your dead."

Shit. But I shake that thought away. I'd deal with that information, and all it implies, later.

"You knew me that night I was here with Colin and the Carpenters."

"Yes," he says, nodding. So, I wasn't being paranoid, thinking he was looking at me here the other night.

"So, you know—have known—what I look like." Of course he did, he'd have gotten that information from my ex when I was in California. Shit, I should have changed my looks more; colored my hair, gained a lot of weight, but I hadn't. Hadn't thought I'd needed to.

"Wouldn't have mattered if I knew or not—you're the spitting image of your mother."

That stops me cold, and I have to brace my arm tighter. "My mother?"

"God, you look just like her."

"You knew my mother?"

"*Knew* her? Yeah, I knew her." There's something in his voice that seems off, but before I can press he asks, "So, how'd you find me?"

"A picture on Nick's computer."

His brows rise in surprise. "Nick has a picture of me?"

I get the impression that's not so much that *Nick* has a picture of him, but that there's a picture of him out there anywhere. Of course he'd be careful about having his picture taken. So am I.

I can see him searching his mind, his memory, and then it catches. "Oh yeah, the night Nick and Carrie went to that fancy company dinner of hers."

"They were dressed up in the picture, yes."

He's nodding his head, a small, chagrinned smile crosses his face. "That's it. One photo, on one guy's computer. And here you are." He motions to me in an offhanded way. As if my showing up is just a matter of bad timing for him.

I raise the gun an inch higher, firming my grip. "Yes. Here I am."

He chuckles now. Chuckles! "I guess it's true, no good deed goes unpunished."

"What good deed did you ever do?"

"Not many, that's true. But I did try to throw some business your way when I could."

"What do you mean?" There seems to be a large piece of

this puzzle that I'm missing, but nothing's fitting. I shake my head slightly, as if trying to clear it.

"When I'd hear people talking about selling their computers, or wanting to buy a used one, I'd give them your info. Try to help you out a little bit." There is a southern, Tennessee drawl to his voice, the slow cadence that everyone around here seems to use. I don't know why, but this fact infuriates me.

He's a New Jersey goomba, he shouldn't have the same, easy twang as does Nick and Colin. But then my brain registers what he's saying. "You gave them my contact info? How did you have my contact info?"

"Your ebay account info. You have it on there yourself, looking for sellers."

"Yes, but how could you possibly know that was me?" I'd used an innocuous user name, and if truly hacked, the ebay info would be in my Michigan name. My safe name.

Not so safe after all.

"Who else knows my Michigan name? Where I live?" He shrugs, and I aim the gun with more force. "Who?"

"I have no idea."

"How do *you* know?"

"Does it matter? I'm not going to do anything with it. If I'd meant to hurt you I could have years ago."

That's true. So, was Chazz not the person who hired my ex to kill me? I want to find out more, ask lots of questions, but my window is closing. If I'm going to do this, it has to be now before the workers show up. I can worry about what he may or may not have known after I get out of Tennessee.

My arm straightens, my grip tightens. This is it. Can I take a man's life?

As if sensing my struggle, he says, "Just so you know, it wasn't personal. Your dad. I always liked him."

It doesn't sway me. "And yet you shot him in cold blood." Much like I am about to do.

He continues on, as if I hadn't spoken. "And he sure did love you. You were his sun and moon. Raven this. Raven that."

"Stop," I say quietly, not wanting to hear it. Not wanting to feel the pain of losing him all over again.

He keeps going, "It sure broke my heart to take your daddy away from you. You were such a cute little thing." It's like he has a death wish—maybe he does. Maybe he wants this all to be over as much as I do. Because that's all it takes.

My hand starts to squeeze the trigger when I hear a very calm, very soft voice behind me. "Easy, Raven, you don't want to do this."

Shit. One of the kids got here early and must have been standing behind the door when we came in. But no, they wouldn't know my name.

"It's Will, Raven. Lower the gun so we can talk about this."

How the fuck did Will get in here? How long has he been here?

"I'm stepping to your side, Raven. Don't panic, I'm just coming out so you can see me."

He comes into my periphery, keeps moving and stands next to Uncle Chazz. Uncle Chazz is not surprised to see Will, but then he would have known he was there when he went out to the Dumpster.

Again, I feel like there's a play going on here that I came in on halfway through the third act. My finger eases off the trigger. Will and Uncle Chazz both notice my movement. For all intents and purposes, this is now over. I can't kill someone with a witness standing nearby, and there's no way I'm going to hurt some innocent bystander. Especially Will. I keep the gun pointed at Uncle Chazz, but my dream of avenging my father's death is over.

For now.

Now I have to figure out how to get out of here without going to jail.

"You don't know what's going on here, Will. You don't know who this man is."

"I know exactly what's going on. And I know exactly who

he is."

I look at Will, things falling into place a tiny bit. "Well, then, who the hell are *you*?"

I look at him, his green eyes both warm and hard. I know I should have figured out something wasn't quite "on" with Will, but I'd been so distracted with trying to make sure people didn't realize I wasn't quite "on" either—that Will had seemed like a port in a storm.

He stares at me. I think he's trying to make a decision, but what? Finally he sighs, reaches into his jacket. I brace myself, wondering what he'll pull out. I'm in no mood for more surprises. I don't point the gun at him, I keep it trained on Chazz.

He pulls out a little wallet and flips it open, just like they do in the movies.

"FBI," he says, just like they do in the movies.

"But…I saw you on the Planet Records website."

He raises an eyebrow and I inwardly cringe at my naiveté. Of course the FBI can find a way to put a bogus executive on a company's website.

"And you're here to protect him?" I ask, motioning to Chazz.

"Not entirely."

"Then you're here because of Carrie's murder?"

He shakes his head. "I'm not here because of Carrie," he says.

"What? Why then?"

"I'm here because of you, Raven."

My mind reels with the new development, but I know I still need to get out of here if I can. "You knew I would be coming here, to do this?"

"We had our suspicions. We didn't know for sure that you'd located Chazz. We didn't know about the picture on Nick's machine. That would have made this whole thing make more sense."

"So, I'm being watched?"

"No, not watched. Your case, Chazz's case, it's all part of ongoing monitoring."

"I don't understand."

Will looks at Chazz, who shrugs at him, then turns back to me. "Chazz is under our protection. He's been Johnny Campos for twenty-two years."

"You'd protect a killer?" As soon as it is out of my mouth I feel foolish. Of course the FBI protects killers, I would imagine half of their informants in the witness protection program are criminals. "You'd let my father's killer go free so you could have testimony on a big fish?"

"That's how it works," he confirms my thoughts.

I wave my hand at Chazz. "He kills an innocent man, takes my father away from me, I live with a woman I've never met, in virtual hiding, and he's allowed to…to…" I grasp for words that could sum up the injustice. None come to me. My arm encompasses the back room… "Run a bar in Tennessee?"

Chazz snorts. "Not exactly a dream life for me either. And not exactly an innocent man."

"What?" I say as Will says, "Shut up, Johnny."

"No. What did you say?"

"Keep your mouth shut," Will warns Johnny.

I raise the gun again, though we all know it's a bluff.

"Raven," Will says softly. Not patronizing, but still very softly. "The kind of life Johnny led then—as Chazz—your father was part of that life too. He wasn't just chosen at random. There was a reason they wanted him gone. Surely you've thought about that in all these years."

I had. Of course I had. I was watching some movie once about hit men—*Grosse Pointe Blank* I think—and one of them says something like, "If I show up at your door, you did something to bring me here", and it had stuck with me.

I just didn't want to admit it.

But now I have to. "What all did he do?" I ask in a whisper.

Chazz snorts again. "What didn't he—"

"Shut the fuck up, Johnny," Will says now with force. But Will knows. It would have been before his time, of course, Will would only have been a teenager when this all happened. But he knows.

"It doesn't matter. What matters now is getting you out of here before anybody sees you."

Still stinging, but knowing he's right, I drop the gun. Maybe I can make some kind of deal. I don't have any information they would need, but maybe they'd just let me go if I promised not to tell anybody that Uncle Chazz was alive and well and running a bar in Mount Juliet. Will steps forward and takes the gun from my hand. I stick my hands out for him to cuff, already spinning with what kind of deal I can make. Surely they don't want me in any kind of testifying situation?

Will sticks my gun in the back of his waistband—just like he had this morning at Jennilee's house—and puts his hands on both my shoulders, then shakes me gently until I look him in the eye.

"No cuffs. This is what's going to happen. Are you listening?"

I nod. I don't really care anymore. I didn't avenge my father. I don't even think my father was a man worth avenging.

"You're going to get in your car and drive back to Michigan. You are not ever going to mention to anyone that you were here, that you've seen Johnny, any of it. Do you understand?"

"I'm not..." I don't finish the thought, reluctant to say it out loud.

"We'll be moving Johnny. He's been compromised."

"Aw, fuck," Johnny says from behind Will, but he ignores him, his eyes stay locked with mine, his warm hands burning into my shoulders.

"So, any thoughts you may have about coming back to finish this off? They're done. He'll be gone the minute you're out the door. Do you understand?"

I nod, emotions swirling around me, some trying to take root, but I push them away. They all seem too heavy, too overwhelming.

"You're going to get in your car—I know it's already packed—and you're not going to stop until you get home...to Michigan."

I nod again. His hands slide from my shoulders down my arms. One hand drops away, but his other gently wraps around mine. He brushes past me and then leads me by the hand to the back door. He opens it up, looks outside. I don't know what time it is anymore, but apparently the kitchen helpers are still yet to arrive.

He gently pushes me through the exit, his hand drops from mine, and I have to control the urge to grab for him. He stays inside. I stand outside, alone, the sunlight making me blink several times.

The enormity of my life in front of me swells, like a huge wave about to pour down on me. My father is not what I thought. My ex may think I'm alive. My reason to keep going—to avenge my father—my drive, is now gone.

"I can't do this," I whisper. I'm not sure what I mean exactly, but the compassion in his eyes tells me that Will gets it.

"Yes you can, Raven. You're stronger than you think."

My thoughts echo to myself. It's not the first time I'd heard those words. Where had I heard that recently? It was just the other…

Our eyes meet, and in a flash, I know. I just know. My head starts a shaking movement in disbelief, but my hands reach out, believing. My mouth opens to say something—anything—to make him stay. To not push me away. To tell him I know.

He smiles, but it never reaches his eyes. He gives me a final push away from the door and his fingers slide away, letting it slowly close in front me. His look is pained, and I know what he's about to say before he says it.

"Bye, bye, Blackbird." He is gone before I can respond.

# Twenty-Eight

I do get in my car and drive, but I know I can't head back to Michigan with my thoughts whirling the way they are. Too much to process while behind the wheel. The motel is an option, but I don't want to sit in a room by myself. I need to be in public so there's less chance I'll absolutely lose it.

I pull into the IHOP, am taken to my regular booth, and realize how much has happened in so short a time as the waitress who brought Will and me breakfast this morning is still on duty and has a cup in front of me seconds after I sit down.

"Just coffee, thanks," I say. The events of the day must be on my face, because she gives me a small pat on my shoulder and walks away, saying nothing.

An hour, and two refills, later I still have no answers. I try to arrange my thoughts clearly, without emotion.

Will is Confessor. And, he is an FBI agent.

Uncle Chazz is Johnny Campos. And, he is an FBI informant and protected.

My father was a man who probably deserved to be killed. And, that's just what happened.

And the piece de resistance:

Uncle Chazz said nobody believes I'm dead. And, that may or may not include my ex.

Four years ago, when I had my miscarriage, I awoke in the hospital to my ex crying silent tears. His beautiful face marred by pain. Emotional pain.

I was the one with the physical pain.

He'd not taken the news I was pregnant well. He tried to get me to have an abortion. I wouldn't. He said it was for our own good. That we'd be in danger if we had a baby, easier targets. I didn't understand then.

Two days later I woke up in excruciating pain, bleeding. He didn't seem surprised, just loaded me up and took me to the hospital.

I didn't know how—still don't—he'd done it, but I knew he was responsible.

He held my hand, kissed it. Told me it was for the best.

"We can forget about this, Raven. Get past it."

I pulled my hand free, the plastic hospital bracelet chafing my skin, but it was still better than his touch.

"We'll be fine. You'll be fine. You're stronger than you think," he said.

I started planning my eventual escape that day from my hospital bed.

"You should be miles out of town by now," a voice says, causing my head to jerk up. Will slides into the booth across from me. The waitress puts down a cup, pours it full and tops me off. She gives me a quick wink.

She probably thinks all my problems are solved now that Will is here.

I'm thinking they've only just begun.

"Do you have some kind of tracking device on me? On my car?"

He shakes his head. "No need. I know how you think."

I start to object to this, but really, he's right.

"You don't have to worry. I'll go back like a good little girl. I just couldn't drive right now."

He nods, takes a sip of his coffee, he'd figured that out. "Wait until tomorrow. It'll be dark soon. Might as well drive during the day."

"So someone can have a visual on me?"

He lifts a corner of his mouth in a half-smile. "No need. If you tell me you're going back to Michigan, I believe you."

"And yet, here you are."

He takes another drink of coffee, sets the cup down and puts his elbows on the table, as if bracing himself. "I figured you might have some questions."

A noise—something between a grunt and a snort—escapes me. "Yeah, a few."

"I'll tell you what I can. Some is classified, obviously, but some you have a right to know."

A thousand questions go through me. About my father. About the FBI and my case. About Uncle Chazz. About how closely I'm being "monitored". If the FBI is aware of my ex, and is my ex aware of me?

But what comes out, in almost a croak, is, "So, none of it was real?"

He knows what I mean. Yes, there are a thousand practical things I want to know…but none of that compares to this.

He leans forward, takes my hand in his larger, rougher one. "It was all real, Raven. You, me. Blackbird, Confessor. It's the most real thing in my life."

A small sob comes out, which I quickly try to cover up. I'd chosen IHOP so I wouldn't lose it publicly, but I am just a fraction away from a complete melt-down. Only now, a good kind.

"So there's a chance? There's a way? You know, I don't have to go back to…" I look around, seeing if there's someone who might overhear. We're the only table that's occupied in this section.

"Michigan," he softly finishes my sentence.

"Right," I answer. "I don't have to go back." Now that Uncle Chazz isn't going to happen, do I even need to live in hiding anymore? "Or maybe that's where you are, too?" The thought that he was so close—had been so close—all along might just put me over the edge.

"No, I'm in DC."

"I can do DC. I can do what I do from anywhere." I try to keep the desperation out of my voice, but it would be a charade to act cool about all of this, and he would see right through it.

Right through me.

He leans back, takes his hands from mine, takes a deep breath. An iciness trickles over my spine. This is not going to be what I want to hear.

"It's more complicated than that, Raven."

My desperation turns to bargaining. "It doesn't have to be, Will. There's always going to be baggage in every relationship."

His sigh is heavy, he rubs his hand through his sandy hair. "Baggage? You think we just have a little baggage to deal with?"

I lean forward, my hands reach across the table, but I can't reach him, he's pulled too far away. I know I should have some measure of pride about this. But I don't. I can't. "Will," I say softly, "please."

He looks at me, his green eyes filled with emotion, but I can't discern what. "There's a hundred reasons why we can't be together. Why we can never be more than we are."

It's not going to happen. I have wanted this man for four years, I am literally inches away from him, and it's not going to happen.

It all boils over. The desperation and bargaining turns to controlled fury. "That's bullshit," I say, the venom in my voice shocking even myself.

"What?" he asks, confused.

"That there's a hundred reasons we can't be together."

"Raven, there's—" he holds his finger up like he's going to start listing them off, but I shoot up a hand stopping him.

"Those are all bullshit. Things that can be worked around. Location. Jobs. You being involved in my case. You can make them important, but they don't have to be."

He opens his mouth to speak, but I press my hand up higher, stopping him again. "No. Those are *obstacles*, and I'm not making light of them, but they *can* be figured out if two people really wanted to be together." I take a deep breath, knowing how much what I'm going to say next will hurt me, but I have to say it. "There's really only two reasons we can't be together. One, you want to be with someone else." I pause here, but not for too long. Will says nothing. "Or two, you just don't want to be with me."

I drop my hand to the table, like it was a great physical toll getting those words out.

I give him a second, but he says nothing. Finally, I reach for my bag and slide out of the booth. I stand at the edge of the table. He's still staring across from him, as if I was still there. "One or two, Will?" Still no answer. "Although I guess it doesn't really matter. I still lose. Maybe it's better I don't know which one it is."

I walk out of the restaurant, slowly, so that I could be caught if chased. I'm not.

My hands don't shake on the steering wheel as I drive to the motel. Tears don't slide down my cheeks. I grab my laptop case and suitcase from the trunk and bring them in my room. I don't take the laptop out. What would be the point?

I sit on the edge of the bed once again numb, just as I was only hours ago when I'd come back after seeing Jennilee's body.

I know I'm probably being melodramatic, but this feels like a bigger death to me.

I'm still sitting there a half hour later when someone knocks on my door. My eyes search for my gun thinking it's Uncle Chazz, but I realize Will still has my gun. Could it be Colin? But no, I never told him where I was staying, although my car is parked outside my door. He could have trolled by the area motels and seen it. It's six thirty on Saturday night, Colin's probably on his way to the Hopeless Heart.

I walk to the door, stand to the side of it and lean over to the peephole, not putting my body in front of the door. My breath catches, my hand reaches out to the knob, then pauses. I rub my hand on my jeans, as if opening this door is so important I can't afford to have my hand slip.

It is that important.

I move in front of the door as I open it.

He stands there for only a second and then his hands come up to my face, cradling it as his body aligns with mine and he walks me backward until we hit the wall across from the door. I hear the door shut behind him.

"Or reason number three," Will starts and then seems to lose his train of thought as he kisses me.

He tastes like coffee and I drink him in like he's my first cup of the morning. His hands feel rough on my face and yet his touch is tender. His tongue swirls into my mouth and I groan and wrap my arms around his waist pulling him even closer.

He pulls away, rests his forehead against mine. "Or reason number three," he repeats, his breathing as labored as mine. He steps back a tiny bit, not enough that I lose my hold on him, but enough that he can watch me. His hands are still on my face, along my jaw, his thumb brushes across my lips. "Reason Three. That I can't think about anything else but you. That I worry about you day and night. That your picture is lying on my desk where most people keep framed photos of their wives. And I like it that way."

I start to speak, but his thumb presses down on my mouth. "That I know I'm not doing you any favors by hanging on to you. That you could have a fulfilling relationship if I stayed away from you online. And I could still easily do my job of monitoring your situation. Probably do a better job of it. And yet I don't. I don't let you go. Every relationship I try to have is doomed because you're the only person I want to be with."

Tears are streaming down my face now and they cascade over Will's hands. He takes a hand away and licks my tears off his finger. "Reason Three; Being with you is against every code I stand for. It puts you in danger. It puts me in danger. It puts an entire FBI case and it's periphery agents in danger. And yet I'm here." He pauses, looks me in the eyes and says, " I'm here because I said Fuck You to Reason Three. And because I love you, Raven Moldano."

# *Twenty-Nine*

I open my mouth to say the words back to him, but he kisses me again, silencing me. And then all coherent thought rushes from my mind as his mouth moves down and he kisses my neck. I tilt my head to the side and feel his warm, soft mouth, the desperation of his earlier kiss gone, replaced by patient, relaxed, I'm-taking-my-sweet-time luxury.

A hum of delight escapes my lips and I feel his smile against my skin, then the flick of his tongue. My hands run up his chest and push his jacket off of him. My thumb snags on what I realize is a gun holster.

The truth of who he is—who *we* are, and what all has transpired today—comes rushing back. He must feel my body tense, because he quickly gets rid of the gun and holster, hearing them softly thunk on the floor as he sets them down. His hands are back on mine where they'd stilled on his chest.

"It's okay," he whispers against my ear, then gently nips it with his teeth. "None of it matters. It's just you and me now. Just us."

The words—or maybe his warm breath against my skin—make me forget about his gun sitting on my motel room floor. As if to further distance ourselves from that reality, Will steps away from me just enough to pull me from the wall and points my back in the direction of the room, walking me backward away from the hallway, his hands firmly holding my waist.

I can't see where I'm going; it's like a mini version of the Trust Game, letting Will guide me.

And yes, I know because of the secrecy and the "oh, by the way I'm an FBI agent" thing that my trust in Will should be diminished, but it's not.

I trust him with my life.

I have to, but I also want to.

The back of my legs hit the end of the bed and I tumble backward, taking Will with me. He braces himself with his arms, not allowing his full weight to come down on me. But I need it; his weight. His body completely covering mine. The feeling of safety. It's what I've craved for the last four years.

No, what I've craved since I was five years old.

My hands, still on his chest, circle around to his back to try and pull him closer when I feel something cold, metallic. Another gun—this one mine that he'd taken from me at the Hopeless Heart—tucked into the waistband of his jeans.

"Are you fucking kidding me?" I lament. Can't we be two normal human beings who just want to tear each other's clothes off? Do firearms—plural!—really have to be involved?

"No problem. One sec." He hops off the bed, away from me, and I make a little pouting sound, which he chuckles at as he takes my gun from the small of his back and places it on the table on the other wall.

He's standing at the foot of the bed, looking down at me, a dangerous smile on his face. "Sit up for a second," he says and I do. He starts pulling the comforter off of the bed, me scooching it from the top, then lifting myself up as he pulls it completely off from the bottom. "I hate those things," he says as he tosses it to the floor. "Same with this," he says as he pulls the pilled-up cotton blanket away and discards that too, so that I'm sitting on the top sheet of the bed. "I always imagined you against plain, white, cotton. Your olive skin contrasting, your black hair…" He doesn't finish. I bite my lower lip at the intensity of his gaze. He whips his tee-shirt over his head and discards it on top of the comforter, but he stays where he is, just looking at me.

"No fair," I whisper, my throat rough with emotion. "You knew what I looked like. It was hard to fantasize about you."

"But you did?"

I don't know if it's a question or a statement, but I truthfully answer, "Yes."

"When?" he asks.

"All the time."

"When you were in bed?" His hands go to the fly of his jeans.

"Yes," I answer.

"Take off your shirt," he says, his voice strong and controlled while I feel anything but. I grab the cotton shirt around my waist with both hands and quickly yank it off, not wanting my eyes covered for long, not willing to lose sight of Will.

"And your jeans," he says while unzipping and sliding his down his legs. He's a boxers man, which, I don't know, just seems to fit him. They're a comfortable blue and green plaid. Should be nothing to write home about, but as he sticks his hand in and stokes himself as he looks at me, I swear they're the hottest piece of undergarment I've ever seen.

I undo my button and zipper and shimmy my jeans over my hips and butt, lifting and twisting on the mattress. When they clear my thighs, Will leans forward and grabs each leg of denim by the inside, brushing his hands across my foot as he does, and yanks the jeans from my legs. The motion knocks me off balance and I fall back, resting my elbows on the bed behind me.

"Jesus, look at you. So much better than I could ever imagine," he says and then he's on the bed, crawling up my body, staying on all fours above me. Planting soft kisses and wet licks along my body as he moves. Finally he reaches my mouth and he bends his head down and kisses me. A nice, deep, want-to-gobble-you-up kiss, but it's not enough. I need to feel him—all of him—on top of me.

I put my hands on his forearms and push at the elbow, trying to make him lower onto me. He takes the hint and slowly lowers his body onto mine. I open my legs for him, giving him space, then sling my calves over the back of his, my feet resting on his legs. The soft, worn cotton of his boxers tickles my inner thighs.

He smells like IHOP and the thought runs through my head that I'll never have a pancake again without thinking of this moment…this man.

As he gets rid of my bra and laves attention on my breasts, my hands play along his body, learning him, trying to commit him to memory. I don't know where this is leading, if we have any kind of chance for anything beyond this motel room. I want every detail I can for fantasizing later on. It may be all I have in the future.

As if he can sense me thinking beyond this moment, he gently bites down on my nipple pulling me back to him.

"God, that feels good," I moan, arching my back to him.

He mumbles some reply, but continues on. My hands run down the hard plane of his back and slide under his boxers, gripping his ass. He groans and then pulls away from me. In a flash he has his boxers and my panties off and thrown across the room. Then he's back, on top of me and it feels even better without the, lovely though they were, boxers.

"Will," I whisper. "I need this. I need…you."

"Tell me what you like," he whispers. Then he holds my face in his hands, like he did when he told me he loves me. But this time, his mouth widens into a shit-eating grin when he adds, "Confess."

I start to laugh, but it comes out as more of a garbled sob and I can feel tears start again.

"No, Blackbird, don't cry. Oh, don't cry, Raven."

He kisses my tears away and I manage to croak out, "It's good tears. It's…good."

He looks at me. "It is good. I knew it would be. And it's going to be so much better."

Yeah, it could have been a corny line, but Will doesn't do

corny. Neither does Confessor.

"Is it weird for you?" I ask, "Do you think of me as Raven or Blackbird in your head?"

He could have looked at me like I'm crazy, but he gets it. Of course he gets it.

"You forget, I know the name you live under in Michigan. Don't you think that's how I'd think of you? As—" I put my hand over his lips, not wanting that name spoken outloud.

"Shhh," I whisper. "There's no place for her here. She's not part of this."

He nods. "That's not what I call you in my head, anyway. Never has been. It's always been Raven." He scrubs a hand through his hair, then places it back on my cheek. "God, how many times did I almost type 'Raven' when we were IMing."

"I wish I'd known your name then."

"Nah, no mystery in that. Plain old Will. You'd have gotten sick of me early on."

I take my hands from his shoulders and cradle his face the way he is cradling mine. "Not a chance," I whisper then raise my head to kiss him.

Discussion time over—thank God, can't believe I went off on that tangent with this man inches away from being inside me—I slide my hand down his stomach, through the patch of bristly hair, and wrap my fingers around him.

"Christ, that feels so good, Raven," he says on a moan, his neck arching back. I lift my head and suck a pulsing vein.

Then I put my head back down and look him in the eye. "Yeah? If that feels good, then you'll really like this," I say as I guide him to me, tilt my hips up for him and let nature take its course.

If feels like coming home. If feels like being a woman. It makes me feel whole. Yeah, all those hokey things and more. But really? No bullshit? It just feel incredibly…right.

"God, that feels so right," he says and my tears start to flow again with the sweetness of our connection.

He seems to give up on trying to stop my tears and finds his rythmn. "You don't know how long I've dreamt about this."

"Yes, I do," I say. "As long as I have, you just had a visual for your dream."

He smiles, which turns into a griMace as he lenghtens his strokes. "Yeah. Four years is a long time for foreplay."

I nod, but Will moves again, his pace quickeing, and the breath is stolen from me before I can respond.

It doesn't matter, the time for talking, even sex talk, is over.

"So, now, for all those questions you thought I'd want to ask when you came to the IHOP," I say later. Much later.

He chuckles. "That's your idea of afterglow?"

I rub my hand down his chest, nuzzle into his neck. His arms are tight around me, we're tangled up in the sheets and I've never felt so safe in my life.

"Shoot," he says and squeezes me to him. "I'll tell you what I can."

"First of all, are you really going to move Uncle Chazz? He's been here twenty-two years."

"We wouldn't want to, but we have no choice."

"Because of me?"

He nods, his chin touching the top of my head as he does. "He's been compromised, yes."

I arch my neck back so I can see his face. "What if I said I wouldn't tell anyone about him and I wouldn't try to…"

"Kill him?"

I wave a hand nonchalantly. "Whatever."

He grasps my hand, brings it to his mouth and kisses it, then starts to suck on each finger.

"Where was I?" I say, my concentration shot.

"You won't to try k—"

"*Contact* him again," I clarify.

He mimics my hand wave. "Whatever."

"Would you be able to leave him here?"

"On just your word?" I nod. He shrugs. "Yeah, I think I would leave him here. The brass wouldn't like it, but I think I could make the case that it would be more detrimental—and expensive—to move him now."

"Really? You'd do that on just my word?"

He looks at me, stares at me for a moment. "You won't tell anyone about him?"

I lift a shoulder, in a half shrug. "Who would I tell?"

"And you'll leave him alone?" I nod. "Then yeah, I'd make the case based on your word."

He told me he loved me when he came here, and yet these words mean almost as much to me.

Almost.

"Raven, I don't think you would have gone through with it, even if I hadn't been there. I don't think you have it in you to gun down an unarmed man."

Maybe. We'll never know.

"Besides," I add, "It doesn't sound like my father was a man worth avenging." I feel his arms tense around me. "Tell me," I softly say.

He waits a few moments, probably weighing what all to tell me. "Were we straight out of 'The Sopranos'?" I say, trying to help him out.

He lets out a long sigh. "Sort of. Things were different back then, from what some of the older agents have told me."

"But my father…he hurt people?"

"That's what the files, and the older agents, say. Apparently he knew too much, or hurt the wrong person and Chazz was sent in to clean it up."

"And then you—well, not *you*—got Uncle Chazz and turned him?"

Will chuckles. "'Turned him'? Yeah, but not then. It was about a year later, they got Chazz on something else and he entered the Program in exchange for his testimony. They never could make the case against him for your father's murder."

"But I was a witness."

"Apparently they couldn't risk the testimony of a five-year-old. Plus, the agent that had custody…"

"My…aunt."

"Right. She got really attached to you pretty quickly and she fought for leaving you out of it. Then they got Chazz on something else and you weren't needed. It was about the time "your aunt" was thinking about retirement, so she left early and, well…you know the rest."

"Was my aunt's car accident really an accident?"

His body stills. "We don't know," he says firmly. "We can't be sure either way."

"And my ex? Do you—or the FBI—know all about him?"

He takes his arm from around me, slides out of bed. I admire the view as he steps over to where his clothes were strewn in our haste. He pulls on his jeans, but doesn't do them up. He walks over to the table and chairs area, pulls out a chair so it faces the bed. He sits down, leans forward, resting his bare forearms on his thighs.

My gun sits on the table, where he placed it in our frenzy to get our clothes off.

I pull up the sheet, covering myself more fully, feeling like I need armor for what I'm about to hear.

"There's a man named Carlo Esposito. Ever hear of him?" I shake my head no, and Will continues. "I didn't think so. You shouldn't have if we were doing our job right, and your aunt kept quiet about it. Anyway, he was, back then, an up and coming figure in the Jersey Syndicate. We believe he's the one who ordered the hit on your father. He's the one Chazz turned on, but for something else. We never had enough to get Chazz on the hook—and then turn on Esposito—for your father's hit."

I wince at the term "hit" when used about my father, and Will starts to lean back as if he wants to spare me this. I wave for him to go on. He pauses, studies me, but then continues.

"So, a couple of years later we turn Chazz, not for murder, but Carlo goes to jail. Case closed. And then, eleven years later he gets out of prison and wants to resume his climb to the top, but he knows he has two loose ends out there, Chazz…"

"And me," I whisper. So, I was never in danger from Chazz at all. It wasn't him who'd hired my ex, but this Esposito guy. I do the math, I'd had just left home to go to California around then. "Did using my real name in California tip him off?"

Will shakes his head. "No, but that probably wasn't a smart move."

"Then how?"

Will drops his head slightly, but then looks me in the eye. "There was a breach on our end."

"Who? Not my aunt?" She was unhappy with my decision to leave Michigan but I can't imagine…

Will shakes his head. "No. No. She loved you, Raven, like you were her own. No, this was…well…let me back up."

He gets up from the chair now, starts pacing. I watch the smooth, strong lines of his back, and then when he turns I admire his chest and shoulders, follow with my eyes the line of hair from his chest down his belly to the open fly of his jeans. I'm half tempted to say forget it, come back to bed, but these are things I've wanted to know since I was five, so I let him pace.

"This was about the time I joined the department. I wasn't put on your case then, someone else from my class at Langley—a friend of mine actually—became one of the junior agents involved. It was considered pretty low priority, a monitoring thing. The agent in charge would be retiring in a year or so, and they were transitioning things over.

"Each case like this, with lots of pieces, but not hot, has a senior agent, a junior agent and a field agent involved, though it's not their only cases."

I nod, but he doesn't see me, he's still pacing. "Well… anyway…we don't know all the details…but we think…"

This is unlike him. "Just say it, Will." I try to lighten the moment. "Confess."

He looks up at me, stops pacing, comes to the side of the bed and sits down next to me. I take his hand in mine, he squeezes mine, and I hang on.

"It appears that when Esposito got out of jail, at some point he contacted our agent, or our agent contacted him—we still don't know—and sold him the information on where you were in California at the time. He didn't have access to Chazz's information yet, or we're sure he would have sold that, too. And he never saw the information on your Michigan safe house, thank God."

"Oh," is all I can say. What can I say? The FBI probably saved my life by placing me with my aunt, can I really hold them responsible for an agent who sold me out? Part of me does. But the other part of me knows that this all starts with my father and the kind of man he was. Which I still haven't fully come to terms with, so I choose to focus on something else. "But you caught this agent? Right?"

He lifts my hand, turns it and softly kisses my palm, while he shakes his head no.

"What happened to him?" I ask, but just as surely as I knew that Will was Confessor as the door of the Hopeless Heart closed on me, I know what he's going to say next.

"You married him."

# Thirty-One

**I** come out of the bathroom after my shower and Will is dressed, sitting at the chair, his elbows on the table, talking on his cell phone. When he sees me he signs off with whomever he's talking to and hangs up.

"You okay?" he gently asks as he rises from the chair.

I nod and make my way back to the bed. Will has straightened it up, the blankets that had been thrown to the floor, neatly back in place. I perch myself, wrapped in my towel, knotted over my boobs, on the edge of the bed.

When I realized that I'd married a rogue FBI agent who'd hired himself out to a mafia boss to kill me I ran to the bathroom and puked. When everything I'd eaten in the last two days was gone, purged, I felt the need to be clean and had brushed my teeth twice and taken a very long, very hot shower.

It wasn't Will's touch, scent, that I wanted to wash off, but I knew he'd be out here waiting, and I could come to him without the grime of all I'd just learned.

It's still with me, but hearing the concern in his voice, seeing the heat in his eyes as he watches the knot of my towel…it helps.

"Everything okay?" I ask, nodding at the cell phone he's still holding.

He nods, but fingers the phone. "I need to go to The Hopeless Heart. The River Rats will be playing," he looks at his watch, "Are playing. And I want to talk to them afterward and let them know what's going on."

"What do you mean? Detective Mosley pretty much did that already earlier. Surely he told them about Jennilee killing herself?"

He gestures to his phone. "That was him. Yeah, he told Nick about Jennilee. I meant I want to talk to them about me. Let them know I'm not really from Planet Records."

Right. A thought occurs to me. "Is your name even Will Fredrickson?"

He gives me a sheepish grin. "Will is right."

"Do I get to know your last name, or will you have to kill me if you tell me?"

He leans over, kisses me, his lips still in a smile, which I have on my mouth when we break apart. "All in good time," he says, then he stands up, walks to the chair where his jacket is and pulls it on, he rests his hands on the back of the chair that is still pulled out from when he told me about my ex. "I want to give those guys the courtesy of telling them myself that the Planet thing was a cover."

"Oh God, that's going to kill Colin," I say, feeling badly for him. He thinks his dream is within reach.

Will doesn't move, he stands very still. "About you and Colin…"

"How should I end it?" I ask. "I mean, it was never anything for sure, he knows I'd plan to leave on Monday, but still, I'd like to say something to him in person, but…"

"You can't go back to The Hopeless Heart."

"No, I suppose not."

"I can set something up for you to see him tomorrow if you want."

"Then he'll think you're involved."

"Aren't I?"

"Yes, but he doesn't need to know that. He can just think he and I didn't click enough to stay in touch after I go back home to Vermont."

Will gives a small snort.

"Really? You're going to get on me about Vermont, Mister Planet Records?"

"But I'm an officer of the law in deep undercover."

"I'm a single woman meeting a guy she met on the internet, we have our own code of security."

"Point taken."

"I'll IM him tonight and see if he wants to meet for breakfast. I'll tell him then that we can stay in touch, but I don't see much future for us with me back in Vermont."

"*Much* of a future?"

"Any future," I say more clearly.

"Because of Vermont? Because he'll probably say he's willing to travel to you."

"Sheesh, you're not helping."

"I'm just trying to think like Colin. He seems like he really likes you, he'll try to head off your excuses."

He's right. I don't really want to hurt Colin, but maybe it would be best if he thought there was no way anything could happen between us. Cold turkey. I shrug. "I could lie and say that I thought it would be a lark, and I really enjoyed chatting on line with him, but couldn't go through with it once I met him because I'm really married."

"You *are* really married," he says with a bit of bite in his voice.

Oh holy shit, he's right, I am married. Technically.

"Technically," he says.

"When we were talking about him before? You didn't say if he thinks I'm dead."

I see Will's hands tighten on the back of the chair, his knuckles turning white, but his face belies any emotion. I'll bet he's great undercover.

"We don't know if he bought it or not. We—well not me, I still didn't have your case yet—went in afterward and cleaned up your efforts, made it more authentic, got the local authorities to sign off on your "death". It was a pretty amateurish effort."

I take offense to that. "I *was* an amateur."

He continues without acknowledging my comment, "He went underground right after. Totally off the grid. We have no way of knowing if he bought it or not."

"Oh," is all I can say.

"Since then, Carlo Esposito has been killed, so, technically there's no reason for him to come after you even if he did think you're alive."

I just look at Will for a long time then say, "How well did you know him when you were at Langley together?"

"Pretty well, we were roommates. But, I guess not so well after all."

"Do you think he won't come after me if he thinks there's a chance I'm alive?" It's not really a question, if he knows my ex as well as he thinks, he knows the answer as well as I do.

"No," he says, then looks away, as if he can't meet my eyes.

"No," I say, defeat in my voice. Uncle Chazz may be off the table, but Raven Moldano must remain dead and buried, and I will most likely be placed back in my nest.

"About Colin," he says, changing the subject. "I don't care how you do it. But I'd like to get on the road by mid-day tomorrow."

"On the road?"

"I'm going to ride with you back to Michigan,"

"And then what?"

"We have a nine-hour drive to talk about it."

"But..." a panic starts to rise in me. Is this it? One day with Will and then it's over?

He raises a hand from the back of the chair, as if to stop my thought process. "To figure out the logistics of us. How to make it work."

"Oh. Okay." I smile at him and he just looks at me for a moment, then shakes his head, but he's smiling now, too. It's going to work, and we both know it.

He picks up his holstered gun from the floor, but does not

put it on. He wraps the strap around the gun and holster, and hangs on to it. I assume he'll stow it in his car while he breaks the news to Colin and Nick.

At last, it seems there's no more need for guns. Amazing that all of this went down without any shots going off at all.

He pushes the chair in, under the table, and comes over and kisses me on the forehead. As he pulls away, I grab onto the front of his leather jacket. "That Billie Holiday CD in your car?"

"Yeah," he says, knowing I now know that he knows who it reminds me of.

"That CD *does not* come in my car."

He chuckles, kisses me on the lips, tousles my hair. "Consider it tossed," he says then leaves the room.

**A** few minutes after he leaves I throw some clothes on and go out to my car and grab my tote bag and the bag with all the stuff that I'd printed out from Nick's machine that I brought along with me. No need to hang on to it all now. I can toss most of it here, lighten up my load.

I also bring the gun out and put it back in my glove box. I don't want it in the room with me.

I don't need it anymore.

I wonder if any questions can be raised by a cleaning lady finding lots of printouts about Carrie's disappearance and murder, but I can't figure out how that could be a problem. At most, they might go to the police, but all was square with them. Obviously Will had been running a little interference for me with Detective Mosley or I'd probably still be at a police station answering questions as to how I came to be so involved in all of this.

The case is closed.

I almost empty the bag directly into the trash can but stop. I know I printed out the logs of all my chats with Colin. Maybe something in there will trigger a thought on how to end this thing with him in a better way.

I don't know how, but maybe he said something once about

never being able to date someone that wears purple nail polish and I could show up tomorrow wearing purple nail polish. Yeah, I know, it's a stretch, and I doubt there'll be anything that easy in the logs, but I've got some time to kill before Will gets back and I don't want to just sit here and think about how much shit has happened in the last twenty-four hours.

Although, the last two hours were pretty damn good.

I toss a lot of stuff out: The print outs of the folders on Nick's machine, a list of all the pictures from different folders. Then I take the logs and settle on the bed, putting the pillows behind my back as I sit against the headboard.

I can smell Will on one of the pillows and I breathe deeply as I shuffle the logs and put them in order by date of the chat.

A smile is on my face as I read through them. I really like Colin. We have so much in common; our love of old movies, the fact we were both orphaned young, we are the same age so our cultural references are the same. There is a strong connection between us.

But it was never the connection I had with Confessor.

That I have with Will.

I wish there was a way to keep Colin as a friend—a chat buddy. I have no idea what the future holds for me in terms of living. Will I still be in Michigan? Will I still need to be in hiding?

If I do, and Will comes in and out of my life as his job allows, I'll want all my chat buddies to keep me company.

Then I remember I irrevocably lost Gammon_89 today, and the intensity of Will's lovemaking, the sweetness of Colin's conversations are lost and I am awash in sadness for Carrie and Jennilee and how horribly wrong it all went.

I push the logs away, wanting to curl up in the sheets and be reminded of only Will and myself. As one of the sheets of paper flits off the edge of the bed, something catches my eye, and I reach for it, picking it up off the floor just as it lands.

It is one line from Colin's chatting software. Something clicks in my head, and I grab my laptop and boot it up. Once up

I call up all the bookmarks I'd made about Carrie's case from the Nashville newspaper's website. I double check the dates and then the date on the chat log.

It doesn't make sense.

Is there a weird time and date stamp thing with Colin's Ims? Like it's incorrect? Or off by a day?

I log in to the chat software as PatsyKlein. There's a message from Colin; "Are you out there? I can't believe what you and Will did for Nick! Call me when you get this. Or, if not, please come by the HH tonight. Miss you."

I look carefully at the date and time he sent it. It was sent at four-thirty this afternoon. Right about the time I was stripping off Will's clothes.

The date is correct. So, if I printed this log out, like I did the others, it would be correct. So, I can assume the one laying beside me is correct.

I grab my tote bag and turn it upside down on the bed, then search through the mess looking for Will's business card. The bogus Planet Records card. What did I do with it after I called him on Friday to go on the stakeout of Jennilee with me?

I can't find the card anywhere. I tear the room apart, throwing things in the trash that I won't need. I go out to the car and look around there. Nothing.

I know I can just wait until Will gets back, but somehow this seems important to me, like it's something he should know now. It's probably not, probably nothing at all, but the feeling grows and I know I'll go crazy sitting her for a few more hours.

I know Will doesn't want me showing up at the Hopeless Heart because of Uncle Chazz, but I won't go anywhere near him. Just find Will, and show him the log.

If I can talk to Colin, let him know I'm leaving for—Vermont—tomorrow and that I don't think there's a future for us...well, then, that just leaves one less thing to do tomorrow. Will and I can sleep in.

I smile at the thought of waking up in Will's arms, then I

grab a jacket, my purse and car keys and leave for the Hopeless Heart.

# Thirty-Two

My hands are loose on the steering wheel as I drive to the Hopeless Heart. I have the chat log print out on the seat next to me. It reminds me of driving to the bank just a few weeks ago with the print out of Uncle Chazz on the passenger seat.

I think about what the print out could mean—if it even means anything—but I come back to one thing: Colin might be involved in this somehow. And I mean beyond giving Nick a fake alibi.

Did Nick do it like I'd suspected all along? Then went to Colin for help, and they concocted their alibi? That makes the most sense to me.

And fits with the  Colin I've gotten to know wanting to help out his best friend.

I enter the bar and my eyes go directly to the stage. Nick is singing one of the band's original songs. Colin sees me right away, as if he'd been waiting for me to arrive.

He had been, of course. Or was hoping I'd see his IM and come by.

He flashes me his aww-shucks smile. I raise my hand half-heartedly in greeting. Some emotion—concern? - fills his eyes, but it's time for the guitar solo, so he returns his attention to his playing.

I see a flash out of the corner of my eye to the right side of the room. It's Tricia, waving for me to join her at her table. The

Carpenters are there, so is Nick's lawyer. And Will.

The table seems to be in celebration mode and I feel sick to my stomach thinking of Jennilee. But, to the Carpenters, their son had a near miss at the hands of an unstable young woman, and was now in the clear.

Reason to celebrate, I guess. I know how they feel. I am sick about Jennilee too—I keep seeing her body—and yet the day has turned out to be a good one for me. Even weighing in the fact that I found out more about my father than I wanted to know.

Will has his back to me, but turns around when Tricia waves. Like a shot he is out of his chair and headed toward the front door where I'm still standing. As he moves to me his eyes search out the bar area and then beyond, to the doors that lead to the kitchen and Chazz's office, which are to my left.

I look over to the other side, but see no sign of Chazz either behind the bar or near the doors. When I look back, Will is on me, grabbing my upper arm, pulling me into his side, blocking me from the direction of the kitchen and office.

"What the hell are you doing here?"

"I need to talk to you."

"You couldn't have called?"

"I couldn't find your card."

He takes another look around—still no sign of Chazz—and herds me back out the front door. He then does a visual sweep of the parking lot. There's no one around, but when Will speaks it is soft and low, though his tone is not. "Jesus, Raven, this is not a good idea. I have to make a case for keeping Johnny here and you show up only hours after I have to stop you from…" He looks around the parking lot before he finishes, but I cut him off.

"This has nothing to do with that. With him."

"What then? What couldn't wait until I came back to you?"

I take a tiny moment to bask in how good that sounds "came back to you", and then I answer. "There's something weird about a chat Colin and I had."

"You came here now to talk to me about you and Colin? I

thought we settled that." He takes a step away from me, drops my arm. "Or is there more to it? Are you having second thoughts about leaving him? Second thoughts about me?"

Men. Such idiots sometimes.

"No. No. Of course not."

His shoulders sag—with relief?—and he takes a step back toward me. "Okay. Sorry. Let's just back up. Tell me what you came here for."

"Remember when I found the emails Carrie and barabino wrote to each other?"

"Yes?"

A thought comes to me…between Will and Confessor—who I told different things to—what all does Will know to be true? "Barabino is Jennilee by the way. *Was* Jennilee."

He nods. "I figured it was something like that. I knew it had to be more than just finding out Carrie and Jennilee were sorority sisters that had you calling me to stake out Jennilee."

There would be time enough later to explain how I figured that all out. It really didn't matter anymore with Jennilee dead.

"Well, anyway, I had the idea to look for those emails because I inadvertently opened up a chat software and I was automatically logged in as Carrie." I get a blank look from Will. "It made me think maybe there was some software on Nick's machine that only she used and would automatically be logged in for her. Like her FaceBook page or like that."

"Okay…yeah, I remember you telling me that at the time."

"And it was. Her webmail was book marked in Safari, in fact all her stuff was. I think she used Safari on Nick's machine and he used Firefox. The bookmarks on them are totally different."

"And?" He looks around the parking lot again, but there is still nobody else but us.

"So that day, when I opened up the chat software and came up as Carrie, Colin was online."

"Yeah?" He is motioning for me to hurry up. I can tell he's getting nervous about us being out here in the open.

"And he said—or typed—'who are you'."

"And what did you answer?"

I shake my head. "I quit out of it right away, but you're not getting it. I didn't get it at the time, but I wouldn't have then."

"You're right, I'm not getting it." He looks around again, but, bless him, there is no impatience in his voice, no patronization. This man knows me better than anyone on earth, and he wants to know what pieces I put together.

If I hadn't loved him before—and let's face it, of course I did, had for years—I would now.

"This chat was Thursday night."

"I got here Wednesday. Met with the band Wednesday night," Will says, I can see him turning the information over in his head, the cogs still not quite fitting. Hey, I had this information all along and they *just* fit for me.

"Carrie's body wasn't discovered until Friday morning."

"And this chat was Thursday night?" There is a lilt, a question at the end of his statement. Not questioning the night of the chat, questioning what it meant.

"Right. So, Carrie is still AWOL on Thursday night. Colin is online, has his chat software up, and Carrie lights up as being online. What should he say to her?"

He has it now. I didn't even finish that sentence before he had it. But he plays along anyway. "*Where* are you?"

"Right, but he says, '*who* are you'."

"Because he knows it couldn't possibly be Carrie online."

"And why is that? A day before her body is discovered."

He opens his mouth to answer my question, but really there's no need. And no opportunity. The door to the bar swings open and Will, lithe and sure, steps in front of me, guarding me from anyone who might be at the door.

It is Colin and I realize that the loud music had stopped. The band must be on break. He looks from me to Will and back to me. There is suspicion in his voice, but not the kind that there should be. No, he thinks he's losing his could-be girlfriend. And what's worse, he's losing her to a man he has to be nice to.

"Hey guys, what's going on?" he asks, trying for nonchalance. He doesn't quite pull it off.

"Colin," I say, and then Will moves his hand behind him to my stomach. Warning me? Giving me strength? "We need to talk."

Colin's shoulders slump a bit at the universal break-up prologue, but that wasn't what I'd meant. "Oh, okay," is all he says.

I'm about to say, "no, it's not that", but I let it lie. It would be *that* soon enough.

"Are you guys on break?" Will asks, still blocking my body from Colin—and anyone else who might hurt me, I suppose. At Colin's nod, Will continues, "I need to talk to you and Nick. Let's do that first."

I put my hand on top of Will's that's still resting on my tummy. He flips his hand and squeezes mine. Again, a warning, a signal or just reassurance?

Confessor knows everything about me—but I don't know everything about him. Although it looks like I'm going to get the chance to do just that.

Colin turns and opens the door. "Let me go get Nick,"

But Will stops him. "No, let's do this in Johnny's office. More privacy."

And no escape route.

Colin nods and goes inside, Will moving to follow him, until Colin is in the building then Will turns to me. "You need to go back to the hotel and stay there."

"No way, I want to hear Colin's explanation."

"Explanation for what, exactly?"

"Why he asked who are you instead of where are you."

"And how do up propose I bring that up. Even after I tell them I'm FBI?"

"What do you mean?"

"That chat log. You logging in. If the chat is explained he's going to wonder how we could possibly know about that. And if they're really smart—and they are—they're finally going to put it together with Nick's sold machine. All Nick would have to do is check his shipping receipt and have your Michigan name, address, everything."

"Oh." So much had happened this week—hell, today—that I'd let that piece of the puzzle slide out of place.

"Exactly. The whole point of this was so you wouldn't have to come forward as the owner of Nick's machine. So that you wouldn't be—your safe house wouldn't be—exposed.

I've thought of my house as my safe place, my haven, for years, but to hear it called a "safe house" in that way, from an FBI agent who used terms like "safe house" and "exposed" with cold efficiency, seems surreal. No, not surreal, just...*too* real.

"Suppose I do bring it up? What do you think his explanation would be?"

I try to think like a liar—it doesn't take much of a stretch. I shrug. "That it was a typo? Or that he knew Carrie hadn't taken her laptop with her so how could it be her? Or that she hadn't gone online the whole time she'd been gone, so it was a likely leap to assume it wasn't her chatting?"

"Yeah, there could be, *there are*, lots of explanation for it. Simple, innocent ones."

"Do you think it's simple? Innocent?"

"What do you think it means?"

I love that he asks my opinion before he gives his own. "I think Nick killed Carrie—probably accidentally—panicked and went to Colin who gave him an alibi."

Will is nodding his head, as if he agrees. "And how does Jennilee fit into that scenario?"

"I'm not sure. We know she sent the emails—or at least knew where they were coming from. Maybe she was helping Carrie out, getting people to notice she was gone so Nick would have to do something?"

"Yeah, that actually makes a twisted sense. But why kill

herself if Nick is the one who killed Carrie?"

I shake my head. "I don't know. Maybe she felt responsible because she'd helped Carrie bait Nick? Maybe she somehow knew it was Nick but couldn't bring herself to turn him in? Maybe that's why she planted the watch and sent the email about that, because it would kill her to hurt Nick. Kind of a passive-aggressive informant."

"And then when we confronted her she figured either she'd be taking the rap for Carrie's death or she'd have to turn on Nick. Neither choice appealed to her."

"So, we drove her to kill herself?"

He puts and arm around me, starts walking me toward my car, which is right in the front row. "She obviously wasn't real stable to begin with. I think the situation put her over the edge. A situation that was originally created by Carrie, not us. Not you."

He takes my keys from my hand, unlocks the car door and hands the keys back to me. "Now, I want you to get in your car. I want you to go back to the motel, lock the door, and don't go anywhere. Understood?"

"Yes. But how are you going to talk to them about this without mentioning the chat log?"

He gives me a "who do you think you're talking to" look of disbelief. "Please. Raven. I am a professional."

I smile at him, give him a quick kiss and watch him as he walks back to the bar.

The door is slow to close behind him and when Will steps out of the way, to the left toward Chazz's office, I see a waitress at the table nearest the door. Her hair is in a long braid and as she pushes in a chair, I can faintly hear the scraping of the chair legs against the floor.

Or maybe I can't hear it at all. I'm close, and the bar is quiet now with the band on break, but maybe it is just seeing the motion that starts my mind racing. Where had I…what did that remind me of…

An image, crystal clear, pops into my head.

Oh, holy shit…Jennilee didn't kill herself.

# Thirty-Three

I start to race to the bar, but stop and go back to the car. I pull my gun out of the glove box, check that the safety is on and put it in the back waistband of my jeans like I'd seen Will do. I grab my jacket and put it on to cover the gun.

Not in a million years do I want to use the gun, but Will is in a room with a killer and doesn't have all the facts. I'm leaving nothing to chance.

Wow, it's a really uncomfortable feeling, the cold of the metal seeping through the thin cotton of my shirt. I wonder if Will is used to the feeling by now?

At the front door I pause. I don't want to deal with the Carpenters, and I wouldn't put it past Tricia to hurry over to me if she sees me come in. I change direction and run to the back of the building, figuring I'd pound on the door until one of the kitchen kids came and opened it.

But the door is propped open and one of the workers is outside smoking. I startle him and he has a moment of fright in his eyes until he looks me over and decides I'm no threat.

Should have seen me here a few hours ago, kid, with a gun in my hand and vengeance in my heart.

"Can you get Ch—Johnny for me?" I say to the kid as I approach him.

He looks me over again, probably trying to figure out why I'm coming from the front of the building to use the back door, but he leans his head toward the open door and shouts, "Johnny, somebody out here to see you."

So, Chazz wasn't in the office with Will, Nick and Colin. No reason he should be, but you never know. I'm almost to the door when Uncle Chazz walks through it. In theory, he's the one who should have fright in his eyes, seeing me here, knowing Will is in the office, unable to save his ass this time.

Instead he walks past the kid, who turns and goes back into the bar, and reaches me in three long strides. "You need something?" I can't really discern his tone. Whether he's asking me because he wants to help, or in a tough-guy kind of way? I'm not sure.

"I need to get to Will, and I didn't want to go through the bar. I didn't want to have to talk to the Carpenters."

"Why not, you'd be welcome at their table, you're their hero tonight."

"Maybe not for long."

"Oh yeah? This thing shaking out differently than y'all thought?" No surprise in his voice. He's been around the block, Uncle Chazz.

"I think so, that's why I need to talk to Will."

"He's busy right now."

"I know. I know he's using your office to talk to Nick and Colin."

"Yeah, those two are going to be pretty pissed when they find out he's not some hot shot exec ready to sign them."

"It's more than that."

He jams his hands in the front pockets of his jeans, tilts his head to the side as he studies me, then says, "Come on in." He steps aside and waves an arm for me to precede him into the back room of the bar.

As I walk past him I say, "You're not worried this is some kind of trick? That I'm back here to …finish…"

"Nah," he says as he follows behind me, "You wouldn't have gone through with it, even if Will hadn't been here."

Why does everybody keep saying that?

Maybe because it's true?

"Is there another way into your office directly from here, or do I have to go out into the bar to get there?"

"You have to go through the bar."

It isn't that big of a deal, the door to the kitchen and Chazz's office are only a few feet apart. Even if Tricia saw me from the other side of the room, I'd be in the office before she would even be out of her chair.

I start to head that way when Uncle Chazz puts his hand on my arm to stop me. "Wait, come with me." He crosses to the far side of the backroom where there's a phone mounted on the wall. "I can listen in to my office on here, see if maybe you shouldn't go in there right now."

"Like an intercom? Will they be able to hear us?" I wave my arms around, encompassing the fairly noisy room. Two kids are flipping burgers on the grill and the third is stacking cases of beer along a wall. All three looked me over when I entered, but Chazz—Johnny to them—must have given them some kind of look because they were now all minding their own business, or seeming to, anyway.

"No. It can work as an intercom, but I set it up to be silent as well, basically just a listening device."

"Why would you do that?"

He shrugs, when he answers his voice is soft so as not to carry beyond me. "When you live like I have for the last twenty years, you learn to—" He cuts himself off, let's out a sigh. "Well shit, you *have* lived like I have for the last twenty years."

I shake my head. "Not really. I didn't live in fear all those years, like you have, waiting for someone to knock on your door—"

"Or come at you from behind a Dumpster?" he adds, raising an eyebrow at me.

"Exactly. I didn't have that all this time."

"But you have it *now*?"

I don't hesitate in my answer. "Yes, I live in fear now."

"Sucks, doesn't it?" he says with no pity, no concern, just the facts, ma'am.

"Yeah, it does."

He knowingly nods, then reaches for the phone from the wall and does whatever it takes so that we're able to hear into his office.

It feels so weird, to be having this little "moment" with the man who killed my father.

"Christ, I can't believe this is still happening." Nick's voice, "Should I go grab my lawyer?"

So, Will has told them something isn't quite kosher with the case. Did he tell them he's—

"I mean, what do you think would be the best way to handle this, Will?" Nick again. There is a pleasing quality in his voice and I'm guessing by the tone Nick still thinks Will is going to sign the River Rats and doesn't want to upset the apple cart.

I can almost see Will raising his hands in indecision when he says, "I don't know Nick. I'm just telling you what I heard… that the cops aren't satisfied and that a couple of officers timed the drive from your apartment to the lodge where Carrie was killed."

He hadn't told them about the chat log. He's letting them believe their alibi has been found bogus. Which I always felt it was, based solely on a glance between Colin and Nick. Couldn't exactly take that to court.

And I couldn't exactly show up in a courtroom, and Will knows it. Whatever tack he takes, he'll try to keep me out of it.

"But we knew they'd do that," Nick says. "You even said they would."

"Yes," Will answers him, "But they did it today. *After* they found Jennilee."

"Shit," Nick whispers.

"What does it matter about his alibi now?" Colin states. "Maybe he was home alone all night and thought nobody would believe it. We know he didn't kill Carrie, Jennilee did."

"Is that why you two cooked up an alibi? Because you thought nobody would believe he was home by himself?"

Both Colin and Nick are silent and I wish Chazz had cameras in his office. Maybe he does. I start to ask him, but he knows where my thoughts are going and shakes his head. "Just the phone in there."

I hear the scraping of a chair and then Will says, "Sit down, Colin." I wait to hear a door open, but I don't. It's excruciating just standing here listening, but I know if I go in there I'm going to kill whatever game Will is playing.

And yet, I need to let him know what I figured out—that this is bigger than just Nick killing his girlfriend and getting his best friend to give him an alibi. I look at Uncle Chazz, noting the irony as I say, "I need your help."

"What do you need?"

"Can you somehow flash a signal on this thing or something? Somehow alert Will that I'm here, that I have information? But not so he has to leave the room?"

"Why not call him? Either on this phone, or on his cell. He never takes that thing off."

He did while he was in bed with me.

I shake my head. "I don't have his number. And even if I did I don't want to take the chance that Colin or Nick would overhear my end of the conversation."

"I have his number. You could text him."

"I don't have a phone that can do that." I wasn't about to explain to Uncle Chazz about buying one of those pre-paid phones once I got down here so there was no way to trace anything to me in Michigan. Besides, the cheap-o I bought doesn't have texting. And, it's in my car in the parking lot.

Uncle Chazz pulls a phone out of his back pocket, pushes a few buttons and then looks at me expectantly. "What do you want to say to him?"

"He'll think it's coming from you, right?" I ask.

He thinks for a moment, then types in "Raven w/ me. We

can hear U. She has info 4 U. Give sign if U get this."

He hits send. Seconds later I hear Will say, "Just relax, Colin, sit back down. Let's work through this. All I want is to help you guys make this go away so we can move forward. I think that— Sorry, I need to check..." There is some rustling. Will must be standing closest to the phone.

"The truth is I was home alone that night," Nick says. There are nerves in his voice now. Nerves that Will will pick up on and press in on Nick. But it's the wrong path.

"Okay, now we're getting somewhere. Let's just go through that night again and then you can get back out there and do your last set. The jukebox is fine until then. They might even have a couple of Beatles songs on it."

"That's it," I nudge Uncle Chazz. "That's the sign."

"It is?"

"Yes, trust me."

Chazz lets out a soft snort. Yeah, I guess that's kind of stretching it. But he holds his fingers poised over the phone's keyboard, waiting for me to dictate.

"Say, 'Not Nick. It was Colin'." Uncle Chazz raises a brow at me, but types it in.

"He just going to take your word for it?" Chazz asks me.

"Yes," I answer without hesitation.

"Why?"

"Because *he* doe*s* trust me."

He hits whatever key it takes to send. I can hear Nick going over everything he did that night—at home, alone. That's good, it gives Will time to get the text and formulate a plan. I'm trying to figure out how he's reading it without letting Nick and Colin know when he says, "I'm getting in information about this as we speak from a good source."

"What kind of source would a record exec have in a police station in Tennessee?" Colin says, suspicion in his voice. No dummy, he.

"We have contacts all over the place in police stations in case one of our artists gets picked up for something. And we get a lot of calls from the Nashville cops. Lots of DUIs with you Country artists."

Good recovery, Will. Sounds pretty plausible. Could very well be true.

Nick is finally done giving the play-by-play of his night at home and Colin says, "You see why we came up with the alibi? Nobody was going to believe him."

"And what about you?" Will says.

"What about me?"

"Where were you that night if not with Nick like you said?"

There is the tiniest of pauses and then Colin says, "I was home too, just like I said. Just that Nick wasn't there. I was alone too."

Will lets out a huge sigh. I hear a chair squeak—he must be getting up. "Okay. I've had it with you guys. I'm just trying to help out. We have lots of resources at Planet if you need them. We want to sign you guys. But not if I don't know what I'm dealing with. Not if you keep blowing smoke up my ass."

I hear him start to walk but then stop as Nick says, desperation clear in his voice, "Jesus, Will, I'm telling you the truth. No way would I ever hurt Carrie. She drove me crazy sometimes, yeah, but I loved her." The emotion is raw and true, but I don't know if it's because he's thinking about Carrie, or because Will—and a record deal—is about to walk out the door.

"See, I know that, Nick. I know you wouldn't hurt your girlfriend. You're not that type of guy. But accidents can happen. Suppose you went to the lodge to see Carrie, tell her to quit with the dramatics. Or, I don't know, maybe you went up there to make up with her.

"Was she with another guy when you got up there? Is that why you fought? Maybe pushed her a little too hard?"

"No. No. Jesus, no. I didn't go up there. Not that night, not the whole time she was gone."

"But you knew where she was?"

"Yeah, I knew. Or I figured she was there. That's where she'd go when she needed a break." The way he said the last had me picturing him doing air quotes around "a break".

"All right. Let's talk about the emails. And the watch," Will says. The change of subject, when Nick is so worked up throws me, and then I realize that's exactly why he did it—to throw everybody off balance.

"What about the emails? That was just a game to try and get me to chase Carrie."

Colin corroborates, "Yeah, playing head games as usual, but this time she got that whack job Jennilee involved. Had her sending emails from The Country Grounds, got her all worked up. Any fool knew Jennilee was head over heels for Nick. This whole thing pushed her right over the edge."

"Got him," I say.

"How?" Chazz asks.

I'm about to answer when Will says, "That's right, she did enlist Jennilee's help in trying to make Nick follow her. And she did send those emails from The Country Grounds. But Colin," Will pauses here, for dramatic pause or to make sure Colin is looking at him I don't know for sure. "How did *you* know that?"

# Thirty-Four

Chazz looks at me with a smile. "Our boy is good at this."

I nod. "Colin must have known about the emails being sent from there."

"It's not what you think. None of it," he says quietly, defeat in his voice. But also pleading. He thinks Will, and the power of Planet Records can make this go away. Just as Will wants him to think.

"I think that you killed Carrie, and then tried to throw the suspicion onto Jennilee. How is any of that wrong?" Will says, almost as quietly as Colin. No accusation, just in a how can I help way.

"Colin? What the fuck? What were—" Nick's voice is cut off, from a look or gesture from Will most likely. Yeah, Nick, don't mess this up now.

"It's okay, Colin," Will says so softly. "Confess."

A chill goes through me. To hear his voice say that word after seeing it typed to me so many times…very surreal.

And yet, this whole thing is surreal. Communicating with Confessor through a keyboard (though a tiny, cell phone one this time) seems so normal. And as normal, I'm on the outside, listening in. But, this is anything but normal.

Colin's sigh is so big we can hear it. "Carrie was an accident. It wasn't supposed to go this far. Jennilee killing herself…that was never supposed to happen. I can't be held accountable for what that nut job did to herself."

"But it sure worked in your favor, didn't it? Her killing herself?" Will says ignoring Nick's gasp of…what? Disbelief? Pain? Betrayal? All of the above most likely.

Colin sighs again, but he doesn't deny it. "It just got out of hand. I went up there to tell Carrie she had to go home, that Nick was going crazy but that he wasn't going to come after her, not again. That she needed to deal with this whole quit the band thing like an adult. It got pretty heated. She said she wasn't going to come back. She knew Nick would come to his senses, come and find her. She started getting hysterical, saying that it was all my fault that Nick wouldn't grow up, throw in the towel, quit the band. That I kept his head full of dreams about the band hitting it big."

I can see it all unfolding the way he describes it—it fit with all I know about Carrie and her need for stability. And with Colin's determination to make the River Rats a success.

"You know how she could get." He must be speaking to Nick now. "She's done it to you tons of times." There is no answer from Nick, which is probably agreement by omission.

"And Will had just shown up—it was really going to happen, we were so close. I told her about Will, about his interest, and she just lost it. It's like she knew you'd never quit the band now, never be the little nine-to-five husband she wanted. Never have the normal family that she'd never had, that she'd always wanted."

I can see that happening too. I know what never having something does to you. How you crave it.

"She came at me, started pounding on me, screaming that it was all my fault. I pushed her off of me—not hard, I swear it—and she tripped on something and fell back. The sound of her head hitting that fireplace thing…it…it was…"

He doesn't finish. There is something between a moan and a sob that comes from Nick. "It was an accident. I never meant to hurt her. I knew I never should have left, but I just panicked. Nobody was supposed to get hurt."

"What about the anonymous emails? Did you send those or did Jennilee?" Will asks.

"Jennilee sent the first one. I sent the second one."

"You were in on it together?" There is surprise in Will's voice.

"No. The first time I went to talk to Carrie—"

"You mean you saw her another time? Different from when you killed her?"

"I didn't kill her," he says quietly. "She fell. It was an accident."

"So you saw her another time? Before…she fell?" There is understanding in Will's voice. He *is* good at this.

"Yeah. I was pretty sure she'd gone to those cabins. When I got there, Jennilee was just leaving. They were hugging, and then Jennilee got in her car and drove away. The way Carrie was smiling, I knew she'd talked that poor girl into doing her dirty work. Jennilee, she'd do anything for Carrie or Nick."

"Did Carrie see you?" Will ask.

"No. So, instead of talking to Carrie, I followed Jennilee. She went to that coffee house, was on the computer for a little while and then went home. I thought it was weird, but I didn't know what to make of it."

"Until the anonymous tip was made public," Will surmises.

"Right. Then I knew how tangled this thing was going to get. I held off a little while thinking Nick would put an end to it and go to Carrie, or she'd get tired of the game, but that didn't happen."

"Christ, Colin," Nick barely whispers. I can tell he doesn't know what to make of this. His best friend killed the woman he loves, but he can see it unfolding the same way I can, the way Colin told it. And Nick knows, apparently, that Carrie probably behaved exactly the way Colin said she did.

"And then I came to town, and you needed Nick on his A game. After you *saw* Carrie, you knew they'd look at Nick first, so you gave him the alibi—which is actually *your* alibi. And when they started to really dig, poke holes in the time frame, you grabbed his watch, sent the second email from the same place that Jennilee had sent the first, knowing everybody would think someone was framing Nick," Will finishes the story. Wow, he's good. I hadn't even gone that far ahead. And he's right. Colin probably snatched the watch from Nick's office the day we were there together. Right after we first met.

"I knew it would look like a frame, Nick. That no one would believe you did it. Raven was with me that day at your office. If it came down to it, she could say she saw the watch on your desk, after Carrie died. I was trying to protect you, bro."

"I didn't need protection," Nick says coldly. "I didn't do anything wrong."

Holy shit, Colin used me that day. That's why he had me meet him at Nick's office, go up with him, go into Nick's office. He wanted me to see the watch in case I'd be needed later. I feel... well, I have no right to feel used, do I? After how I used Colin to get into the Hopeless Heart, and into all these people's lives. How I'd planned on Colin being *my* alibi that first night at the Hopeless Heart.

"I feel sick about Jennilee, I really do," Colin continues. "But there was no reason for her to kill herself."

"Other than the fact that you were framing her?"

"She didn't know that. I was just trying to throw suspicion off of me. And Nick."

"She probably figured it out," Will says, and I silently agree. She might have been deeply troubled, but Jennilee wasn't stupid. I'd played backgammon with Gammon_89 too many times to think that. She knew exactly who would have had access to Nick's watch. That's probably why she'd gone back to the coffee house last night—to try and find something incriminating on Colin. Or maybe to cover her own tracks from the first email. We'd never know for sure. A few of these pieces will die with Jennilee.

But she won't have died in vain.

"One more text," I say to Chazz. He nods for me to go on, and I tell him what to type.

"Colin killed Jennilee."

# Thirty-Five

"How do you know that for sure?" Chazz asks as he types and transmits the text.

"I don't know anything for sure, but I do know someone else was in Jennilee's apartment with her after Will and I left her this morning. When we left her place she put our coffee mugs in her sink and pushed all the chairs in around the table. It made a screeching, nails-on-a-chalkboard kind of a sound."

"So?"

"When I was back later, when I saw her…body, the chairs were out, the mugs were back on the table, it looked like Will and I had just left."

"Somebody wanted it to look like…" he drifts off, he's not really sure. Neither am I.

"I think he wanted it to look like Will and I were there, accused her of knowing something about Carrie's death, and her guilt drove her to kill herself right after we left."

"And you think Colin did this?" There is major doubt in his voice. I don't blame him, Colin is the quintessential boy-next-door, I'd thought so from the moment I saw his picture on Nick's machine. Even after he'd just confessed to accidentally killing Carrie, it's hard to believe he'd kill Jennilee in cold blood.

But, I also know he saw his chance with Planet Records and wasn't going to let anything stand in his way.

"He's the only person involved in this not accounted for.

Nick, his parents, Tricia, were all with me at his place with the cops."

"That's kind of a stretch to assume Colin's the only other person involved. Carrie could have been fucking around, there could be all kinds of other people messed up in this."

"Yeah, could be," I say. I don't go into the chat log, there's no time. Besides, deep down I know it's Colin.

"I need proof," Will says.

"What kind of proof?" Colin asks, confused. As well he should be, because Will is talking to me.

"Type no proof, just gut," I tell Chazz and he quickly complies.

"Shit," Will says when he sees my text. He knows, as I do, that now that there is suspicion, a closer look can be taken at Jennilee's body, the crime scene, everything. You can't just go in and slit a girl's wrists and not leave behind some kind of evidence. But that's not going to help now, not when he's close to having Colin confess it all.

He's about to ask something further when Will speaks again. "Colin, we know about Jennilee." Taking a straight shot at it. Why not, either he'll get more out of him, or not and we'll just wait for evidence to back up my claim that Colin killed Jennilee. Either way, three people heard Colin confess to killing Carrie. Four if you count Nick, but who knows what way the wind will end up blowing him.

He might think he has a high-powered record company exec who's going to help him out of this jam, but Colin is going to jail tonight.

"I don't know what you're talking about," Colin says. There is suspicion in his voice now. "Who are you getting texts from, anyway?"

He's too sharp, Colin. He's not going to trip up again. Kind of a miracle he did the first time. And now he's thinking something's not right with Will.

Ten points to the gentleman.

"Colin, remember I said that you couldn't possibly know where Jennilee sent the emails from?"

"Yeah?" full blown suspicion now.

"I knew that because only Raven and the FBI agent that was with her, following Jennilee, knew the actual location of where Jennilee sent those emails."

"But *you* were with—" Nick's voice cuts off as he gets it. Colin hadn't said a word; he'd gotten it right away.

"So, no Planet Records?" Colin says, disbelief in his voice.

And really, that sums this whole thing up. He's just confessed to a—in his mind accidental—killing to an FBI agent, and what has him reeling is the fact that the chance, the break, the future he fervently believed was finally going to happen for the band, is not to be.

That desperation for his dream to come true is what sent him to see Carrie in the first place. What sent him into the cabin the second time, after Will had shown up.

The sequence of events play in my head and a horrible thought occurs to me.

"Oh my God, I set this whole thing in motion."

"What do you mean?"

"Carrie's dead because of me. So is Jennilee. Colin went to the cabin to confront Carrie the second time because Will had shown interest in the band."

"So, Will being a bogus record exec set it in motion. How does that come back to you?"

"He did that because of me. Because he thought I'd come here. He didn't know for sure I knew about you, but he couldn't take the chance that I'd come here to…"

"Which you did."

"Which I did," I say quietly. God, the weight of this is all too much for me to deal with right now. I can drive myself batty with the "what ifs" later, the main thing is this is all coming to an end. And Colin will pay for what he did.

Still, I should have just stayed in Michigan, I should have

never left my nest.

As if reading my thoughts, Chazz says, "But then you wouldn't know about your father, would still be wishing you could…" he stops. He's not sure I wouldn't be better off without that knowledge anyway. Neither am I.

There is still silence from the office as the truth of Will's identity seeps in. I imagine Colin and Nick are battling the crushing fact that their dream is indeed dead with the harsh reality that Colin is out of the band—permanently.

Time to find a new guitarist, boys.

"Oh, fuck," Chazz says.

"What?"

"Does Will have a gun on him?"

He left mine at the motel which is now on me, and unless he had put his holstered one on during the drive over…but no, I think I would have felt it on him as I hand my hands on him when he stood in front of me out front. "I don't think so. Why?"

"Because Colin knows where I keep mine."

"You mean in your office?"

"Yes."

"Isn't that kind of dangerous?"

He looks at me like I'm an idiot. Yeah, I guess that sounded pretty stupid considering the life he's led…and that random people could just march in his back door and point a gun at him fairly easily.

I point to Chazz's cell phone, in his palm, at the ready. "Text that to Will. Gun is wherever it is. Colin knows about it."

"It's in the bookcase," Chazz tells me as his thumbs move over the keys. He's not as fast as I've seen kids text (not that I've seen a ton in person), but he's not bad. Certainly faster than I'd be. "Behind a stack of dirty aprons and dishcloths."

Give me a full-size keyboard and I'm a whiz…all that time online. But not so much with the little ones.

"Colin, why don't you sit down, there's no use getting edgy," we hear Will say.

"Where are the chairs compared to the bookcase?" I ask Chazz.

"On the other side of the room. He's trying to move him away from the bookcase. It's not that big of an office. A desk, a couple of chairs in front of it, a couple of filing cabinets and the bookcase."

I pull out my gun from the back of my waistband and start to leave the kitchen, to get to the office, but Chazz's hand clasps around my upper arm. "What the hell do you think you're going to do in there?"

"I don't think Will has his gun. I think it's in his car. I'm just trying to level the playing field."

"Or get you and Will shot."

"Blackbird, get out of here," Will says through the phone. I turn around like there's a camera pointed at me or something, but no, it's just that Will—Confessor, really - knows me so well that he can tell what I'm about to do.

But it also tips off Colin and Nick, not that it matters much now. "Who the fuck is Blackbird? Has your phone been on this whole time?" Colin's voice grows a bit fainter as he speaks, he's moving across the room.

"Colin, just stay where you are." Will's voice is firm under control. "Get her out of here, Chazz," he says. He uses names that Colin and Nick won't know. Even now he's still protecting me.

I try to pull away, but Chazz's grip on me tightens.

"Colin, step away from the bookcase," Will says. "Nick, stay in your seat. Colin, I said move away from there."

"He doesn't have his gun," I say. "If he did, he'd have it pulled and Colin would have stopped moving the first time he told him too. If he'd known there was a gun in the room he probably never would have let them know he's FBI."

"Fuck," Chazz spits out, "You're right. Give me your gun."

I hold my other arm—the one he's not grabbing—away from him, hold the gun up high in my hand, like two little kids playing keep away. "No. Why? What are you going to do?"

"Get it to Will."

"How?"

"It's my office, why wouldn't I just walk in, tell the boys they need to get back onstage. They don't know we've been listening to them."

It makes sense, we're already heading across the back room as I hand him my gun and he says to one of the workers. "Call 911, tell them to get Detective Mosley over here pronto." The worker - the same kid that was smoking when I came to the back door - looks confused but regroups quickly and pulls a cell phone out of his back pocket.

Chazz doesn't stop moving and I'm right behind him. "Stay here," he says as get to the door which leads to the main floor.

"Not on your life," I answer.

"There's no reason you'd be with me. That won't fly."

"I can't stay back there and just listen to it," I say.

He must see the determination in my eyes. "Okay. Stay in the hallway here. When I go in, you stand well away from the door. Stay there until Detective Mosely shows up. When you see him come in, knock on the door. Yell that you need me at the bar. Got that?"

I nod and follow him the several feet from the door to the backroom to the door to his office. I keep my head down, hoping nobody from the Carpenter's table happens to be looking over here. I walk past Chazz when he stops in front of the office door. I go a few more feet and stop, putting my back against the wall.

He sees that I'm in a good spot—able to see the door when the Detective arrives, and nearby in case I'm needed, and yet out of the way.

"What are you planning to do?" I ask.

"Pretend I'm looking for the boys. Try to diffuse the situation, and get the gun to Will."

Seems like a tall order, but who knows what all Chazz did in his former life. This could be an easy Sunday drive to him.

He stands in front of the door and looks at me. I nod to

him. He puts his hand on the knob, takes a deep breath, opens the door, enters the room as he says "Are you two still in here, there's a packed—" I don't, can't, hear the rest as the door shuts behind him.

Shit, I thought I'd be able to hear what was going on. But the extended lack of a band on stage had caused someone to put on piped in music, or a jukebox—very loudly. And the wooden door is thick and heavy.

But not too heavy to muffle the gunshot I hear about thirty seconds after Chazz enters the room.

I push the door open and take three steps into the room and stop. Nick is standing to my right by the desk. In front of me stands Chazz, gun in his hand.

He's standing over Will's body.

Suddenly I am five years old again and Uncle Chazz is standing over the dead body of the man I love most in the world. He even slowly raises his non-gun hand to his mouth, his index finger straight up—pointing to his scar—in a "shhh" motion.

Oh, God, this can't be happening again. And with my gun. Chazz shot Will with my gun. The gun that was meant to kill him. All these thoughts rush through me in no more than a second or two.

But no, something's not right. I'm not five years old, it is not my father lying on the floor, and there's another piece to this puzzle unaccounted for.

The door shuts behind me and Colin steps from behind it, puts his arm around my neck, pulling my back to his front, the steel barrel of the gun he's holding to my face still warm from shooting Will.

# Thirty-Six

"**R**aven?" Colin says, surprise in his voice that he's holding a gun to my head. Uh, yeah, me too. "What are you doing here?"

I look at Uncle Chazz for answers. He moves his head in the tiniest of shakes. Don't let on I know what's going on.

"I came to see you. Tricia told me you guys were in here. Colin, what's going on? You're scaring me. Who is that, and why did he hurt Will?" I try to sound like I don't know what's going on. Like Chazz is the one to be afraid of.

My words are barely audible as Nick starts freaking out. "Christ, Colin, you killed a federal agent. What the fuck were you thinking. What are we going to do now?"

"Shut up," Colin screams at Nick and it does the trick. "Let me think." His hold around my chest and neck tightens.

There is pounding on the door behind us, and someone is trying the knob, which Colin must have locked as he shut the door. "What was that? Are you okay? Was that a gunshot?"

Colin nods his head toward Chazz who says loudly, "Everything's fine, Lacey, just a little accident. Not a gun. Go back to work."

"You sure?" The voice—Lacey, I guess—says again.

"Yes. Sure. Nothing to worry about," Chazz says, then says in his normal tone to Colin, "That'll buy you some time, but if she doesn't see me in the next few minutes she's going to call the police."

"Fuck," Nick whispers, then shuts up again as he looks at Colin.

I look at Will's body and I see blood pumping out of the wound on his chest. So much blood. It reminds me of Jennilee and all the blood around her body. Wait. That's good, right? Blood wouldn't still be pumping if he's already dead. I look up at Chazz and he sees what I've realized. We need to end this now, one way or another so we can get help for Will. He won't make it much longer. It's amazing he's still alive judging by where the bullet hole seems to be.

"Colin," I say quietly. "You need to let me go now so we can talk about this, so we can straighten this all out." Like there's a chance maybe it can all go away? He almost seems to buy it for a second and his grip loosens every so slightly before tightening again.

"Jesus, Raven, I can't believe this is happening," he says. "All I ever wanted was to get a chance. For people to hear our music."

I take a deep breath, try to keep my voice calm. This isn't the first time I've dealt with a killer. Not even the second.

"I know, and maybe you still can, Colin, but you have to let me go. We have to get help for Will. We can't let him die. That will make this thing a whole lot worse."

As soon as it's out of my mouth I see Chazz go on alert. Shit. Does Colin think Will is dead? Will he assume it's better to have one less witness?

We don't have time to guess. Can't take that chance. Suddenly Chazz says, "Do you trust me, Raven?"

I look at him, know what he's going to do, and am for the first time happy I know a trained killer. I still my body, keep my head even as I say, "Yes." Before I even finish the slur of the esss, Chazz has put a bullet in Colin's brain.

His body falls from mine and before it hits the ground I am moving toward Will, falling on my knees at his side. Chazz passes me on his way to Colin and I see out of the corner of my eye that he picks up Colin's gun—Chazz's gun.

He comes back to join me, I have my hands over Will's wound trying to stop the blood flow, or at least slow it down. Chazz turns and leaves the room, he's back in seconds with a stack of laundered bar towels from a supply shelf. He throws them down to me and I take several and put them down over Will's wound and press harder.

Chazz goes back to the door. There is a woman standing there and he calmly tells her. "Nice and slowly get everyone out of the bar. The police are on their way, but call 911 and tell them we also need an ambulance. Tell them officer down, that will get them here quicker. And keep everyone the hell away from here."

I see the young woman's eyes go big as she listens to Chazz, then looks beyond him at me hovering over Will, Colin's dead body and Nick, bent over, hands covering his face, in shock. But she nods to Chazz then turns, closing the door behind her.

"Give her a raise," I say. Chazz lets out a snort then joins me on the floor and applies pressure by putting his hands on top of mine.

Will moans and I try to soothe him even though he probably can't hear me. "It's okay. It's all going to be okay. Colin's dead. It's all over. Hang in there."

A small smile crosses his mouth and his eyes are tiny slits, but they are open. "Bye, bye –"

"No!" I say as I take a hand away and grab his chin, pointing his face in my general direction. "No Bye bye. This is not Bye bye, God damn it. You are *never* telling me bye bye again, do you hear me?"

The smile gets a little stronger and I feel his jaw move under my hand. A nod. A tiny nod. I try to pull it together—there'd be time for sobbing later—and bring my attention, and my hands, back to his wound.

"Got to get her out of here," Will whispers.

"I'm not leaving," I say.

He turns his head to Chazz. "She can't be here when the Feds show up. Mosley owes me, but the Feds can't know she's flown the coop."

"They don't know she left her safe house?" Chazz asks.

Will shakes his head then griMaces at the movement. "Only I knew…didn't want her…on radar…for…get her out of here."

Chazz looks at me. "He's right. You have to get out of here."

"No way in hell."

"It's not just about you being in danger. If he didn't tell his superiors that you're out of your target zone, and he's known all this time, he's as good as toast in the bureau."

Seriously? I have to leave him here, bleeding all over, to protect his career? "Fuck his job," I say.

Will starts to chuckle, which turns to gasps of air. "Please, Blackbird…for me. You have to get out of here."

Now I start to cry. "I can't. I can't leave you like this."

"I'll find you and let you know what's happening," Chazz says to me.

I nod and start to reluctantly pull my hands away from Will's body. "I'm staying at—"

"I know where you are. I even know what room," Chazz says.

Of course he does. I was never going to get the jump on him. Not with Will in his corner. He hands me two of the clean towels. "Wipe as much blood off as you can. Then put my jacket on over yours to cover the blood. When you walk out of here keep your head down. Don't make eye contact with anyone. Go through the kitchen, leave through the back door. Blend in with the crowd that's probably out front by now. Wait until the police come inside before you get in your car and drive away."

I do as he says, wiping my hands, getting his jacket that hangs on a hook on the back of the door and putting it over my own. I look back one more time trying to come up with something profound to say to make Will hold on.

"I love you," is all I have to offer up, but it's enough. He smiles, and lifts a hand a few inches off the ground, in a small wave.

I take the few steps to the kitchen without looking at the bar area. No eye contact. I don't make sure, but I get the sense that most people have been cleared out. The kitchen is deserted. Lacey had done her job well. Chazz is right, as I round the front of the building on the front side, most of the people that were inside are milling about, sticking around to see what's going to happen.

I keep low, but not like I'm trying to hide, and skirt a wide birth behind where the Carpenter party is trying to get a couple of the kitchen worker kids to let them in. The kids most likely had been positioned at the entrance by Lacey and were taking their duty seriously, not letting anyone in.

Squad cars are pulling into the lot now followed closely by—thank God—an ambulance. I reach my car without anyone really noticing me. As soon as the cops and EMTs are in the building I get in the car and pull out of the parking lot.

I can't stop crying as I drive to the motel. It takes me four tries to swipe the stupid key car so that it works.

I take off Chazz's jacket and look down at all of Will's blood on me. Knowing I have a window of time before Chazz can get free to contact me, I strip out of my clothing, rinse out all the blood as best as I can from my shirt and jeans and take a shower. I hang the clothes over the shower rod to dry after I'm done and pull on some clean sweats and a turtleneck, but I can't seem to get warm. I wrap the comforter around me.

And I pray.

**"W**hat happened to diffusing the situation?"

"Yeah, that didn't go like I thought."

"No, not quite," I say to Uncle Chazz as I open my motel door to him at ten the next morning. Nearly eleven hours of sitting, shivering in that God awful comforter until he called and told me Will was out of surgery and expected to recover. Another hour until he was standing here now, with a huge cup of Dunkin' Donuts coffee in his hand which he hands to me. He takes a sip from his own cup and hands me a bag—presumably of donuts—

which I toss onto the table.

I sit back on the edge of the bed while he makes himself at home, pulling a chair up to the table, pulling a donut out of the bag and taking a bite.

"I guess I need to thank you for saving my life," I say to him.

He smiles. "Bet that's not easy for you to do."

"No, it isn't. But I am grateful."

He waggles a finger at me, crumbs dropping onto the table. "See, if you had taken me out when you'd wanted to, I wouldn't have been there to save you."

I don't bother going into how fucked up that logic is…that I never would have needed saving if Uncle Chazz hadn't killed my father in the first place, but I let it lie.

I let it all lie. A sort of peace comes over me and I know that my nightmares will, if not completely disappear, at least lessen.

"So when can I go to the hospital?"

"You can't. The place is swarming with Feds."

"How did you explain my being in the office when you shot Colin, but disappearing afterward?"

He shrugs. "I never mentioned you. Colin's dead. I think Nick is still in shock about the whole thing—especially that Colin killed Carrie. There's a lot of police work to do to follow up on Colin killing Jennilee. You never came up."

"What? Are you serious? Nick will mention me. Lacey saw me. The kitchen workers."

"Yeah, and if they questioned everybody to find out what really happened, they'd hear about you. But they have a Federal agent and a Federal informant who told them the same story. They don't need to dig any further."

"But I'm all over Detective Mosley's reports, I'll bet."

He takes another bite of donut and shakes his head. "No, I guess Will kept you out of that. A little payback for handing Mosley Carrie's killer. And now Jennilee's. Made his job a whole lot easier."

"The system can't work like that," I say with disbelief.

Chazz nearly does a spit take with his coffee, but then safely swallows it. "Are you kidding me? These guys scratch each other's backs all the time. That's exactly how the system works."

Yeah, well, I guess he'd know better than me.

Speaking of the system… An odd thought occurs to me. "How often are you in contact with Will? I mean normally. Are you online with him a lot?" I ask Chazz.

Not that it really matters, I guess, but I hate the thought of Confessor having the same relationship with all his work cases. Well, not the *same* relationship, but you know what I mean.

Chazz shrugs. "Same as with the agent before him. Check in call once a month. Maybe once a year they show up, just to make sure there's nothing hinky going on. What do you mean being online with him? Like an email or something? No, they need to hear your voice, once a month, at a phone they can definitely trace to your set location."

I almost let out a sigh of relief. So, Will was being honest when he said Blackbird and Confessor were—are—real.

"Isn't that how it is for you?" he asks me.

I shake my head. "No, I never knew I was part of the program."

"Well you do now," he says. I only nod, but I get up off the bed and grab myself a donut and settle into the chair opposite him.

"If I can't go to the hospital, what now?"

"Sit tight, Raven, sit tight."

Four days. Four excruciating days before I feel Will's arms around me. Before I can hold him and reassure myself that he is indeed going to be okay.

I spent the days getting updates on Will from Chazz, finding a Laundromat when I ran out of clothes, reading all about the case and the shoot out in the papers (I'm never mentioned once), playing online backgammon with eatmeee!!! (his championship is mentioned often—by him) and worrying.

One of the mornings when Chazz brings me donuts he spends a few hours telling me about my father. Nice stories, funny stories. Appropriate stories that help ease the pain of finding out exactly what he did for a living.

I asked about my mother but he quickly changed the subject. I didn't push it, though I sort of wanted to. But, in the end, I figured my instincts about my mother were right. If my father wanted to tell me anything about her, he would have.

Besides, even though I hadn't killed Chazz, and he had saved my life—and Will's probably—it isn't like Johnny Campos is someone I feel I can push on a topic he doesn't want to talk about.

But now…now I lie in bed with Will in my motel room, his good arm around me, my hand on his bandage and we sleep.

I have no nightmares.

We spend another three nights there in that motel. Me running out for food so Will can rest. Waiting until he has enough strength to travel. On the third night we find out he has more strength than we'd thought…in the most delightful way. We decide to head to Michigan the following morning.

He's not expected to report in for a month or more and we figured he can rest and recuperate in Michigan as well as anywhere.

He gets grumpy as I load up my car, him not being able to lift anything and so not able to help. Chazz had dropped off a suitcase of Will's things while Will was in the hospital. I didn't ask where Will had been staying all along, but I figure it was somewhere close by. The black SUV Will had driven is gone, returned to somewhere by some sort of Federal fairy.

"That's everything," I say and he just grunts.

I wrap my arms around him, kiss him softly which doesn't stay softly for long. I break away and say, "Come on, crabby. I bet you're going to be like this the whole way home, with me having to do all the driving."

"Don't remind me," he says, but he smiles and kisses me again.

He moves to the door and I go to the table to retrieve my

laptop case which is the last thing to pack. As I pick it up my baby name book falls out of a side pocket.

Unable to resist, I flip it open from the back until I find what I'm looking for. I smile as I read the entry, then tuck the book into my bag, turn toward Will who waits for me. He opens the door, standing to the side so that I can pass.

"Let's go, Blackbird," he says. No bye, bye. No leaving before I can respond. I brush past him as he leans down to whisper, "Let's fly away."

*Will—William (English). Determined guardian.*

## Acknowledgments

A big thank you to Colleen Gleason and Holli Bertram, who are even better writers than they are critique partners. (And that's saying a lot!)

A shout out to my besties Kelly Campbell and Amy Pellizzaro who have been incredibly supportive as I made my way through these uncharted waters.

Kelly Young and Patti Kearly, among others, were early readers and gave insightful and thoughtful feedback. Thanks, ladies!

And a special thank you to my agent Jodi Reamer, who took me on with this book…and its many renditions.

My apologies to the online backgammon community and backgammon tournaments for my artistic license with the online community and national tournament that I created, and any other inaccuracies of the game.

Try Mara Jacobs's romantic mystery series

## AGAINST THE ODDS
ANNA DAWSON'S VEGAS, BOOK 1

## AGAINST THE SPREAD
ANNA DAWSON'S VEGAS, BOOK 2

Try Mara Jacobs's *New York Times* bestselling Worth series

Worth The Weight

Worth The Drive

Worth The Fall

Worth The Effort

Totally Worth Christmas

Worth The Price

Worth The Lies

Find out more at
**www.MaraJacobs.com**

Mara Jacobs is the *New York Times* and *USA Today* bestselling author of The Worth Series

After graduating from Michigan State University with a degree in advertising, Mara spent several years working at daily newspapers in Advertising sales and production. This certainly prepared her for the world of deadlines!

Mara writes mysteries with romance, thrillers with romance, and romances with…well, you get it.

Forever a Yooper (someone who hails from Michigan's glorious Upper Peninsula), Mara now resides in the East Lansing, Michigan, area where she is better able to root on her beloved Spartans.

You can find out more about her books at **www.marajacobs.com**

www.ingramcontent.com/pod-product-compliance
Lightning Source LLC
LaVergne TN
LVHW020041110826
845155LV00029B/576

* 9 7 8 1 9 4 0 9 9 3 9 8 0 *